The smoke hissed li… Wolf raised his weapon. Berika climbed onto the bed as the prince advanced toward the hellfire apparition writhing above the brazier. A tongue of hissing flame flicked toward the sword and withdrew without touching it. Berika couldn't hear the Web's music; she gathered her courage and her *basi*, just the same. Another tongue of flame leapt from the creature's mouth. The Wolf slashed downward, severing the coil from its source. He gave his wailing war-cry and thrust the sword between its smoldering eyes.

As she had done so many times in the fields beyond Gorse, Berika sent her *basi* leaping out of her mind. . . .

BENEATH THE WEB

Lynn Abbey coedited the popular fantasy series *Thieves' World*™ with author Robert Asprin. Abbey is also the author of several fantasy novels, including *The Black Flame, The Guardians,* and *The Wooden Sword.*

Ace Books by Lynn Abbey

DAUGHTER OF THE BRIGHT MOON
THE BLACK FLAME
THE GUARDIANS
THE WOODEN SWORD
BENEATH THE WEB

The Thieves' World™ Series
(Edited by Robert Lynn Asprin and Lynn Abbey)

THIEVES' WORLD
VOLUME 2: TALES FROM THE VULGAR UNICORN
VOLUME 3: SHADOWS OF SANCTUARY
VOLUME 4: STORM SEASON
VOLUME 5: THE FACE OF CHAOS
VOLUME 6: WINGS OF OMEN
VOLUME 7: THE DEAD OF WINTER
VOLUME 8: SOUL OF THE CITY
VOLUME 9: BLOOD TIES
VOLUME 10: AFTERMATH
VOLUME 11: UNEASY ALLIANCES
VOLUME 12: STEALERS' SKY

BENEATH THE WEB

LYNN ABBEY

ACE BOOKS, NEW YORK

This book is an Ace original edition,
and has never been previously published.

BENEATH THE WEB

An Ace Book / published by arrangement with
the author

PRINTING HISTORY
Ace edition / August 1994

ISBN: 0-441-00084-3

ACE®
Ace Books are published by The Berkley Publishing Group,
200 Madison Avenue, New York, NY 10016.
ACE and the "A" design are trademarks
belonging to Charter Communications, Inc.

PRINTED IN THE UNITED STATES OF AMERICA

10 9 8 7 6 5 4 3 2 1

Chapter One

The war between the kingdom of Walensor and its mightier neighbor, the Arrizan empire, had lasted for ten bitter years and cost a full generation of Walenfolk lives, lost to hellfire, the corrosive weapon of Arrizan conjury. The high plains donit of Norivarl was desolate, pocked with ash and slag. Its hardy inhabitants had been reduced to beggary in the other donits of the kingdom: Survarl, Arl, Escham, Pennaik, and Fenklare.

The eleventh annual muster had gone out in the springtime week of Lesser Hunger. The Walensor army massed and marched north to Tremontin Pass, where the harsh winds of Norivarl funneled into Arl. Four thousand war-weary men awaited the Arrizi host. The Pyromant known only as Hazard, a conjurer who'd wrought many nightmare miracles throughout the war, led the imperial army.

The Walenfolk were led by Prince Rinchen sorRodion, a brooding young man with no miracles at all to his credit.

The Walensor army arrived at the Arl end of Tremontin on the seventh day of Greater Wind. Obedient to their noble officers and the prince's command, they camped throughout the surrounding forest and set about creating earthworks among the ancient trees. Walenfolk scouts spotted the forerunners of Hazard's army on the last day of the week of Lesser Wind, thirteen days later. The Arrizi host, ten thousand strong, arrived during Greater Rain and the outnumbered Walenfolk honed their weapons, and their nerves, to razor sharpness: If Hazard broke out of Tremontin, his army would winter in Walensor, foraging in the fertile lowlands of Arl and Escham, and the kingdom would be a memory by the spring.

Prince Rinchen refused to lead the army into the desperate battle everyone expected. He kept them digging in the forest and kept counsel only with himself. Hazard goaded the prince with disorderly sallies through the gullet of the pass. The Walenfolk army, noble- and commonfolk alike, threatened mutiny, but the prince was protected by two dozen fiercely loyal Pennaikmen. He safely ignored the Arrizan bait and cooled his critics with stony silence.

A dusty summer haze settled over Tremontin as the Arrizi drilled and the Walenfolk threw up piles of earth, stone, and sticks according to their prince's whim. Summer became autumn. Cooling winds carried dust deep into Walensor, and still the young prince kept his army camped in the forest. Snow glazed the dark granite peaks above the pass. When the snow did not melt in a day, a delegation of noblemen led by Prince Rinchen's younger brother and longtime rival, Alegshorn, confronted their commander in his sparsely furnished tent.

"There'll be snow under the trees in another week," the handsome, golden-haired Aleg said to his seated brother. "The men would sooner die in hellfire slag than be frozen beneath summer blankets. How say you now: Do we ride forward and fight, or run like whipped dogs?"

Rinchen raised his head. Firelight reflected in his ice-colored eyes, lending them a hellfire glimmer. "We wait. Hazard will come to us. He must. He's waited too long to take his army back into the empire. He winters in Walensor or he watches all ten thousand starve and freeze. He *must* bring his army into the gullet. We'll crush him then."

"You best hope we do, brother," Aleg said for himself and the noble warriors behind him. "Or, by all the gods awake and asleep, you'll be the one who gets crushed."

The dark prince smiled, a feral smile with ivory teeth. He'd been born on the last night of the year, an untimely moment which made him, by longstanding tradition and his grandfather's royal decree, a cursed, tainted creature. While there wasn't a man in the tent who doubted Prince Rinchen's intelligence or his loyalty to Walensor, there also wasn't a man who hadn't prayed for his convenient death.

Including Prince Alegshorn, second in line to the throne.

"If I'm wrong," Rinchen said without emotion in his voice, "I will forfeit my life to your judgment, but if I win—if I end this war—I expect nothing less than your support, total and public."

Ten years of underdog warfare had turned the Walensor noble-folk into gamblers. Prince Aleg calmly raised the stakes:

"If the Walensor army leaves Tremontin to the last man as strong as it entered, I'll kneel before Grandfather and renounce my own claims to the throne."

Even those in the tent who believed Prince Rinchen's strategy might succeed knew that any battle wrought casualties on both sides. They expected the Wolf—the name they gave to Prince Rinchen in private—to spurn Aleg's offer. Soldiers died in the field whether there was battle or not, and the weight of trust between the brothers could be measured with a single grain of sand.

But Prince Aleg knew better than Hazard what bait to dangle before Walensor's Wolf. He was ready when his brother surged out of the camp chair, sealing their agreement with clasped hands and a rib-battering embrace, and he was braced for it—unlike the peers who held their collective breath a moment before letting it out with a sigh.

After twenty-three years, and with the help of Walensor's mortal enemy, their long-unheard prayers seemed certain to be answered.

"Double the scouts," Rinchen said, still clinging to Aleg's hand. "Let me know when the Arrizi break camp. And, dear brother, remember this: Our agreement has no force if any man disobeys orders. *Any man.*"

On the fourth day of Lesser Fallow, scouts raced to Prince Rinchen's tent with the long-awaited news: Hazard's army had broken camp and entered Tremontin in battle ranks.

After armoring himself in blue-black mail, the Wolf summoned his noblemen. His unsheathed sword lay across his thighs when they arrived to receive his final orders.

"You will instruct your seconds to lead your men in retreat from Tremontin and form a defensive ring beyond the pass mouth. This battle belongs to us alone—those of you in this tent, me, and our kingdom's sorcerers."

"Have you lost your mind?" Jemat sorLewel, the kingdom's marischal, withdrew his sword partway from its scabbard.

Prince Rinchen was fast, in many opinions, unnaturally—even cursedly—fast. He pressed his sword against sorLewel's throat.

None doubted his willingness to kill. In other seasons, when Walensor's army had engaged the Arrizi host, their cursed Wolf wrought carnage second to none. Glory-seeking men who on other days argued for the privilege of thrusting their knives between the heir-presumptive's ribs drew lots on battle days for a place at Prince Rinchen's side.

More importantly, he had slain so many would-be assassins that Walensor's native mercenary murderers refused commissions, and the prince's enemies had been reduced to hiring foreign amateurs.

SorLewel's expression froze between contempt and fear; he released the hilt of his sword. The sound of oiled steel slipping against a wooden scabbard was the only sound in the tent until, after lowering his own sword, the prince spoke.

"I mean to bring Tremontin down on Hazard as he brought Kasserine down on us."

Which was to say, with sorcery, as Hazard had used Arrizi conjury ten years earlier to drown a generation of Walenfolk men—including King Manal's only son, Vigelan, father of both Rinchen and Alegshorn—in a sudden lake of hellfire and molten rock.

Walensor's sorcery was, however, restrained by an ancient Compact with its gods, some of whom dwelt in the features of the land. The gods did not interfere directly in mortal lives and mortals did not invade, much less destroy, the dwelling places of the gods. Instead, the kingdom's worshippers entrusted their prayers to the Web, an irregularly shaped dome of sorcerous power and wisdom unique to Walensor; and trusted their basilidans, sorcerers whose special talent was divine communication, to interpret the gods' responses.

"No basilidan speaks for Tremontin," the prince explained. "All the gods-awake avow that these mountains are godless. The destruction of Tremontin will not violate the Compact."

"But how will you destroy a mountain?" a faceless voice demanded. "There's not enough Brightwater beneath the Web to tumble Tremontin."

"It can't be done. It mustn't be done," another insisted.

"It can." Prince Rinchen did not look at either man. "It will. Even now the magga sorcerers are moving through the forest, anointing the groundworks with Brightwater and bonding them to the godless stone of Tremontin. When we break apart the groundworks—which we shall do together—the pass will crack and crumble—

"And Hazard will be buried with his army!"

"What of Norivarl?" asked a man whose high-plains accent betrayed his origins and concerns. "With Kasserine filled with hellfire and Tremontin filled with rubble, what will become of the noblemen and honors of Norivarl?"

"The noble honor-estates of Norivarl," Prince Rinchen replied, "are desolate. A full quarter of Walensor's remaining honors is without noblefolk to oversee them or commonfolk to work the land. In time the slag will have cooled, the rubble will have settled, and the honor-land of Norivarl will be reclaimed. Until then, a different order will prevail."

Until then, yes, and possibly forever. Every man in the tent knew that there was no way back to the world they had known before the war. Walensor had not been a warrior's kingdom. Their sorcery, in particular, was ill-suited to the demands of battle. *Basi*, the intangible essence of sorcery inherent to all life and reverently imparted to sanctified artifacts, focused on mending, communication, and the accumulation of knowledge in the Web. Noblefolk defended Walensor, but, to balance this privilege, they were Severed from the Web: forbidden to wield the *basi* they had been born with. Within days of their birth, noble children were plunged into cold fountains of sorcerous Brightwater where sanctified knives Severed them from their innate inheritance.

All the men in the Wolf's tent, including the royal brothers, were headblind. Their power was measured by the breadth of their honor-lands. Noblefolk defended their honor-land, and incidentally the kingdom, with their swords, and dispensed justice from a hierarchy of family courts. What the Wolf proposed was not merely possible, but necessary. Without the rule of noble justice, the kingdom would cease to exist as surely as if Hazard had conquered it.

But that did not make the Wolf's words easier to swallow. Perhaps if the other prince had said them, the golden prince with the winning smile and easy manner whom every lord favored for the throne. While he lived, Prince Vigelan had nurtured a savage rivalry between his tainted, but incontestably legitimate, firstborn and the more attractive Alegshorn. On long winter evenings, after supper was cleared away, Prince Vigelan had set his sons to brawling with threats and promises. As the boys thrashed each other in the straw, the noblemen had wagered on the outcome, with a hundred gold marks promised to the man who correctly bet the night when young Aleg solved the dynasty's succession problems. After Vigelan's death those hundred marks were spent on swords and armor, along with all the other coins in the treasury. The brothers, no longer goaded by their father, scorned each other's company unless royal rituals or the well-being of the kingdom forced them together.

Face-to-face in the cool, drafty tent, they created an unnatural calm between them, like thick air before a summer storm. The noblemen turned to Prince Alegshorn, expecting him to rebuke his tactless, but truthful, brother.

"My lords," said Prince Alegshorn, assuming a place midway between his brother and the other noblemen. "The sorcerers say it can indeed be done without violating the Compact. You will all know how much it grieves me to raise my voice for *him,* but we cannot risk Walenfolk lives, including our own, unnecessarily."

"Well said, little brother," the Wolf replied. "You've grown into wisdom, at last. How sad you find that it fits you grievously."

Prince Aleg spun in a fighting stance: feet apart, fists raised, and staring down the naked steel of his brother's upraised sword. Aleg's partisans surged, but stopped when the Wolf pressed the honed steel into the hollow of his brother's throat. The message was Brightwater clear: Although Prince Rinchen could not hope to prevail against the assembled noblefolk, his brother would not survive to sit on the throne.

Aleg himself broke the stalemate, beating Rinchen's sword aside with the back of his fist, which he left poised in the air between them.

"You hold all Walensor hostage to your arrogance. Flaying is too good for you, Wolf. The day will come when I'll chain you in a cage."

Prince Rinchen lowered his sword and, with his off-weapon hand, pointed two fingers at his brother. "Better a wolf than a begging dog."

"Enough!"

It was a new voice from outside the tent. A wedge opened through the noblemen. Feladon, master of the kingdom's sorcerers and a man known to favor Prince Rinchen's eventual succession to the throne despite his curse, thrust his silver-tipped staff between the enraged brothers.

"Neither of you will reign nor rule if Hazard is not defeated. Arrizi drums are already echoing down the pass. If we do not move the mountains, we must make a stand and fight. So—do we bring Tremontin down, or do we not?"

With calm defiance, Prince Aleg turned his back on his brother. "Go ahead: Bring it down. I can cage a rabid wolf any time."

* * *

Sixty Walenfolk—all high-born noblemen and disciplined sorcerers of magga rank—brought down Tremontin that day. Magga Feladon and the other Walenfolk sorcerers braced themselves for Hazard's counterattack when the granite began to crumble, but no gouts of metal-colored hellfire transformed the sky as Tremontin began to move. For a moment the screams of ten thousand trapped Arrizi soldiers filled the air; then the sound of crashing rock dwarfed all else. A fraction of the vanguard was cut down emerging from the doomed pass. No one could guess how many men from the rearguard might have escaped out the nether end, but no one doubted that the heart of the Arrizi host had been crushed.

At sundown, when the dust was still thick and occasional screams still erupted from the rubble, the Walensor army took its own measure and found fifteen men unaccounted for. They were veterans fully capable of obeying the retreat-and-withdraw order. Prince Rinchen claimed their disobedience nullified his side of the bargain. Led by Prince Alegshorn, the noblemen insisted fifteen Walenfolk deaths nullified their side as well.

Noble prayers once again went unanswered: The Wolf survived and the stalemate rivalry between the princes was doomed to continue. But even that could not inhibit a genuine celebration of Walensor's stunning victory. Only a few prisoners had been taken; to a man, the Arrizi survivors insisted that Hazard had ridden into the gullet, dying with his army before he could launch any counterattack. Without his ruthless, brilliant commander, the Arrizi emperor would be condemned to eat the bitter fruit of defeat for many years.

And together the cooling hellfire of Kasserine and the dusty rubble of Tremontin sealed Walensor's vulnerable northeastern border.

The war was over.

The celebration in the Walensor camp was short-lived. The men were weary. Winter storms were coming. Although the basilidans assured one and all that the deaths of godless mountains and the ancient forest beneath them had not jeopardized the Compact, no one, noble or commonborn, could look comfortably upon the ruins of Tremontin. And they stood aside when Prince Rinchen walked among them, making ward-signs behind their backs if the Wolf's shadow crossed theirs.

Following their noblefolk lords, the army began to disperse before the dust had settled from the Tremontin sky. By the end of Greater Gleaning only a handful of noblemen, magga sorcerers, and those men who had given their oaths directly to one of the sorRodion princes slept on the frosted plains. By the time the first snow fell on the fourth day of Lesser Gleaning only fifty veterans remained. They had hunkered down in an old stone fortress which had survived the destruction of the pass it had once guarded.

Shattering Tremontin had not improved the winter weather. It came out of abandoned Norivarl with blizzard vengeance. Storms roared off the far northern iceland every few days. Life was cruel until the gritty snow drifted deep enough to bury the barracks. Then the men dug rat tunnels and lived in relative comfort. They congregated by their hearths. When they were not stropping steel with cold-black whetstones, they gambled furiously for stakes of black coins—and to keep their names from rising to the top of the reconnaissance roster.

Reconnaissance didn't venture outside during a blizzard, but even the worst blizzard eventually came to an end. As the winds died down and the sky brightened to a dull grey, the commander mounted a bench by the barracks hearth. Aided by an eminently bribable quartermaster who tallied each veteran's debts, he announced the new reconnaissance roster to a grim and generally silent audience, among them the nomad Vinoch.

Vinoch had a Pennaikman's wild, black hair. Before living memory, Pennaik had not been part of Walensor, and the Pennaikmen had been no better loved than the Arrizi buried in Tremontin. In those days, border skirmishes had occurred every summer, and hot-blooded men, Walenfolk and Pennaikmen alike, had earned a lifetime of glory and honor fighting each other. Until Rodion, a silver-eyed Pennaik chieftain, changed everything by leading a horde into the heart of Walensor.

Rodion had slaughtered Walensor's rightful king with his own knife and bedded the royal widow before he washed his hands. Rising from the bloody marriage bed, Rodion had crowned himself king and ruled with more wisdom than anyone had a right to expect. Since then, five generations had held the throne. Courtesy of Rodion's summary intermarriage and less-hostile unions ever since, the sorRodion both looked and acted like the established noblefolk lineages their eponymous ancestor had conquered. With the exception of the tainted Wolf prince whose ice-colored eyes harkened back to his ancestor and, by Pennaik tradition, betokened a man of singular destiny.

Vinoch's eyes were of a similar pale hue. He was a marked man among his kind and served in Tremontin to avoid his kith and kin. "Why bloody me?" he demanded of no one in particular when his name was called. "I went out last Ninthday. I'm paid up. I'm not busted. There's been a bloody mistake. It's not as if there's anyone or anything out there, and if there was, don't we have a bloody spook sitting in his steam-bath to spy it out?"

Another veteran, Maudan, grumbled cautious agreement. Reconnaissance had ventured the length of the rubble to the remains of the Arrizi camp. They'd found a few frozen corpses, nothing more. So far as anyone, including the garrison's lone sorcerer, had proved, they were absolutely alone.

A third voice entered the conversation. "Leszuk's been eating steam all week. He's green with Brightwater mold."

Maudan ventured his opinion: "Seems to me when a spook spends so much time in the steam, he's got gods gnawing his mind."

"Then let the bloody spook make his own reconnaissance." Vinoch hawked loudly into the hearth.

Pennaikmen had little use for gods or sorcerers. Before Rodion had developed a lust for civilization, they'd been a simple nomadic folk, with their own magic, their own shamans, and a clutch of shadowy spirits with easily mollified tastes for hot blood and distilled liquor. Now Pennaik was beneath the Web, subject to Walensor's traditions, but, Compact or no, Vinoch placed greater faith in the old ways. He reached into his belt-pouch to finger a tasselled talisman, and touched his five carved-bone dice as well.

"Anyone for Iron-in-the-Fire?" He fished deeper in the pouch, then fanned three irregularly shaped silver coins. "I got three flakes for the man who beats my throw. Loser takes my place."

Winter was long in Tremontin, and though the gambling was incessant, the stakes were generally black-money grit until after Calends. Risking silver so early in the season, Vinoch reasonably expected his bet to be accepted.

Instead the barracks fell uncommonly quiet, all eyes looking past him to the door. The Pennaikman felt a tingling at the base of his neck—like a spider scuffing all eight feet.

The Walenfolk called it *basi.* Pennaikmen stubbornly refused to give it a name. Everybody had a little; it was the life force. A few had a lot; they were spooks. Vinoch had enough to know he was in trouble.

"So, blackhead, you think I should go alone, eh?" grey-robed Leszuk said softly as he closed the door.

Sometimes an Eyerlon sorcerer relaxed enough to enjoy the latest spook story, and sometimes a black-haired Pennaikman referred to himself and his kin as blackheads, but more often the epithets were fighting words, no quarter asked or given. Vinoch straightened to his full height and matched the spook grin for toothy grin.

"I say there's no need to risk men's lives for the curiosity of a spook who hasn't got the pull."

The barracks remained silent except for the crackle of firewood and the occasional drip of water through the snow-covered roof.

Leszuk was a stumpy man, with thick arms and thicker legs. His neck bulged beneath the twisted silver torque that proclaimed his sorcerer's prowess. He wore his plain grey robe belted up over cavalryman's leggings. The torque proclaimed he had more *basi* than most; the ratty, unadorned robe warned that he was among the least of his sorcerous peers, a spook who had never been initiated into one of the several disciplines. As Eyerlon's sorcerers were measured—and they were measured into more ranks and disciplines than the army—Leszuk was just another unlucky veteran serving time in Tremontin.

"I can pull the Web down, all right," the sorcerer responded slowly in icy, hanging tones. "It's what pushes back that I'm worried about."

Vinoch felt beads of sweat on his forehead. Tremontin was dead. There was nothing larger than a field mouse left out there. Even the vultures had finally departed for warmer corpses. Dead was dead, as Vinoch saw it. There were no ghosts beneath the Web and nothing to account for the howling men heard on windless nights or the dreams that reduced hellfire-hardened veterans to gibbering cowards. Vinoch hadn't endured a nightmare—yet—but he'd felt them nosing the verge of his dreams. He knew there was something out in Tremontin, and that it wasn't going away.

"I might pull too hard," Leszuk continued. "I might pull the push clean inside these walls. You wouldn't want *that* to happen—would you?"

Vinoch shook his head, his tongue a speechless, sour rag.

"So, it's better that I go out and see with my eyes. No pull. No push. No danger." The spook's smile broadened. He clapped Vinoch on the shoulder.

Stinging sparks radiated along Vinoch's nerves from his shoulder. He wanted to curse but his voice had failed and, anyway, the sparks weren't the spook's fault. From deep within himself, Vinoch heard a voice that might have been his mother's, but might have been much, much older:

A day to meet your destiny, it whispered. *A good day to die.*

Pennaik language was consciously ambiguous; everything was subject to interpretation.

Vinoch's heart stuttered. When its rhythm returned, it beat with Leszuk's: Their destinies were linked. They were both going to die. Vinoch wrested away from the spook. Then, leaving his three flakes of silver on the table, he sought his sword and quilted surcoat.

In the pale light of a winter afternoon Vinoch rode with Leszuk into Tremontin. Steam funneled from their horses' nostrils, but they were swaddled and kept their living heat to themselves—for a little while. Leszuk led them deep into the ruined pass. The fortress slipped from sight. They were alone.

Vinoch listened anxiously to every hoof-crunch in the dry snow. He expected death to come when the shifty ground yawned beneath him. He imagined frozen dirt filling his nostrils. An hour passed, and despite the swaddling, his feet throbbed with cold. He stopped imagining dirt and began to think of ice crusting his flesh. Finally he closed his eyes and tried to think of nothing at all.

The attempt failed. Vinoch's horse balked each time Leszuk exchanged one aimless angle for the next complicated curve. Vinoch had to pay attention to the sorcerer's movements. He saw the large circular path of unfrozen ground at the same instant Leszuk did, and reined his horse to an immediate halt. He was twenty paces back when the sorcerer dismounted and walked unsteadily toward the center of the unfrozen dirt.

"I'm going out to the middle. I'm going to open myself up as I would in a Brightwater steam bath. But I won't be in a bath, and I won't reach for the Web—so nothing will happen and I'll walk right back."

Vinoch worried his chapped lips with his teeth. It didn't take sorcery to see that nothing natural kept this forsaken patch from freezing. And knowing what was buried in the ruins—the Arrizi army and, one devoutly hoped, the Arrizi commander as well—it didn't take genius to equate unnatural with unfriendly and unhealthy. A man could not outrun his destiny, but nothing said he couldn't try.

He applied shifting pressure against the horse's ribs. The beast blew steam as it turned toward the hidden fortress. It took a step. Behind them, the spook let out a blood-freezing shriek.

Vinoch clutched his cloak in panic, surprised that he was still alive. He didn't look back. The shriek broke, then restarted, weaker and warbling. He heard a crackling sound, smelled the bitter gall of hellfire and refused to turn around, hoping against hope that he might survive if he did not look. His spurs gouged the horse's flesh.

The warbling ceased.

The horse was useless. Its hooves were rooted to the ground, which, Vinoch realized, was covered now by slush, not snow. Warmth caressed his back, swirling toward his heart. With a bark of terror, he kicked free of the stirrups, leaping to the ground. His legs buckled and he crawled until his heart stopped; then he used his last strength to roll onto his back.

A good day to die.

But Vinoch did not die when the hellfire swept over him. Without body, mind, or will, the nomad confronted ten thousand Arrizi, fifteen foolish Walenfolk, one unlucky spook, and the countless trees and animals of the buried forest.

He had two last notions before his soul merged with the rest: they were all waiting for something beyond his imagination; and they wouldn't have long to wait.

Chapter Two

Braydon was nervous. After Tremontin and to his great surprise, Prince Alegshorn sorRodion had selected him, a country-common shepherd, from a hundred other men to serve in his personal guard. He applied himself to his new duties: standing watch in one of the many palace towers when the free-spirited prince did not require an escort. But after a mere three months in Eyerlon, the narrow maze of streets remained unfamiliar and frightening to him, especially at night, especially when he found himself last in line as the prince led them all who-knew-where. He was completely lost. If he became separated, it would be dawn before he found his way back to the palace, and by noon he'd be walking all the way back to the wretched village where he'd been born.

There were real threats to the prince's well-being on this, the second night of Calends in the forty-seventh year of King Manal sorRodion's reign. In addition to the obvious dangers posed by the ice-covered cobblestones, there was always the Wolf, who might be lurking in any shadow. When he marched with the common men of Fenklare during the war, Braydon had had no personal contact with the Wolf, but legends of the cursed prince's depraved habits and blood-lust circulated through the smaller, close-knit royal guards. As Braydon followed his prince through the dark streets, he wished he had a spear in his hand instead of a sputtering torch.

He was breathless and oozing sweat beneath his surcoat when Prince Aleg called a halt outside a nondescript building and divided up his men.

"You three make yourselves scarce, but keep your eyes open. Hal, you stay with the torches. And you— You with the torch—Brandon—?"

"Braydon Braydson, midons prince."

"Right. Give Hal your torch. You're coming with me."

"Midons prince?"

Braydon had, he believed, gotten his promotion because he was a brawny lad who, as a rule, did exactly what he was told. Still, it didn't take much to guess that this was no ordinary assignation and whoever went inside might witness events that might render him expendable. Any reasonable man would hesitate.

"*Now,* Brandon."

He swallowed hard and followed his prince through the dark door. The lamp-lit vestibule was blessedly warm and blessedly empty. The prince shed his drab cloak and cowl. His golden hair shone against the embroidered blue velvet of a tightly fitted dalmatic. One after the other, Prince Aleg propped his boots on the stairs for Braydon to polish with his sleeve.

"Do I seem sufficiently princely?"

Braydon collected the castoff clothing. "Yes, midons prince."

"Look at me, Brandon, when you answer me."

"Braydon, midons prince. Braydon Braydson." He folded the garments over his arm as he obeyed. "The whole kingdom knows you are a prince, midons, how could you seem otherwise?"

Prince Aleg flashed a smile that men followed eagerly into battle and women into other, equally dangerous places. "For a start, I could look like my misfortuned brother." The prince's smile cooled but did not vanish—as if he shared a private joke with himself.

Braydon followed Prince Aleg upstairs. The two men bracketing the upper doorway recognized the prince and stood aside. Like Braydon, they wore nothing that could identify them—but unlike him, they were armed: one with a shortened spear, the other with a sword. The swordsman opened the door.

Chair legs scraped as a double handful of noblefolk rose and gave the golden prince the honor he was due. Braydon recognized most of them. Many were the prince's personal friends; a few were older men who'd befriended his father. A few, concealing their faces behind decorated masks, weren't men at all. These women worried Braydon. Prince Aleg had a very comfortable hall and privy chamber in the palace; he did not need to wander the frigid streets of Eyerlon when he wanted to meet a lady.

The seat of honor at the head of the table stood unoccupied, but honor be hanged, if Prince Aleg sat there he'd have his back to another door. Braydon was still wondering what he should do if the prince moved toward the indefensible seat, when the prince nudged the chair of Eudalig sorJos, a cruel-faced young man whose reputation was almost as unsavory as the Wolf's. SorJos scowled but surrendered his place at the table. Braydon, much relieved, stood at the prince's back.

"We're honored by your presence, midons prince," one of the unfamiliar men announced. "Your blessing—"

"Don't confuse my blessing with my presence, Skulpen," the prince snapped. The rest of the room stiffened. Prince Alegshorn picked up a wine ewer and filled the nearest goblet before Braydon could intercede. "Quickly tell me everything no one would tell me in the palace, so I can stop pretending I don't know why I'm here."

Conscious of his duties, Braydon kept his eyes on the just-named nobleman, whose lips became pale, thin lines when he scowled. Skulpen was old enough to be Prince Aleg's father, and for an unguarded moment Skulpen's eyes flashed with undisguised contempt for Prince Vigelan's charming second son. Braydon marked that; then all true emotion vanished beneath a partisan smile.

Driskolt sorMeklan, Sidon of Fenklare, the prince's most frequent companion for both revelry and quiet conversation, answered his friend's question. "We believe that the Wolf plans to disassemble our estates. We believe he means to restore his treasury by ransoming them to the highest bidder. We believe he intends to pollute our honor lands with upstart common merchants who grew rich while we defended Walensor. We are not pleased."

Prince Alegshorn seemed surprised, although Braydon knew that Sidon Driskolt had invited his prince to this seditious gathering. "And to think," the prince said, "I had thought it was the king's treasury that needed filling, and the king's notion that vacant estates be offered to those merchants who kept the army clothed, fed, and armed."

"Godswill, midons prince!" Oxlike Black Moreg sorMoreg (so-called to distinguish him from his identically named, equally massive, but red-haired, cousin), another of Prince Aleg's contemporaries, but a less-frequent visitor to the palace, pounded the table with his massive fist. The goblets tottered. "Since Tremontin, the Wolf lurks inside King Manel's ear. While he's whispering, no one else can be heard! Only the gods know what the Wolf's got in mind once he has a full treasury."

"The gods and the spooks," Eudalig corrected.

Braydon's ears turned red as the assembled noblefolk spewed abuse upon Walensor's sorcerers and its crown prince. To his relief, Prince Aleg silenced everyone with a soft-spoken question: "What do you expect of me?"

Eyes turned uptable to the sidon of Fenklare, who kept his hands folded and his mouth shut.

The fateful words fell to Black Moreg. "Godswill! *Remove* the bastard!"

"In an eyeblink—if the Wolf *were* a bastard, but he's as legitimate as I—or you, Lord Moreg. Challenge my brother's right to the throne of Walensor and you challenge the right of every son to inherit from his father. To speak of *removing* the Wolf is to talk treason against the traditions which have ruled the kingdom for a thousand years. Do we dare to talk treason tonight?"

A lump clogged Braydon's throat. They were already talking treason. They were all dead if word of this meeting reached the wrong ears. He wanted to bolt from the room, but he didn't, nor did any of the partisans standing behind their lords, though their faces grew pale.

"Your father first talked treason the morning you were born," Eudalig drawled. "Just ask Lord Skulpen: He was there. It was always Prince Vigelan's intention that you should be his heir."

Growing up on Fenklare's northwest frontier, Braydon had never laid eyes on Prince Vigelan sorRodion. He'd known nothing of the nursery-war between the Wolf and his slightly younger, slightly bigger brother until he joined the army. Since Prince Alegshorn plucked him for his guard, he'd heard rumors of vicious beatings that left *both* young princes at the menders' mercies for weeks at a time. If the rumors were true, he thanked all the gods that he'd not been born a sorRodion, but had to wonder, very privately, if either prince was fit to rule. Stealing glances at the other common partisans, Braydon wondered if others had begun to share his doubts.

"Godswill," swore a beardless youth of no more than fifteen years. The youngster, wearing a sorMeklan badge of dark green and deep ruby on his sleeve, sat beside Driskolt sorMeklan.

"Godswill, midons prince, if you don't act soon, it may be too late. Our king is old and could die at any moment."

Driskolt, an only son and confirmed donitorial heir, had no need to wear the family's colors. He did not clout the boy across the head, and so Braydon inferred that the stripling spoke with Fenklare's approval.

"You will, midons prince." Red Moreg spoke for the first time, a voice as deep and formidable as his cousin's. "We place our lives and our honor in your hands."

The prince contemplated the swirling wine in his goblet as if the surface patterns held private omens. "Need I remind any of you good lords that the price of treason is not merely death, but anathema? To raise a hand against the Wolf is to raise a hand against the Crown. Get caught and you lose not only your life, but your soul's eternal peace. Personally, I'm content, of late, to let Fate weave her own cloth."

"The war's over; the Wolf will turn on you." Skulpen spoke with certainty. "He might prevail: He's fast and sly, pays no heed to honor, *and* you've never gotten the best of him. Maybe you'd both die. Then who'd inherit the crown? Gilenan?" The sneering lord named the third prince, a boy born after his father's death. "No one wants your mother for regent; her Merrisati kin would swarm like flies and we'd never be rid of them. A nobleman, like myself, might wed one of your sisters, might make a bedstead claim on the crown. But it would be easier for us all if you clear your own path to the throne, as Prince Vigelan always intended."

Prince Alegshorn stared at the older man a long time. "I am truly heartened by your faith, Lord Skulpen avsorLewel." The prince's voice held a touch of bitterness Braydon had never heard before, but it had no effect on Skulpen, who smiled for the first time as he said:

"It is an honor to place my honor in the hands of Prince Vigelan's favorite son. You are all that my heart's-friend prayed for. Walensor will be in your debt."

Braydon's tongue stuck to the roof of his mouth. Growing up, he'd held the usual commonfolk perception of noblefolk: powerful men and women whose loyalty to each other was exceeded only by their greed. He'd clung to that perception during the war, but a few months in the prince's guard had changed his opinions completely. If Prince Alegshorn ascended the throne as a result of conspiracy and treason, he was going to be in debt to the noblefolk, not the other way around.

As with the misplaced chair, Braydon's prince didn't need the concern of a country-common shepherd. "Were the throne to become mine, I would want no debts surrounding it, either owed or owing."

"But will you have the crown and throne, midons prince?" Eudalig toyed with the feathers dangling from his hat.

"I would not refuse, if they came cleanly. But, and hear me well, good lords, while King Manal rules and reigns, I abide no talk of treason against my kin."

Driskolt sorMeklan leapt to his feet, brandishing his goblet at the rafters. "Hail Manal sorRodion, King of Walensor!"

Everyone matched the gesture, saluting the monarch who had already reigned for forty-seven years—the last twenty as an invalid ensconced in a Brightwater-filled throne. King Manal had brought Walensor to unprecedented prosperity and, inadvertently, aroused the greed of the Arrizan Empire. Most common men, Braydon included, wouldn't have minded if Manal sorRodion remained king forever. He believed in his heart that the king, not the Wolf, had planned the audacious strategy of Tremontin.

Driskolt's young companion voiced Braydon's sentiment: "May our king rule and reign a hundred years!"

Arms stretched again; then the noblefolk sat and drank. Or Braydon assumed that they did; Prince Alegshorn, the only nobleman whose mouth he could actually see, merely wet his lips without swallowing. Braydon was relieved when the conversation meandered to slightly less dangerous subjects.

"I'm opening my hall for a feast tomorrow," the prince announced. "After all, twenty-three years ago there were only three Calends' nights between the winter solstice and the rising of the next new moon. It has become my custom to celebrate the precise anniversary of my brother's birth."

"Will he attend?" one of the Moregs asked. Braydon did not see which, and their voices were very much alike.

"My brother marks his anniversary on first of Greater Ice, as you well know. A Calends birth, when the sun is cold and the moon is hiding, is too cursed for public celebration, especially by a prince who wishes to be crowned king. But I am pleased to remember what the Wolf would forget."

One of the masked women spoke for the first time. Braydon recognized the voice of Wektianne barSulwynde, whose long, slender legs he'd last seen wrapped around the prince in his privy chamber. "Is the celebration for lords only, midons prince, or are ladies invited?"

"Beauty is always welcome in my hall. Yours above all, dear lady. We'll dance away the cold and make merry until dawn."

"As you command, midons," she replied huskily.

Prince Alegshorn leapt to his feet so fast that the grim partisan behind Wektianne wrapped his fist around the hilt of his sword and Braydon lurched forward to protect his prince with his life, if necessary. But the golden prince merely reached across the table to raise the lady's hand fashionably to his lips. "Say 'request,' *merou.* Not even a prince can command beauty."

The odd-sounding endearment was one of the few Pennaik words the prince used with any frequency. Braydon didn't know what it meant, but from the flush surrounding the edge of Wektianne's mask, it was a word she had heard in more intimate circumstances. Braydon held his prince's chair, expecting him to sit again, but the prince remained standing.

"I cannot stay here all night, so, tell me, do I understand you right, my good and loyal friends? It is your opinion that for the good of Walensor, and especially for the good of Walensor's noblefolk, the Wolf must die?" Aleg stared at each of the conspirators in turn.

Braydon caught sight of Aleg's smile and was grateful he did not have to meet the eyes above it.

Eudalig moistened his lips. "It would be sufficient if he renounced his claim in your favor, midons prince. He knows it was Prince Vigelan's wish, for the good of Walensor. You said it yourself: He's Calends-born, cursed in form and spirit. Because he is legitimate, and a hand raised against him now is a hand raised against us all, he must be brought to a proper understanding."

"While hearts beat blood, the Wolf will not renounce his rights," Prince Alegshorn assured them all. "If you would plot against my brother, *you* must understand that. He'll kill anyone who crosses him."

Eudalig studied his fingernails with seemingly rapt attention.

The prince broke the tension with a grin. "For that matter—in this one thing, we are in complete accord."

"That is understood, midons prince," Driskolt agreed, meeting his prince's stare. Braydon knew the sorMeklan counted a dozen kings of Walensor and elsewhere in their lineage; he supposed they could meet the eyes of any upstart sorRodion without flinching. "The question seems to be: Which prince wants the throne more? The donitors would like to have an answer before the Wolf sells our honor-land to ennoble commonfolk merchants."

Prince Alegshorn caught Braydon's eye, and jerked a commanding knuckle toward the door before saying to his friend and everyone else: "You shall, Dris. My word: You shall be the first to know."

Braydon reached the door in time to open it for his prince, who strode through without a backward glance or farewell. They were alone in the vestibule again. While Braydon draped the prince's cloak around him, Prince Aleg studied the now-shut upper door.

"Well, we've spiked their wheels for a while," he said, fastening the cloak with a plain bronze brooch.

"'We,' midons prince?"

Prince Aleg sighed. "A figure of speech, Bandron."

Braydon opened his mouth, then closed it again: If the prince couldn't remember his name, he might yet survive this brush with treason.

Prince Aleg waited until they were in the tunnel between the older and newer portions of the royal residence before questioning the men he'd left outside the conspirators' bolthole. They reported seeing nothing suspicious; Aleg dismissed them for the night. Braydon started with them. He got half a step before he felt a drag on his cloak.

"Follow me."

Quenching his torch in the snow, Braydon hurried after the prince. They took the empty backways to Prince Aleg's hall, where body servants awaited them. A half-dozen hands helped the prince remove his heavy clothes; Braydon was left to his own devices, and the prince was comfortable in silk and soft wool while he was still arguing with his surcoat. Prince Aleg sent a boy to the kitchen for cold meat and sweetbreads. By the time the plate arrived, Braydon was warming his back by the brazier, wondering how much longer he had to live.

From a sideways sprawl in a high-backed chair, Prince Aleg dismissed the boy. He began gnawing on a chicken leg. Braydon stood stiff and grim.

"Have some," the prince said amiably.

Braydon shook his head, though his mouth was watering.

"Suit yourself. There's enough for two."

"It is not my place, midons prince."

The prince tossed the bone into the brazier, where it sizzled. He began dividing a sweetbread into bite-sized pieces. "What do you make of our conspiracy?" he asked casually, as if asking about the weather.

Braydon wished that his prince would stop implying *we*. "It is not my place to make anything of it, midons prince. I wish to the gods that my ears had been sealed with wax."

"But they weren't—and I asked you a question."

"It is not my place to answer such a question, midons prince."

"Braydon Braydson, born in Gorse on Weychawood in far Fenklare, and, by my grandfather's assart decree, exempt from sorMeklan taxation and justice until his death. You're the son of Brayd (who else?), a shepherd, and the woman, Ingolde, a weaver recently raised into the Web as a hedge-sorcerer. Your father died at Kasserine—with mine. Your brother, Indon, died what—two summers ago in High Norivarl—?"

"Three."

The prince shrugged. "Very well, three summers ago. It was four years ago that you first answered the muster-call. You marched with Santar barFlayne avsorMeklan, because, though your village is assarted land, your family sells wool at the Flayne market where he was lord. You, yourself, are a lordless man. Have I missed anything significant?"

"No, midons prince," Braydon whispered to this toes.

"I know things about you, Braydon, that you don't know about yourself. But I'll spare you the details if you'll concede that I am not in the habit of choosing my guardsmen haphazardly, *and* do me the honor of answering my questions when I ask them."

Braydon couldn't speak, but the prince was blessed with—or had learned—patience. He waited until his guardsman mumbled:

"I concede, midons prince."

"That's good. I was beginning to fear that I'd misjudged when I chose you."

"I thought it was the luck of the draw." The words were out of Braydon's mouth, without the proper honorifics, before he could stop them.

Prince Alegshorn scowled. "Iser's iron whiskers, not hardly."

"Midons prince, you knew who I was when you walked the line picking your men for the winter?"

"Let's say I knew *what* you were, and let's say you answer my question: What do you make of our conspirators?"

The momentary pride Braydon gained from the knowledge that he'd been chosen by plan, not luck, vanished. "Midons prince, it isn't my—"

The prince hurled another half-gnawed bone. It struck hard on bone beneath Braydon's eye. A finger's breadth more and it would have blinded him. He realized that luck had nothing to do with his prince's aim or, presumably, anything else.

"Midons prince, I believe they despise Prince Rinchen above all else."

"Everyone despises my brother. He despises himself; all else follows naturally. Should I make common cause with them?"

"They support you, midons prince, because they believe you're noblefolk, like them, not royal."

"Well put!" Prince Aleg sat straight in his chair. His smile left Braydon blooming like a flower in the springtime sun. "I'll remember that, Braydon—noble, not royal. Anything else?"

Braydon raked his sweat-damp hair, wondering if he should mention the contempt he'd seen on Lord Skulpen's face, and deciding against it. "I don't know, midons prince. I don't know you. And I know even less of the Wolf, your brother. Begging your pardon, midons prince, but you are not what I expected. Is it not possible that the Wolf is not what he seems either?"

"Ah—now that's a very good question. I knew you would be clever enough. But you ask the wrong person. Everyone knows that my brother and I are hardly in each other's confidence. He meets my expectations, but who can say if he truly is what he seems to be? Go on."

"I've gone far enough, midons prince. I see that a prince's life is treacherous, and I have already made too many errors—"

"Fortunately for both of us, I haven't." Prince Aleg took a bite of sweetbread, then wiped his fingers on his breeches. "Braydon Braydson, to whom have you sworn enduring oaths?"

Braydon recognized a commanding question and came to attention. "Midons prince, I'm sworn to your personal service."

"For which I pay you well. I had something personal in mind. Have you sworn your honor or loyalty to another?"

Braydon shook his head. "I was born in an assart village. Our land belongs to the Crown, our personal oaths, too. I'd need royal permission to swear a personal oath. . . ." Understanding burst in Braydon's mind. "I could freely swear to you, midons prince," he murmured, raising his eyes to meet the prince's.

"Have you enough *basi* to reach the Web?"

"I am headblind, midons prince. Surely you know that our hedge-sorcerer, Auld Mag, swore so when I was born. Even if I had the *basi*, I could not use it."

"Can't miss what you never had," the prince added with a knowing look. "Can you read script or tallies?"

"Not a word, midons prince. I can count sheep in my head and coins on a board."

"Make certain it stays that way if you value your tongue or your fingers."

The prince bellowed for another servant. The man appeared so quickly that Braydon assumed he had been eavesdropping. "Summon the spider. Tell him I'm taking an oath."

The servant's eyes wandered. Braydon realized the man was a sorcerer reaching for the Web. He shouldn't have been surprised that his prince would have spooks in his personal service, but he was.

"Taviella attends. My ears are her ears. My eyes are her eyes. All that is done shall be recorded within the Web."

The prince disappeared momentarily into his privy chamber at the rear of the hall. When he returned, he held a length of braided silk cord in the sapphire and grey colors he'd made his own. "You're right-armed, aren't you?"

Braydon nodded, and shivered involuntarily when the prince knotted loops of silk over his right shoulder.

"Braydon Braydson, lordless man of the assart of Gorse, surrender yourself into my safekeeping. Swear to me your life and honor; I will protect them from all harm beneath the Web of Walensor as you henceforth honor me above all others." Braydon tried to kneel. "Stay on your feet, fool—I'm not ennobling you," Prince Aleg hissed, "merely asserting, before the spooks, that I'm the only one who can legally kill you."

Braydon's jaw dropped. "Midons prince—"

"The lordless man understands," the spook chanted. "He is lordless no more. He is Braydon Braydson no more. Braydon avAlegshorn, what you do henceforth is done by Alegshorn ruVigelan sorRodion, Prince of the Realm. Whatever is done to you, is likewise done to the prince."

The hall echoed with the sound of something breaking. Braydon wondered what was wrong, then felt boiling moisture streaming down his right arm and was shamefully relieved when the prince seized his shirt to keep him from falling. The burning stopped; his right arm was completely numb. The sleeve shimmered with Brightwater, and the clasp binding the cords to his sleeve gleamed with unnatural light before fading to ordinary silver.

"The oath is bound!" The spook closed his eyes, breaking contact with the Web. "Will you be needing me again, midons Prince Alegshorn?"

"No, go back to bed."

When the spook was gone, Braydon succumbed to dizziness.

The prince helped him sit in the high-back chair and once again suggested that he eat.

"Your first Brightwater oath takes a lot out of you."

Braydon took a drumstick awkwardly with his left hand.

"You'll feel fine by morning," Prince Aleg assured him. "But I'd think twice before I raised my hand against anyone wearing my colors—especially against me."

Holding the drumstick in his teeth, Braydon arranged his numb arm in his lap. He fingered the braided silk and took the drumstick out of his mouth. "What does it mean? What have I done, midons?"

"You've become an oath-bound partisan—*my* oath-bound partisan."

"What do I do, midons prince?"

"Whatever I tell you to do—mostly messenger duty. I'll give you a scroll to take to someone, or send you to fetch one. We headblind folk can't rely on the Web, can we?"

Braydon still didn't like it when the prince used *we*. "Does it come off, midons prince?" He fingered the silver clasp.

"Of course. I expect everyone in my service to change his shirt at least once a year."

Braydon blushed like a maiden. "What if I lose it, or it gets stolen?" Once again he forgot the proper honorifics.

Prince Aleg merely laughed. "You won't lose it; Brightwater silver doesn't get lost. And it doesn't take kindly to being stolen or otherwise removed."

"'Otherwise removed,' midons prince?"

"I don't promise you that you'll be safe from my enemies or my friends, Braydon avAlegshorn, but I swear you'll be avenged."

"I'm honored, midons prince—I don't know what to say . . . or do."

"Say 'good night' and go back to your barracks. Wektianne's in the inner room and she'll keep me up past dawn if I linger out here much longer."

Chapter Three

A steel needle flashed in the lamplight of a shuttered bedchamber in a noblefolk residence of Eyerlon. Following a pattern pinned to a sawdust-filled pillow, the needlewoman made knots from fine, white thread. It was the simplest of needlemade lace patterns. An experienced lacemaker would create it quickly and by fingertip feel alone, but for Berika Ingoldesdaughter each stitch of the web required and received her full concentration.

Not long ago, in the week of Lesser Gleaning, Berika had been a daydreaming shepherd in the faraway village of Gorse. She'd come a long way from there to a bedchamber in the sorMeklan residence, but she knew she hadn't come to the end of her journey. The days of rich food and soft mattresses would not last forever, so she practiced her knots until her fingers ached, determined to be prepared for whatever fate befell her.

But sometimes even the most diligent thoughts wandered from their proper path, or were pulled—

"Berika?"

The voice came from the depths of Berika's daydreams. Faint and empty, it set her thoughts adrift. The needle slipped through her motionless fingers. In her mind's eye, she returned to Gorse when the night air was raw and she was damp to the skin from the rain.

The thongs of her cloak pressed against her throat. Her fingers were numb, nearly useless on the wet leather bindings that held the wooden bar locked in place across the fane door. The harder she struggled with the bindings, the tighter they became until she went to work with her teeth.

Berika was determined to get into the little open-roofed building where her village worshipped Weycha, the forest goddess, the one god they were allowed to worship until She forgave them for cutting down Her primeval trees.

Weycha had already forgiven Berika—or so Berika had believed. Locked inside the fane was a harp formed from a single piece of Weycha's wood and sealed in a golden acorn as large as half-grown sheep. Berika had received the *basi*-laden instrument that past afternoon. She meant to take the instrument all the way to Eyerlon, where, somehow, it would become the key to unlock a better future than the one she'd have here in Gorse.

Taking wasn't stealing. The harp *was* hers, just as the demon calling her name as she bit through the bindings was also hers. She'd fetched them both with a wild, whirling, and desperate prayer. The mortal world was no place for a demon. He'd brought the harp, the true answer to her prayer—it couldn't very well have fallen straight out of the sky—and now, his task accomplished, it was time for him to return to his proper world. Demons couldn't die, couldn't feel pain, couldn't ache with loneliness and fear—

Although that was what Berika heard in the demon's faint voice, both in her memories and in her daydreaming thoughts, as he repeated her name.

The bindings fell away. The fane door swung open. Through the almost-darkness Berika glimpsed the harp, snug within its huge protective acorn. The demon crouched beside it with glowing-ember eyes and wild hair. She should have been afraid of him. Beneath the Web of Walensor, everything unnatural was dangerous. She should have escaped with the acorn, counting herself beloved of the gods who'd answered her prayer. But what she wanted to do was kneel beside the demon and hold him gently in her arms until he died—if demons could truly die.

That frightened her more than the demon himself. He roused something worse than pain from deep within her. Hold him until the aching was gone and she'd be left with love. And love was the last thing Berika wanted to feel. Love was a woman's special enemy. It left her blind, weak, and helpless in the world of men. Berika's mother had told her so every day of her life, and if Berika believed nothing else Ingolde told her, she believed that one thing.

Love was the enemy. The demon was the enemy because she loved him.

She ran away, tears mixed with the rain, leaving the harp and the demon behind.

"Berika? Can you hear me?"

His voice came from another dark corner of her mind. She hurried toward it and a giant fir tree.

The demon was there, nestled within her cloak, just awakening from a peaceful sleep. Her head was on his shoulder and his touch was gentle as he wriggled free.

Hirmin Maggotson was coming: her hellfired husband whom she feared and hated, but never, ever loved. The demon had done what no one could do—what no one had even tried to do: challenged Hirmin's right to her and taken her beyond his reach. But she was the world to crippled Hirmin. He was coming after her and the demon was leaving. She could forgive him. He'd come for her once, that was enough. The demon didn't have to fight Hirmin a second time.

The demon had left the harp, left a path she could follow by herself. If she chose, she could continue to Eyerlon with her cloak to keep her warm, her mother's hoard of little silver coins to buy her food, and the acorn-harp to buy her future once she reached the city. With the demon between her and Hirmin, she might well succeed.

But Berika chose against leaving, without asking herself the reason why.

She stayed nestled in the cloak, thinking the demon was gone, waiting for Hirmin to reclaim her. And Hirmin did come to the fir-tree clearing, armed with a fresh-sharpened scythe, but the demon had not gone. Armed only with righteousness, the demon fought for a second time against the crazed and desperate Hirmin.

Demons bled.

Hirmin's wicked long-handled scythe slashed the length of the demon's forearm. The gushing blood was as red and free as any mortal man's. Perhaps the demon could die . . . would die fighting a battle that didn't have to be fought. Berika knew she could survive her husband. She didn't love him. A woman could survive anything . . . except love.

The demon retreated toward an ancient, skeletal tree where, Berika was certain, Hirmin would put an end to whatever life he possessed. And although she knew she could survive years of life with her husband, she was suddenly uncertain if she could survive the death of Dart, her demon.

Then the tree exploded and Dart disappeared, replaced by something wholly demonic and wielding a wooden sword that shone with its own crimson light. Two heartbeats and it was over: The seething sword slashed her husband's neck. His head and body fell separately. Her deliverer came toward her carrying that strange, deadly sword, smiling Dart's warm smile. Only he wasn't Dart, or Dart wasn't a man. Ingolde was right: Love was the enemy, but terror was stronger than love. She fell on her knees, eyes closed and begging for her life.

"Berika? I'm lost."

Blinded by tears long since shed, Berika followed her heart until memory's vision cleared again.

They were in a tiny room with slanting walls and a shifting floor: a river boat's tiny cabin. She could stand up straight, but Dart had to be careful that he didn't strike his head on the deck beams. He was warmly dressed in the fine, comfortable clothes of the noblefolk—as she was, too, she realized—and holding a harp she had just given him. A child's harp with rotted, broken strings.

They were on their way to Eyerlon, no more stops or missteps. Dart was not a demon; he was the younger brother of Lord Ean sorMeklan, the donitor of Fenklare, who had died eighteen years earlier, been resurrected and preserved by Weycha as her champion until Berika's wild prayer had drawn him out of the forest. Demons were unnatural and dangerous—but the Compact absolutely forbid resurrection; it was anathema to the revenant and to those who associated with him. Dart was headed to Eyerlon because the most powerful sorcerers in Walensor were there, sorcerers who had questions and who meant to have answers to those questions, whatever it took to get them. Berika knew all this because through accident, coincidence, and the ache of love—both denied and feared—she had betrayed her demon into the hands of sorcerers and his family; betrayal which destined her also for Eyerlon, not with the acorn-harp but as the leman-lover of Driskolt sorMeklan, the donitor's son and Dart's nephew.

Driskolt had taken her into his bed to spite Dart, his resurrected uncle; and, looking at Dart's face as he handled the crumbling harp string, Berika knew that Dris had succeeded.

Dart set the harp aside, thanking her politely, acidly. The words flayed her heart, exposing the love, the fear, and a new sense of shame. She wanted to be gone from the cabin . . . from him forever . . . before her tears burst through, but he caught her at the door with his own, unnecessary apology, and she put her arms around him instead.

By then Berika wanted to touch a man, and be touched in return. She had Driskolt to thank for that. What had begun in betrayal and vengeance had, with unnerving speed, transformed itself into comfort, even friendship—but not love. Berika had never loved Driskolt and never feared him. She didn't cringe when Dris touched her, and he had proved, from the first, not to be cruel or heartless. Hirmin ceased to be the only man she remembered, and when Dart's arms circled through hers, she was no longer afraid of her demon or of love—

Until Driskolt came into the tiny room and fear grew in her heart as never before. Dart and Driskolt sparred with each other, but Driskolt wasn't Hirmin, and Dart was in no position to fight for her ever again.

Dart said, instead, that the passionate embrace which Dris had interrupted was merely retribution: his way of teaching Berika a lesson for betraying him.

Ingolde's lesson: Love was the enemy. The light went out in her world. The pain was too great for tears.

"Berika? Where are you?"

She wandered outside her own memories. Pain became endless in the emptiness and the dark. Berika was in the fane, the forest, and the river boat all at once, and somewhere—nowhere—as well, with Dart's plaintive voice all around her. The echo of relentless, probing questions undermined Dart's voice, and moment by moment, Berika caught the swirling drift of memories—answers—that were not her own.

Her demon was in the ungentle care of the Eyerlon inquists, potent sorcerers who could glean the least motes of truth from anyone's memory. They picked him apart with questions, destroying the barriers the goddess had placed in his mind when she resurrected him. They wanted Weycha, the proof that the goddess had violated the Compact, and the reason why—and they did not care about those pieces of Dart's life they found but did not need.

"Berika! Have a care for me. Help me find the way!"

Berika did care, although she wished she did not. They'd hurt each other evenly, but how could anyone hear such a plea and not care? She was a shepherd. She knew how to find the lost and the helpless, how to guide them home.

Her face—not the true-face she knew was hers but the face Dart remembered—welled up in the lonely darkness. There was light which she could not bear, because it came from her. She fled back to herself, to her own darkness, dreams, and memories.

Berika's thoughts and self returned to the quiet bedchamber

where hot tears dribbled from her chin to her hands. She'd dozed off, Berika told herself. Lost herself in sad dreams. Without conviction. It had all happened before, although never during the day. Dart *was* in the Basilica. The inquists *were* interrogating him.

And when he was so lost that he could not find himself, her demon still called her name.

Berika drifted through her memories of Dart, unmindful of her tears, until her hands recognized the fine thread twisted around her fingers. The simple needlelace web on which she'd been working since dawn was a tangled ruin, thoroughly ink-stained by the crinkled parchment pattern pinned beneath it. With a hopeless sigh, Berika set the sawdust-filled lace-making pillow aside. She slid from the chair to the floor and warmed her hands above a cast-iron brazier set, for safety, in a small sandbox.

"Here I am, in an Eyerlon noblefolk residence and it's colder than it ever was in Gorse."

She talked to herself quite often, now that she passed her days alone in the drafty bedchamber on the residence's second floor. Superficially, it was a fine room. The bed was huge with two mattresses, one of horsehair and the other filled with feathers. Heavy curtains in the sorMeklan colors—deep green and rich ruby red—hung from carved bedposts. There was a knotted carpet on the floor, and tapestries hung against the walls.

But the residence itself was falling apart.

When she'd asked Driskolt why the sorMeklan residence was more ramshackle than a country-common shepherd's home in Gorse, he'd explained that all the noblefolk residences had been hurriedly raised twenty years ago after King Manal was crippled in a hunting accident. With their king dependent on Brightwater and unable to wander from one clan stronghold to the next, as had been the custom of Walensor's kings for untold generations, the noble clans were compelled to come to him.

Convinced that Prince Vigelan would soon become king and return to the traditional, wandering ways of monarchy, the sorMeklan and their peers had cobbled their residences together. None of them had anticipated that King Manal would reign another twenty years, or that the second half of those years would find Walensor in a desperate war.

And no one had noticed that they were building their residences on a flood plain.

Since its construction, the sorMeklan residence had sunk about three feet and listed noticeably toward the river front. The chimney flues were cracked and, except for the huge hearth in the lower hall, the only source of heat was a multitude of braziers. The kitchen was unusable; all the sorMeklan food was cooked field-style in the courtyard. During the bitter days of Calends, meals weren't merely cold, they were often frozen. There were gaps in the walls larger than Berika's fist. The tapestries were in constant, noisy motion. Flakes of snow as well as plaster drifted on the carpet.

Berika's numb fingers warmed and began to ache. She wrapped her hands in the full skirt of her wool gown and rocked on her knees. Eyes closed, she concentrated on the cow-headed image of the women's goddess. "Mother Cathe—weep for me. I've never been so cold in all my life!"

The image did not weep. Instead, the voice of Berika's conscience reminded her that she didn't have to spend her days as well as her nights in the drafty room. She was the sidon's leman; she had the run of the residence.

"Just like his hounds."

Berika's hands stopped burning. She unwrapped them and held them above the brazier again.

"No, it's not like that," she corrected herself. "Midons Driskolt isn't what I thought he'd be. He reminds me of Indon. . . ."

When he'd died three summers ago, Indon was not much older than the sidon who visited her whenever he pleased and came through the door without knocking. They were both burly young men with unruly light brown hair over nut-colored eyes. Driskolt seemed to resemble his kin in the residence. Indon resembled neither of his dark-haired parents—although, for that matter, neither did she nor Braydon. Their hair was lighter still and their eyes were blue-gray. Ingolde said they looked like their grandmother. She never said anything about Indon.

Berika returned to her chair, taking the pillow into her lap. The ink stains would never come out, but the pattern was salvageable and the medallion itself was only the third one she'd made. Her work was still far too coarse to sell in the market even if the thread had been pure white. For practice it didn't matter if the thread was stained or not. She set to work carefully untangling the snarls.

Two days after arriving in Eyerlon, she'd asked midons Driskolt if a woman could survive in the city without selling herself. He had laughed aloud, but Berika had persisted and he'd mentioned the lacemakers whose work was more precious than gold. Then he'd arranged for an old woman to teach his leman the rudiments of stitching in air, as the lacemakers called their craft. Perhaps the sidon had thought Berika would be discouraged by the crone's appearance. If he had, he'd thought wrong.

"I'll be ready," Berika promised, after defeating the snarl. "When he throws me into the street, I'll be able to take care of myself. I won't have to go back to Gorse and I won't have to live above a gaming house. I'll find a little room with a big window and I'll sell lace to noblefolk ladies—" Without warning, the half-finished web tore loose from the parchment pattern pinned to the pillow. This time the lace could not be salvaged. The day's work was ruined.

"Mother Cathe, *please*, let me learn. I don't have very much time—"

But the image that sprang into Berika's mind wasn't the women's goddess, it was a fire-blackened tree.

"Weycha!"

The name was off Berika's tongue before she had the wit to swallow it. Weycha's was not a name Berika wished to utter. The goddess hadn't been pleased when Berika fetched Dart out of the forest. She could hardly be happier now with her champion under inquist interrogation in the Basilica.

"I thought he was a demon. I thought he broke the Compact. I was afraid for my soul." That was a lie and Berika knew it. "My mother always said love was the worst fate a woman could have. She said hate could make a woman strong, if she seized it by the throat; but love would make her weak. Better to marry a monster like Hirmin than be flayed by love." That was partly true, but if the goddess could hear, then she should tell the complete truth. "I'm sorry, Weycha. I didn't understand. I pray he'll be all right—you know that I do. I pray your champion will leave the Basilica safely. I pray he will return to you. I listen when I hear his voice in my dreams. I guide him back to himself. But I could not bear to see him again."

Berika dried her eyes on her sleeve. She threw the ruined lace on the brazier and started again with a new thread. Lacemaking was tedious, hour-eating work. Nothing else could occupy her thoughts while her fingers worked the needle; that was why she enjoyed it.

The door opened; someone entered the room—a sour-faced young woman bearing an armload of dark green cloth.

"Godswill! Look at you! The little spider at her web—even when no one's watching! You don't fool me. You're not fooling anyone."

Berika slid to her knees. The sawdust pillow hit the floor with a thud.

"My lady—Midons?" Lady was a title of courtesy. Anyone could be called a lady, even a country-common leman. But *midons* acknowledged the explicit right of one highborn man, or woman, to judge lesser men and women. From the few times she had been downstairs where the real sorMeklan gathered, Berika recognized the angry young woman as a highborn member of the clan.

"Don't 'midons' me, snivelling bitch. Don't you dare! I'm nothing to you, thank the gods! You're just another bony whore midons plucked out of the gutter. And I know what will become of you. Godswill, you'll curse the day he found you."

"I'm sorry, my lady. What should I say? What should I do?" Berika, sensing that her unhappy visitor was dangerously close to hysteria, stayed on her knees.

With a wail of rage, the noblewoman heaved the cloth to the bed. "There's nothing you can do! It won't last. I know it won't. It can't," she shouted. Red blotches bloomed on her haggard cheeks. "You *bore* midons, you know. You whores intrigue him while you're floundering in the gutter, but you *bore* him afterwards."

Berika wisely did not say that Driskolt sorMeklan had not found her in the gutter, but some glint of defiance evidently showed on her face, because the noblewoman laughed like a godstruck crone.

"You don't know!" she crowed. "You think midons will let you play here forever. Look your country-common best and smile your simpering little smile— Midons plans to sell you!" The noblewoman gripped the latch-handle. "Godswill, I pray he finds some hellfired veteran with silver to burn!"

The noblewoman slammed the door as she left. The planks were warped, like everything else. The door struck the frame and bounced open. The entire residence shuddered. Berika leapt up, lunged for the swinging door and caught it before it could rebound off the wall, then eased it shut.

With her heart pounding against her ribs, she slumped against the wall, feeling the floorboards shift as her visitor stormed down the stairs. Although slavery had been outlawed for generations in Walensor, Berika did not doubt that the sorMeklan heir could sell a commonborn girl for coin or favors. Still, it wasn't the prospect of being bartered that terrorized her. Through sheer coincidence or knowing malice, the noblewoman had summoned the image of Berika's husband, Hirmin Maggotson.

A piercing shriek shredded what was left of the afternoon peace.

It broke the image in her mind and she began to breathe again. Then, a crash. Berika squeezed the latch; there might have been an accident. The noblewoman, blinded by her anger, might have tumbled down the treacherous stairway. The sorMeklan residence was a community not unlike a commonfolk village: There were no secrets, and no excuses. Berika eased the door open.

"—You can plead your case to the donitor when he gets here. Until then do as you're told and stay out of my sight."

Berika hadn't heard Driskolt use that tone of voice since the night she betrayed Dart. Shutting the door silently, she willed herself to hear no more of that conversation and turned her attention to the bundle in the middle of her bed. The colors were green and ruby; the fabrics were velvet and satin brocade tied up with a girdle of braided silk.

"Oh, Mother Cathe—" Berika brushed her fingertips across the velvet, then retreated as far as the wall would allow.

The woolen gown Berika wore was worth more than the flock of sheep she'd left behind, but the gown on the bed with its gold-figured brocade was worth more than her whole village. It had to be a very special, very prized garment, and the fact that it was in her room, coupled with the way it had arrived, left her witless. Moments passed before she noticed it was the same colors as the bed curtains—the colors the sorMeklan wore when they wanted everyone to know who and what they were.

Nothing short of a thrice-witnessed marriage contract to the sidon or one of his very close kin could transform Berika Ingoldesdaughter into Berika sorMeklan. . . .

Midons plans to sell you.

She'd certainly fetch a better price wrapped in clan colors.

Berika's hands throbbed. Her fists were clenched so tight that blood no longer flowed through them. Slowly she willed her fingers straight. Tears blurred her vision again as she returned to the bedside and stroked the soft velvet.

"What's to become of me?"

None of the possible answers was appealing. Her eyes fell on a suede pouch peeking through the bodice. Desperate for distraction, she opened it and spilled gem-studded jewelry across the brocade skirt. The stones were rubies and emeralds, to match the gown, set in gold. Her fingers trembled above the glittering metal. She bit her lower lip and took the necklace in her hand.

Commonfolk wisdom asserted that gold was different from all other metals and that its purity could be verified by taste. All Berika tasted was salt tears and blood. She worked her teeth on the soft metal until one of the stones slipped beneath her tongue. The necklace spilled from her hands to the carpeted floor.

A shameful flush spread across her face as she spat the emerald into her palm and dried it on her skirt. Then she reached under her gown and found the pouch-knot in the corner of her linen. Blindly, she loosened the knot and dropped the gemstone in with the black-money grit and rough-shaped silver flakes that, until this moment, had constituted her entire worldly wealth. She told herself that stealing from the sorMeklan wasn't a crime, not if the sidon was planning to sell her. But her face remained heated after she retied the knot. She fumbled with the shutter latches and thrust her head out into the pale light of a Calends afternoon. A frigid breeze cooled her cheeks and dried her tears.

She watched the clouds part above the golden dome of the Basilica. A shaft of sunlight set the metal glistening. For a heartbeat Berika thought she could see the Web itself within the shaft of light, descending from the heavens, but that was only a trick of the tears frozen on her eyelashes. The breathtaking radiance of the dome vanished as the clouds sealed out the sunlight again.

She looked beyond the Basilica to the sprawl of the Palestra buildings where the sorcerers lived, learned, and worked. She wondered if Dart saw the sun anymore. She shivered, but not from the cold, and wrapped her arms tightly over her breasts.

"You were right, Ingolde—love is the worst fate. Look what it's done to your daughter."

She no longer felt the cold, or anything else. One arm drifted upward, reaching toward the golden dome and beyond. She lost all sense of time and place. The door opened, the floorboards sagged; she failed to notice either.

"Iser's whiskers! What are you trying to do, Beri? Freeze to death?"

Berika was startled; her mind was empty. She didn't recognize the roofs of Eyerlon, the room around her, or the man who stood behind her. He laid his hands on her shoulders and lowered her arm before he closed the shutters.

"Indon?" she murmured.

"Do common shepherds have no need of warmth?"

Her mind restored itself, and she succumbed to a shiver-fit. The man held her tightly and pressed his freshly shaved cheek against her bare neck.

"Godswill—you're cold as ice!" Driskolt released her and busied himself feeding charcoal lumps to the brazier. "You are, beyond all doubt, the strangest girl in all Walensor. What possessed you to open the shutters in the midst of Calends?"

She chose not to answer. The heir of Fenklare secured the lid of the brazier. She could feel the salt tracks on her cheeks and was certain that her eyes were still red and puffy. Driskolt took a step toward her; Berika retreated. His scowl deepened as he considered her and the shuttered window. Berika flinched, though he made no other move.

"Forget about him," Driskolt advised in a tone that held more compassion than threat.

"Forget about who?"

"My late uncle. Your late travelling companion."

"Late?" The word customarily referred to the deceased. Dart had been, but was no longer, deceased. It could be no more than her lover's heavy humor. Or it could be something more. Either way, the word had escaped before she could censor it, and it lingered in the chilly air between them.

Driskolt nudged her pillow aside with his foot, grabbed the heavy wood chair as if it were kindling sticks and spun it front to back, then straddled the seat as if it were his horse. With his arms folded across the top of the chair and his chin atop his arms, he settled to stare at her through half-closed eyes.

She should have been frightened; he surely meant to frighten her. She'd found that there was a mean streak running below the surface in all the noblefolk she'd encountered, even Dart—though he'd restrained himself better than the rest. If it had been Dart slouched silently in the chair, she wouldn't have known what he was thinking and she would have been frightened. But Driskolt sorMeklan straddling a backward chair with a scowl on his still-boyish face was the image of Indon, and she knew she could wait him out.

The cord-wrapped joints of the chair creaked when Driskolt finally sat up straight. "All right—he's not dead . . . deader. I don't know what the spooks are doing to him, but I'd know if they'd done something they couldn't undo. But that's all I know, and I can't *do* anything. None of us can do anything—not even my father, with all the rights of justice short of a crown."

The sidon was probably telling the truth. He was very precise where his rights and the prestige of his clan were concerned, but she was unimpressed. "Would you do anything, even if you could?"

Driskolt's eyes opened wide. Otherwise, his expression remained the same. She feared she'd finally overstepped herself.

He'd never beat her, and swore he didn't dishonor himself by using main force against a mere woman. By his own admission, though, he'd broken his oaths more than once, and she'd had ample opportunity to explore the excessive strength in his thickly muscled arms. He could break her neck without trying, or thinking, and repair his damaged honor afterward.

"Dart is *inconvenient*." The sidon chose the word carefully. "Inconvenient," he repeated with a more normal inflection. "He complicates a situation—my situation—that was never complicated. I've never had a rival, Beri. My place and future have always been secure—until now."

Berika relaxed. Growing up with older brothers had given her skills and talents that had their uses in the sorMeklan residence. "I don't think Lord Ean would turn his back on you," she said. "You're his only son. I don't think Dart can threaten you."

"But you don't know. No one knows—that's the nub of it. I don't want to stand against him. I've seen what happens when rivalry runs rampant." Driskolt's eyes pulled suddenly to one side. Berika followed them, but he wasn't looking at the bed. "I couldn't live like that," he said softly. "He'd have the better of me in a week. I can't think around corners; I never had to learn. But Dart— If he is my father's true brother, resurrected, then he's as crafty as the Wolf."

Driskolt ground his knuckles against the bridge of his nose. Another moment and Berika would have wrapped her arms around his shoulders, kissing him on the forehead as if he had been her brother. But he glanced at the gown on the bed and stood up before the moment arrived.

"So Cathera brought it after all!"

Her heart sank. She stared at her feet. Her worst suspicions seemed confirmed as Dris rose from his chair. He examined both the gown and jewelry . . . including the necklace which he poured slowly from his right hand to his left before turning around.

"Godswill—Beri, what's wrong?"

She gulped down the sharp-edged lump in her throat. The necklace returned casually into his right hand. At any moment she expected fire and smoke to billow out of the pouch-knot beneath her skirt; in the meantime nothing—especially her tongue—was within her mind's control.

Dris tossed the necklace on the bed and faced her. "What's wrong?" his voice was sharp with concern. "Berika—talk to me. Say something." He shook her at the shoulder, and when that failed, seized her chin and raised it until their eyes met. "What's wrong?"

She had a choice between accusation and confession; she took the easier course. "She said you were going to *sell me.*"

"Cathera?" Driskolt's eyebrows disappeared beneath the fringe of his hair.

"The woman who brought the gown. She stood in the doorway and said you thought I was a bony whore, that you were bored with me and were going to sell me."

Driskolt's hand fell away from her chin. He spun around and indulged himself with a peal of laughter. "And you believed her?"

All of her swirling emotions funneled into righteous indignation. "Why shouldn't I believe her? Why would she lie to me?"

Driskolt shook his head. "I wouldn't know where to begin, but Cathera's only ambition is to marry me. She regards all other women as the enemy."

"But did she lie? Did she? Why is that gown here if you're not going to sell me?"

"Because Prince Alegshorn is holding court tonight, and I'm taking you—not Cathera—with me."

"Mother Cathe—" Every fiber in Berika's body was roused for flight, but there was nowhere to run. "Sweet Mother Cathe." When she could bear looking at the sidon's broad grin no longer, she turned around and hid her face in her hands. "I don't know what to believe. I don't understand anything anymore. And please stop laughing at me."

"I'm the sidon of Fenklare. This is my house and I can do whatever I want here. Right now I'm laughing because you're not bony and you're not a whore. You are a country-common shepherd, but you've got an uncommonly bold tongue. You talk to me as if I were . . . just another country-common shepherd like yourself."

"I'm sorry."

"That should be: 'I'm sorry, midons sidon,' from your knees and preferably kissing my boots with your arms wrapped around my ankles—"

Appalled, Berika hurried to do exactly what he suggested. He caught her arms before she knelt.

"But then I *will* find you very boring, very quickly. Be yourself, Berika Ingoldesdaughter, and we'll remain friends."

Berika dared a glance at his face. The softness had vanished from his features; his eyes could cut steel. Men like the sidon were most dangerous when they were most honest. "I don't belong here; I'm a fool."

"Cathera is a fool; trust me. You're not a fool."

"I still don't belong here—"

"You belong where I say you belong."

The strength was gone from Berika's legs. "No one else in this house wants me here. They despise me. Why do you keep me here?"

"I've already told you. I find that your uncommon ways please me. In the sorMeklan residence, that is sufficient. Now—take off your gown. We don't have much time."

Driskolt released her. Berika caught her balance by grabbing his arm. "Yes, midons." She untied the laces at her throat; he undid the ones along the sides of her wool gown.

Chapter Four

The Web was far older than the kingdom of Walensor, and the crypts beneath the Basilica were older than the golden dome above it. In the time before memory, *basi* had begun in cold, pure, underground water and even now there were occasions when maggas trekked below the polished marble baths to work sorcery at its source.

The ancient downward corridor formed a spiral with rough-hewn walls shimmering in the rainbow colors of Brightwater. Near the top of the spiral, forbidding black doors with rune locks loomed at odd intervals: the sealed private sacrams of reclusive maggas whose lifework was the mystery of the Web itself. In the middle of the spiral the rugged sacrams were available to any disciplined sorcerer whose needs could not be met in the Cascade. No one had used the mid-spiral sacrams in a generation. And the spiral below the mid-level was entered most frequently these days by terrified neophytes fulfilling rash promises made to their dormitory peers.

Two young sorcerers wearing the brown robes of undisciplined neophytes tramped through the mid-level. Their buskins slapped loudly against the Brightwater-slicked stone, obliterating other sounds. Between them they supported a third man dressed only in a dripping-wet shirt. The third man's feet were cramped and twisted. He tried to walk, but mostly his companions dragged him along.

The rough-hewn walls gave way to the water-wrought tunnels of the depths where Brightwater mist rippled across the convoluted stone. The neophytes left their companion beside a puddle while they bound their robes beneath their belts. The shivering man clambered to his feet and hugged himself for warmth.

Green mist seeped between his naked toes. It surrounded his ankles and reached toward his knees. For a moment he stood straight and relaxed.

Then the neophytes were ready again. They caught him below the shoulders, trying to drag him as they had before, but his feet were rooted in the mist and they all crashed to the stone.

Stifling curses, the neophytes got to their feet. By then the green mist was gone and there was nothing to account for the mishap. The third man wasn't moving.

"Corby, is he—?" red-haired Wrast asked anxiously.

Corby pressed his fingers into the hollow of the witless man's neck. "I feel something." He wiped his fingers on his sleeve.

"They say he was dead once before. Maybe he can't die again."

"Maybe."

"Maybe we should leave him here and bring midons magga to him?"

Corby weighed their choices. Halwisse sorJos had a fearsome reputation in the undisciplined ranks. A word from her and a neophyte could find himself doing tedious webwork for weeks. "Dead or alive, she's going to want him in her sacram, and we're going to have to get him there. We can carry him. The sooner we do, the sooner we'll be out of here altogether."

Getting out quickly appealed. They wrestled their limp companion into an arm-sling. His eyes opened briefly; they shimmered like the Brightwater mist.

Wrast stifled an oath and urged: "Let's run."

They tried, but the tunnel was too treacherous for any pace above a one-step-at-time walk. They came to the first sacram of the depths: an inky, yawning hole set in the floor.

"Midons magga Halwisse?" Corby whispered. The answer was an echo.

"Why us?" Wrast whined.

"Because I got stinkin' drunk and you fell asleep. Because we're commonborn and no amount of *basi* will convince the noble bastards otherwise. Start walking."

Wrast obeyed. "As the gods will, I'll never fall asleep during lecture again. Gods will it."

"Gods will we get rid of this noble bastard while he's still alive."

Two more empty sacrams yawned before the light of active sorcery spilled into the tunnel. With renewed spirit and strength, they hauled the unconscious man forward, stopping outside the sacram's water-carved rock entrance.

Magga Halwisse, ten years a magga mender and still among the youngest to wear the magga's jeweled blazon on her breast, dozed in a rocking chair in the far corner of the small chamber. Her gown was the pale blue reserved for the mender's discipline, but the hem bands were thick with silver thread and pearls as befitted a daughter of Escham's richest clan. A private smile tugged the corners of her mouth as she rocked. Corby supposed she could hear the subtlest rhythms of the Web while, here at sorcery's source, he could only hear a numbing drone.

"Magga Halwisse?" Corby whispered. There was no response. "Magga Halwisse? Sister mender? *Midons?*"

Halwisse's eyes opened. The gentle smile vanished from her face, replaced with the masklike graciousness noblefolk displayed to inferiors. But even that false smile vanished when her eyes fixed on what they hauled between them.

"Why didn't you call me?" she demanded.

Corby met the noble mender's glower without flinching.

"Midons magga, I would not presume to enter this sacram without your direct invitation and I would not disrupt your privacy through my clumsy touch on the Web."

Halwisse didn't argue. "Enter, then, and bring him in. Quickly. Carefully. What hap—"

The ancient sacram wasn't large enough to hold four adults—especially when one of them entered feet-first and had to be stripped of his soggy shirt before he could be deposited on the solitary cot.

"Out!" she commanded Wrast, banishing him beyond her threshold. Then, with Corby's help, she yanked off the wet shirt. "What happened?"

Corby shrugged—no small accomplishment with a naked and unconscious man hanging in his arms. "Nothing—until we entered the depths. He stumbled and didn't get up. That was it, nothing more. I touched him—to count his pulse—" He looked up at Halwisse, this time without insolence or defiance. "They say he was dead. Is that why . . . ?"

Halwisse looked at him—and lost her grip on her patient's ankles. Despite Corby's best efforts, the unconscious man landed on the stones with a groan.

"I guess he's all right," Corby said with a forced smile.

"He is not all right! Take his shoulders."

With one gasping effort they swung his body onto the creaking cot. Halwisse shook open one of several blankets piled beside the cot and followed it with several others before, with apparent reluctance, she placed her hands on either side of his head and closed her eyes. A visible shudder raced from her fingertips to her toes and the man's shivering stopped.

"This is a disgrace!" Halwisse's hands trembled. "Did Magga Feladon attend the ordeal? Does he know about this?"

"I did not see him, midons. The new basilidan did not seem concerned—"

Halwisse straightened slowly. "The new basilidan?" Her voice was ice and scorn. "What place does *she* have at an ordeal?"

"I don't know, midons." Corby retreated toward the threshold. This was the imperial magga Halwisse every neophyte feared. "There were black robes and one white," he said rapidly. "It was not my place to ask questions—" His voice faltered.

Halwisse had seized the Web with palpable anger. When her mind shouted Magga Feladon's name, the moist walls of the sacram glowed bluer than her gown and every hair on Corby's body stood erect. He cringed, expecting a painful reflux when she released the Web. But Halwisse was magga rank with more than enough *basi* to control her anger and the Web. Her face was serene and dangerous when she turned around.

"You may go," she said sweetly—and Corby did, grabbing Wrast's sleeve as he hurried away. The two of them slipped and swore as they scrambled out of the depths. Halwisse allowed herself a bitter, indulgent smile.

Commonfolk youngsters were welcomed in Eyerlon if they had the *basi* to reach the Web. They learned Webwork quickly enough, but it took them decades to master subtlety.

The Web descended. It whispered her name and the Magga's signature. Halwisse pushed it away and, with a curt gesture, inhibited it from returning. She wasn't interested in sharing her own thoughts with Feladon. Let him hike down here and *see* what the inquists and Weycha's new basilidan had done. In the meantime she gathered her anger and disgust, banishing them as she'd banished the neophyte dolts. Then she focused her attention entirely on the cot.

Driskolt ruEan barRelamain sorMeklan.

With the back of her hand, Halwisse swept stray hairs from her forehead, leaving her hand covering her mouth. She was twenty years older now—but Driskolt sorMeklan hadn't changed at all. A woman did not forget the face of the man who stole her maiden's heart, even if he had not noticed the thievery. She'd recognized him straight away, though he called himself Dart now, and hadn't recognized her when she mended his body after each interrogation. She cast a tiny thanksgiving prayer into the Web, begging that he remain ignorant of that. The black-robed inquists complained that Dart's memory was in more pieces than a drunk's goblet, memories which he showed neither the ability nor the inclination to reassemble.

She shivered. Gods grant him the strength to resist forever, for her sake and, she prayed with a strangled sob, for his own. When Magga Feladon arrived, she'd ask that another magga mender assume her responsibilities. Until then . . . For the last time . . .

A miniature silver horn dangled from a silken cord around her waist. Her fingers steadied when she unhooked it and caressed the polished amber sealing each end. When the stones were warmer than flesh, she pressed her thumb over the smaller stone and the other one gently between Driskolt's—between Dart's—eyes. Then, when she was certain he was asleep and would not resist, she began mending the damage of his latest ordeal.

Inquists were not torturers. They used their *basi* to summon the truth out of a guilty conscience. When, as occasionally happened, fear or some other emotion was stronger than guilt, they concocted potions to expel the inhibitors and, if necessary, to protect the answerer from himself. Halwisse moved her Brightwater-filled silver touchstone across Dart's forehead, along the curves of his skull behind his ears, and down his neck. Everywhere she felt weariness that could not be mended and the stew of inquist alchemy. An ordinary man with ordinary *basi* would be long dead. Even a sorcerer would have confessed every tattered secret.

Dart was not ordinary.

Halwisse's fingertips tingled when the amber cap passed above Dart's neck. Not at all ordinary. He could not be Weycha's champion, as he claimed—the gods had basilidans and the Web; they did not need champions—but he had died and the forest goddess had, for her own as-yet-unknown reasons, resurrected his dead body. Mostly Dart sorMeklan was a man, but here and there, where only a mender could detect it, forest merged with flesh, producing amalgams Halwisse was loathe to touch.

But she had to touch them: The amalgams were the precise places that tore apart when the inquists asked questions Dart could not answer.

The touchstone slipped through Halwisse's fingers. Swallowing bile, she picked it up again and held it above an unnatural injury. Her lips were thin, straight lines when she closed her eyes and pulled down the Web.

Dart awoke with the unpleasant sense of something warm and prickly wriggling in his neck. It took great resolve to remain motionless while the mender did her work. But then, he had great resolve, and the mender had been very careful to restrain him before she started. He didn't know what she was doing, although he knew he could have done just as well, and with far less discomfort, himself. When Weycha restored the body he'd squandered with drink and debauchery, she'd made certain he could take care of it.

The wriggling ceased. Dart forced himself to relax while the mender continued her examination.

Knowing that he was Weycha's champion was hollow consolation when life consisted of frigid ordeals in the Brightwater Cascade and his mender's brutal mercy. He'd lost the track of time. It might have been days since this unhappy phase of his life began; it might have been weeks or months. And although he had not lost faith with his goddess or his still-unclear purpose, he did want to see the sun again and play his harp.

Failing that, he wanted to die again forever.

An intangible needle pierced between two ribs. The shock surpassed his self-control and he growled as he tried to move his arms. It took all his strength, but he had his hand above the blankets before the mender circled his neck with a lash of sorcery, renewing the paralysis from there down to his toes.

Growling louder, he met her eyes.

"Damn you, leave me *alone*!"

Halwisse could not look away. Dart's eyes were both terrible and fascinating. The pupils were black and rayed like a dark star. The irises were dark, too, but alive with sparks of amber, gold, and emerald green. They filled her with nameless dread.

"Anathema," she muttered. "Anathema." The touchstone slipped from her fingers as she spread her thumb and little finger wide and folded her other fingers against her palm: Mother Cathe's ward-sign against all things unnatural.

Dart closed his entrancing eyes with a groan. Halwisse watched with horror as the sorcery she'd loosed when she dropped the touchstone raged through his helpless body. Muscles heaved and a blistered rash spread across Dart's skin. She spotted her touchstone among the blankets. Holding it with both hands, she pressed it hard against his breastbone, recalling the lash into herself, then returning it to the Web. For a pair of heartbeats, she felt his agony, and hated herself for what she had done.

Their hearts returned to separate rhythms.

Dart reopened his eyes. They were quiet now, without sparkle or fascination. He studied her a moment, then twisted his neck to stare at the wall.

"I'm sorry," Halwisse murmured. If she told Magga Feladon what she had done—lashing a patient with vengeful sorcery—he would have to replace her with another—and strip her of her magga mender's blazon. She was trapped—not as trapped as Dart, but trapped all the same. She poured herself a goblet of nectar.

"Would you like something to drink?" she asked, knowing that his mouth tasted as awful as hers.

No answer. Not even a twitch of consideration. So he knew about the potions she stirred in the thick, sweet liquid. She wasn't entirely surprised.

"It's pure. There's nothing in it. Look—I'm drinking it myself."

He turned his head slowly toward her. "You're a magga mender. If the inquists wanted your secrets, they'd hardly bother with poison, would they?"

Halwisse blanched. "The inquists don't use poison—" she began, then abandoned the thought. "I'll swear by whatever you hold sacred that the nectar's pure . . . and that I'm sorry for what I did just now. I'm going to ask the Magga to relieve me. You're—You're not—"

"A demon? A fetch? An animated corpse? What was that last thing you said? *Anathema?* I'd completely forgotten anathema. Excluded from the Compact. Banned from the Web. So unnatural that Brightwater boils when it touches me and self-respecting sorcerers resort to the lash. Have I become anathema to you, Halwisse?"

She sank into her rocking chair. "Cathe weeps. You remember."

The angle was wrong. Dart couldn't see her and didn't try. "I remember everything, Halwisse. *Everything.* I can't always put names with faces, or know their order in time, but thanks to the inquists, I can remember everything now."

"Oh, gods." Halwisse took a long swallow from the goblet. The cloying liquid soured in her mouth. She wanted something sharper and stronger. Something that would help her forget.

The sacram remained silent. Halwisse got to her feet and saw that Dart was asleep. He cried out when she removed the touchstone she'd left on his chest. In the brief contact, she felt the bleeding places. She should have mended them, but having already broken all her Brightwater oaths when she lashed him, she judged it a lesser offense to leave Dart alone, as he wished, to mend himself.

Halwisse rearranged his blankets and, when that didn't disturb him, smoothed the wilder locks of his hair. She'd been told that by sunlight Dart's hair was many-colored, but here in the sacram it was an unremarkable shade, midway between light and dark—exactly as she remembered it.

She had returned to her rocking chair, feeling soul-weary and miserable, when she heard footsteps in the tunnel—Feladon hurrying to see for himself. He wasn't alone. Halwisse dampened her temper before it flared, and stood up from her chair. The water-carved tunnels were treacherous. She should not have expected an old man to enter them alone.

After touching Dart's flesh and feeling the slow, steady rhythm of sleep beneath her fingertips, she renewed the sorcery that kept him restrained. Then she fussed with her hair and robe. Appearances must be observed: the elderly Magga Feladon was her equal in birth and her superior in *basi*. She bowed her head and extended her hands gracefully—the traditional greeting gestures between noble peers—as his shadow fell across the threshold.

"Magga, I'm honored that you've come so quickly."

"Hadn't much choice, had I? when you kinked the Web." Feladon took her outstretched hands and let them go just as quickly. "You were distraught. Show me why."

Halwisse straightened. "The ordeals go on too long. The inquists—" She forgot the words in her mouth when she realized that Magga Feladon's companion was not a sturdy neophyte, but a nubile girl robed in purest white: Weycha's new basilidan.

"Good greetings, sister," the girl said politely, but without the courtesy Halwisse had given Feladon. "I have often wished to see where my goddess's champion is kept when he is not under inquiry. When I perceived your distress, I made haste and met Magga Feladon along the way."

Halwisse was dumbstruck. In Eyerlon, where the Web was most potent and compressed, it was impossible not to eavesdrop. It was also unthinkably rude to take advantage of it.

"He was so close to my goddess this last time," the girl continued, evidently unshamed by her indiscretion. "I was about to enter the Cascade myself, to open my heart for the first time to my goddess, when he collapsed and the inquists could not revive him."

"You knew?" Halwisse accused, but the girl was more brazen than bright; her smug expression never wavered. And Halwisse turned to Feladon. "I was not told. The neophytes brought him here half-dead from cold and inquiry, but no one told me anything precisely. It's hard enough to mend a man who is like no other man, without the burden of ignorance. I can't—I can't—"

The fire went out of Halwisse's anger. The basilidan had her hand on the blankets covering Dart's thigh, and the look on her face went beyond lust. Before this girl, the forest goddess had chosen *men* to speak for her. Did Weycha miss her champion-lover so much that she'd chosen this nubile girl to be her basilidan—her voice, her body?

Magga Feladon laid a fatherly hand on Halwisse's arm. "You can't what?" he prompted, coincidentally blocking her view of the cot.

"I can't allow it. I won't allow it. I demand to know why a basilidan attends an ordeal. I demand to know why Dart is harried until his muscles bleed. Why is he dosed with potions that would kill another man, that make my work a thousand times more difficult? What purpose can this serve?" Halwisse tried to see Dart, but Magga Feladon moved with her and the effort was wasted.

"Let's step outside the sacram a moment," the Magga urged.

Halwisse jerked back. She was jealous and mortified. She was fifteen again—the age she'd been when she'd fallen in love with the handsome, reckless younger son of Fenklare's donitor. "I want to know the meaning of all this."

"Midons magga," Feladon said firmly, reminding Halwisse of her heritage and obligations. "Outside, please."

A sacram was no place for hysterics. The wiser part of Halwisse understood and followed the older man across the threshold—but not before the jealous part hissed a warning in the basilidan's ear: "You may fool all the others, but you're not fooling me!"

The girl's stark terror was not quite the expression Halwisse expected. She swept out of the sacram—leaving the basilidan alone with Dart. "What's going on?" she demanded of Feladon beyond the threshold.

The Magga frowned. "That poor child is having a hard ordeal as it is without a mender making it worse for her. She's so young to endure the basilidan transformation, and completely alone because the goddess who chose her has vanished from the Web."

This was known. Every sorcerer in Walensor knew how, not long after the destruction of the Tremontin forest, Weycha had made the Web quake with three accusations. The first, that Walensor had broken the Compact between mankind and the gods when the forest died; the second, that the Arrizi pyromant, Hazard, had survived the destruction of his army; the third, and most important to the goddess, that someone had stolen her champion.

Then, before anyone could respond, Weycha focused her anger on her basilidan, and slew that hapless man the instant she herself vanished.

Two days later a newly disciplined communicant sorcerer had taken sick with a raging fever. Her hair had fallen out, her flesh lost its natural color: unmistakable symptoms of the basilidan transformation. When the fever broke, the girl had donned white robes and proclaimed that her name was Ash and her goddess was Weycha.

But Weycha would not answer Ash's prayers.

Halwisse glanced into her sacram. The girl had turned back the blankets. She crowded beside Dart on the cot. Her hands caressed the most private portions of his flesh. Gall rose in Halwisse's throat; she swallowed with difficulty.

"This is not right."

"You've said yourself that there's evidence of regeneration more typical of a tree than a man. If he was dead it does not matter *why* Weycha brought him back to life. The goddess broke the Compact, and her champion—if that is what Weycha meant him to be—is anathema."

Anathema—Halwisse had used the same word herself, but she did not like its sound from Feladon's mouth.

"Weycha must return to the Web to answer her own accusations, and those of the Compact," the Magga continued. "If Ash thinks straddling this dead, anathematized creature before, during, or after his interrogation will lure Weycha back, then we are compelled by the Compact to help her. If, in the end, she destroys Dart, so be it, but it serves us naught to have him destroyed before Weycha returns."

Ash did straddle Weycha's self-proclaimed champion, moaning

as she swayed from side to side. Halwisse bit her lip until it bled. Dart must be awake by now, but still within her restraints, unable to resist. Or cooperate.

The moans grew louder. Halwisse turned her back on the sacram.

"Gods and goddesses have disappeared from the Web before and we did not countenance *this.*"

"It is not simply that Weycha has vanished," Feladon said with evident distress. He could not look at Halwisse without seeing what was going on behind her. "We cannot find Leszuk ruLeszuk—and that damned blackhead spook the Wolf keeps in his guard insists our man was swallowed by a hole in the Web."

Halwisse shook her head in mute denial. "That can't be. The blackheads are charlatans; they know nothing. The Web—"

"Over Tremontin—where Weycha apparently had an avatar she did not see fit to reveal to us—is gone," Feladon concluded. "I have ascertained this for myself. There is a hole . . . No, worse than a hole: a hardened darkness that cannot be entered. I've told no one else but the king, Halwisse: I trust you will keep it in strictest confidence. That poor half-mad child in there does not know and I especially don't want that man, or whatever he is, in there, to know. It is our king's wish and command that we observe Ash closely, but allow her complete freedom with that man."

"What about . . . Hazard? Is he—?"

"We cannot peer inside the Arrizan empire. Ten thousand died—more than twice as many as died at Kasserine, and almost all of them, including Hazard, weren't born beneath our Web. Most likely the Web simply needs time to recover from the influx of so many foreign souls. You needn't worry about Hazard or the Web. Precautions have been taken. Your task, magga Halwisse, is to keep that man healthy enough for Ash to use as she wills. Do you understand?"

Halwisse steadied herself against the shimmering stone walls of the tunnel as she closed her eyes and nodded obediently.

Chapter Five

Wrapped and ribboned like a New Year's present, Berika climbed into the sorMeklan coach-sleigh behind the legitimate ladies of the residence. She settled herself in a drafty corner of the rear bench and pretended that she was invisible. The ruse worked. Not one of the other women deigned to notice her.

All but the last night of Calends whirled with obligations and festivities as noble- and commonfolk alike nurtured the ties that bound Walensor together. Only royalty stayed home; obligated to no one, they entertained their friends and enemies lavishly until the last night, when godsfearing folk gathered with their close-kin to eat a solemn dinner of bitter food, honoring their dead. As this was merely the third of ten Calends' nights—the exact number varied between three and fifteen and was proclaimed through the Web at the autumn equinox—Eyerlon's streets were thick with mounted noblemen, blazoned coaches, and clan partisans.

Whips cracked as the sorMeklan partisans struggled to sort out protocol and precedence on the icy streets. Clouds of uncomplimentary perfumes competed in the suffocating coach. The ladies fidgeted and tempers frayed.

Berika longed to unhook the leather window-coverings for fresh air, however frigid, and a clear look at the palace. Dris said its walls were freshly painted with murals commemorating the

Tremontin victory and that torch sconces protruded from every toothlike merlon. A country-common shepherd imagined a wonderland of firelight and color and was deeply disappointed that she could not see it. But her companions would notice the draft, even if they would not notice her, and their complaints would sour her lover's mood.

So Berika imagined what she couldn't see. The acid gossip swirling around her became faint and incoherent. She was in a pleasant drowse when a cold, lonely cry shuddered through her soul.

Not all the sorMeklan were going to Calends revels. One of them languished on the anvil of sorcery. Berika waited to hear her name called again, but the cry was not repeated. She shivered despite her cloak. Maybe her demon had broken free to rejoin his goddess at last, but maybe he'd become so lost that even a shepherd could not find him. She blotted a tear before it streaked across her fashionably rouged cheeks.

Four of the ladies got out just inside the portcullis; they were bound for the chancery hall in the new palace where King Manal dwelt in Brightwater solitude and the dowager princess Janna avsorRodion, widowed mother of the princes Rinchen and Alegshorn, presided over boring pomp and splendor. The coach stopped again alongside the tunnel that separated the old palace, where both princes lived, from the new.

Sidon Driskolt sorMeklan, frosted slightly around the nose and chin, helped his ladies, one-by-one, from the coach. He greeted Berika by name, raised her hand to his cold lips, then passed it into the keeping of another man whose cloak and cowl left him a stranger. A second lady emerged, and a third. Driskolt hesitated when he took the hand of the fourth.

"Why, Cathera—what an unexpected and utterly unwelcome surprise."

The sidon's gracious tone belied the hostility of his words. Anyone an arm's length away would have been fooled, but Berika was close enough to catch a second, silent exchange between her lover and her unknown escort. Cathera clung to Driskolt's side, and the former shepherd of Gorse entered the palace on the arm of a man she did not know.

Liveried servants stripped Berika of her cloak. She chided herself when she became flustered from the attention: Dris had made certain that she was more than presentable. The dark sorMeklan colors complemented her hair, which had been brushed until it glistened, then expertly dressed with jeweled pins. Nervousness and cold contributed to the already fashionable attractive blush on her cheeks. And the look she received from Cathera was pure malice. She stayed close to her escort, who proved a pale, beardless youth with sheepish eyes.

Music, laughter, and the aromas of a feast wafted down the nearby staircase.

"Shall we ascend?" the sidon asked, as if there were a question.

Prince Alegshorn's hall was a shepherd's wonderland. Flocks of ladies in bright gowns and glittering jewels fluttered among men bedecked in equal luxury. A pair of bards in gaudy purple silk and Brightwater silver made the air shimmer with their storytelling. Minstrels sat on a brocade-covered dais strumming their instruments, though no one was dancing. Servants in the prince's sapphire-and-grey carried gilt platters filled with rare delicacies, while impassive guards wearing the same colors flanked the doors, keeping the hall safe for noble frivolity.

"I'm a shepherd," she mumbled. "I don't belong here."

"If midons sidon has brought you," her escort corrected, "midons prince would not ask you to leave."

Midons prince, indeed.

Prince Alegshorn sorRodion presided royally over this calculated and lavish display. He greeted the sorMeklan heir with a rowdy embrace and Cathera with a kiss that left her blushing. Berika judged his eyes and, especially, his smile . . . as dangerous; she hoped he would ignore her and, for once, her hopes were realized. Prince Alegshorn took Cathera's hand from Driskolt's, and Driskolt took Berika's instead. She noticed that the sidon's velvet dalmatic matched her gown perfectly.

"You're gaping," he hissed. "Close your mouth."

Berika obeyed, but not before whispering, "Midons prince—" in a thoroughly awestruck voice.

"—Is my friend," Driskolt countered and led her to the sideboard, where silver-gilt goblets stood in symmetric ranks around the punch bowl and stools had been thoughtfully provided for those who became giddy after drinking it. "If you must gape, gape at Killeen. He's besotted already."

"Killeen?"

Driskolt cocked his head toward her beardless escort. "He worships you almost as much as he worships me."

Berika's mouth closed naturally. She caught her reflection in the half-filled goblet Driskolt handed her. If she hadn't known better, she would have said it was a pretty face. Knowing better, she looked away just in time to see a black-clad giant beckon Dris from across the room.

"Smile," Driskolt advised, touching his goblet to hers. "No man will touch you without my permission. Half the women here aren't as wellborn as you and the other half wouldn't notice you if you swooned at their feet. There's nothing to be afraid of."

Berika smiled wanly and watched him disappear into a knot of men. With her teeth clenched to keep her jaw from gaping, she looked around the crowded room. She didn't believe what her lover said about the men, and was careful not to meet their eyes, but he was probably right about the women. Several had the easy manner of doxies, spilling out of tightly laced gowns onto the swains at their side. Remembering the fate from which the sidon had rescued her, Berika took a sip of the punch. It was pure Brightwater liqueur; she resolved to go thirsty.

Killeen wasn't the only man watching her, though he was the most obvious about it. In her private thoughts Berika dubbed him "the puppy." She would have wandered toward the bards and become sincerely enrapt by their blend of sorcery and storytelling—but Killeen was already there, so she strolled toward the minstrels.

A possessive arm slipped familiarly around her waist before she arrived. The arm wasn't attached to anyone she recognized.

"I beg your pardon, midons," she stammered. "I'm sure you have mistaken me." It was not quite what she'd meant to say.

The nobleman's smile was sly while it was directed at her, but it and he vanished once he'd looked beyond her shoulder.

Berika turned around. Her lover had his back to her, but the matched colors were unmistakable. So, the gown was a sort of armor, and while she wore it, Driskolt's assertion about the men in the room held true.

She stood between the wall and the minstrels, listening to their ribald songs, playing with her unemptied goblet. The servants brought her sweetmeats and bits of honey-baked fruit, but no one else came close. Driskolt smiled occasionally, but remained on the far side of the hall, near the resplendent prince. Berika begged Mother Cathe to send him to her; Killeen came instead and stayed too long. By the time she was rid of him, Cathera and the respectable women were hovering by the bards, the less respectable women were laughing in the laps of the luckier men, and Berika's feet hurt from standing. She dragged a stool over, bumping into one of the guards as she did.

"Pardon me . . ." she said, and barely kept herself from

gaping. The guard had a full beard, and his features were squared off by a chain-mail coif. Nonetheless, he was very familiar. "Braydon? Braydon Braydson avGorse?"

The guard blinked and spoke through tight lips. "Berika? Is that you?"

Berika wanted nothing more than to hug her brother, but even a shepherd leman understood that such a breach of protocol was unthinkable. "I never dreamed—" she began, then remembered that before she left Gorse she had learned that Braydon had joined the prince's guard. "You never said which prince."

"I didn't think it mattered—you and Mother were in Gorse. Not here. Why are you here? How?"

With carefully chosen words, she described her journey across Fenklare to Relamain in the company of Weycha's champion, and her longer, easier river journey from Relamain to Eyerlon in the closer company of Fenklare's sidon. She didn't lie; nonetheless, she omitted everything that was truly important. Braydon did not seem to notice the omissions.

"I knew you had run off," he confessed. "And I'd heard that a dead man had appeared at Relamain stronghold: The spooks accused the sorMeklan of breaking the Compact with resurrection and demonry—" This was more than Berika had heard. She shivered anxiously, but Braydon didn't seem to notice that, either. "I guess I'd heard it all. I never imagined it all went together." He looked her over without moving his head. "Does Mother know?"

Shamefaced, Berika shook her head. "I wouldn't know what to tell her, even if I could. Maybe later. When it's over. She wanted me to come to you."

"You're way above me now, Beri."

Berika observed Prince Alegshorn's colors on her brother's tabard and hanging in a silk braid from his shoulder. "You belong to the sorRodion."

The beard and moustache twitched. "I serve Prince Aleg, not his brother nor any other sorRodion—praise all the gods awake and asleep. I have not risen above myself. All my duties are public."

There was much Berika wanted to say, more she wanted to hear, but Braydon cut her off.

"And I'm on duty now. We've talked too much already."

"Can you visit me? I'm at the sorMeklan—"

"No."

"Can I visit you?"

"No." Braydon swore, then he softened. "We're not in Gorse

anymore, Beri. It's better—safer—if we forget we've seen each other."

Nodding, Berika accepted her brother's wisdom. "Can you at least tell me where the ladies go—the real ladies—instead of using the straw?"

A grin split his facial hair. "Straw's not good enough anymore? All that silk and velvet's gone to your head?"

Berika stuck out her tongue, as she had done countless times at home. "I'd like a little privacy."

Braydon rolled his eyes. "Privacy—now there's a royal habit. What the Wolf and his mother do in private . . . Anyway, you'll find a garderobe near the end of the corridor. Go straight, then left, then right. You'll hear the stream below."

"If someone—someone like that undergrown puppy yonder—tries to follow me, throw the bone the wrong way, please?"

"For you, midons: the sun, the moon, and everything in between."

Berika trod firmly on Braydon's instep as she went off in search of privacy.

Straight, left, and right were meaningless in the old palace. Globes of Brightwater-dampened moss shimmered in hand-baskets, casting just enough light on the narrow, twisted corridors to get Berika thoroughly lost in very little time. Most of the doors she found were locked; the ones that were not opened into cavernous, dark rooms. She heard music and laughter rising from several directions, but no running water. The corridor she'd judged most promising ended in a dusty cul-de-sac; she backtracked and lost her way again. A half-dozen times she thought she'd returned to her original moss-lit corridor, but eventually conceded that she hadn't any notion where she was.

Trying to remain calm, she tracked the loudest sounds she could hear. Her lover wasn't much of a gossip; even so, he'd told her enough tales of sorRodion unpleasantry to keep her wary as she walked. She didn't want to wander into the wrong room or gathering.

Prince Alegshorn was Driskolt's boon-friend; naturally Dris described the prince in savory terms. King Manal never left his Brightwater throne, not even to eat or sleep. The king's crippling accident supposedly had destroyed his lust for manly pleasures as well; Dris hinted at the unnatural pleasures Walensor's king pursued from his throne. The dowager princess Janna amused herself at night with commonfolk lovers, then fed them poison with breakfast and watched them die. Dris claimed she ate their hearts and livers, too. When Berika challenged that claim, he laughed and admitted there was no proof either way.

But Driskolt had never laughed when he talked about Prince Rinchen. The Wolf was not like other men. He could not bed a woman, by love or force; still, he had *appetites.* Dris swore to the gods that the Wolf fornicated with animals of every kind and, in the company of his blackheads, enacted bizarre and bloody rites on the palace roofs, rites culminating in perverse, unmanly orgies.

Berika had never seen the Wolf, which allowed her imagination free rein as she wandered. Once his horrific portrait began to loom in her mind, she could not chase it out until she made Cathe's Horns with both hands and allowed herself to think of Dart. She called her demon's name, as he called hers, but there was no response. She continued wandering.

She climbed the stairway and from there entered a tiny room that was dark and empty and lined with benches—but not a garderobe. She was farther than ever from Prince Alegshorn's hall, and panic was that much closer. She found another unlocked door and another dusty stairway going up. Then, she came to a set of double doors virtually identical to the ones her brother guarded, and although the merrymaking noises were a faded memory, she wished for a miracle and opened them.

The dark room was as large as Prince Alegshorn's hall, but completely empty. A sliver of ruddy firelight shone beneath a distant door. Summoning what remained of her courage, Berika crossed the darkness and hammered the door with her fists. She heard footsteps and the slide of a well-oiled latch. Then the door swung open.

"Arkkin, this had better be *very* important."

The masculine silhouette confronting her was Driskolt's height but leaner. Its face, what she could see of it, was also lean.

"A thousand pardons for disturbing you, midons," she yelped.

The outlines of the hall were visible in the threshold light. There were other doors leading who knew where, and yet another stairway leading up.

"It goes to the roof, *merou,*" he said softly, cautiously.

Berika was country-common, more comfortable without walls or ceilings. To her, the roof meant freedom and, disregarding his warning, she bolted for it. The stranger was blindingly fast. He seized her forearm and spun her backward against the wall. His free arm rested against her throat, the other, still locked around her left forearm, had somehow captured her right arm as well. He could break either arm if he chose, or choke the life out of her. The light fell on his face and she could see him clearly: soot-colored hair: straight, thick and ragged; icy eyes, and a thoroughly grim demeanor.

"There are Pennaik archers up there, *merou,* cold and unhappy. They'll put ten arrows through your heart, just because they're bored." His expression remained deadly. "I do not think the roof is where you wish to go."

The pressure on Berika's neck eased enough for her to gulp down her panic. Then he released her arms and they stood as they had in the doorway. Berika did not doubt that he could catch her again, and did not try to escape.

"I left the prince's revel and got lost."

One sooty eyebrow arched doubtfully. "I did not know the princes were revelling, *merou.*"

Berika spoke the native Walens language, and though she knew that there were other languages in the world, hearing foreign words sent shivers down her spine. She glanced at one of the closed doors; his arm fell heavily on her shoulder.

"Truly, midons, I am simply lost. I've never been here before and I never meant to disturb you. Midons Driskolt sorMeklan, Sidon of Fenklare"—Berika prayed she got his title right—"brought me to Prince Alegshorn's honoring of his brother's birthday."

The arching eyebrow vanished completely beneath a fringe of like-colored hair.

Berika was certain she'd gotten something wrong. "Not the sidon's brother. He doesn't have a brother. The prince's brother—Prince Alegshorn's brother, the Prince Rinchen, who everyone calls the Wolf—"

"And is the Wolf there?"

Berika had no reason to lie: "Midons, I do not think he was invited."

His face softened, as if she had passed some obscure test. "Do you wish to return?"

"I must, midons. The sidon of Fenklare—" She couldn't find the words that would describe her ambiguous relationship to the sorMeklan clan. "I came with the sidon, midons; I must leave with him." She hung her head. In the dim light, the green of her gown was barely perceptible and the red had gone to black.

"Does he misuse you?"

His fingers traced a line across her cheeks. She shook her head, saying nothing. The fingers settled beneath her jaw. She raised her head and, unable to interpret his expression, didn't know what to say or do.

"Please, midons—the sidon has been kind and generous. But I—" Words failed again. "I'm lost and will disgrace him."

The hand withdrew. "Everyone gets lost in the palace; it's no disgrace. I'll escort you to the hall myself. Come in, warm yourself a moment while I make myself presentable."

The room was small and very cluttered. Huge parchment scrolls were spread in layers across a worktable and piled haphazardly elsewhere, including across the narrow bed. Swords and other weapons angled from and against racks on the panelled walls. Chain mail spilled out of coarse-cloth sacks, and piles of cloth that might be equally shirts or rags were scattered across the floor. He ignored them all and opened a carved clothespress instead.

"Are you thirsty?" he asked with his head inside the clothes-press. "The wine on the table might be drinkable."

Berika demurred and asked about a garderobe instead. The stranger pointed to a gap in the panelling. On investigation, she found herself in a drafty alcove, staring through a plank at cold, windy nothing. With three layers of skirts and long, trailing sleeve plackets, the garderobe was an uncommon challenge. By the time she returned, shivering, he had exchanged his nondescript shirt for a fine black dalmatic trimmed with braided silver cord and ruby velvet.

While the stranger grappled with the laces and buckles that molded the dalmatic to his body, Berika spared a moment to wonder who he was and how he came to be living in such isolation beneath the palace roof. But she also lived without servants beneath the sorMeklan roof. If she did not wish to answer questions, and she did not, she decided she ought not ask any either; so she waited quietly by the table instead.

The topmost parchment was marked with irregular lines and blotches in a variety of colors. There was writing scattered about—none of it intelligible to her—though she cocked her head and made an effort to memorize the patterns.

"It is a map of Walensor."

Berika leaped into the air. He caught her effortlessly when she stumbled regaining her feet.

"A map, midons?" The word was not as foreign-sounding as *merou*, but just as meaningless.

"A sketch of the realm as it might appear from the Web. This is Eyerlon—" He tapped a script-surrounded dot. "Here is the River

Escham flowing from the west, and here is the River Arl from the east, absorbing the Escham and continuing down to the sea."

Narrowing her eyes, she committed that portion of the map to memory. "Fenklare?" she asked, without using an honorific.

He looked at her gown and smiled as he indicated a green-bordered shape.

"It's very large," she said, comparing it at once to the shape of Escham around the Eyerlon dot.

"Smaller than Pennaik, and almost as empty. Here is the sorMeklan stronghold of Relamain."

Berika stretched her fingers across the parchment: two hand-spans and a finger's breadth between the sorRodion palace and the donitor's stronghold.

"And the Weychawood?"

"From here and beyond." He indicated the entire northwest corner of the parchment where there was very little writing but several drawings of demons and wild, gnarled trees.

Gorse could be anywhere along the sawtooth line. Once again Berika narrowed her eyes and committed the images to memory. She had many more questions, but the stranger had gone to the door where two crude spikes jutted from the panelling. Taking a heavy, intricate golden chain from the upper spike and an unadorned sword belt from the lower, he finished "making himself presentable."

Berika held her breath. Driskolt was wearing a chain like that; so were Prince Alegshorn and half the other men in his hall. But they weren't wearing swords. The only armed men in Prince Alegshorn's hall had been commonfolk men like Braydon. Finally, judging a sword more important than a chain, she let her breath out with a sigh.

"Shall we go?" he asked when he'd adjusted the weapon to his satisfaction.

She nodded, and as he had not used any honorifics with her, she ceased to use them with him.

This nameless and presumably common stranger knew his way around the palace. Berika hiked up her skirt to keep up with him as he wove through moss-lit corridors and empty rooms. The sounds of merrymaking began to grow louder and, at last, they entered a recognizable corridor. Thinking of Braydon, and how he'd not wanted to talk to her while she was wearing sorMeklan colors, Berika thought her escort would send her into the hall alone. But he caught her wrist before he forced the double doors apart.

She'd no choice but to accompany him into Prince Alegshorn's hall, where conversation came to an immediate halt and all faces turned toward them.

Driskolt looked like he'd swallowed something sour. Braydon gaped. And even Prince Alegshorn was frozen in a noblewoman's embrace. "The Wolf's among us," someone whispered hoarsely from the safety of a crowd. She tried to replace the man who'd invited her into his private chamber with the Wolfish demon she'd imagined in the corridors, but the man—cold and dangerous, perhaps, though not entirely unkind, and no more a demon than Dart—prevailed; Berika wished the ground would swallow her whole.

"This girl came to my door," the man beside her said. "Lucky for me she chose my door, else I'd never have known you were revelling in my honor."

Prince Aleg extricated himself from the woman, who dashed to safety. Berika was numb below the knees, but the Wolf's firm grip on her wrist kept her upright.

"And here I thought my beloved elder brother was shunning me again." Aleg showed his teeth as he smiled and opened his arms.

"I would never decline an opportunity to carouse with my younger brother and his very dear friends." The Wolf's silvery eyes were sharp; his smile toothier than his brother's.

"Say 'our' friends." Aleg strode forward. "Eat what you will, drink whatever you wish. Make merry with one and all. We celebrate the unsung twenty-third anniversary of your birth."

At the last moment, Prince Rinchen released Berika's wrist and seized his brother, pounding both ribs and shoulders. The blows were loud and surely painful, but once again, the Wolf fell far short of the demon she'd imagined. She'd have sworn there was an eyeblink's embrace between the pounding, and that it had been reciprocated. But everyone else in the room was pale-faced and breathless, clearly seeing deadly malice in the Wolf's every gesture.

And as everyone else knew the Wolf better than she, Berika dismissed her own judgment and tried to bolt toward Dris.

But whether he was man or demon, the Wolf was indisputably faster than she.

"Did you send me this woman? Is she your birthday gift, or someone else's?" he asked, squeezing the bones of her wrist together.

"Alas, no, dear brother. I never beheld her before tonight; she didn't come from me. My gift is in the stable. He's foul-tempered and unbroken and—sad to say—a gelding. But a virgin guaranteed. I'm sure you'll find him suitable for your pleasure."

The hand circling Berika's wrist turned precipitously cold. Despite Driskolt's assurance that everyone knew about the Wolf's perversions, she could scarcely believe that Prince Alegshorn would flout his brother this openly. And judging by the deepening pallor of their audience, she was not alone. Prince Rinchen released her. He flexed his fingers and she feared he would reach for his sword. Aleg was the taller of the brothers, and broader across the shoulders; but only a fool would try to survive on the difference. They glowered at each other and neither blinked.

The bards were silent, transfixed, and no wonder. Berika didn't have enough *basi* to reach the Web, but even so she could feel the malice and hatred swirling between the brothers—and wondered how she could have thought that there was anything else between them. It fell to the unsorcerous minstrels to break the tension with a ragged melody. Berika, who remained as close to the brothers as they were to each other, felt the tension drop.

"Music saves us again," the golden prince said. "Will you choose a partner and lead us all in an anniversary dance?"

Berika felt disaster looming as the ice-eyed prince turned toward her. She didn't know one foot from the other when it came to noblefolk dancing.

Mother Cathe—help me!

She could see Driskolt sorMeklan's face beyond the prince's shoulder. There was no satisfaction in knowing he was as anxious—and helpless—as she.

Weycha—rescue me!

It was reckless beyond measure, but it worked.

"A thousand pardons, midons prince, but the lady has sworn her first dance to me and her honor would be compromised if she broke her oath."

Berika was speechless as Killeen's arm slid around her waist. So, too, were both princes.

Prince Alegshorn found his voice first: "The *comes* of Kethmarion, Killeen barKethmarion avsorMeklan—"

Berika's eyes widened. Driskolt had taught her the meanings contained in noble names: The puppy was the last of his lineage and therefore in full possession of his rights and titles despite his youth; moreover he'd been formally adopted into the sorMeklan clan.

"—And a man of rare passion and loyalty."

"And luck," the Wolf added. He smiled at Berika until she was ready to faint; then he turned back to his brother.

Killeen eased her out of harm's way.

"I find myself unpartnered," the Wolf said to Aleg. "*Our* friends seem to doubt my intentions where their ladies are concerned. Should I leave?"

"Never! I'll dance with you myself, to show my good will and your innocence."

"Will you lead, or I? Unless we know who rules before we start, no amount of good will and innocence will keep us together."

Tension soared again. This was, after all, the bitter core of their rivalry. Could the elegant, amiable Alegshorn accept his cursed and tainted brother's right to rule? Could Prince Rinchen retain the crown when the great clans preferred his brother? The guards wore Prince Alegshorn's colors, but Prince Rinchen wore a sword.

Prince Alegshorn shook his head. "I won't fight with you tonight, brother. Another time."

"Whenever, brother. I'm always ready."

Prince Rinchen paused before departing. His eyes sought Berika in the audience. He did not smile or otherwise acknowledge her, but she knew he'd taken her into his memory, just as she had done with his map. Prince Alegshorn called everyone to join him in dancing. Killeen, wisely, led Berika to the sideboard where the punch bowl waited. She emptied two goblets and was halfway through the third before the ice melted from her throat.

Chapter Six

Two nights after he'd seen his sister consorting with the sidon of Fenklare *and* the Wolf, Braydon avAlegshorn sat on the edge of his cot, listening to other men snore. His worries had overthrown his dreams in the depths of the deadwatch, and now, hours later in the predawn darkness, it was unlikely that the sound of one man groping for his clothes would disturb anyone. But Braydon was cautious; he was always cautious. Growing up with an iron-willed mother and an elder brother and a younger sister who took after her, Braydon had looked to his father and learned caution's lessons early.

He smoothed two layers of linen carefully around his torso—wrinkles could pinch and plant the seeds for frostbite. Over the linen he wore a quilted shirt and quilted breeches, cinched at the ankles, wrist, and waist with reliable double-knots. Beneath the cot he found his buskins and made certain that their fleece lining was flat and dry before lacing them to their proper snugness. Frigid deadwatch air could slip through any gap, but a man could swaddle himself too tightly. Winter survival lay in compromise and unwavering attention to detail; both were skills Braydon had mastered long before he saw the walls of Eyerlon.

While he wriggled his toes in the fleece, Braydon pondered the message he'd gotten last evening from his mother, Ingolde Braydswidow.

After his first sleepless night, Braydon had sent his mother a message through the Web, in which he described his meeting with Berika. He confessed that despite his favor with Prince Alegshorn, there was nothing he could do to protect her from royal ruthlessness. The message was as concise as four hours of fretting could make it, and the communicant-spider still demanded a whole silver mark before she'd recite it into the Web.

Braydon was especially cautious with money. He hoarded his monthly stipend with a passion other men reserved for squandering theirs. The shepherd's son had a bit of gold with every jeweler in Eyerlon; he wouldn't entrust his entire nest egg to any one man's hands. Although his stipend hadn't changed, the Brightwater oath had already enlarged his treasure: The palace laundry would take his linen on Thirdday and Seventhday, thereby saving him the three black grit coins he'd been giving another man's wife.

Prince Alegshorn's newest partisan could afford a silver mark for Webwork and he could afford the two marks he'd paid to hear Ingolde's reply recited by a different spider. But he had truly resented that additional mark. His mother was the hedge-sorcerer of Gorse now. She didn't have to pay anyone to recite her words to the Web or retrieve his, but surely she understood that her rambling gossip came out of his purse.

Did she think he needed to know that wolves were crossing the Weychawood stream in unusual numbers? Did he need to know that the old woman, Bourge, had vanished one night and was found torn and frozen two days later in that same stream? He certainly did not care that the charred tree trunk in the village fane had burst into flame for no good reason and reduced itself to char and ashes. No matter how frightening, such things were irrelevant to *his* message. The only words Braydon had hoped to hear from Ingolde were: *Send her home at once!* What he got instead, buried in the middle of the message was: *Weycha has a mother's anger toward those who fail without trying.*

The spider himself had demanded to know what the hedge-sorcerer meant. Braydon had said—honestly at the time—that he hadn't any notion. But a possible meaning had come to him tonight: Weycha's anger with Gorse would pale in comparison to Ingolde's wrath if her only surviving son allowed noble youths to ruin her daughter. Braydon wasn't afraid of Weycha; Ingolde was another matter. So long as he lived beneath the Web, Braydon had no doubt that his mother could find him.

He reached under his cot. The silk cords and always-warm clasp of the prince's badge rolled into his fingers. Prince Alegshorn was right: An object that had been ensorcelled with Brightwater had its own *basi* and was unlikely to become lost. His arm tingled when he fixed the clasp in the shoulder seam of his shirt. The sensation faded quickly, but Braydon didn't think he'd ever become accustomed to it.

Still, the prince's badge could work small wonders and Braydon wasn't about to surrender it. When, at the first rays of dawn, he presented himself to the deadwatch officer to request permission to enter the city, the officer took one look at the braided silk and raised the portcullis immediately.

Eyerlon was already awake. Bakers and other morning tradesmen were hard at work, and a man could find himself a bowl of steaming porridge if he were willing to lay a bit of grit on the counter. Braydon dropped two angular black coins on the board and ate his breakfast behind a warm bread oven.

By the time he'd licked both spoon and bowl clean, Braydon had changed his plans twice. He wouldn't go to the sorMeklan residence as he'd first intended. Even if the sidon granted him an audience, which was not likely, the nobleman was more likely to report his visitor to the prince—jeopardizing the Brightwater badge—than to defend a commonwoman's honor.

Nor would he bother speaking directly to Berika. His sister's usual response to good advice was to do the precise opposite.

Leaving the spotless bowl behind, Braydon pursued his third plan. With his collar hunched against his ears, he trudged through crunchy, sun-dazzled snow to the bridge that separated the Palestra from the royal city. As Prince Alegshorn's partisan he wasn't challenged until he reached the inner gate.

"State your business," a grey-robed sorcerer demanded. His beard was the same color as his robe; most likely he'd been born with enough *basi* to reach the Web but through a cruel trick of fate had not amassed enough since then to rise through the ranks. Obviously bored and bitter, the spook did not bother turning back his cowl for a look at Braydon's face.

Braydon broke the rime from his beard. "I'm looking for the man called Dart sorMeklan, who is held here under the Magga Sorcerer's writ."

"You're daft," the grey-robe sputtered, fumbling with his cowl. "What's a fighting man want with the likes of him?"

"The prince's affair," Braydon lied steadily. He opened his short cloak so the gatekeeper could see the clasp that was made from the same metal he wore around his neck. Belatedly, Braydon considered that this could be much more foolish than seeking an audience with the sidon.

"Gods have mercy. There's no end of strangeness in this world. First they move him out of the depths, now midons Golden Prince has *affairs* with him."

Braydon's gut churned, but he was a combat veteran and he knew how to conquer fear and dominate lesser men. "Midons prince will be displeased if I am unable to deliver my message."

The sorcerer eyed the clasp a moment. "He's warded into a room in the northwest tower. Do me a favor, one commonborn man to another: Don't tell them I told you." Before Braydon could voice his consent, the grey cowl had descended over the sorcerer's eyes again.

But the prince's badge was even more potent in the northwest tower, where the maggas of the various disciplines had their large, comfortable quarters. These people knew the prince and protocol. They weren't about to challenge or misdirect an oath-bound messenger. Braydon was escorted to an open door by a dour red-robed communicant.

A plainly dressed man sat at a table engrossed in a massive leather-bound book. His back was to the door. The communicant, who undoubtedly refused, on principle, to learn merchants' scribbling, made intricate gestures above the threshold.

"You may enter and leave whenever you wish. Will there be anything else?"

Braydon cast a distrusting glance at the empty doorway. Being headblind, he could not sense the strongest sorcery, but he wasn't immune to its effects, as the oath ceremony had proved. He wondered briefly what would happen if, after leaving the room, he tried to reenter it. He decided not to ask.

"No. This won't take long. No need to wait. I remember the way out."

The spider left immediately. Braydon filled his lungs and strode across the threshold. He felt nothing untoward and let the breath out with a sigh.

Laying a ribbon across the parchment, the reader marked his place and swivelled in the chair. He studied his visitor impassively. "Do I know you?"

"You are the one called Dart, who appeared in the assart village of Gorse in the week of Lesser Gleaning and has been claimed as close-kin by the sorMeklan in Relamain?"

"I am. You have the advantage over me." Dart stood slowly—like a recuperating man, still uncertain of his strength.

Braydon shuffled his feet and mopped melting rime from his beard before answering: "I'm Braydon Braydson. You know my sister, Berika. She's living high in a world she doesn't understand, attracting the wrong sort of attention—"

"And you think *I* could help her?" Dart chuckled, jeopardizing his balance. He steadied himself against the chair. "I'm a dead man. Gone and forgotten for over eighteen years—so I've been told. *I'm* living in a world I don't understand, attracting all manner of dangerous attention. In no small part because your sister chose to betray me—with my clan, as it turned out—but she had no idea of that at the time."

Braydon had gone from cold to hot. This was a part of the story Ingolde might not have known and Berika had not seen fit to tell him. "I'm sorry to have bothered you, Midons. I didn't know." He turned to leave.

Weycha had refined Dart's instincts. They were keener than his inborn judgment and he trusted them absolutely. "Wait. My name is Dart, not midons."

Berika's brother stopped short of the threshold. He turned around, but said nothing. Dart caught him staring at his eyes; he pushed his hair back to give the man a better look. The guardsman gulped, and stared out the window instead, still saying nothing.

Dart moved cautiously away from the table. There was no place for hatred in his resurrected self. The man he'd been would have sworn bloody—albeit futile—vengeance on the sorcerers who'd plied him with mind-rotting drugs. These last few days, since he'd been brought out of the underground sacram to this room, his food had been pure. He had Ash to thank for that, and he did each time she visited.

"I harbor no ill-will for your sister. Whatever else you may have heard, there was only convenience between us, and when that failed, she did what seemed best. The last I saw her, she was in the hands of midons Driskolt sorMeklan, Sidon of Fenklare. He has the means to protect her. He's close-kin to me, but not a friend; you'd be wiser to make your appeal to him directly."

His visitor continued foot-shuffling silence. In the process, the braided silk was briefly visible beneath his cloak. Dart recognized it for what it was: a mark of Prince Alegshorn's protection. He suspected he, too, had a royal protector—how else to explain the massive chronicle of the Arrizan War sitting on the table when he awoke yesterday morning? Script-shunning sorcerers did not keep chronicles, but clans did and the one he read had a distinctly royal flavor. It was tempting to see Braydon's visit as more than a brother's concern for his sister.

"Does midons prince know you're here?"

The guardsman blanched above his beard. "No, midons," he stammered.

If the younger prince was Dart's patron, this anxious guardsman didn't know it. "If the sorMeklan won't, or can't, protect Berika, appeal to a more powerful man. That's the only advice I can offer."

"I've only been in Prince Alegshorn's service a few months, and it's the Wolf's attention I'm afraid of."

Dart shrugged, and regretted it as the room spun again. He clutched the back of the chair, fighting nausea. His disordered memory had just flashed a vision of the young princes wrestling savagely. Bets had been placed on the supper table and the dark-haired prince was winning—until Vigelan waded in. He hurled the boy, his firstborn son, against the wall and proclaimed his yellow-haired second son the winner. Rinchen crouched where he fell, blood and tears streaking his face, never making a sound while Aleg sat stiffly on his father's lap. Vigelan was dead—he'd read that far in the chronicle. It was just as well. He doubted they'd still be friends, but what had become of those two boy princes?

"You know best. After eighteen years, what I remember of the princes is useless to us both, but you've given Prince Alegshorn a Brightwater oath, and even a prince owes a man for Brightwater; *that* surely hasn't changed."

"I'll think about it, midons," Braydon mumbled, retreating across the threshold at last. A white-robed sorcerer was running toward him. She was young—no more than fifteen—and her short hair was pure white: the unmistakable mark of the god-bugged basilidans. Braydon started to tell her that Dart was ill, but her malice-filled glower froze the words on his tongue and he hurried away in silence.

After leaving the Palestra, Braydon meandered through the royal city. If he had any sense, he'd go back to the barracks and try to sleep. He started night-duty again tonight, and a man could get very tired standing outside some lady's bedroom. Usually Braydon was a sensible man, but today he walked through the palace tunnel to the practice fields where noblemen and soldiers traded blows day in and out.

He spotted a sapphire-and-grey banner and headed toward it, never noticing who else might be on the field. From a safe distance, he watched Prince Aleg and another nobleman spar with arm-long double-edged swords. Neither weapon was bated. The nobleman wore leather gauntlets and a metal-studded surcoat. The prince wore an ordinary shirt: the city-sword he wielded was designed for private skirmishes where the etiquette of combat was not honored and armor was seldom available. Neither man pulled his strokes.

Men died on the practice fields. There was fresh blood on the nobleman's thigh, but the prince was unmarked and clearly enjoying himself.

This was the first time Braydon had watched his new patron using the weapon all noblefolk loved best. The experience was sobering, especially when the prince brought the contest to an end by reversing his sword and knocking his opponent senseless with its hilt. Braydon stared at the groaning, bleeding man and did not realize the prince had noticed him until a hand fell upon his arm.

"Sing a song of steel, Bandron?" Prince Aleg suggested with his reckless smile.

Braydon retreated. "No, midons prince. I've never held a sword."

The clot of men who practiced with the prince jeered at him for taking such a bumflower into his personal guard. Then they turned on Braydon himself, who blanched with shame.

Prince Aleg clapped his arm around his partisan's slumped shoulders. "And I don't suppose you can ride a horse, either, can you, Braydon avAlegshorn?"

When it mattered, the prince remembered names.

The mocking stopped. Braydon's hollow expression was all the answer Prince Aleg needed. He rolled his eyes toward the heavens and the Web.

"You're a lucky man, Braydon avAlegshorn. My horse is in the stables; you can't learn to ride today. But I won't have it said that a man sworn to my service has never sung with steel. Take his—" The prince pointed at the sword beside the stunned man. "He won't be needing it again today."

Braydon's dread was momentarily overcome by excitement. What commonborn boy had never dreamed of having a sword in his hand? He picked up the weapon carefully with his right hand and thought he'd done well until he saw the prince's sword coming toward him. He *was* expendable. Prince Alegshorn was going to carve him into bits for the amusement of his noble companions—intent was clear in the prince's gold eyes.

"Godswill, midons prince—have mercy on the bumflower.

He's tighter than a virgin. He'll only spill his guts or worse." The smirking nobleman proved his point by slapping Braydon's sword with his own.

Braydon lost his grip on the sword and dropped to his knees. The man's satisfaction was short-lived: The tip of Prince Aleg's sword pointed at his heart. Braydon recalled the words of his oath: *Whatever is done to you is likewise done to the prince.*

"Raise that sword again, Sarl ruMareden, and you'll be raven-food by sundown."

Sarl's sword dragged in the dirt as he retreated.

"All of you." The prince raked his companions with a scowl. "Leave me!"

They left immediately. Braydon wished to leave, too, but he knew the command had not included him.

"It will never come to me, midons prince. I'm a shepherd's son. I'm good with a crook or a spear—"

"You're sworn to me. A spear won't do you or me any good if we're backed into a corner. You'll learn to use a sword whether you will it or not, by my command and for your own safety. I cannot teach you the song of steel myself, but the men who taught me will, every day from dawn to noon. Do you understand?"

Braydon remembered Dart saying that in the aftermath of a Brightwater oath, Prince Alegshorn owed him, and not the other way around. But flush with the prospect of learning the song of steel, he forgot completely about the favor he wanted on his sister's behalf. "I—I don't know what to say. I shall try. I shall try very hard to learn everything, but I pray to all the gods awake and asleep that your life never depends solely on me."

Prince Alegshorn looked into the distance. Braydon followed his eyes and saw another banner, black and bloody red.

"Prayer isn't enough."

Across the field a line of spearmen knelt to receive a mounted charge. The black-clad warrior crouched behind his stallion's neck with a longer, heavier battle-sword cocked high above his head. The spearmen held their ground. The horse swerved through the line, the warrior slashed one side then the other, and smallish spheres went spinning through the air. The shortened spearmen toppled sideways, still clutching their weapons.

A feral war-cry Braydon had heard on the war-fields of Norivarl echoed over the field. His knees turned to water and he vomited onto the frozen mud.

Prince Alegshorn doubled over laughing. "They're strawmen!"

he roared. "Strawmen! Iser's cast-iron balls, you're more innocent than a newborn kitten. You're as innocent as an egg. Did you think we let the Wolf practice on living men, Egg?"

The answer appeared on Braydon's green-tinged face.

Chapter Seven

For the last twenty years, King Manal sorRodion's throne hall lay in the dark heart of the new grey-stone palace. The consciously bleak chamber had bare walls, sealed windows, cold hearths, and a massive dead-black pyramid centered against the back wall. While the king was awake—and Manal sorRodion had been awake since the start of the Arrizan War—he kept himself sealed at the apex of his throne.

Four magga menders attended the throne in day- or night-long shifts from stools mounted in the pyramid corners. Through their constant diligence and Webwork, the menders controlled the Brightwater that circulated through the king's battered body and had sustained his life for more than twenty years.

The king's accident—he had fallen from his horse while hunting stag in the nearby royal forests; the horse had fallen on him, crushing his lower back and pelvis—had transformed his kingdom far more than the Arrizan War. Warfare, with its eternal handmaidens, death and deprivation, was a too-frequent visitor in Walensor's history, but never before had its king been rooted in a single place, intimately dependent on sorcery, and isolated from the folk he ruled. If the donitors wished to confer with their ruler, they either journeyed to Eyerlon or confided everything to communicant sorcerers who whispered what they gleaned from the Web into King Manal's ear.

Other sorcerers—pragmatic men and women whose innate, ever-growing *basi* had lifted them into the disciplined ranks but would not likely lift them to magga rank in a normal lifetime—left the Palestra, where, since time immemorial, their kind dwelt in a single community. For the first time ever, they themselves swore Brightwater oaths, giving their greatest loyalty not to Eyerlon's Magga Sorcerer but to one or another noble clan. They became partisans wearing colors not associated with any of the sorcerous disciplines.

If King Manal's immobility had served to disperse sorcerers throughout the kingdom, it had also transformed the sorcerers' city of Eyerlon into a royal city. Eyerlon was no longer just the intellectual and religious heart of the kingdom, it had become Walensor's largest city—the fixed center of its wealth, trade, and government. The city sprawled and brawled with the raucous vigor of an adolescent. On the coldest day of Calends or the darkest day of war, Eyerlon throbbed with promises.

In almost every way Eyerlon was King Manal sorRodion's singular creation, but the city never saw him and he had never seen it.

As the first days of his infirmity became weeks, months, and finally years, the king succumbed to bitterness. He banished everything he had loved from his presence. He ordered that a new palace be built, alongside the old one but free from memory or association. His new throne hall in his new palace never echoed with the sounds of feasting and revelry. Tables and benches gathered dust along the walls until, during one particularly cold winter, they were burnt. Bright tapestries commemorating his own triumphs and the triumphs of his ancestors were likewise burnt or rolled into storage for another reign.

In time, Manal sorRodion grew jealous of the free-roaming clouds beyond his windows. He could not command clouds, so he commanded masons to seal the windows with mortar and stone.

The king ruled Walensor through the Web, and though his subjects flocked to Eyerlon for the opportunities it offered, they did not come to the throne hall. Only his wolfish grandson and a handful of aged counsellors regularly stood before the pyramid throne—except during Calends.

Royalty and noblefolk had always come to Eyerlon for the long, moonless nights that filled the ill-omened space between one year and the next. The Web recorded a time when Calends was a time of noble feasting and royal sacrifice; those days were long gone. The feasting continued, but the sacrifice had been replaced with politics until the First of Greater Ice: New Year's Day when the royal family, now excluding the king, stood naked in the frigid Basilica Cascade giving thanks to the sun and moon together and, toward noon of that same day, the noblefolk reaffirmed their liege-oaths to royalty.

King Manal lulled the assembling court, pretending to doze while observing them with ears and narrowly slitted eyes. Brightwater sharpened his senses: he could see in the dark, hear a whisper in the farthest corner of the hall, and for the moment he relished his worthy subjects jostling each other across the cold stone floor.

The noblefolk assembled to the king's right: donitors, hereditary chancellors, and their close-kin partisans. Feuds were temporarily suspended. Ean sorMeklan stood cheek by jowl with Jemat sorLewel, in strict adherence to protocol, notwithstanding the blood-debt that had hung between them for a generation. Water-rights and land-rights had been confounded when the Escham River had jumped its banks early in Manal's reign. He'd wisely left the issue unresolved and reaped the benefits as the kingdom's two most powerful noble clans dissipated themselves through murder and intrigue. With a kinsman under wards in the Palestra, the sorMeklan were vulnerable, but it was unlikely that the sorLewel would avenge their losses.

The noblefolk were united this year. Manal knew why. His treasury was empty. The kingdom had mortgaged itself fighting Hazard's army. To preserve their own kingdoms, his brother monarchs had eagerly supplied everything Walensor needed to fight the Arrizi. Their neighbors had been relieved when they seized a decisive victory, but now they fretted that Walensor had grown too mighty. The long left side of the throne hall was cluttered with foreign emissaries, merchants, and moneylenders with their duly witnessed account books. Such wealth as the kingdom still possessed lay in the honor-estates and behind the treasure wards of its noblefolk. Reckoning was due.

Immediately to the king's right the dowager princess Janna stood amid her three eminently marriageable daughters. She gripped her youngest son, Gilenan, firmly by the shoulders. She was Merrisati by birth and temperament; Manal had never trusted her, nor she him. Janna lusted for the throne, first for her husband, now for Gilenan—she'd lost the affections of her other two sons years earlier. Not that she'd ever wanted Rinchen's affection. No one *wanted* anything of that silver-eyed boy. Janna had tried with

Aleg, but she was a poisoner, start to finish, souls as well as bodies. She'd estranged her golden child before he left the nursery, as surely as she'd lost the Wolf.

King Manal thought he might have had to kill her after Vigelan's death, but the crown prince had done his dynastic and marital duty before going off to Kasserine, and Janna's womb was lined with iron. Gilenan was born early in the spring after his father's death. Janna never let her last hope out of her sight, and Manal let her live: Her locked cabinet of poisons was a convenient asset when anyone else was not.

The time would come when he'd have to kill her—unless she died before Gilenan attained his majority rights at the age of twenty-two. They'd be enemies then. For now they were allies, with Rinchen and Aleg between them.

Prince Alegshorn was in the very rear of the hall, with his back to everyone. He amused himself with a ring-toss toy which he wielded expertly in his off-weapon hand: Young Aleg had learned from the Wolf, his brother; he was more cunning than his supporters suspected. Aleg wouldn't trade one avowed enemy for a horde of noble masters, not unless he had to and not a moment too soon if he did. Moreover, Aleg was not ambitious. He could play princely games well enough to survive in comfort, but had never shown an interest in the kingly variations.

Unlike his older brother.

Manal did not look at Prince Rinchen standing on a patch of fur carpet directly in front of the throne. The Wolf was indeed cursed: cursed with an excess of intelligence, ambition, and guile. He had the earmarks of a capable king—and for that reason alone, Manal feared his grandson as he feared no other man or woman. He'd needed a capable prince to roam the kingdom while war raged, but now that war had ended . . .

As appalling, constricted, and grim as his invalid's life was, it was preferable to death. Manal did not intend to die, did not intend to abdicate. He intended to live forever, ruling through capable, but expendable, princes.

Manal had agreed to Prince Rinchen's scheme to crush Hazard beneath Tremontin. Brash and bold, it had had the earmarks of genius; he'd not been surprised when it succeeded.

But the Wolf was supposed to have died beside his enemy, a convenient martyr to Walensor's greatest victory. A king had to be publicly grateful that only fifteen Walenfolk died, but he could privately wonder what, by all the sorcerers in the Web, had gone wrong. He smiled at his eldest grandson; he'd planned other opportunities.

The Wolf returned his king's smile.

Smile now, boy, Manal thought. *You won't be smiling when this is over.*

Rinchen caught the malice in his grandfather's eyes. It made his heart skip a beat—the old man was planning something—but he kept his rising anxiety well-hidden. He'd never grown completely accustomed to the constant flow of betrayal and disappointment that was—to his own mind—the tangible confirmation of his curse, but he'd long since mastered the art of icy indifference. Sometimes he convinced himself that he truly did not care about the emptiness.

His grandfather thumped his scepter loudly against the resonant, Brightwater-filled pyramid, signalling that the afternoon court was open.

The scepter had been hammered out of a chunk of iron that had fallen in flames from the stars. Rinchen himself carried it to the Basilica on New Year's Day. It had the weight and balance of a battle axe, the general shape of a short thrusting spear, and, as a symbol of royal authority, it was a formidable weapon. His grandfather remained trapped within his throne but, courtesy of his scepter, his weapon arm was as powerful and steady as it had ever been.

Half the audience clamored for King Manal's ear. The king levelled the scepter at the donitor of Arl and the rest of the hall fell silent.

Alden sorMoreg spoke for his clan and for his peers. His words were carefully chosen and punctuated by the vigorous nodding of the noblefolk gathered around him.

"Midons king, the Wolf, your grandson, has brazenly sent his spies onto our honor lands. They ask questions of everyone and about everything: What was this worth before the war? What tax was paid then? What is it worth now? What tax is paid now? What should it be worth? And *what tax could be paid?* When we challenge these spies, they brandish a royal writ and refuse to answer. We have sacrificed our blood and gold for the kingdom's cause. The land we fought for is all we have left, and we will fight to keep it before we surrender it to foreigners and merchants."

"Our grandson brought us a great victory," King Manal countered mildly. "But there were no battlefield spoils to collect, no conquered Arrizi cities for plunder. Our treasury doors stand open;

there's nothing inside. What should we do, except allow our grandson to take a census of Walensor's wealth and potential?"

"Repudiate the debt!" someone muttered from the depths of the noblefolk pack. "We owe nothing to foreign maggots and commonborn profiteers. We met and vanquished Hazard while they sat safe in their countinghouses."

That brought an uproar from the opposite side of the hall, where debt, not land or blood, was honor, and repudiation was unthinkable. King Manal leveled the scepter at a red-cheeked Merrisati moneylender.

The king nodded sagely and seemed to sympathize with the foreigner's argument—though Prince Rinchen knew better. Manal sympathized with gold, his own, and the more of it, the better. When the Merrisati finished his speech, the king swivelled the scepter and allowed another nobleman to vent his spleen. Three more times the scepter arced over Prince Rinchen's head, ignoring him while tempers unravelled and words were said that would not easily be forgotten.

It was not the way Prince Rinchen would have handled the audience. The noblefolk, the merchants, and the foreign moneylenders had legitimate grievances and he had devised a way that would satisfy them all equally. He'd explained each detail to his grandfather, exactly as a prince ought to explain himself to his king, and he had secured the king's permission, attested to in the royal writs his census-takers carried. Rinchen thought that because he promised to fill the empty treasury with gold he had his king's support, but his way was slow and subtle. It required a degree of compromise that he'd never achieve if this acrimony went on much longer.

Rinchen remembered the smile and the malice. His gut contracted; he willed the muscles to relax and waited for the scepter to point between his eyes. The moment came soon enough. He didn't blink.

"Midons grandsire, my intentions have been known to you since before the fall of Tremontin." His voice was loud enough to carry throughout the hall and carefully modulated to reveal respect, nothing more. "I have ridden with the army and have seen how both noble and common Walensor has suffered. Every estate, town, and village needs time to restore itself. Our census seeks to determine what Walenfolk *need,* not what they have. It will also tell the Crown which parts of the realm might be teamed together for the benefit of both. I have proposed that we exercise only our customary tariffs, dues, and taxes, and that we grant our creditors the free use of our roads and rivers until we have discharged what we owe to them. It is my thought—which I have shared with you from the start—that ten years of nurturing will see our debts repaid, our realm restored, and our treasury stacked high with gold and silver."

Rinchen knew his ideas were honest, solid things, fair to noblefolk, merchants, and foreigners alike. If they'd come from the mouth of anyone else—from his grandfather or Aleg—the kingdom would have rallied enthusiastically behind them. But they were his ideas—the Wolf's ideas—and he doomed them with his own cursed self. As arguments swirled virulently around him, Rinchen offered no defense of himself or his ideas.

When the court was on the verge of anarchy, King Manal pounded his scepter again. He restored quiet by levelling the symbolic weapon once again at his grandson.

"We do not have ten years, boy. A kingdom must be ruled today, for today, not tomorrow. And you do want to rule, don't you, my proud prince? You cannot please them all, so choose among them. It shouldn't be hard for you. A little arithmetic. It's no secret you're as fond of numbers as any chiseling pedlar. Who will you squeeze? Who will you pay?"

The short hairs at the base of Rinchen's neck prickled in hatred and distrust. Cursed by his birth and every day thereafter, he should have realized he'd never truly had his grandfather's approval—not for Tremontin, not for the census, not for anything. All he'd gotten was enough rope to make himself a noose. His tongue tasted of ashes, and for a moment he was a boy again, withered by his family's scorn.

The clacking of his brother's wooden toy was the only sound in the hall.

Then he raised his head and stared calmly down the iron scepter. "Midons grandsire, my king, unless you mean to crown me, I have all the time in the world."

"Share Walensor with you, boy? Put a crown on *your* head? How long do you think it would stay there?" The king's complexion darkened dangerously before the entranced blue-robed sorcerers amended the Brightwater circulating in the throne.

No one came to Rinchen's defense; no one ever had. He stood alone and spoke for himself with his doomed words and cursed voice. "Make me a king beside you, midons grandsire, as you raised Vigelan. I do not care if I am loved or hated, but I will not be hated for another man's greed and deceit—not even yours, midons."

At the back of the hall, Aleg failed to catch the tethered ring on his toy's wooden spindle. His exhaled curse drew the attention of the tense hall and made Rinchen cringe. While he was skirmishing with his grandfather any untoward move on Aleg's part—any move at all—could alter the balance irrevocably. Then Aleg found his rhythm again—probably he'd shifted the toy to his surer weapon hand—and Rinchen took a breath.

"Boy, you're not ready to be king of anything except fools. There's another way, boy, though I'm not surprised you haven't thought of it."

The king prodded Rinchen's cheekbone with the scepter; Rinchen valued his sight and was forced to retreat before speaking:

"I've relied on my family for my education, midons grandsire—my lord and king. I remain ignorant in many ways."

Rinchen felt the probing eyes of the audience, and lifted his chin. He did what he needed to survive, always. He wanted to wear the crown; that and that alone could justify his curse—but the longer he survived, the more they hated him. He could live with hate.

"I beg enlightenment, midons grandsire, what have I overlooked?"

"Marriage, boy, *marriage.*"

Rinchen's shoulders sagged ever-so-slightly. He *should* have foreseen this. "I— There have been—" His world was crumbling; he scrambled for high ground. "Walensor's heiresses—"

"Are as poor as their fathers and brothers. Look beyond Walensor, boy. Look to our neighbors who've grown fat on our gold—the gold we gave them while we fought their enemy. We've saved their precious necks, my proud prince, and they owe us a princess or two—"

The clack of Aleg's toy ceased abruptly, but the king's eyes never left Rinchen's face. The clacking resumed and Rinchen said:

"May I assume, midons grandsire, that an offer has been made?"

No child of royalty, nor even the upper reaches of the clans, could hope to negotiate his or her own marriage, but some were more wary of the prospect than others.

"There have been several, boy. By some accounts you're quite the hero—moving mountains, crushing pyromants. But there was only one that offered the solution to *all* our problems."

The king had rattled him as badly as he'd ever been, and with witnesses. He felt naked and violated, with his back exposed for all to see. He wanted to run, but did not dare. Survival lay in never running, always standing firm—no matter how much it hurt. Even when it was his mother walking toward him with a smile on her painted face and a brocade-wrapped parcel in her pudgy, short-fingered hands.

"Humility flatters you, my son," she whispered, offering him the parcel.

"I'm gratified, *merou*." The parcel was transferred without touching hands. "I'd feared only my death mask would ever please you."

The brocade concealed a dark wood portrait case, inlaid with mother-of-pearl. Its simple, elegant design aroused his direst suspicions, but he kept his hand steady on the clasp. The open diptych revealed two miniatures: one a full-length profile, the other a vapidly smiling face. "Merrisati," he murmured, recognizing Janna in both paintings. "A cousin, *merou*? A niece? Surely she is close-kin to you? Have you sent your condolences? A little box of poisons?"

The dowager's face contorted; her voice turned shrill and penetrated to the farthest corner of the hall. "You miserable whelp—*cursed*, miserable whelp of my womb. I should have choked the life from you with my bare hands when you crawled out of me. If my women had not held me down, I would have wound the cord around your neck—"

"Princess!" King Manal shouted, thrusting the scepter between them. "That will be all."

Janna retreated to Gilenan, enough venom in her eyes for him, grandfather, and absent Vigelan, whose untimely death ensured that she would forever remain merely a princess, never a queen.

"The princess Thylda is much-beloved by her royal father, King Trench—who no longer worries that the Arrizan empire marches toward *his* tidy borders. In his eagerness to express his gratitude he has offered his favorite daughter and a dowry train of twenty ox-carts each filled with gold, jewelry, and other precious wares. And he has offered to repudiate all debts between our kingdom and his. Think of it, boy: Our accounts drawn through with the Merrisati, a brimming treasury, and a bride for your bed."

But Rinchen could only think of the face staring out at him, and that thought left him speechless.

"What say you?" King Manal thundered, pounding the pyramid through with his scepter. "It should not take half so long. We have indulged your whims. We allowed you your secret pleasures while the kingdom was at war, but you ended the war. Will you take the

Merrisati princess to wife? There should be only one word on your tongue!"

The hall buzzed as men and women measured the king's pronouncements. Marriage. Another Merrisati princess cluttering the sorRodion lineage. Undoubtedly there were secret codicils to the agreement the two kings had concocted. Rumors were conceived and born, but the loudest sound remained the steady clacking of Aleg's toy.

"An answer, boy! A king's first duty is to his kingdom. His second is to his dynasty. An impotent king is an abomination before the gods: Anathema! If you would wear a crown, you must honor your duties."

"I cannot marry." A lie would be easier, but he could not lie, not about this.

King Manal cocked the iron scepter above his head. "Cannot! Cannot—by all the gods beneath the Web, boy, I'll have the truth: Are you incompetent with women or only uninterested? Have you inherited *all* the Pennaik vices? An answer—*now*, and a truthful one." He dropped the scepter in a mighty arc toward Rinchen's head.

The air of the throne sizzled, as though lightning had struck nearby, and assumed an acrid tang. Rinchen staggered backward, his hand covering his cheek. The portrait case shattered on the stone floor, and, at the corners of the throne, the magga menders were jolted from their Webwork trances. They exchanged wary glances while Magga Feladon shoved his way to the front of the noblefolk with a smaller, silver scepter held ostentatiously across his breast.

Rinchen lowered his hand. He studied red-stained fingertips and touched them to his lips. Taste confirmed what flesh had suffered and eyes could see. But he had not been touched, not, at least, by the scepter.

"An answer!" the king repeated, raising the scepter a second time.

Rinchen wiped the zigzag trickle from his cheek; there was no open wound on his skin. The king lowered his scepter slowly. Magga Feladon covered his touchstone with his sleeve. The audience knew something uncanny had occurred. Most of them, being noble or foreign, were headblind. The commonborn merchants, whose *basi* remained their own, lacked the training to interpret what they had perceived. Magga Feladon, the magga menders on the throne, and the smattering of sorcerers among the partisans on both sides of the hall could not—would not—believe that anything had happened.

Licking the last blood from his fingers, Rinchen strode into the scepter's range. His worst fears had been borne out. "For the sake of Walensor I would marry the twenty oxen pulling the princess's dowry, but I will not marry a Merrisati princess unless I can spare her from my dear mother's bitter disappointment. On the day of our marriage, she must be enthroned beside me as my queen." He'd relocated his confidence and his fleeting smile on the far side of fear. "How say you, midons grandsire?"

The scepter shook in the king's white-knuckled grasp. "The marriage contract is for a princess, not a queen. A new agreement will have to be struck. Twenty ox-carts are not enough for a queen."

"I'm certain you will get what you want, midons grandsire."

He bent his neck in the abbreviated courtesy between equals, then turned his back on the throne. Aleg was still playing ring toss with his weapon hand; the fingers of his off-weapon hand were splayed widely, awkwardly against his thigh. Rinchen made a weapon-side fist and then spread it out as he stalked out of the throne hall.

The mood was merrier later that evening in the great hall of the sorMeklan residence. Ean ruEan sorMeklan, Donitor of Fenklare and undisputed lord of his clan, was tired, but satisfied. He'd foundered two horses getting to Eyerlon in time for today's court, but the effort had been worthwhile. With the sorRodion squabbling as never before, he and his own peers had little to fear from royalty or each other. Creditors could be put off with promises of the Wolf's impending marriage, and the marriage itself would undoubtedly be put off many times before it was consummated—if it ever was.

From his chair at the head table, Lord Ean presided over the boisterous feast his only son had arranged in his honor. A brace of acrobats cavorted in the center of the hall, drawing bursts of applause and laughter from the family and their most honored guests. Minstrels played furiously in the gallery, doing their best to rise above the din. There was more welcoming going on than he'd expected or needed, but he smiled and ate without complaint. Compared to the vipers in the palace, and notwithstanding the troublesome resurrection of his younger brother, the sorMeklan were a clan of uncommon unity and affection.

But, then again, the sorMeklan were better bred than the

sorRodion. With only slight poetic license, they traced their lineage back to the legendary elders who raised the Web. The sorRodion lineage led quickly back to ragged-fur nomads who drank the blood of their enemies and worshipped nameless, shapeless spirits who'd never found a place in the Web.

When Driskolt marched to the head table beneath a fanfare of trumpets, Ean ruEan regarded his son with love and pride, not fear. He embraced Driskolt without a thought for his back, kissing him on both cheeks and ruffling his hair ever-so-slightly. His son beamed with pride as he returned the residence keys and the clan spear. After handing the keys to his wife and replacing the spear in its ceremonial bracket beside the door, Ean accepted his partisans' salute as sturdy kitchen drudges carried the first course of the feast triumphantly into the hall.

Berika was braced for a long evening. Cathera wore the green and ruby gown and sat beside Driskolt at the high table. She sat on the awkward salt-cellar border between the close-kin, who ate off silver plate and linen, and the partisans, who made do with bread and bare wood. Berika hadn't attended great hall suppers since her arrival in Eyerlon, and she hadn't wanted to attend this one. Though food was plentiful and delicious, she ate little of it: The necessary rituals of summoning the appropriate server and transferring morsels from the platter to her plate were beyond her comprehension.

To make the meal more tedious, Berika found herself sharing a plate (in the respectable up-table direction) with Killeen, the puppy who'd rescued her from the Wolf two evenings past. The *comes* of Kethmarion would graciously get her anything she wanted, if she were willing to pay his price—which she wasn't. He crowded against her until she was sore from balancing on the edge of the bench that fate, or more likely, Driskolt, had assigned her. The puppy offered wine from his own cup and sweetmeats delicately impaled on the tip of his knife. If she refused too often or too loudly she knew she'd attract attention, so she ate and drank and countered Killy's questions with grudging one-word answers.

She was relieved when the last of the meats, fish, and fowls had been whisked away. Trumpets heralded the final course; acrobats cleared a path from the courtyard kitchen to the high table. Lanterns dimmed, and finally, a marzipan reconstruction of Tremontin Pass entered the dining hall on the shoulders of the cook's strongest apprentices. Once set on a special table at the center of the hall, it began to quake and crumble. In the last moment before it collapsed, the dessert released a flock of frightened doves that immediately sought refuge in the soot-covered roof beams.

Led by the donitor, the sorMeklan hall erupted with wild cheering.

Driskolt stood and bowed from the waist, his face flushed with relief. He had fretted over this grand finale for weeks. Earlier in the day Berika had helped him confine the doves in their cage beneath the table. She was genuinely glad that everything had gone exactly as her lover had hoped. Perhaps *now* he would not mind if she went upstairs to her room. She leaned forward to catch his attention, then pointed toward the door. The sidon nodded curtly and she sat back with satisfaction.

"I'm leaving," she told her too-attentive companion. "I have permission from midons."

Killeen also merited "midons" courtesy, but Berika hadn't offered it to him all evening. The puppy hadn't objected, which lowered him even further in her commonborn opinion.

"I'll escort you, my lady."

"Thank you, but I know the way."

"I insist, my lady."

The puppy latched onto her hand and would not relinquish it, even when she rose to her feet. "You don't understand—" Berika could see her lover easily and had no difficulty recapturing his attention. The look he shot back at her was neither pretty nor kind. She was the one who had not understood. Suddenly, she was cold and shivering.

"You're not feeling well, my lady?" Killeen stood up, released her hand, and wrapped his arm protectively around her shoulder.

She looked beyond the puppy's shoulder. Driskolt was still watching her. His expression had softened somewhat; he thought she understood.

"Berika?" Killeen asked solicitously.

Contradictory thoughts clamored in Berika's mind, then merged into one. Killeen was enthralled with her and he'd done Driskolt and all the sorMeklan an immeasurable favor when he risked the gods-alone-knew-what to rescue her from the ice-eyed Wolf. In return, the puppy had been thrown a bone: her. Berika retained a choice: She could throw a tantrum the way Cathera did—and wind up on the ice-covered streets. Or she could choose to accept her fate. She made her choice, and felt as if she were falling from a very great height.

"Berika, my lady—are you well?"

"Yes, midons," she replied with an awkward, brittle laugh. "Well—maybe not. It's the wine. I'm not used to it and it's made me foolish. Suddenly I am not at all sure I can find the way to my bed by myself." She chose the words, but they burned her mouth.

"Then you must not refuse my offer. I know my way around."

The puppy's paw slid beneath her arm, clumsily caressing her breast. She shuddered; he held her more tightly. They walked together to the door. Berika was careful not to glance at the sidon as they passed behind his chair.

Chapter Eight

Halwisse sorJos dawdled in the dim passageway between the Palestra and the Basilica. She'd left her blue magga mender's robe in her quarters and wore plain grey wool instead. With the cowl up and her neck discreetly bent, she was simply another tired sorcerer with the right to restore herself in the Brightwater baths, but she was ashamed of her need and clung to the shadows.

The Basilica, with its polished marble floor, Brightwater-filled baths, soaring pillars, and immense dome, was meant to impress everyone who entered it. Halwisse had lived in the adjacent Palestra all her life without becoming immune to its grandeur. The thundering Cascade, which overwhelmed ordinary folk with ordinary *basi*, sprang into existence unexpectedly after the dome was sealed some four hundred years ago. Its abundant Brightwater had reinvented Walensor's sorcery, but for a trained eye, it was the crystalline structure of the Web itself, weaving through the Cascade, that inspired the greatest wonder.

And fear—especially when Halwisse imagined its power corrupted by an undisciplined mind.

A solemn group of neophytes, led by their tutor, came down the passageway. Halwisse made herself inconspicuous against the wall. The neophytes marched across the marble floor and formed a circle on the rim of the large pool at the bottom of the Cascade.

Following the chanted commands of their tutor, they descended into the swirling Brightwater, joined hands, and began the nightly Webwork rituals. The crystalline Web shimmered and the cold Brightwater grew warmer. Soon, steam wisps danced across the surfaces of a ring of smaller, still baths along the outer wall.

At midnight, when bells pealed the end of nightwatch and the start of deadwatch, the neophytes broke their circle, and sorcerers of all ranks and disciplines headed for the heated baths. Halwisse adjusted her cowl and followed the curving wall. She walked past the nearest baths which were also the most crowded. The sorcerers were like any other tight-knit community and the hours of the deadwatch were hours of friendship, courtship, and gossip—all of which Halwisse wished to avoid. She made her way to the great doors, where a steady draft of wintery air created a thick fog above the empty pool she chose.

Shedding the warm robe, Halwisse extended a trembling toe toward the Brightwater, worrying not about the temperature of the Brightwater, but about how the *basi*-charged liquid would react to her presence. When she'd come to the baths after mending Weycha's resurrected champion, her exhaustion bloodied the limpid Brightwater. But Magga Feladon had finally granted her wish, and just this afternoon she had returned to her customary duties as one of the king's entranced menders. Tonight, exhaustion should be pure, pearly white.

King Manal was like no other man, but he was not like Dart, not anathema. The Webwork his shattered body required did not violate the Compact. Halwissa did not sully herself mending him as she had mending Dart. There was no reason to be fearful of what the Brightwater would reveal.

Grimly, she plunged her toe beneath the Brightwater. A sheet of exhaustion sloughed away. It was dense and sank quickly, but—thank all the gods awake and asleep—it was an honest white. Halwisse dared to believe that the afternoon's disturbance in the throne hall had occurred only in her imagination. She lowered herself into the pool. More opaque tension drifted away from her body. The Brightwater clarified itself and began to restore her depleted *basi*. She sank onto the sitting ledge beneath the pool's surface.

Eyes closed, Halwisse convinced herself that she hadn't felt sorcery lash out between the king and the Wolf; she'd simply felt one man's rage against another. Inquists experienced the anger of others all the time, but, as a mender, she was unaccustomed to such raw emotions and had mistaken them for anathema. King

Manal had been Severed. His *basi* was bound to the Web and he was headblind. He couldn't violate the Compact with the lash. The king had been enraged by his cold, stubborn grandson—but he'd done nothing out of the ordinary, nothing another man would not have done if faced with the same insolence. Relieved of her fears, Halwisse allowed her thoughts to drift with the music of the Web.

"Magga Halwisse?"

A masculine voice jolted her from her reverie. She opened her eyes, but before she recognized her visitor, she saw strands of crimson seeping away from her. As the destructive potential of sorcery was measured, the filaments were pinpricks of annoyance, but their mere existence shattered Halwisse's peace. She stared at them, oblivious to the man who had startled her.

"Magga Halwisse?" he repeated. "May I join you?"

Dumbfounded, Halwisse recognized the Magga Sorcerer and, almost as quickly, knew why he'd sought her out. He'd been there, too.

"May I, magga Halwisse?"

Halwisse nodded. She felt weary, but not as weary as the Magga looked. His hollow face was the color of old parchment with dark holes for red-rimmed eyes. Sculling the Brightwater with her fingers to disrupt the telltale crimson threads, Halwisse felt a surge of *basi* as another sheet of milky exhaustion spread from the opposite side of the pool. Then, to her horror, a blood-colored strand slithered toward her.

The headblind king had usurped them all.

"Cathe weeps."

"If She knows," Feladon replied. "He pulled only a little from each of us. A goddess might not notice."

"The lash was small. I didn't know what had happened. I still don't." Halwisse confined the strands within the curve of her arm, then swept them below the surface.

"You faced the king from your stool. You didn't see the mark appear on Prince Rinchen's face. Blood. When he wiped it off there was no wound."

Halwisse's arm sank. "How?" she murmured. Like a sword, *basi* was double-edged: neither inherently beneficent nor malignant. Nonetheless, powerful sorcery was surrounded by mysteries of mind-numbing complexity; it was not easy to abuse, especially by a Severed man.

"I was about to ask you," Feladon countered. "Were you in special empathy with our king? Were you doing anything unusual when he forged the lash?"

"No." She shook her head. "The Webwork we do from the throne is primitive, far below conscious thought. The focus is very narrow. Sometimes my own thoughts are leagues away. I was completely unaware of our king and the Wolf. It was over so quickly." She stared at the crimson that continued to trickle through the Brightwater. "I was usurped before I knew I was in danger."

Feladon thought a long while before answering: "Hedge-sorcery."

Since all living entities accumulated *basi* with the passing of time, it followed that men and women who lived long enough accumulated enough for the simple undisciplined sorcery known as hedge-sorcery. Hedge-sorcerers did not come to Eyerlon for training. They were never given silver touchstones filled with Brightwater. They worked by instinct, which though prone to misuse, was severely limited in power. In the countryside, where disciplined masters of Webwork were reluctant to serve, hedge-sorcery was the only sorcery, but in Eyerlon, where the maggas congregated and accumulated *basi*, hedge-sorcery was beneath discussion.

"Impossible!" Halwisse laughed nervously. She recited an old proverb: "'A headblind man may live for six-score years but his *basi* will never pull down the Web.'"

"Who knows what a hundred-and-twenty-year-old man might do, headblind or not. But even the meanest bumflower, if he were as old as King Manal is now, would likely have accumulated enough for hedge-sorcery. He might be too dumb or senile to use it, but it would be manifest.

"And consider this, sister Halwisse," Feladon continued. "For the last twenty years, we've bathed our king in Brightwater. *Basi*—yours individually and that of the others who have toiled with you—sustains him, and you sustain yourselves by drawing *basi* from the Web. No one knows if King Manal was headblind from birth. Headblind from the Severance ritual . . . yes, but perhaps there's a difference between inborn headblindness and Severance. Most of our Severed noblefolk die before their sixtieth birthday; *all* the sorRodion have. I searched the Web myself. It is true that the few Severed souls I found who'd attained our king's age were as headblind on their deathbeds as they'd been all their lives, but King Manal has survived his deathbed. And King Manal"—the Magga lowered his voice—"is descended from Pennaikmen. We may laugh and say there's not one Pennaikman in a thousand with the *basi* to reach the Web, but perhaps we're just not measuring the right ability. They were not utterly without magic before the Web was stretched above their lands. All that drumming and drinking can create something very much like hedge-sorcery; I've seen it myself. The Wolf's man, Arkkin, is no fraud."

"Anathema," Halwisse whispered. Until this Calends—and there could not be a more inauspicious time for such thoughts—she hadn't given anathema a dozen thoughts in her entire life. Now it dominated them.

"Anathema? Isn't Severance the very opposite of Anathema, Halwisse? Don't we bind the infants of the noble families more tightly to the Web and Walensor than we are bound ourselves? We compel them to surrender everything; what might happen if one of them learned to take?"

Halwisse shook her head."Why tell me?" she asked, grasping the potential catastrophe's full scope. "What can I do—?" She stopped herself with a gasp. "No, you can't expect the menders . . . You can't expect us to . . . We don't kill, Magga. We may open the door to eternity, but we may not do more than that. If a soul is not ready to join the Web, we wait until it is."

If Walensor's Magga had hoped the youngest and presumably most flexible of his magga menders would say something different, he hid his disappointment well. "I would not suggest otherwise, but all the suffering Walensor endured in the war will pale before what we could now face."

She gathered her courage. "What do we face, Magga?"

"King Manal is undisciplined. He does not understand the mysteries of the Web. He fears death, as all unenlightened folk fear it . . ." The Magga left the implications of that fear unspoken.

"No. Our king is a wise man and thoughtful. He will find enlightenment. He won't chase immortality."

"Our king has been my friend since childhood, but he is a sorRodion, with all the cruelty and wildness of that lineage. He can be wise and thoughtful, and he would not hesitate to lash the Wolf. Only a fool would think it will not happen again, or that he will not learn to wield it expertly."

"The holes? All the problems we've had with the Web since Tremontin— Could it be—?" Her thoughts swirled like the milky, blood-threaded exhaustion dissipating in the pool. They made knots of their own volition, knots too awful to articulate. "King Manal—?" She raised her head in incoherent frustration. Could everything ominous be flowing from their king, the man they'd sustained past death with Brightwater? As luck would have it, she caught sight of Ash leading her paramour, Dart, into the Cascade. The pair settled into one of the shell-shaped baths that rose gracefully through the torrent. Halwisse shivered involuntarily. "Weycha," she said, offering herself an alternate explanation. "Think of the trouble She's caused: slaying her basilidan, then choosing a hoyden to replace him. Resurrecting the dead; breaking the Compact . . ." Halwisse shivered again. Thinking about Weycha and the king didn't lessen her concerns; it enlarged them. "I'm frightened," she whispered, looking to Feladon for reassurance. "What are we going to do?"

The Brightwater between them was crystal clear, but Feladon's face was as weary as it had been when he entered the pool. The Magga hesitated, then said:

"Nothing. I fear we have already done too much. From the moment we learned of our king's injuries to the moment the Wolf asked if we could bring Tremontin down, we've asked only one question: Does this act violate the Compact? We never asked: What is the pattern? Does this pattern violate the Compact? I think the time has come for us to do nothing more than pray that the Web, which we've stretched and twisted beyond all recognition, will restore itself." The Magga's tone did not inspire confidence. "A year ago, even a month ago, I was certain of everything we did. Now I'm certain of nothing except that our meddling will make a bad situation worse. The *basi* of four hundred generations dwells within the Web. If that is not enough wisdom to set things right, then nothing you or I decide will make a difference. It will be best, I'm sure, if we hold firmly to our faith in the Web and the Compact."

Appalled by what her noble heritage termed cowardice, Halwisse turned away from her mentor. Faith was for commonfolk. If *she* were Walensor's Magga and she confronted problems of such magnitude, she wouldn't wring her hands with prayer. "This is more than we alone should decide. We must go to the noblefolk. All the clans are here for the New Year's oath-giving. We must confront King Manal—"

"No!" Feladon interrupted sharply. "The king must not be told anything. I forbid it!"

The plain silver ring Feladon wore on the index finger of his right hand shone with exceptional brilliance, reminding Halwisse that the Magga had the right, and the power, to command her obedience. She hung her head like a chastened neophyte. The Brightwater surrounding Halwisse turned an icy blue.

"Yes, Magga Feladon. I thought if our king understood the dangers we face on his behalf, he would be better able to resist temptation—"

"You thought wrong. I know his heart and his mind as I know my own. I cannot contemplate what would happen if my friend learned what he had done, what he could do. But, beyond even that, I do not want some other sorRodion wondering if he has inherited some wild Pennaik talent to draw *basi* out of the Web."

Halwisse knew exactly which other sorRodion Feladon had in mind. Thoughts of the Wolf and the lash together were the precise reason why noblefolk were Severed. But if the Magga could keep secrets from his friend the king, Halwisse could keep secrets from her friend the Magga. As quickly as politeness allowed, she left the bath.

She climbed the stairs to her quarters in the Palestra and roused the trio of women who served as her maids. One she sent to her wardrobe after her warmest clothing and the second to the Palestra stables to requisition a horse and escort. The third, a woman her own age who had given a Brightwater oath many years ago, remained at her side.

"Can't you wait until morning, midons?" the oath-bound woman pleaded. "The night streets are no place for you."

"I must talk to my uncle tonight, Ani, or not at all. If I wait until tomorrow . . ." Halwisse left her thought hanging in the air. She wasn't impetuous by nature, and if she waited until sunrise she'd find a reason to do nothing.

"Midons Faerilen will want concessions," Ani warned, her arms folded before her.

The sorJos clan enjoyed disproportionate prestige in the noblefolk hierarchy. Although they were merely a sept of the sorLewel clan, the royal city of Eyerlon sat on their honor-land. The sorRodion royalty declared itself exempt, but the sorJos collected rents from everyone else. They were very rich and could become richer through whim or vengeance against another clan now that they all must maintain residences in the city.

After Halwisse's father and all four of her brothers died during the Arrizan War, sorJos leadership had fallen into the hands of Faerilen, a man who always had the strength and energy to do what he wanted, but suffered convenient infirmities whenever the army needed him. Currently, Faerilen wanted his son, Eudalig, to succeed him, rather than any of Halwisse's brothers' children. A magga mender's steadfast support of her young nephews' birthrights had ruined many a sorJos celebration in recent years. But birthrights paled in the light of a sorRodion threat to the Web.

"If Eudalig adopts two of the boys as his heirs, I'll grant the rest—provided Faerilen and Eudalig listen to what I tell them and act accordingly." Conceding defeat to Ani was more painful than conceding it to her uncle and cousin would be. Halwisse pulled down the Web for comfort.

When she released the Web, her three women stood in a grim row before her. Ani spoke for the trio:

"You're not feeling well. You shouldn't go out on a frigid night like this. We'll get you a warm posset and put you to bed—"

Halwisse stood up. She shoved her way past the women. "I'm made of sterner stuff than Faerilen. It takes more than a cold night to stop me, thank all the gods."

The fur-lined travelling gown lying across her bed weighed as much as a man's chain-mail shirt and was almost as difficult to put on without assistance. Nonetheless, she shook out the heavy garment and fought a good fight against the voluminous skirt until the women bowed to her determination.

The declining moon was a thick crescent in the deadwatch skies when Halwisse left the Palestra. Calends would last another five days until it completed its waning. The new year began when the light of the waxing moon was first seen after the winter solstice. Halwisse knew that the moon whirled around the world as the word whirled around the sun in an endless, mechanical dance; there was no danger that the new year would fail to begin at its appointed time, as ignorant, commonfolk believed. Even so, Halwisse could not completely repress a feeling of dread as her escort formed around her: sorRodion kings and princes usurping the Web. What could possibly be worse?

The sorJos had always lived in a substantial residence outside the Palestra. Its stone walls stood on high, solid ground and it looked very much like the stronghold it was. The gate was shut and the gatekeeper protested that he lacked the authority to admit anyone during deadwatch.

Without a word, Halwisse pulled down the Web and shattered the dreams of the oath-bound sorcerers inside. Moments later a servant appeared in the snow-covered courtyard. Halwisse and her escort were let through the gate without further discussion. Faerilen, bleary-eyed and irritated, met her beside the cold hearth in the lower hall.

"This is a surprise," he said sardonically. "Whatever could have driven a magga sorcerer to her close-kin at this godsforsaken hour?"

Halwisse touched the Web again, restoring sensation to her hands and feet. "I have learned of things more important than our quarrel—"

"It is not a quarrel, Lady Halwisse. It is a question of rights. In the absence of heritable issue in the senior branch, the title devolves to the next branch and its heirs. It is only a quarrel because you persist in denying my rights."

Faerilen's son Eudalig appeared at the top of the stairs. He was fully and impeccably dressed despite the late hour, with a glass of steaming wine in his hand. Although Eudalig was only a few years younger than she, he represented everything Halwisse disliked in men, especially those who'd first clotted around Prince Vigelan and now gave their allegiance to his golden son. But Eudalig had the courage his father lacked and was devious by nature. She spoke to him directly:

"If you'll swear on Brightwater to adopt two of the boys as your primary heirs, not to be displaced by legitimate or natural children, I'll withdraw my objections and return the sorJos regalia."

"Don't do it!" Faerilen erupted. "She's trying to trick you. My grandsons must inherit!"

Eudalig came down the stairs slowly, never taking his eyes off her face. "Unless I'm mistaken, my dear cousin believes she knows something that makes a mockery of inheritance. Am I right, dear lady?"

The stones beneath Halwisse's feet felt as shifty as springtime mud. "It is not a time for little boys to lead clans," she admitted. "Do you accept my terms?"

"Will you tell us why you've come if I don't?"

Before Halwisse could answer, Faerilen seized his son's arm. "Don't listen to her!"

A dark wine stain spread across the pale silk of Eudalig's shirt.

"You must die, midons sire." Eudalig's voice was tight. "And I must die before her brother's whelp could inherit. I'm not planning to die soon. Are you?" The son stared at his father, and, after a long moment, the older man stepped aside. "I accept your terms," Eudalig said to Halwisse. "May I assume you're prepared to take my oath?"

Halwisse produced her touchstone. "I am."

While Faerilen fumed, Halwisse extracted a binding promise from her cousin on her nephews' behalf. Then she told Eudalig what had actually happened the previous afternoon in the throne hall—how King Manal had used the lash of sorcery on his grandson—and all the unpleasant implications associated with it. She told him about the dead area in the Web above Tremontin and the disappearance of the forest goddess, Weycha. She told her cousin about the anathema Weycha had resurrected. She did not say who Dart had been while he had lived, but Eudalig already knew Lord Ean sorMeklan's younger brother had returned from the dead. His smile dripped acid when he said:

"That must have been *very* difficult for you, Halwisse. How long has it been since you touched a man with his parts intact, and a one-time lover, to boot?"

Halwisse flushed, more with rage than embarrassment, and wished she'd stayed in the Palestra. But it was too late. Oaths had been given. Events had moved beyond her control.

"There are possibilities here," Eudalig sorJos mused to his goblet. "And rewards for the man bold enough to seek them."

Chapter Nine

Dawn had broken. Pale light seeped through shuttered windows in the palace barracks, but Braydon failed to recognize the man standing beside his cot. The shepherd had long since learned the lessons of military life. His arm muscles bunched, his fists clenched.

"Your prince has sent for you," a gruff voice whispered. "Gather your clothes. You can dress in the watchroom."

"Wha–?" Braydon could fight before he was fully awake; thinking was more difficult.

"You heard me. Get your worthless butt over to the palace before the golden prince comes looking for you!"

Braydon's arms and hands relaxed and he flattened against the horsehair mattress with a deep sigh. "Iser's frozen balls—do you know what he wants? What hour of the watch is it, anyway?"

"It's the dregs o' deadwatch. As for the other—nobody in the palace tells me their secrets. Get up and get gone!"

The man walked away. Braydon sighed a second time. Now that he practiced with a swordmaster each morning, he'd been removed from the regular duty roster—to the anger of his commanders and the envy of his comrades. The way things were going, he'd be looking for somewhere else to eat and sleep by the end of Calends.

Still, the lessons made everything worthwhile. The sword was the noblefolk weapon. If a man aspired above his birth he had to sing the song of steel. Braydon had discovered his aspirations, but he had yet to pick up a sword. Prince Alegshorn's swordmaster had kept him busy dodging pebbles and hopping from one foot to the other.

Bracing himself for the cold, Braydon sprang out of bed in a single movement. By the time his naked feet lodged protest with his skull, he was in the watchroom trussing up his breeches. An iron kettle was spitted over the fire, a wooden ladle, too. Braydon dipped out a measure of dark, oily liquid and gulped it down with a grimace. The men on deadwatch brewed their tea strong enough to make a corpse piss brown.

A wind had come up with the sun on this, the sixth day of Calends. Ominous clouds hid the sunrise and filled the air with stinging crystals of ice. Braydon raised his cowl before crossing the empty courtyard between the barracks and the old palace. The tunnel gatekeeper passed him through with a quick nod. The guards outside the prince's hall hailed him by name.

"Braydon, lad—what took you so long? Midons prince sent for you at the top of the watch. He's been awake and waiting since." The guard paused before adding darkly: "By himself."

"I came as fast as I could. No one saw fit to wake me."

The second guard scowled. "That may be true, lad, but don't make excuses for yourself. If midons prince takes the watch officers to task, your life will get that much harder. Now—luck to you; you'll be needing it."

Braydon gulped nervously and strode into the hall. The large chamber was empty except for the prince, a brazier, and two high-back chairs. Prince Aleg knelt between the chairs. As Braydon approached, the prince tossed a little ball into the air, then contrived, one by one, to collect misshaped bits of iron from the floor. A shower of metal fell through his fingers as he lunged after the ball.

"Seven, always seven," the prince complained. "Six is no trouble at all, but seven beats me every time. Care to try your luck, Egg?" He scattered the bits before offering the ball.

Braydon shook his head. It seemed to him that all noblefolk, including his prince, spent entirely too much time gambling or playing children's games.

"Suit yourself, Egg," the prince said, tucking the ball into his sleeve and leaving the iron bits where they were. "But my swordmaster tells me that a pole-axed ox has faster feet than you and your off-weapon arm should be lopped off at the shoulder; you can't use it and you'd never miss it. Egg, my man, if you want to rise above your birth-place, you'd do well to improve your nimbleness." He sprawled across the larger of the two chairs.

Appalled that his thoughts were so transparent, and that the prince was taking such close interest in his lessons, Braydon blushed from the roots of his beard to the roots of his hair. "I will, midons prince." He shed his outer garments as he approached the scattered metal.

"Not now, Egg. Take a seat and tell me what you think of this." The prince gestured toward the second chair with a tube of parchment. The scroll bounced to the floor when Braydon failed to take it quickly enough.

It was Braydon's morning for morbid embarrassment. "I can't read, midons prince," he explained. "You asked me that before you took my oath. You were satisfied with my answer."

The prince's eyes—a darker shade of gold than his hair—narrowed. "I recall I was not so satisfied with your readiness to do as you were told. Pick it up, open it, and tell me what you think."

Truly frightened, Braydon fumbled the scroll twice before he got it unfurled. The ranks of scribbling blurred. "Midons prince, I cannot make anything of it."

"Try, Egg. As you value your life, try!"

Braydon tried. He shifted the parchment by quarter-turns. His vision cleared, but the sheepskin did not yield its secrets. The marks were writing—any fool could see that—but aside from a few squared-off symbols that looked like names, they held no meaning for a country-common shepherd.

"I understand noth—"

Searing pain shot from the silver clasp. His arm went numb; he couldn't breathe, and he couldn't escape the horrifying thought that his heart was about to burst into flame. The pain ended quickly. The prince had warned him not to raise an arm in rebellion; lying, apparently, was a form of rebellion. Braydon picked up the scroll a third time.

"This mark here—" Braydon jabbed at a particular mark. "I've seen this before. When I make my mark on the paymaster's tally, these marks are close by. But I don't read them."

Prince Aleg retrieved the scroll and laid it in the brazier. "It's your name, Egg, and the assart village where you were born."

"My name is Braydon, midons prince."

The golden eyes rolled upward. "Very well, it's the name you were born with: Braydon Braydson, from the Fenklare assart called Gorse. Of course, you're looking at it upside down.

Reading's a matter of perspective. I know many men who read better from the wrong side of a writing table."

Braydon watched as the parchment sizzled. "Why did you test me, midons price? Right side up, upside down—I swore it was meaningless."

"Spoken like a true illiterate. Reading isn't magic, Egg." The prince emphasized the nickname Braydon disliked. "It's merely recognizing symbols like faces in a crowd until you know whether they're your friends or enemies. I wanted to know which one you recognized and what you made of them."

"I made nothing of them, midons prince. I beg you, believe me."

"I believe you. If a man reads that he's been condemned to death for crimes he could not have committed, certain expressions are apt to appear on his face; none appeared on yours. I believed you from the start. I hadn't counted on the oath's power over you. You're a bone-out honest man. I like that, Braydon avAlegshorn, though it limits your usefulness."

"I'm sorry, midons prince."

"Why? Do you have any notion of the uses I have for dishonest men?"

Braydon hung his head in the faint hope that the prince would not see another blush burning on his cheeks.

"Stand up straight, Egg, and be grateful that I value the service of an honest man. You can take this to Jeliff the pickler—"

The prince produced another scroll from the depths of his chair. Braydon couldn't help noticing that though the parchment had been sealed, the glossy wax had not been embossed by any signet. Braydon had never heard of Jeliff. He didn't know what a pickler did, or why a prince would be sending him an anonymous message. Braydon allowed himself to wonder about all these things while Prince Alegshorn recited directions to the twisted streets of the Eyerlon river front. When the prince asked his messenger to recite the directions back to him, Braydon was too ashamed to blush.

"I'm a patient man, Egg—but I have my limits. Pay better attention this time."

The morning watch was up when Braydon left the palace with the prince's directions impressed firmly in his memory. He ignored their jibes, and with his shoulders hunched against wind-driven snow, hiked to the frozen river front. The narrow harbor streets were clogged with barrels and crates. Work crews added to the chaos, shuttling goods from the huge sleigh-boats that supplied the city during winter to the merchants who sold them. Braydon lost his way amid unexpected detours through truly unsavory alleys, but the river front was safest during these morning hours when most of its lowlife was asleep. Eventually and without mishap, he found himself in front of a particularly pungent door upon which he knocked loudly.

A bald little man with leathery skin and a full white beard opened the door. "You're too late, lad. We sold out before dawn. Come back to—"

"I've come to see Jeliff the pickler. I have a message from the palace."

"There's two hundred people in the palace—which one sent you?" the bald man complained, but he let Braydon into the workroom and shut the door behind them.

The aroma of salt, pepper, and vinegar rising from the open barrels crowding the workroom was acid enough to put an edge on a dull knife. A pickler, apparently, was a man who pickled things. "Are you Jeliff?" he asked, wiping his nose on his sleeve.

"I am."

"Then I've come from Prince Alegshorn with a written message." Braydon found the belt-pouch beneath his cloak.

Jeliff's eyes widened. "Upstairs!" he whispered, seizing Braydon's wrist.

The air in the upper room was easier to breathe, and the room itself was somewhat brighter. Platters of the pickler's wares were laid out on tables that stretched the length of the shop. Braydon's empty stomach reminded him that bitter tea was no substitute for breakfast. Pickled eel with cabbage was standard winter fare in the barracks' mess, and there was plenty of it on Jeliff's tables. There were also delicacies that made Braydon's mouth water, and a few strange-looking creations which interested him not at all. His gut betrayed him with a groan.

"Sent you off without a proper feed? Well, never mind. Give me what you've got there, and help yourself—but mind the little peppers and all the dark sauces unless you eat fire or fear poison like royalty."

Thus forewarned, Braydon ate only the foods he recognized while Jeliff broke the seal on the scroll. It was caution, too, that kept his eyes focused on the pickled food, not the pickler sucking his teeth as he read Prince Alegshorn's message.

"What other orders did the prince give you?"

Braydon watched the scroll burn in the pickler's hand. "He said I was to bring your answer straightaway."

"Did he, now?" The pickler stared absently at the parchment until the flames approached his fingers; then he dropped the remains on the floor and ground the fire out beneath his heel. "This will take time," he said. The smell of charred parchment vanished quickly in the overall pungency of his establishment. "Surely midons Prince Alegshorn didn't expect me to keep you here?"

A faintly menacing tone had crept into Jeliff's voice; Braydon wished he had a sword hanging at his hip. Two lessons into the Song of Steel, surely he was already a better swordsman than any pickler. Still he was a veteran of the Arrizi campaigns, a man of the guard, and a prince's oath-bound messenger; he was not about to be intimidated by a scruffy pickler. Drawing himself up to his full height, he wiped briny fingers on his cloak. "Midons prince said I was to await your reply."

The pickler met Braydon's glower. He distracted Braydon's attention, then threaded a sailmaker's straight awl through the coarse cloth of his shirt near the neckband. The neckband tightened like a noose around Braydon's neck and, with a final twist of his hand, Jeliff pricked the soft flesh beneath his chin with the steel point. Braydon couldn't see the tiny weapon, but he could feel it, and imagine it piercing his tongue. If the awl didn't kill him, some briny poison clinging to the metal surely would.

After a very long, motionless moment, Jeliff lowered the awl. "No lies now, lad. What, exactly, did the prince say?"

"He said I was to await your orders. I assumed—"

"Never assume, lad. You're already in over your head. Assumptions will get you killed."

The pickler withdrew his weapon. Just as Braydon feared, greenish oil shimmered on the awl. His mind was still asking itself useless questions when Jeliff slid the awl into the flesh between the bones of his own forearm. Against the advice he'd been given, Braydon dared another assumption: The pickler wasn't committing suicide; therefore he was an assassin. There was no guessing, or assuming, what other weapons his body concealed.

Jeliff's face twisted into a sly smile. "You'll come back tonight, before the top of the deadwatch. Don't come to the lower door again, there's a stairway at the back. Come alone and make certain you're not followed. You can do that, can't you?"

Swallowing hard, Braydon grunted agreement. He couldn't take his eyes from the liver-colored spot on the merchant's arm where the awl had disappeared.

"You're an honest man," the pickler said, echoing the prince's earlier words. "Your oath will protect you only if you don't ask questions." His arm hung normally at his side. "Now, have you had enough to eat? Can I give you something for your lunch?" Jeliff plucked a wrinkled ball from one of the platters Braydon had ignored. The ball was mottled brown and about the size of a man's eyeball. "These are punau eggs, worth their weight in silver. They say eating a punau egg on the last night of Calends will keep you alive till the next one."

Braydon wasn't tempted; his appetite had vanished. "It's not the last night of Calends," he said, whispering because he could not speak any louder.

The snow squalls had blown over and the sun was shining when Braydon left the pickler's establishment. Braydon gauged the angle of the light on the rooftops and saw the scarred, scowling face of Prince Alegshorn's swordmaster in his mind's eye: he'd been inside longer than he'd thought. But the sunlight had melted the icy streets and made them treacherous. There'd be no running unless he wanted to risk his neck. Braydon made haste slowly toward the practice ground.

Prince Rinchen had entered the tunnel from the opposite direction. The Wolf was dressed in his customary black with flashes of silver and ruby. He was fresh from practice with a bit of color in his pale cheeks. A wolf-pelt cloak overflowed the arms of one of the middle-aged chancellors laboring to keep pace with him.

Braydon flattened himself against the wall. He had no reason to think the prince would recognize a man from his brother's guard, but prudence made men wary when the Wolf was near. Prince Rinchen stopped in front of him. The chancellors stumbled against each other.

"You're late for your lesson, partisan. My dear brother's swordmaster gave up on you and left the field."

"I was—" Braydon hesitated. Both Prince Alegshorn and the pickler-assassin had hailed him as an honest man, but every fiber in Braydon's body counselled him to be less than honest now. "—I was irresistibly detained." Among the guardsmen *"irresistibly detained"* meant only one thing: *I was with a woman.* Braydon could only hope the Wolf understood the passions he was not presumed to share.

Prince Rinchen appraised him thoroughly and with a scowl. Braydon felt sweat on his forehead.

"A man in your position"—the prince did not say what that position might be—"can ill afford to miss his lessons. Or don't you wish to serve my brother with a song of steel?"

Wishing with all his will that he'd taken a little longer to get from the river front to the palace, Braydon lowered his eyes and shook his head. "No, midons prince."

"No—you don't wish to serve him? He will be displeased to hear that."

"I serve with all my heart, midons prince, but I cannot sing with steel."

"Then perhaps you'd like a lesson from someone who can teach you tricks that golden Aleg's swordmasters do not know?"

It was scarcely believable. The Wolf—one of the finest swordsmen in the kingdom and certainly the most devious—seemed to be offering a lesson in the song of steel. Braydon's knees froze, and the remnants of his pickled breakfast churned loudly in his gut. "I am a rank neophyte, midons prince. Such a lesson would surely be wasted."

No one in the passageway spoke while Braydon got a foretaste of eternity.

"Some other time—if you have another time."

The Wolf continued into the new palace. Braydon stayed where he was, leaning against the wall, waiting for his heart to beat normally again.

In another part of Eyerlon, Berika was also staying very still and feeling trapped. The puppy was asleep with his head on her shoulder and an arm draped across her body. Driskolt always left her alone after lovemaking, but Driskolt had his own suite of rooms while Killeen slept on a pallet in the lower hall. Reckoning that the lower hall was at least as crowded with sorMeklan partisans as the shepherd's house in Gorse had been with women, children, and sheep, Berika supposed she shouldn't begrudge him a night uninterrupted by coughing, snoring, or the occasional nightmare. And she probably wouldn't have, if he'd curled up anywhere else in the huge bed except on her.

She'd been awake since dawn. At first she'd tried to wriggle free, but the puppy slept lightly and awoke with one irresistible thing on is mind. So Berika gritted her teeth and tried not to move. Inevitably she was overwhelmed with itching. She wanted to scratch the bottoms of her feet, the backs of her knees, the base of her spine, and, of course, the tip of her nose. By the time she heard the mid-morning peal, she was ready to kill herself or the puppy; it no longer mattered which.

She resisted the urge and sought refuge in her *basi*. If she lived long enough, she'd make a fine hedge-sorcerer. Her endowment of *basi* had fallen just short of what she would have needed to reach the Web before her seventeenth birthday. In the weeks since her seventeenth birthday—roughly the same time that she'd been living in the sorMeklan residence—she had not bothered exercising her talent on which she'd wasted so much hope. Using it again was like putting on winter clothes after summer: heavy and awkward.

Berika stuck with it, exploring and exercising until she was moving within herself more freely than ever before. She found the itchy places and soothed them from the inside. She numbed her feet and made her hands hot. Wherever she focused her *basi*, her body revealed another mystery. In an afterthought, Berika dove as deep within herself as she could.

Mother Cathe—what's that*?*

But Berika knew, even as despair and outrage boiled through her. Whether it was sheep or people, village life shielded little from its children, especially Berika who had fallen prey to her betrothed many years before their marriage. Berika said her prayers earnestly every night and repeated them as she contemplated the burgeoning presence within her.

Mother Cathe—make me not with child.

The cow-headed goddess, protector of women and guardian of childbirth, had kept Berika safe from Hirmin and Dris, but not the puppy. On her own, Berika forged a barrier in the deepest recesses of her body. Nothing was destroyed: nothing was conceived—it would simply slide away when the right time came. Berika released her *basi;* her mind tumbled into more ordinary awareness. She was exhausted, drenched with sweat, and shivering.

Killeen woke up. "Berika, what's wrong?" He was gentle, kind, and adoring in the manner of puppies everywhere. He would have doted on his firstborn; he might even have married that child's mother and removed the stigma of her commonfolk birth. It wasn't Killeen's fault that she found him utterly unappealing.

"I must be more careful—now that I know how to be careful."

"What are you talking about?"

Berika hadn't meant to speak aloud and didn't want to answer Killeen's question. "I was dreaming," she insisted, then kissed him on the lips, knowing it would drive any question from his mind.

She was enduring her success when someone pounded once on the door and flung it open.

"Out!" the sidon of Fenklare bellowed.

Berika lunged for the larger share of the bed linens. Killeen tumbled onto the cold floor, sputtering incoherently at his patron.

"Out!" Driskolt repeated. He was loud, but he didn't seem angry—yet.

Killeen grabbed his garments and ran. Driskolt closed the door firmly while Berika twisted the linen around her. She wasn't about to start an argument, but she was ready to finish one if Dris gave her half an opportunity. He tried to caress her cheek; she swerved away.

"Iser's balls—you're in a foul mood this morning."

"You pass me off to a boy who doesn't have a whisker on his chin. Then you come storming in like a rutting bull and you're surprised I'm not overjoyed to see you?" Berika had adopted the noblefolk habit of asking questions that did not require answers.

"If there was any passing off going on, I was passing Killy off to you, not the other way round. You were handling everything well enough when I came in. I don't see what you're complaining about."

Berika struck him in the face with her pillow, and regretted it almost immediately. Dris seized her wrist and twisted it until her fingers stiffened. They were face-to-face and a hand's width apart. Berika's breathing was shallow from the pain, but she didn't blink.

"Godswill, you're a stubborn woman, Berika," Driskolt said admiringly as he twisted her wrist a bit more. "I'd have to kill you before you broke—and then I'd never have the answers I need." He released her as abruptly as he'd grabbed her.

"What answers?" Berika replied, cradling her wrist in her lap, no longer pretending that it didn't hurt.

"Does Dart, my uncle, have spook's *basi*?"

Berika almost forgot the pain. "No, that was the first thing our hedge-sorcerer said about him. Auld Mag said she'd touched newborn babes with more and that he was as mad as his hair."

"You're certain?"

Berika nodded, then curled up around her throbbing wrist.

"Did I hurt you?"

Berika made a sound deep in her throat that meant yes.

"You shouldn't be so aggravating. My father and I were called to the Palestra this morning—a roomful of spooks with their silver showing and a mouthful of questions about Dart. I thought you'd rather answer me than my father."

Gut-wrenching fear worse than the pain in her wrist brought tears from Berika's eyes. "Why ask me? Don't the sorcerers know everything? I'm just a godsforsaken shepherd."

"Whatever the spooks know, they're not telling anyone, even the palace." Driskolt laid his hand gently on Berika's shoulder. She jerked away from him and he didn't try again. "I'll get the mender. I'm sorry; I truly am. You bring out the worst in me, sometimes, but if you know something about Dart that you haven't told me, you should think about telling me now. It's very important."

"I don't know anything. I wish I'd never met him. Go away."

Berika felt Dris stand up and heard him sigh. Her anger was fading. Men like Driskolt and Killeen had power, real power, and it didn't pay to stay angry with them. If she and the sidon had been talking about anything except Dart, she would have swallowed her tears and called him back to the bed. But they were talking about Dart. She hadn't heard her demon calling her since the night of Prince Alegshorn's party. She'd begun to think that meant he was dead, begun to think death was a good thing for him. Now she thought he was alive, but unable to call her, and she was deep-in-the-gut afraid.

As soon as she was alone, Berika pulled the pillow against her face and screamed into it. She had to talk to someone. If it couldn't be Dris or Killeen, it would have to be her brother, Braydon. She knew no one else in all Eyerlon.

Chapter Ten

When the midday peal rang the change between the morning and afternoon watches, Prince Rinchen had completed a day's work with his grandfather's chancellors. He'd listened to petitions, sealed grants, dictated decrees, and attended to every other thing the chancellors brought to his attention. But he'd also compelled them to rush after him through narrow corridors and endure the frigid Calends weather on the practice ground.

This particular morning Rinchen had, additionally, distributed alms to crippled soldiers, bartered like a fishwife with foreign emissaries, and battered his way through three sparring partners. The older nobles and sorcerers who governed the kingdom from one day to the next were red-faced and exhausted when he returned them to the chancery behind the new palace throne hall. They gratefully shed their cloaks and warmed themselves at the hearth while servants put goblets of steaming mulled wine into their stiff-fingered hands.

"Midonès, will that be enough? Have we covered everything?" he asked from the doorway.

There wasn't a hint of irony in his voice, but the chancellors weren't fooled. He'd run them mercilessly if they intruded on his precious private hours in the afternoon.

"Exactly enough, midons prince," Jemat sorLewel said from a

cushioned chair. There wasn't a hint of irony in his voice, either.

With a thin-lipped smile, Rinchen spun on his heel and left the chamber. A brace of surly Pennaikmen with baggy breeches, shaggy coats, and an excess of knives in their belts escorted him through the warrens of the old palace. Seen through strict Pennaik eyes, every sorRodion was a mongrel bastard. The rest of the kingdom might think the Wolf—Rinchen sometimes thought of himself as "the Wolf," especially when he was thinking about his curse—was a throwback to his nomadic forebears, but his own guards knew better. His hair was as black as theirs, but lusterless and arrow-straight. His skin was too pale, his features too sharp and narrow. The men who served him so loyally would not share food with him or sleep where he slept but—because of his eyes—they offered him their lives and souls.

Ice-colored eyes, they told him, were the marks of destiny. Ice-eyed men rode the high road to greatness—or doom. The nomads were gamblers of the first water, ready to seize any risk—except the soul-deep contamination that came from eating or sleeping with a mongrel.

Two dozen Pennaikmen camped in a barren chamber below his hall and on a flat expanse of roof adjoining it, re-creating, with considerable success, a bit of the steppes wilderness in the midst of Eyerlon. The two who'd flanked him since the chancery joined their brethren. Only Arkkin ever climbed the last flight of stairs to his private hall and chamber without explicit invitation.

Alone and smiling for the first time since dawn, Rinchen took the stairs two at a time. His smile vanished when a particular swirl of carved wood above the doorway caught his eye. An untutored eye could not decipher the long-dead woodcutter's art, or notice that a tiny segment had been given a quarter-turn. But he knew his sanctuary's secrets. He knew where to look among the curling vines and coiled snakes: A message awaited him behind another panel in the hall itself.

The Pennaikmen were the best men blood or money could buy. They watched the roof, the shuttered windows, and the stairway, all from a measured distance. But there were other ways to reach his lair, as the young woman in sorMeklan colors had discovered. He had no friends, but he was not completely without allies, although none of them wished to be seen in his company. Boltholes scattered throughout the palace and kingdom enabled the Wolf to remain one step ahead of his enemies.

By habit, Rinchen glanced left and right coming through the door, reading the empty shadows as he entered his own territory.

If his allies knew the hidden ways, so did his enemies and their hired assassins. Not long ago he would have stood in the doorway inspecting every shadow before he strode into the hall, but he had relaxed a bit since Tremontin.

Ten steps into his hall, a weight dropped from the rafters. It was man-heavy, man-sized, and armed with steel. Rinchen protected his throat and felt a blade slice his forearm. Denying pain and shock, he twisted his shoulders and sought a handhold on the assassin's body with his uninjured arm. The assassin knew his trade. He didn't scream as blood gushed from a torn ear; screaming would alert the Pennaikmen. He gouged the air where Rinchen's neck would have been, if he weren't both lithe and quick. The assassin knew he was going to be thrown before his feet left the ground, flowed with the motion rather than fighting against it, and righted himself, catlike, before he struck the floor.

Rinchen retreated, respecting his opponent now that he'd taken his measure. With his good hand he drew a small knife from his boot. His injured arm was numb below the gash, tingling above it. He suspected poison, then banished the suspicion from his thoughts. Pressing the numb hand against his thigh, he tried to flex his fingers. They were sluggish and without strength; they'd have to do better when he needed them.

The assassin advanced in the balanced stance of a master. He held his knife in his left hand. He feinted to take the measure of his opponent.

The Wolf didn't bite. Tensed and motionless, he studied the assassin's face. If there were more in the shadows, eye movement would give them away. When nothing broke the man's stare, Rinchen offered his own feint. The assassin's knife drifted off-center; it was all the opening Rinchen needed. Shrieking his war-cry as he seized his opponent's weapon wrist with his clumsy hand, he thrust through the assassin's defenses. His knife plunged hilt-deep between the man's ribs. He wrenched it a quarter-turn before ripping it along the bone. The wound was fatal, but assassins often stoked themselves with illicit decoctions, and a single fatal wound was not sufficient. He twisted the hilt again to free it, then shoved it into the assassin's groin.

His heart had beaten eight times during the attack—Rinchen measured such things habitually: he was slow as honey in winter.

The assassin did not react to his two gaping wounds, but struggled with unnatural strength. Rinchen abandoned his own knife just as his weakened arm collapsed. He wrapped his good arm around the assassin's neck and spun the man around, much as he had spun the sorMeklan girl—it was one of his favorite moves—but this time he continued to squeeze.

Choking and desperate, the assassin stabbed wildly at the Wolf's midsection. The blade slid over the fine mail he always wore beneath his shirt when he walked amid the kingdom's chancellors. The assassin slashed at Rinchen's face, but he wasn't nearly fast enough and his neck snapped like green wood. This time his body went limp.

Coldly methodical, Rinchen wrenched the dead man's head around until their eyes met; then he snapped his neck a second time.

Life faded from the assassin's eyes. His bowels loosened and Rinchen released the reeking corpse.

He looked at his arm for the first time, raising it toward his parted lips. But dizziness overtook him before he could taste his own blood, and he reeled into strong, supporting arms.

"Poison," he whispered before his eyes closed.

Magga Feladon had been right when he claimed that not one Pennaikman in a thousand had enough *basi* to reach the Web, but Arkkin, who cradled the Wolf's head in his arms, was one in ten thousand. The shaman wet his fingers in the wound and, using blood as more timid sorcerers used Brightwater, struck the Web like a bell. When he was satisfied that a mender was on the move, he released the Web and pressed his fingers into the hollow of the Wolf's neck, slowing his pulse and keeping him alive.

Several hours later the heavy shutters in Prince Rinchen's hall were wide open. The barren room was as bright and cold as the Calends afternoon outside. Magga Feladon, who'd been summoned for a private audience, kept his cloak clasped and his hands tucked into its fleece lining. It was unlike the prince to keep invited guests waiting. Promptness was among that young man's limited virtues.

To keep warm, Feladon paced the width of the hall and one half its length, avoiding the part closest to the prince's inner lair because three palace drudges were scrubbing the wood floor. He'd been pacing a while before he noticed that their rags wrung out a rusty red. He reconsidered the wide-open windows, then reached for the Web.

Even in the palace, with the Basilica's golden dome visibly brilliant in the afternoon light, Feladon could sense the echoing hole over Tremontin when he caught the Web. "Frightened" was too strong a word for his reaction, but not by much. He couldn't imagine life without the Web binding him and all the other sorcerers together, and thanked the gods that he'd never have to.

Propelled by *basi*, Feladon's thoughts migrated to the center of the Web where he acknowledged the afternoon communications. They shared awareness of Arkkin's thoroughly uncivilized summons. Feladon reached out to the mender who had responded. Halwisse reported that the Wolf had been wounded by an assassin whose body had vanished by the time she arrived. She'd purged fish toxin from the prince's blood and mended his flesh. She'd done her duty; the Wolf would survive, but she was more concerned about the missing assassin. Shaking his head slowly, Feladon withdrew from the contact.

Near his private nexus, Feladon found a confidential annotation from the deadwatch communicant: An exceptionally dense pall had sprung up above the sorNesil residence just before dawn.

Neither illegal nor uncommon—at least among the wealthy—palls were artifacts of sorcery that obscured a physical location. Walenfolk had a right to secrecy. The donitorial residences and strongholds were under palls more often than not, as were many of the larger mercantile establishments. A hedge-sorcerer could create a pall as dense as any Feladon himself could create. Foreigners passing beneath the Web moved in palls only a magga communicant could penetrate. Arrizan conjury had palled the entire Norivarl donit. The possibility that the emptiness above Tremontin was a pall resulting from the burial of so many foreigners burst into Feladon's mind. It was a welcome explanation for disturbing phenomena, but Feladon had more immediate thoughts to ponder while he paced.

The sorNesil were bound by marriage to the donitors of Escham and by debt to the sorJos sept within that clan. The sorNesil would have a wealth of excuses for that dense pall above their residence. Magga Halwisse sorJos, so concerned about the Wolf's would-be assassin, would have excuses too, but he wouldn't ask her for them. Magga Feladon tucked his suspicions into the recesses of his mind, not the Web.

Extending his hands through the slits in his cloak, he reached for the Web again and made a diamond shape with his thumbs pointed at his heart and his fingers aimed at the lye-bleached floor. In a voice that could not be heard an arm's length away, he recited the orison for the dead. The Web around him vibrated gently, absorbing the mordant *basi* his prayer had released, and for an unwelcome but not unexpected moment, the dead man's thoughts passed through Feladon's mind on their way to the Web. He felt the precautionary drugs that not only stoked the man against pain or injury, but created a thick tangle of confusion to protect his employer and his past from inquist inquiry. The hours between drinking the decoctions and death were the only clear thoughts, but they were very clear. Feladon winced when he saw the Wolf's face for the last time: not at all cold, but full-lipped and flushed with passion.

He released the Web quickly and rubbed his eyes.

Prince Rinchen stood in the doorway to his private lair.

"When you're ready, Lord Magga."

Feladon noticed the fringe of a linen bandage peeking from the sleeve of the prince's somber shirt. He waited until the door was closed and he had wrought a pall around them before asking: "Are you all right, Lord Prince?" Rinchen was not his lord. The Wolf did not have justice rights over Walensor's Magga sorcerer that merited a "Midons" honorific. Nor was he anyone's shirt-name friend.

The Wolf flexed his injured arm. "I'm alive."

Only someone who knew the young man well would notice the change in his expression, or guess what it masked. Feladon noticed. "I'd hoped Tremontin would stop this once and for all."

"Only two things will stop it: the crown above me and the throne beneath me."

Feladon did not mention the third alternative: death. "What happened?"

"The usual." The prince massaged his shoulder. "He tried to take me by surprise, but surprise wasn't enough. He looked foreign. Maybe the Merrisati don't want their princess to marry a wolf. I had the Pennaikmen dispose of the body."

Feladon didn't ask for more details. Since their appearance on the prince's sixteenth birthday—the day a nomad boy became a man—the Pennaikmen had insulated the prince with the privacy he craved. Those who had "disposed of the body" were undoubtedly headed north, never to be seen in the heartland again. In a few weeks the guard would be at full strength again. Feladon turned his attention to the more obvious:

"You were wounded seriously enough to require a mender."

The prince averted his eyes. "I *was* a little surprised, and there was poison on the knife. Arkkin didn't want to take chances."

'A little surprised'? *That* was quite an admission from this young man. And a poison that had affected him? It was not generally known—except to a handful of magga menders and, of course, Feladon himself—that thanks to his mother's many attempts to poison him in infancy, Rinchen was immune to the more common deadly substances; Rinchen himself did not know—one hoped—how in this one instance his curse contrived to protect him. Usually it served the Palestra's needs to encourage the prince's belief in his curse, but now, with his grandfather, the king, wielding sorcery, another tactic was required.

"My lord, will you please consider telling the king what has happened?"

"No." The Wolf's voice was soft, but emphatic.

"You just said he seemed foreign. Surely if the Merrisati—"

"No," Rinchen repeated, more softly than the first time. "He never lifted his voice to help me when I couldn't help myself. He's used me as his stalking-horse all along; I know that now. He's first among those who wish me in the ground, last to admit it. I don't need his help and I won't ask for it."

Feladon made himself look at the prince's face. If he could not imagine life without the Web, neither could he imagine what Rinchen saw through those ice-colored eyes. Born a month early and at exactly the wrong time of the year, the ill-omened infant had been sick—poisoned by his mother, mostly—and given up for dead many times before he reached his first birthday. By then his fortune-favored brother, Alegshorn, had been safely delivered from Janna's womb.

Somehow Rinchen survived in the malignant nursery where he and his brother were confined every night, and any other time protocol or education did not require their presence. While Prince Vigelan lived, the boy sometimes evidenced a forlorn hope that he could win someone's approval, but after Kasserine, the Wolf kept his hopes, if he had any, to himself.

"You don't have to ask for anything, lord prince—simply tell the truth: an assassin confronted you and you killed him in self-defense. Tell your own side of the story instead of letting others tell it for you."

"Others?" the prince asked with a sour laugh. "Do you think anything I say will change what others say about me? Let *others* whisper rumors. They make me stronger than I could ever make myself. Rinchen sorRodion—the Wolf Prince, demon's spawn, cold of eye, cold of blood, deceiver, murderer, and defiler of innocent beasts. What I cannot have in love, I will accept in fear and hatred. I am what *others* have made me and I have accepted their curse."

"But you're not the man your enemies say you are."

"By what sorcery do you know that? Look around you, Feladon. This what I've made of my life. You say I'm not my enemies' man, but do you invite me to dine with your wife? dance with your daughters and nieces? Do you trust me? Did you ever?"

Feladon looked at the window. He'd been Prince Rinchen's principal tutor. He'd felt compassion for a lonely, angry boy, been impressed by his crisp, eager intelligence. But while Prince Vigelan lived, no sane man lent a hand or smile to his son. And after Prince Vigelan died, it was too late: He'd become the Wolf, moody and abrasive. He'd killed more men with his bare hands than most men had slain with their weapons during the war and—Feladon had seen that look of passion through a dead man's eyes before—enjoyed it.

The Wolf's behavior was hardly surprising and almost excusable, but he wasn't a man another man trusted or befriended.

"Why did you summon me?" Feladon asked abruptly, wanting to be gone from this sad, untidy room. "I'm no mender or inquist."

"This was the second attempt on my life in as many days. Yesterday nothing would have protected me from the king, if he had known what he was doing, or if he had intended to kill me before witnesses—"

Magga Feladon opened his mouth to object, but the prince silenced him with a curt gesture.

"Don't deny it. The king is as old as you are and you've stoked his heart with Brightwater for twenty years. What did you think was going to happen? Is the Basilica going to do anything about it? *Can* the Basilica do anything about it? The Web is dying—"

"No one's said the Web is dying—"

"No one's said King Manal lashed me with sorcery, either, but it happened. Since I gave the order to bring Tremontin down, a goddess has gone missing, the Web's dying, and my grandfather's developed a dangerous penchant for sorcery. And there's a man under wards at the Palestra—at least he was a man until that missing goddess had her way with him. He claims he's Weycha's champion, and the sorMeklan concede he's one of theirs. But no one claims him as strongly or as frequently as that nubile basilidan—your niece, isn't she?—who calls herself Ash."

"Midons prince—" Feladon mumbled, dropping into reflexive subservience, while wondering how the Wolf had learned so much.

He knew the Palestra leaked. He'd been known to whisper a secret out of turn himself, sometimes to this very man. Talking to Halwisse sorJos during the deadwatch had been a calculated risk;

the attempt on Prince Rinchen's life was not unexpected, but the prince had taken care of himself before. Feladon's surprise rose from the completeness of Rinchen's knowledge. The Wolf was too clever by half; he inferred more from an offhand remark than most men absorbed from a sermon, but he could not have inferred that Ash was his niece. Someone inside his household had told him.

"Yes, Lord Magga?" The prince feigned innocence. The guise wasn't particularly successful; it didn't have to be.

"These are difficult times. While you and the king repair the kingdom's visible damage, we who weave the Web are repairing the less visible damage. Everything is flux. What was strong yesterday, might be less strong today, or more. We must all be very careful. The Basilica will not do anything rash. There are many pots simmering in the hearth; we keep our eye on all of them. A little soup may sizzle on the stones, but you may be certain we have everything well in hand." Feladon congratulated himself on an adroit recovery.

Prince Rinchen retrieved a sheet of parchment from his worktable. "I mean to help you by taking one of your pots into my own care: the man you have under wards—the one who calls himself Dart sorMeklan. It isn't fitting that a donitor's brother spends his days in the Palestra. If the sorMeklan won't shelter him, I will. Send for him—now."

Feladon protested for the better part of an hour: Dart sorMeklan was a resurrected man. Every breath he took violated the Compact. He was anathema. He belonged below the Basilica; it was charity to keep him above ground in the Palestra. But the prince would not relent.

"If he is the Driskolt sorMeklan of old, then I remember him fondly. It is customary for friends to take care of each other, isn't it? Instruct me, old tutor: Do I misunderstand the mystery of friendship?"

Feladon squared his shoulders. "Driskolt sorMeklan was as old as you are now when he disappeared, and you weren't more than four. Forgive me, but the two of you were not friends and have no friendly interest in each other now. He is anathema and rightly belongs to us. I beg you to reconsider."

Rinchen refused, and eventually Feladon reached through his pall. The Magga's thoughts and reluctant commands reached their destination instantly; it took much longer for Dart to be escorted from his warded room to Prince Rinchen's lair atop the old palace.

The prince and the sorcerer passed that time in awkward silence. Rinchen sat behind his worktable, studying his maps and scratching notes on scraps of parchment. Feladon had swallowed pride and learned the rudiments of script. He used the Web to see exactly what the headblind prince was writing. But the Wolf had mastered languages the way he mastered weapons, and Feladon could not decipher the marks he saw.

While Feladon fumed, Rinchen drew a stream of arrows, each pointed in the sorcerer's direction.

Feladon had Severed the prince the day he was born. He knew as surely as he knew anything that Rinchen could not perceive the simplest sorcery; the Wolf was inferring again. Feladon ended his Webwork abruptly, giving himself an instant, throbbing headache. He rubbed his aching temples until he noticed that Rinchen was smiling. After that he bore his pain discreetly.

Dart arrived with two neophytes beside him and four Pennaikmen beyond them. Weycha's champion walked by himself. His parti-colored hair was tucked into a shapeless hat and his eyes were hidden by its shadow. In Feladon's opinion, he looked properly worried.

Prince Rinchen rose to his feet, transfixed by his visitor's face. "Leave us," he commanded. "All of you. I will speak with Lord sorMeklan alone."

The neophytes and Pennaikmen retreated but Feladon stayed put. "Rinchen—"

"Leave us."

Feladon had seen the look on Rinchen's face before: hopelessness, fear, and pain layered beneath implacable stubbornness. The Wolf was always ready to fight to the death; he'd become very hard to kill. Feladon admitted defeat. "We will not be responsible," he warned as he hurried after the neophytes.

The footfalls of seven men faded. Dart stood just inside the room, waiting for the prince to speak first. Dart remembered dying and the face of a goddess. There wasn't much that surprised him and even less that truly frightened him. He had the patience of a man who'd spent eighteen winters inside a tree trunk.

He could outwait any more-ordinary man, even Walensor's Wolf.

"They told me who you were and what you'd become while you were still on the river from Relamain. We knew each other . . . *before*." The prince moistened his lips. "You tailed with Prince Vigelan, my—my—You befriended me once. I was much younger. You might not remember. But you haven't changed at all. You're exactly as I remember." He picked up a stylus, scratched at a vagrant dot on the map, and ignored the man he'd invited into his most private lair.

Dart approached the worktable. "I seem to recall a wet-nosed brat who wanted to ride my stallion, and who bit me when I lifted him up behind. Is that what you recall?"

Prince Rinchen kept scraping at the parchment. "Riding behind wasn't worth the effort. I couldn't see anything, or feel the wind on my face."

"I was the only one who'd risk your father's wrath by noticing you. Biting me like that, you risked being left behind . . . again."

"But I wasn't, *and* I rode in front."

"Just like your brother—except Aleg rode in front of us all with your father, and you were sitting in front of a man who loved his family no better than yours loves you."

The prince laid down the stylus. "Vigelan didn't dare haul me off; you were his closest friend. I stared at his back the whole morning. I got what I wanted."

"That's a lie if I ever heard one—and, Rinchen, I remember telling a lot of them."

Rinchen remembered the truth. In a childhood full of fear, pain and helplessness, merciless beatings, the truth about that autumn day stood clear in his mind. Dart—Driskolt then—*was* Vigelan's closest friend, always at his side and sometimes winning the reckless games that preoccupied young noblemen long before the war.

He himself had still been young and stupidly trusting of Vigelan's promises: Behave yourself, and you can ride the Tenthday hunt. He had behaved—gone four full days without a beating or even a swat—and gone down to the stable at dawn to collect his reward. But Vigelan had Aleg before him in the saddle already. *Aleg* who was still afraid of horses. Aleg had outgrown that fear soon enough. Scrupulously fair, Rinchen always made himself acknowledge the precise measure of another's strengths and virtues. But there was no misremembering the terror in Aleg's eyes up there all by himself, or the ache in his own heart when Vigelan laughed and said there was no room.

He'd run away blindly and drawn an ass-over-elbow swat from Driskolt sorMeklan. He'd been about to run into a misplaced pitchfork, and Vigelan's friend had saved his life. It was an unprecedented act: the saving, not the swat. Wary to the bone, he'd picked himself out of the straw, ready to dodge another swat, foolishly hoping he wouldn't have to.

And Dart asked him if he wanted to ride. Too frightened by dreams-maybe-coming-true to answer with words, he'd merely nodded his head. Dart swept him up and plunked him down on the padded cantle *behind* where the rider would sit. He'd see shirt all day, nothing more, and the wind wouldn't touch his face. It wasn't enough—better to be on his back in the straw than seeing shirt all day. He hadn't just bitten Dart, he'd kicked, scratched, and used the words he'd learned from Vigelan.

Dart had swatted him—swatted him forward before he mounted behind him, securing him in the more precarious pommel-perch with his weapon-arm. Vigelan swore when they joined the hunt, but Dart laughed and they thundered off with another twenty horses. It was joy, and he'd surrendered to it willingly through fields and across streams until they confronted a briar-covered stone wall.

The stallion changed leads, adjusting its stride for height, distance, and speed. Joy doubled and Rinchen had leaned forward to taste the wind when they rose into the air. Then Dart changed arms, gripping him off-handedly and turning him slightly away from the wind. He struggled, the grip grew painful, and he understood: Dart meant to fling him to the thorns and stones.

An accident. The accident Vigelan longed for.

A gift—one friend to another.

He'd never wanted to die. And never, then or now, understood why he wanted to keep living. But he'd closed his eyes, ducked his head, and clung with all his strength. Dart reined the stallion in once they'd landed safely on the other side.

What's wrong, little prince? Think I'd let you fall?

He had, of course: fallen, thrown, or trampled.

Dart switched arms again, held the rein off-handedly and him on the other side, the weapon side, the important side, now that he was more important than guiding the stallion. Rinchen had never felt important before, but he hadn't tasted the wind, and finally he'd shamed himself bawling like an orphan calf.

Dart hadn't said a word, just reined the stallion to a full stop, holding him tight until all the other riders were far from sight and sound. Then he turned the stallion toward the wall again.

Keep your eyes open this time, runt.

He had. It was everything he wanted it to be—and more, because they had to jump again if they were going to catch up with the others. Dart told him how to hold the rein and move his hands;

he'd never been afraid of horses. The third time was joy beyond measure.

Dart waited patiently as before. He waited to see if the prince did remember jumping the wall three times. By then the runt'd been so excited and they were so far behind, he decided they might just as well spend the rest of the day together, one rogue with another. He taught him to swim in a damn cold stream. What else did you do with a four-year-old prince? Buy him a whore? Get him drunk? He'd done the best he could—

"You were gone. Dead. A week later."

He looked across the worktable where Rinchen was hiding his face, talking to parchment. Weycha had been wrong: Her champion had been missed by someone after all. His own instincts counselled him to wrap the prince in a roughhouse embrace. It was Weycha's gifts that held him back. Rinchen needed affection, as he'd needed it that autumn day, but he'd become a man in the last eighteen years.

"Well, I'm not dead now. I hear you've become a fair horseman, now that your feet reach the stirrups."

The black-thatched head didn't move.

"You haven't changed either, Rinchen. It's still your way or nothing."

The prince raised his head and raked hair out of his eyes. "That is as it must be. I'm crown prince. I will be king." Then he peppered Dart with questions about his confinement.

"You already know all the answers, my prince: I live comfortably among my enemies."

"Do you know that Lord Ean sorMeklan has sworn vengeance if one odd-colored hair on your head is harmed?"

"And Prince Alegshorn will purge the noblefolk the moment you're safely dead, my prince. Our families are like that."

Rinchen did not argue. "You were a rogue, but everyone liked you; you were welcomed everywhere. You had friends," he said softly, more wistful than bitter.

Well, not *everyone* liked him. Dart leaned against the table and told the prince about Berika.

"It's for the best," Dart insisted when he saw vengeance brewing in the prince's icy eyes. "If she hadn't betrayed me, the inquists would have eaten her alive. As it is, she's come up safe amid my kinfolk. And her brother's given a Brightwater oath to your brother."

"That assart shepherd?"

Dart nodded. "They're good folk, common or not—which is more than I can say for my other so-called friends." And he spoke of Halwisse sorJos but not of the leather-bound royal chronicles. He suspected that his benefactor was Prince Rinchen, but he was not sure—it could still easily have been Prince Alegshorn. After reading about the fraternal rivalry, he didn't want to risk a mistake. Lastly Dart spoke of Ash, the lusty basilidan who used him in her desperate quest for her missing goddess.

"She's got the whole Palestra whispering. No one believes her when she says we're merely looking for my lady."

"I don't suppose you mind what anyone says. She's pretty enough, if you like women with snow-white hair—"

With a lopsided grin, Dart shook his head. "Red." Armed with his restored memories and the leather-bound chronicle, the erstwhile Driskolt ruEan sorMeklan could play the noblefolk game of intrigue and information when the stakes were right.

The prince's face stiffened unaccountably.

"It's the color of fire, which she takes as a bad omen considering the goddess who's supposed to have chosen her. Almost as bad as getting born in the blind moon of Calends. She's terrified someone will notice, so she's bleaching it as it grows," he explained, hoping the prince had sense of humor.

"Maybe once she reaches her goddess it will turn white. The Magga Sorcerer and the other basilidans are sure the calling is a true one. Do you have doubts, knowing them both—the goddess and the girl—as well as you must . . . ?"

Thus assured the prince indeed possessed a sly and somewhat lewd wit, Dart nearly lost his composure. "Let's say I'm willing to bide my time, midons prince," he said, dropping into the more formal mode of address. "Weycha sleeps alone this winter, and nothing I do, or Ash does, will change that. Perhaps when Quickening comes, a pattern will have emerged."

"That might be too late." The prince shared what he knew about the Web and, more importantly, his grandfather, the king. "I've heard the largest hole is above Tremontin. One might think a pattern has already emerged. A forest has died, killed by sorcery and by a prince's command. One might think that a cursed prince was to blame. He broke the Compact and now no one—man, goddess, basilidan, or king—need abide."

"You left out champion," Weycha's champion said with a deceptively casual shrug. "And I don't think you're to blame. My lady fears Hazard of the Arrizi, not some misbegotten Pennaik mongrel"—Rinchen bristled—"but I wouldn't go walking naked past any large, old trees if I were you."

The ice-eyed prince grinned unconvincingly and said nothing.

"If you were my lady's enemy, I'd have killed you by now."

Dart spoke with flat confidence, notwithstanding the Wolf's reputation. Rinchen slowly took his measure.

"How would you know if I were her enemy?"

"I'd have the same feeling behind my eyes I get each time I see Ash."

"You haven't managed to kill her."

"I haven't tried. Weycha said she needed a mortal champion because only men understood the threats of other men. She said she chose me because I was 'willful, stubborn, and clever.' Ash is not Hazard. I don't know what makes her Weycha's enemy. If I kill her now, I'll never know. So I wait. After you've died once, waiting is easy."

"I'd imagine that depends on what you're doing while you're waiting." This time the smile was unforced.

"To tell the truth, I'd rather be free to open a window or leave my room."

"I can arrange that." Rinchen brandished a sheet of parchment.

Shielding himself with his arms, Dart took a step back from the worktable. "No oaths, midons prince. I'm already sworn to my goddess and my brother. There's nothing left. Whatever you want from me, I can't give it."

Rinchen's shoulders sank. The parchment rolled to the floor. "That shepherd—your leman's brother—I offered to teach him swordwork today; he refused. A godsforsaken country-common shepherd from a godsforsaken assart, and he refused. Then someone tried to kill me. Right here in my own hall. That's our blood and his shit they're scrubbing up out there. I don't know who he was, or who sent him—the possibilities are endless. Once my grandfather finally let me lead the army, I saved his godsforsaken kingdom. We lost fifteen men at Tremontin. Fifteen! We'd lost fifteen thousand while other men led it. And they're *still* trying to kill me." He kicked over his chair rising from it, and stood beside a shuttered window, staring at the bare wood planks as if he could see something beyond them.

"Go away. Go back to the Palestra, back to Ash—back to your gods-be-damned forest. Go anywhere. Let me feel like a fool by myself."

While the prince sulked, Dart scanned the messy room, looking for something to drink. It took a while, but he spotted an ewer and a single tumbler precariously balanced atop a bundle of scrolls. The tumbler was almost clean and the wine smelled reasonable.

"Why feel like a fool by yourself when you can have company?" He filled the tumbler and gulped it down. Sour wine burned a path clear down to his navel. He swirled his tongue around his mouth to do what he could about the aftertaste, then contrived to speak with a sober, level voice: "There's more than enough for the two of us in here." He swept the map onto the floor where it rolled up by itself and blended with others already lying there. "Only one cup, so we'll have to share."

Rinchen stayed beside the window, very much a wary wolf—or a too-frightened boy. He glowered at Dart and the tumbler before snatching it out of Dart's hand. Another long moment and he took a tentative swallow—one got the feeling that this particular prince didn't do much high-handed carousing. Yet another silent moment passed before he set it on the table. Their eyes met; this time Dart didn't wait.

"Don't entertain many friends up here, do you, runt?"

"No—"

"Not surprised, if this oxblood's the best you can offer them." Dart picked up the tumbler and forced another swallow down his throat. "A man's got to have fortitude, if he's to be *your* friend." Either the prince cracked, or Dart was giving up; he couldn't possibly gulp down another mouthful of vinegar.

Rinchen navigated through the rubble to a dangling rope that presumably connected with his guard or the distant kitchen. "I think I can get something a bit less vile."

Dart's gut released a prodigious and relieved belch. "And not a moment too soon." He emptied the ewer into the sand surrounding the brazier, picking up the discarded roll of parchment when he was done. "Can you get my harp with this piece of parchment? I don't give oaths for friendship, runt, but it's been too long since I heard my lady's voice."

"I can try," the prince replied, letting their fingers touch as he reclaimed the roll.

Chapter Eleven

It was the last morning of Calends and the second consecutive morning that Ean ruEan sorMeklan, Donitor of Fenklare and patriarch of his clan, had been rousted from his warm bed before sunrise. Yesterday he'd been grilled by inquists, vulgarly referred to as the stepmothers because they were all women and all old enough to have grandchildren. Today he'd been treated to an unnerving display of sorRodion unity in the throne hall.

All because godswilling Faerilen sorJos thought he could buy the Wolf's death. The old goat had hired a foreigner—a solitary bungler, when the netherworld clans insisted it would take three master assassins to dispatch the crown prince. Not that masters were available. Those same netherworld clans would no longer waste their time, and their members' lives, pursuing Prince Rinchen. They fervently believed the Wolf was cursed and his death belonged to the gods. So Faerilen had hired a foreigner and the sorJos were going to forfeit an honor-estate for their folly.

The matter should have ended there. Lord Ean told the stepmothers that the sorMeklan did not stoop to assassination, and the women had believed him. He told King Manal the same thing, and the king, with that godswilling Wolf cozied up to the throne, said he'd like to put the question to the donitor's son. Bargaining without strength, Lord Ean had agreed to surrender his brother's gods-be-damned touchstones into sorRodion hands to keep his only son away from the stepmothers.

He returned to his residence in a fine rage. His tirades penetrated every dusty corner. Inanimate objects suffered his wrath against walls, ceilings, and floors. People and pets stayed out of sight—except for Driskolt, the beloved target of his relentless anger. Ean had routed his son from one room to the next, until the young man was cornered in the stairwell.

"Who gave you leave to think?" Ean thundered, cocking his many-ringed weapon-hand above his off-weapon shoulder. "Who gave you leave to consort with scoundrels like Eudalig sorJos? Who gave you leave to plot with Prince Alegshorn? By all the godswilling gods asleep and awake, what did any of you think to accomplish by plotting *with* royalty *against* royalty?"

He lost control and clouted his son across the face. Driskolt's head cracked the wood panelling behind him. Blood streamed from his nose and lip. He stanched the flow on his sleeve and kept his mouth shut. That showed some measure of wisdom; Ean knew full well he wasn't ready to listen to anything his son had to say. The time for talk would come later, when he'd purged his rage.

They would talk. Ean loved Dris; his son was the light of his world—which was why he lost control when the boy did something utterly stupid. Something utterly stupid like delivering a back-handed clout with his rings on. Pain radiated past Ean's elbow and he could see his knuckles swelling. Anger faded quickly in his own pain. He stepped back, ending the hostilities; Dris scrabbled to the next landing.

A feminine hand offered a camphor-soaked handkerchief through a barely opened door. Dris held it against his nose a moment before saying:

"Midons sire, my lord—" He had the sense to use a properly subservient tone. "I notified you when I learned of the Wolf's intention to seize our estates and break our backs redeeming them. I asked you what position we should take. When you did not reply, I thought I should pursue our interests as I saw them. It was clear to everyone here in Eyerlon that something had to be done quickly. Decisiveness is the hallmark of wise rule. You said so yourself, midons sire, yesterday when I told you what had already happened."

Ean's knuckles had begun to throb. The last of his rage vanished. "You didn't tell me everything, Dris. You didn't tell me about Prince Alegshorn. Whatever possessed you to plot with royalty? Except in war, our interests never lie with royalty."

"Aleg's my friend and he's our best hope against the Wolf. You told me to tell Aleg about Dart. When Aleg asked if there was anything brewing, I told him. He said he wanted to know more, so I went back to the others and we decided to let him join us. Aleg's got the most to lose. If we help him, he'll be in our debt forever." Driskolt lowered the handkerchief. The blood had stopped flowing, but the nose needed mending. "Godswill—you don't think *Aleg* told the Wolf about the harp and sword?"

Ean snapped the fingers of his good hand. The stairwell echoed as women went in search of the mender. Until she arrived, he furthered his son's political education:

"No—of course not. Alegshorn's not in question here, not directly. But someone did. One of the spooks. Surely they've unravelled my poor brother's memories by now. If Weycha's gone missing—if that's what's had the spooks riled—then they'll want anything that might lure her back. No spook has the right to take our property, but Feladon raised the Wolf. He may hold the boy at arm's length now, but no one's fooled. The pair of them were simply waiting for the right moment, and Faerilen's bungling gave them their moment.

"The touchstones aren't important, Dris. When the time was right we'd have surrendered them, but, courtesy of you and your friends, we can't choose the time. *That's* important."

"But, midons sire, whatever happened in the Wolf's hall didn't have anything to do with us."

Ean closed his eyes. His son was truly perplexed: he wasn't a good enough actor to be otherwise convincing. Growing up in a time of war left his son's generation ill-prepared for the more subtle dangers of peace. He consoled himself with his good health. He was ready for another twenty years, whichever prince inherited the throne. By then Dris would be ready.

But he wasn't ready yet.

"You said Faerilen sorJos admitted to the stepmothers that he'd hired an assassin. Faerilen wasn't part of our group and we'd decided against assassination. I don't understand why the sorRodion are so riled . . . and united. It's not as if it's the first time someone tried to assassinate the Wolf. The king never cared before."

Ean's hand hurt less. Frustrated anger seethed back into his consciousness. "Blood is thicker than water, Dris, and your head is thicker than stone. Faerilen sorJos is protecting Eudalig; King Manal's protecting Alegshorn; and I'm protecting you because you let yourself get drawn into a plot with royalty, against royalty.

There's only one thing our sorRodion hate more than each other and that's owing favors. Alegshorn will make a good king, if he can clear his own path to the throne. If he can't, the sorMeklan will live with the Wolf. Iser smite me, I thought you were clever enough to stay out of plots or I wouldn't have left you alone in Eyerlon!"

Driskolt slumped against the wall. Politics defeated him. He couldn't reconcile Aleg, his lifelong friend, with the Prince Alegshorn sorRodion his father distrusted. He wished the mender would appear; his nose felt like a spike had been driven through it. "We may be fools in your eyes, midons sire—" He turned his hands palms-up, the traditional gesture of submission. "But we're honest and honorable. I'll talk to everyone. I'll tell them what you've said. We never *did* anything, but when I'm done it will be as if we never thought about doing anything."

"I'll take care of it," Ean said wearily. "Drink with your friends, Dris. Hunt with them, whore with them, but if I catch you plotting with them again— By the gods, Driskolt, I'll drag my poor brother out of whatever hell the spooks have left him in and inherit him in your place."

Ean walked away without saying another word. A moment later Dris kicked the wall hard enough to shake the residence; then he got up to look for the mender. He hadn't gone far when Killeen ran up to him.

"I found her," the boy announced.

Dris was in a mood for violence. He raised his arm, unconsciously imitating his father. The mender appeared before any damage was done. She was a bit older than he and had a truly condescending frown.

"You never learn, do you, Driskolt? Midons Lord Ean clouts you. You can't think of anything to do except clout your friend."

Dris was embarrassed; that made him reckless. "I could hit you instead."

"And your nose will point past your ear for the rest of your life." Menders were sacrosanct, the only spooks everyone respected. Maryele could speak her mind whenever she chose. "Sit down and behave yourself."

Maryele fingered her Brightwater torque and reached for the Web. She placed her fingertips spiderlike atop Driskolt's shoulder. *Basi* surged through him; his nerves deadened and his muscles were no longer his to control. He slid to the floor, alert but helpless. Maryele knelt beside him, rearranging his nose and knitting up the broken blood vessels. Neither she nor any other mender could heal a wound, but when her sorcery was finished, sleep and a good meal would see Dris fully restored. She touched his shoulder.

Feeling—a steady, sharp ache—returned and he could move on his own again.

"Don't touch," she warned.

"You didn't . . . didn't twist it around?"

She sighed and stalked away without giving him any reassurance.

"She didn't, did she?" he asked Killeen. His legs were lead; he wasn't going to get to his feet by himself. "Point me toward a mirror."

"Upstairs, midons."

"Iser's cast-iron balls, Killy, I've just been mendered by my steel-fingered cousin; I'll never make it that far."

Killeen hauled him upright. "Try, midons," he whispered. "I don't want to talk where we can be overheard."

They climbed the stairs slowly and walked the narrow corridor to Berika's room, which was empty.

"I heard what midons Lord sorMeklan said—"

"Who didn't?"

"I was thinking—I know who told the Wolf about the touchstones."

Driskolt shrugged off his muzziness. "Who?"

"Berika."

He shook his head in disbelief—a monumentally bad idea—and barely made it to a chair where he gingerly supported his throbbing head.

"Midons, listen to me. Remember how she disappeared from midons Alegshorn's celebration? And how she came back with the Wolf?"

Dris lowered his hands carefully. "Berika didn't know who she was with."

"It wouldn't matter what *she* knew. All that would matter would be if the Wolf knew who she was—"

"He said he didn't."

"As if the Wolf's never lied! Midons, think a moment: *She* was the one who led you to the harp and the sword in the first place. You said she frets over your demon-uncle. She probably thought she was helping him."

"I'd sooner be warded away below the Basilica than have the

Wolf take an interest in me." Dris sipped water from the bed-table ewer, groaning after each swallow.

"But she didn't *know* it was the Wolf," Killeen said triumphantly. "Don't you see?"

"No, I don't see. Berika's not like that. She's canny the way commonfolk sometimes are, like animals. They know who they can trust. She's a shepherd. She wouldn't trust a wolf."

Killeen stood in front of him. "Well, she trusts somebody who doesn't live here. She was up and dressed and out with her cloak this morning before I could stop her. I didn't put it together until I heard midons Lord sorMeklan. I watched her from the window, midons—she was headed for the palace."

"Half of Eyerlon is between here and the palace, Killy." He'd trusted Berika and confided in her. He thought he knew her as well as he knew Aleg. Of course, if his father were right, he was wrong to trust Aleg. Without thinking, he rubbed his eyes and touched his nose. "Godswill! I can't think, Killy. I'm dead tired and mendered. I want to sleep."

With Killy's help Dris collapsed onto Berika's bed. He moaned when his face touched the feather pillow. "A mirror. I want to see what she did to me."

"You look the same as before. Get some sleep. I'll stand watch. Berika will come back here, and we'll get some answers. Midons Lord sorMeklan will think twice before he dismisses you out of hand—"

But Driskolt was already snoring softly through his tender nose.

Killeen's guess was correct. Berika threaded her way through unfamiliar streets to the palace gate. Her cloak was clean and mended. Her hair was respectably dressed. Her wrist had healed without mending and she'd arranged the plaits herself—it was a bit like weaving or lacemaking. She'd learned enough of the noblefolk ways at the residence to easily pass as a poor relation living on clan charity. The gatekeepers listened when she asked the whereabouts of Braydon Braydson of Fenklare and sent her to the watchroom, where the duty rosters were kept. An older man challenged her as she approached the watchtower.

"Midons, I'm looking for Braydon Braydson. He serves in Prince Alegshorn's personal guard."

"He'll be on the practice fields most likely, my lady." The officer pointed toward the tunnel.

Berika studied the dark tunnel between the old and new palaces. It was not an inviting passageway.

"Is he expecting you?" The question was rife with speculation.

Berika shook her head slightly to show that he was not.

"I could prepare a message for him. Come inside a moment—"

The officer seemed too helpful. Braydon's voice warning her not to visit him echoed painfully in her memory. "No, midons, I'll go by myself, if I may."

He smiled with perfect politeness; still Berika felt ashamed as she hurried through the darkness. She became the only woman on the noisy practice fields and her presence drew immediate, unwelcome attention. Tears came to her eyes, blurring her vision. She could barely distinguish the sapphire-and-grey banner on the far side of the frozen dirt. But she kept her back straight, her head high, and pretended not to hear the whistles and worse that marked her progress toward the banner.

Berika watched a man separate from his fellows and come toward her. She didn't realize the man was Braydon until he was directly in front of her; then she fairly threw herself into his arms. Braydon freed himself and held his sister at arm's length.

"Please, Braydon—I need your help. The spooks are asking the sorMeklan about Dart and the sorMeklan are asking me. I don't know what to tell them. I'm afraid for myself and afraid for Dart. The inquists do terrible things below the Basilica. You serve the prince. Can't you ask him to do something? One word from the prince and everything would be all right—"

Braydon released her; she stayed where she was.

"I told you not to look for me—especially not here. You've made fools out of us both."

Her chin dropped.

"Dart's not in danger anymore," Braydon said in a much softer voice. "He's noblefolk; he can take care of himself. You should answer the sorMeklan—"

"But what if I say something that they use against him?"

Braydon repeated the pickler's advice: "Take care of yourself first. You're no good to anyone if you haven't taken care of yourself. I've got to take care of me, Beri. Midons Prince Alegshorn has me running messages between the palace and the river front every midnight. He's given me a sword; I can't ask him for more. You'll have to rely on the sorMeklan."

Berika sniffed her tears. She hadn't known what to expect, but she hadn't expected complete rejection. "We're family. We're supposed to stand by each other."

Braydon snarled. "Not in Eyerlon. Not when we're caught up in noble things. Go back to the sorMeklan—and if they ask, don't tell them about me, especially don't tell them we're family."

Shaken to the core, Berika left the practice ground and the palace. Her mind wandered in useless directions, but her feet were wiser and brought her safely to the courtyard of the residence where she was hailed by name. She was hungry and cold, and although the residence was not where she wanted to be, she had nowhere else to go. The baker was unloading his field kitchen oven. He handed her an undersized loaf. She used it to warm her hands climbing the back stairs to her room.

Her heart sank when she saw Killeen in her chair and Driskolt snoring on the bed, but her spirits had not been high and she scarcely noticed the tumble.

"Where have you been?"

Berika set the bread on the bed-table before unfastening her cloak. With Driskolt asleep, she didn't think she had to answer. Killeen caught her shoulder, knocking the cloak to the floor. He asked his question a second time, and Berika realized that her puppy had cut his teeth in a single day. She was frightened and the truth spilled out of her mouth—all of it. She mentioned Braydon by name both as her brother and as a partisan in Prince Alegshorn's guard. Killeen awakened Driskolt and made her repeat everything.

The sidon was cross-grained and bleary. He made her go through it all a second time before saying: "We've got to tell midons sire. We've got to find my father."

Dris walked unsteadily toward the door. Killeen took a firm grip on Berika's elbow. She tried to retrieve her bread, but the puppy wouldn't permit it. They found the donitor in the counting room with his moneyer. Ean dismissed the young folk with a wave and a frown. Driskolt pulled himself together and insisted that the moneyer depart instead. Lord Ean appraised them all with hooded eyes. At length he dismissed the moneyer. The door was closed and the questioning began.

"Well, girl—speak up."

Berika had seen Lord Ean ruEan sorMeklan only once before, at the welcoming dinner. The donitor was not a large man, and travel-weary as he'd been then, he had not seemed particularly imposing. He was rested now and no one would doubt for a moment that his word was law throughout Fenklare. Reminding herself that she was assart-born and took her law from the king, not the donitor, Berika found her voice.

"Midons Lord sorMeklan, today I went to see my brother. He's in Prince Alegshorn's guard—"

The donitor silenced Berika with a glower and turned the same expression on his son. "Why didn't I know this before?"

Dris smiled nervously. "The only brother she ever mentioned was dead."

Grimacing, Ean returned his attention to Berika.

All the years in her mother's house served her well in the donitor's counting room. "I did not know my brother served Prince Alegshorn until I saw him in the prince's hall the other night."

The donitor asked if she'd spoken to Braydon at that time, and when she admitted that she had, he asked what they'd talked about.

"He was surprised to see me in Eyerlon, much less wearing sorMeklan colors. We couldn't talk for long; he was standing guard. I told him how I got to Eyerlon. I don't remember all that we said—"

"That can be remedied," Lord Ean said, ringing a hand bell. The moneyer opened the door. "Find Nishrun and bring him here."

Nishrun was a tiny, sharp-nosed man with a fawning manner and the red-trimmed robe of a disciplined communicant of less-than-magga rank: the very image of a sorcerer who'd pledged his skills to the noblefolk rather than the Basilica. Wringing his hands in anxious anticipation, Nishrun listened while Ean explained what he wanted.

"Midons donitor, I am not an inquist," the little man whined. "The mind of another person is a maze in which I might easily lose my way." Lord Ean's expression did not change and Nishrun was forced to abandon subtlety. "Midons donitor, it is dangerous for the girl and for me, also. An inquist knows ways to counter a mind's natural resistance. It is a woman's discipline and unknown to me. May I summon an inquist?"

Ean ruEan toyed with the coins on his worktable. Casually, he isolated a trio of gold marks and scooted them in the sorcerer's direction. "Come now, Nishu, you have to learn a little bit of everything before you're accepted into a discipline. I'm sure you'll manage. Berika will certainly not resist—"

The donitor scrutinized Berika, who was stiff and speechless. Although other realms with other magic, other gods, had horrifying ways of unlocking a man or woman's memories. Walensor, constrained by the Compact, had stepmothers, but the prospect of inquist Webwork, especially as performed by an untrained man, frightened her. She accepted Killeen's hand and was reluctant to release it when they sat her in the donitor's chair.

Nishrun settled his silver torque above the woolen cloth of his robe. Only maggas had individual touchstones; all the lesser sorcerers wore torques around their necks that limited the amount of *basi* they could draw from the Web.

"May I know that I will be absolved and forgiven if I fail, midons donitor?" the spook asked.

"No, Nishu," Lord Ean said condescendingly. "I would not want you thinking you could do less than your best."

Clearly disappointed, the sorcerer rubbed the knobs at the ends of his torque vigorously with his thumbs. "Look at me, child. Listen to me, and do what I say."

Berika didn't know what to expect. She gripped the donitor's chair with white knuckles.

"Child!"

Nothing *made* Berika raise her head or look straight into Nishrun's eyes. She did it of her own free will, or thought she did. She'd seen Dart's eyes when they seethed with fire; she didn't think any other eyes could frighten her. And Nishrun's eyes didn't, but once she looked into them, she couldn't look anywhere else.

"Tell midons sorMeklan everything he wishes to know."

Berika *wanted* to do what she was told, but she couldn't pluck questions directly out of Ean sorMeklan's mind. She began to tremble. She fought for each breath with strangled screams, slipping toward madness with each frantic beat of her heart.

Driskolt clenched his fists and teeth. In his heart he'd known it would come to this. They had to have the truth, at least the truth as Berika understood it, and beneath the Web there was only one way to get the truth, although like his peers, Dris was repelled by sorcery's bloodless methods. He had no qualms about intimidating Berika, twisting her arm until she cried, but he hated seeing her helpless on sorcery's anvil. This left him with a simple choice: He could take himself elsewhere, or he could take ratty little Nishrun by his silver-clad throat and smash him against the wall.

It was an easy choice, and he had ratty Nishrun by the collar until his father interceded, but not against him. Lord Ean, in his second rage of the day, backed the frightened spook into a corner.

"I tried to warn you, midons sorMeklan." Nishrun wrung his hands as he whined. "She resisted me."

"You asked her a question she couldn't answer, you godswilling fool!" Dris dared to snarl.

"She resisted me," the sorcerer maintained, then confessed: "I couldn't command her. She's got too much *basi*. You didn't tell me she had enough *basi* to reach the Web."

Dris shouldered in beside his father, their backs to the rest of the room and Nishrun cowering in their combined shadows.

"She told me," Dris snarled, "how she tried every day in her dirty little assart village to reach the Web. If she'd had the pull, the spider would have sent someone to find her."

But weaselly Nishrun stood his ground. "In Escham and Arl, where the Web is concentrated, children must reach the Web with their own strength, but in the wilds of Fenklare, midonès sorMek-lan, it is the responsibility of the hedge-sorcerers. It's too late now, of course. I'd guess she should have been brought to Eyerlon at least ten years ago."

"Are you saying she's a *spook*?" Killeen interjected eagerly from the center of the room. "I've bedded a godswilling spook?"

Dris felt his fists clenching and noticed that his father's had also tightened. Most of the time he liked Killy well enough; other times he firmly believed his father's new ward was the most bumbling fifteen-year-old ever to blink at the sun. By the time he'd reached that age, he knew when to keep his mouth shut; and if he made a mistake he got clouted, hard. Of course, Killy wasn't going to be donitor. He'd been raised on a quiet estate by women—mother, sisters, and aunts—after all the other men of the family died at Kasserine. The women kept their precious Killeen out of the muster these last three years; he hadn't been hardened by the sights of war. After Tremontin, when it was safe, they made him a donitorial ward and sent him to Relamain for "seasoning." Lord Ean had saddled Dris with a shadow and the order to "make a man of him."

Easier to make a man out of snivelling Nishrun, who was clinging to his torque as a flood-swept man might cling to a log.

"She's too old to train. She's hedge, at most, but she's younger, stronger, and more clear-headed than most hedge-sorcerers. She has *influence*," Nishrun muttered. "That's the essence of sorcery. Be careful, midonès; this girl gets what she wants. She's made her luck."

A sour lump filled Driskolt's throat. He'd been Severed, and was headblind, but still susceptible to sorcery. Killy's untimely words echoed in his ears. He'd bedded a spook for weeks, months, now enjoying her company and conversation more than anything else. Iser's cast-iron balls—what might Berika have done to him?

Chapter Twelve

Berika returned to her room in a daze. Nishrun's words were more real than the residence walls, more real than Driskolt and Killeen, supporting and confining her as they climbed the stairs together. In her mind's eye she saw the Wolf's parchment map: the sawtooth line of Weychawood, as far from Eyerlon as anything could be. If she'd been born anywhere else— But no—she'd been born in Gorse, where a talented child needed help to pull down the Web for the first time.

Memories swarmed like maggots, revealing the bones of truth. The two women who should have helped her reach her dream—her mother and her mother's aunt, Auld Mag the hedge-sorcerer—had connived against her. Berika blamed Ingolde for preaching that she should make the best of her fate, but she blamed Auld Mag more. The old woman had wanted a wife for her loutish son and hadn't quibbled over the price. All commonfolk expected to feel the weight of noble feet on their necks, but for Berika, the weight came from her close-kin.

Driskolt granted her privacy. He covered her with a blanket when she curled up on the huge bed, and he took Killeen with him when he left. Bitterness soon stanched her tears. She stared blindly into the afternoon gloom, mourning what might have been.

Her privacy was strictly limited. There was a guard outside the door. She heard him scuffling his feet and wished he would go away. Nishrun had implied that her wishes were sorcery, but this wish had no effect. She caught herself wishing for Dart. She wanted to hear his voice and the haunting music he made with Weycha's harp. She began to hear hauntingly beautiful music. It enthralled her—until she realized that after a lifetime of futile struggle, she'd pulled down the Web.

A presence approached. She couldn't see it with her eyes, hear it with her ears, nor feel it with any other sense, yet she knew for certain it was coming to her.

This is how they find the children. This is how they know who should come to Eyerlon for training—

Blind rage and despair dropped her back to the sorMeklan residence. Her tears flowed in awful silence until the guard said, "Good evening, midons," and the door opened.

If it had been Driskolt carrying a candle and her supper, Berika might have looked on him as her savior. Her lover could be brutal, but he was quick to forgive and had no guile. At a moment when everything else was shattered, Driskolt sorMeklan would be solid and reliable. But it wasn't Dris who set a bowl and candle on the table before caressing her shoulder.

Berika knew that Killeen barKethmarion was the sole surviving son of a once-proud lineage, that his female relations had made him a donitorial ward, and that, like her, he was dependent on sorMeklan charity. But she didn't *know* Killeen until he pinched and twisted her flesh. The youth's taste for power was less clean, less innocent than his patron's. She wished he would leave, and when that had no effect, Berika used her voice:

"Go away, midons. Leave me alone."

"Midons Driskolt said you've had two shocks today: what Nishrun did and what he said. He said you shouldn't be alone; you should be with a man." Killeen's hand moved through Berika's hair, down her neck, across her breasts.

"Then he should have come himself," Berika snarled.

Pain begat pain, not compassion, in the constricted world of noblefolk charity. Berika gouged the back of Killeen's hand with fingernails that had grown strong on sorMeklan food. When she was satisfied that she had drawn blood, she flung his arm aside and rolled to the far edge of the bed, hissing like a cat.

Killeen examined his wound by candlelight. "You'll be sorry." He took the candle and her supper with him when he left.

There was nothing, Berika whispered to herself, that Killeen or the entire sorMeklan clan could do to make her more sorry than she already was. Then her stomach growled and her resolve weakened. Commonfolk, especially country-commonfolk, understood the difference between hunger and starvation. Berika knew she'd do almost anything to avoid starvation, and absolutely anything to avoid another encounter with Nishrun. The sorMeklan, she realized, retained the power to make her sorry.

Maybe it was time to return to Gorse, where she was the equal of her enemies.

The guard outside Berika's door hadn't coughed or scuffled his feet. When she thought about it, Berika realized he hadn't said anything when Killeen left. She crept to the door and tested the latch. It lifted cleanly; the lock wasn't jammed. She eased the door open. The corridor and stairwell weren't as dark as her room. She could see that the guard's stool was unoccupied.

Pulse pounding in her ears, Berika shut the door again. The knotted linen where she kept her wealth beat against her leg. She'd always known it could come to this, hadn't she? She was wearing the wool gown that belonged to her, not the sorMeklan. Her homespun cloak was on the peg behind the door. Except for the emerald, she could leave precisely as she'd arrived, and the emerald would take her anywhere she wanted to go—once she changed it into coins.

Berika didn't know how to change a gemstone into silver coins. Not gold coins. Gold coins would be as incriminating as the emerald. She'd be accused as a thief the moment she revealed her treasure to a goldsmith. She'd wind up in the king's dungeon, surely worse than any room in the sorMeklan residence. She added sorRodion punishment to the list of fates she'd do anything to avoid. She was stymied until her thoughts skewed toward the palace rather than away from it.

Braydon.

Braydon, whose sapphire-and-grey could vouch for his integrity, and hers. Braydon, who hoarded coins religiously and surely knew a reliable goldsmith. Braydon, who'd told her that he carried messages to the river front every midnight. He wouldn't be happy to see her, but Braydon was headblind, and she had a sorcerer's *basi*. Braydon would help her convert the emerald into coins.

Sitting on the floor, Berika fished up the pouch-knot and pressed it between her eyes. Everyone said that real sorcerers had to be trained before they could make the Web sing their song. And everyone had lied.

"Help me, Braydon," she whispered. "Help me get away from here. Help me get somewhere safe."

But before Braydon could help her, she would have to find him.

Calends nights were long in Eyerlon. The nightwatch had barely begun. Midnight—the start of deadwatch—was hours away. It was too early to head for the river front, just the right time to plan her escape from the residence.

Berika reopened the door. The stairwell echoed with the sounds of the household assembling for the last supper of Calends. The last meal of Calends was a somber celebration honored in every household from the palace to the least country-common cottage. If Berika had been in Gorse, there would have been plates on the table for her father and Indon. She wondered idly if Ingolde was setting out a plate for her tonight. The last supper of Calends was for family only, wherever it was served. Berika had not been adopted into the sorMeklan clan; she would not have attended the family feast under any circumstances, but she could be reasonably confident that everyone else would be in the great hall.

The hours of nightwatch passed. Smells of bitter herbs and spices wafted up the stairwell until the hall doors were closed and the echo of dirges drifted upstairs instead.

Berika headed downstairs. A floorboard creaked; she flattened against the wall. What if it was Killeen? What if Killeen's *you'll be sorry* was the same as Hirmin's *you'll be sorry*? Berika gulped down bile. *Basi* could protect her from the consequences of rape but not from the assault itself.

She wished for a knife, realizing that she'd have to arm herself if she was going to wander the Eyerlon river front on a night when all respectable folk stayed home. There were knives in the kitchen . . . along with the cook and his small army of assistants. Cooks prepared the last-night supper; they were excused from memorial rituals. Besides, Berika couldn't defend herself with steel. The only weapon she could wield was a shepherd's crook.

There wasn't a crook within a day's walk of Eyerlon. There were harmless poles in the stables. They were heavier than crooks, longer too, and surrounded by horses and hostlers, but they were the best substitutes Berika could imagine until she remembered the sorMeklan spear.

She'd asked Driskolt why the sorMeklan kept a battered spear outside the door to their great hall when their armory had better weapons. He told her that an ancestor had withdrawn the spear from his dying horse, then slain seven Pennaik warriors with it in the battle that brought Rodion sorRodion to Walensor's throne. Then Berika wanted to know why they kept a relic of defeat.

"To remind us and our kings that the sorRodion never defeated the sorMeklan. They hold the throne because we did not choose to take it."

That short spear would have the weight and feel of her shepherd's crook, *and* the sorMeklan would be hard-hit by the loss of their relic. Berika's conscience fluttered; Driskolt would get another beating when she and the spear turned up missing. But Driskolt was the sidon of Fenklare. He had menders to soothe his body's pain, prestige to restore his spirit. And, anyway, the story was a lie. Even a country-common shepherd knew that the sorRodion owed nothing to the sorMeklan or anyone else.

The clan was singing another dirge behind the closed, unguarded doors of the great hall. Berika very carefully unhooked the spear from its bracket.

There were a few armed partisans in the courtyard, for appearance's sake. No one expected trouble on the last night of Calends. Even so, the gate had been closed at sundown, and getting to the streets was going to be a problem. Then horses stopped outside the gate, and the partisans admitted a parti-colored sleigh into the courtyard, reminding Berika that some noblefolk belonged to more than one clan. While the partisans escorted a young family into the residence, Berika dashed through the shadows to freedom.

Atop the courtyard wall, within a miniature tower that looked like granite but was merely painted plaster, one blanket mound crouched beside a glowing brazier while another peered through a tiny arrow-slit window.

"There she goes, midons," the watcher announced. "Iser's balls—she's carrying a stick—No! A spear—"

The other mound lurched toward the wall. It widened the arrow-slit with gloved fists and stuck its head into the cold night. "Godswill! She's taken *the* spear. Come on, Killy."

Driskolt leapt to the courtyard. His cold-numbed legs buckled and he yelled as he hit the hard ground.

The partisans didn't recognize their sidon or his companion. They split apart. One group shut the gate while the other surrounded the unidentified strangers. They snared Killeen quickly, but Driskolt drew his sword and threw back his cowl. Cursing everyone equally, Dris beat aside the nearest sword; he kicked a partisan in the gut, sprawling him on the frozen ground. He charged another, capturing a second sword with his off-weapon hand. The partisans who had not recognized his voice recognized the quality of his swordwork and stood down. Their officer dropped to one knee.

"A thousand pardons, midons sidon—we had no idea."

Driskolt flipped his extra weapon in the air, deftly catching the flat of the blade in his gloved hand. He extended the hilt toward its rightful owner. "Just open the gate, and if midons sire asks, tell him I'm already looking for it."

The sidon did not linger to answer the inevitable questions. He was through the gate as the partisans opened it. Killeen shrugged out of his confinement and snarled curses at everyone as he caught up with Dris. Dris raised his hand, signalling for silence. There was a good chance they'd lost Berika already, but she wasn't the only lucky person on the streets. Pausing in the nearest intersection, he listened for out-of-place sounds and caught a flash of starlight glinting off the spear in another intersection. He signalled Killeen.

They followed Berika through streets neither man recalled. She crossed and doubled her tracks more times than the wiliest stag. The palace watchtower chimed the fourth of the seven nightwatch hours. Killeen was convinced that Berika's tortuous path proved she was guilty of something. Driskolt, watching her pause and cock her head in another intersection, had a different explanation.

"She's lost. She's using *basi* to find her way."

"Midons, you make too many excuses for her."

Dris bristled at the suggestion.

Killeen persisted. "It's bumflower sorcery—*influence.* Hedge-sorcery. Hedge-sorcery should be anathema, and commonfolk should be Severed at birth. All of them." He sliced the air with his weapon hand.

"Like we are? They'd rise up in bloody rebellion if we took away all their hope."

"*We* shouldn't be Severed; we shouldn't have to beg Webwork from bumflower spooks."

Berika made her choice; Driskolt took off after her without responding to his friend's provocations. He believed in the righteousness of the Compact, and although he sometimes wondered what *basi* and sorcery felt like, he accepted Severance as a reasonable price for noble rights and responsibility. Of course, he was Fenklare's sidon and would become its donitor. The only charity he knew was the charity he meted out to lesser men, including Killeen barKethmarion.

And Berika.

He'd seduced Berika because he thought she was Dart's woman, and he thought he wanted to humiliate his revenant uncle. It hadn't worked out that way. Berika was a bewildering combination of ignorance and intelligence. She asked unthinkable questions, and when he answered them, they were both wiser. He was smart enough to value wisdom when it flowed toward him. He'd learned it from Prince Aleg—although where Aleg learned that lesson, considering *his* family, was a mystery. Still, Berika was wise, and he'd enlisted her—without telling her, of course—in his campaign to make a "man" out of Killeen. It wasn't working; at least it wasn't working the way he'd hoped it would. He'd thought it was the suffocating influence of the women who'd raised Killy; now Dris was worried about the influence of Berika's undisciplined sorcery on another susceptible noble mind.

When he and Killy caught Berika, he was going to have some unthinkable questions for her, and he prayed silently that her answers would ease his mind.

They heard the unmistakable groan of ice thickening and knew they'd come to the river front, where men admitted no close-kin and the last night of Calends was no different from any other. The taverns would remain open until New Year's dawn. There were a few people on the street, most of them drunk and reeling. Those few who were sober made Dris glad he had a sword. Berika stopped some fifty paces ahead, at the mouth of a shambles alley which—sword or no—Driskolt would have shunned.

"Don't go down there," he whispered. He was Severed, so he was headblind; he was alive, so he had to have *basi*. If Berika had influence, maybe he did too. Driskolt repeated the words with thoughts alone.

Killeen surged forward. "She's getting away!"

Driskolt ran after Killy. In some places the leaning buildings touched together and the alley became a tunnel. Frozen offal made the footing treacherous, and the air was pungent. Driskolt grabbed the hem of Killy's cloak.

"This is blind. It's got to be blind. She's got to turn around and come out—"

Then they heard her calling a name: *Braydon*. At the very least she was going to wake someone who didn't want his sleep disturbed. Dris shouldered past Killy. He fingered the hilt of his sword, making certain that it hadn't frozen to the scabbard.

"Keep an eye behind and your hand on your hilt."

"Aye, midons."

The shambles emptied into a derelict courtyard where ice-crusted snow reflected starlight and revealed Berika's silhouette.

"Braydon!"

A brilliant rectangle appeared on a dark wall far above the

courtyard. Two man-shaped silhouettes filled it. Dris and Killeen dove behind rank, ruined barrels.

"Berika? Berika, is that you down there?" The voice had a familiar Fenklare accent.

Driskolt raised his head. "Godswill."

With the sorMeklan spear balanced against her shoulder, Berika climbed to the light. The silhouetted men let her pass between them and the door was closed.

"Godswill," Dris repeated.

"What do we do now?"

"We wait."

"We'll freeze!"

"Then go home, Killy. But I'm not leaving here without our spear *and* Berika."

Killeen grumbled, then hunkered down. They wrapped themselves snugly in their cloaks and watched the stars creep across the sky. The palace bells rang the fifth hour of nightwatch. Not long after, the upper door reopened. Driskolt prodded Killy, who had fallen asleep.

"Get ready. They're coming down."

"Wha' do we do?" The youth was groggy and shivering.

The trio filed silently down the outside stairs. Berika, recognizable by her lesser height and longer cloak, was in the middle. She still had the spear. Driskolt fingered his sword again. The lubricating oil had frozen. He braced the scabbard carefully against his leg and hit it once with his fist to loosen it. Berika had the only visible weapon; Driskolt dismissed her as a threat. Her brother, Braydon, belonged to Prince Alegshorn's guard; presumably he knew how to sing a decent song of steel—but he wouldn't be a serious threat to a well-trained nobleman like himself. The man in the rear was an unknown quantity—assuming, of course, that it was Braydon who was in the lead.

Driskolt wished they'd say something so he could sort them out, but they crunched silently past the barrels where he and Killy hid.

Killeen chose that moment to check his sword. It was frozen, and Killy, his mind clearly fogged with cold, pounded the scabbard without bracing it. The jangling metal against wood was the loudest sound in all Eyerlon and instantly identifiable to any veteran. The man behind Berika drew a sword, and with flat Fenklare vowels, ordered his companions to the rear. Berika obeyed. The man in front of her did not, although he did not draw a weapon.

Giving Killy a shove in the unarmed man's direction, Driskolt scrambled over the barrels to engage Berika's brother, whom he hoped to disarm without injury. Braydon retreated, holding his sword awkwardly. A neophyte. Dris couldn't guess what a neophyte swordsman was doing in Aleg's guard, but it was a complication he didn't need right now. Neophytes were unpredictable. The sidon feinted broadly, hoping to draw a clumsy attack. And he did, but he couldn't take advantage of it because Berika, using the spear like a quarterstaff, was pummeling his back. Dris wore mail beneath his cloak and surcoat; he wasn't hurt, but he had to retreat, catching a glimpse of the other skirmish as he did.

Against all reason and expectation there were three silhouettes circling in the shambles' mouth: Killy, the unarmed man—and another man, with a sword.

Two country-common shepherds, regardless of their weapons, were no match for a donitor's son who'd sung steel since he turned four. If he hadn't been determined not to injure either of his opponents or damage the spear, he could have slain them both with two strokes and gone to help Killeen. As it was, Dris used the same tactics he'd used in the courtyard: beating Braydon's sword aside, delivering a solid kick into a well-padded gut. Berika cracked the spear butt across his skull, dropping him to one knee, then rammed it into his short-ribs. If he'd been unarmored, she'd have had the better of him. Instead, he reached out and seized the spear with his off-weapon hand, giving it an underhand twist as he got to his feet.

The enveloped weapon popped out of Berika's hands. She assaulted him futilely with her fists. Driskolt dropped the spear and backhanded her above the ear. There were flat metal strips sewn into the back of his glove. She went down and stayed down.

Driskolt turned his attention to the other skirmish just in time to see one man miss his parry and take a glancing stroke along the ribs. Killeen was wearing mail. He shouldn't have been injured. So, when the man dropped first to his knees, then onto his side, Driskolt believed his friend had won. But before Dris could shout congratulations, the third man in the shambles' mouth—the apparently unarmed man—made a sudden move with his hand.

He dodged reflexively and felt something catch the quilted wool sleeve of his surcoat. Glancing down he saw a spindle-shaped dart.

The unarmed man was an assassin.

Dris knew the netherworld clans where assassins learned their craft were as old as the sorMeklan themselves, and inextricably bound to their way of life, but he considered assassination an affront to everything honest and honorable. Simply on principle, he'd vowed to exterminate any assassin he encountered, or die in the attempt. The assassin cocked his arm again. Dris was ready; he knew the dart was aimed at his face. He dodged it successfully, but pretended to have been struck. He staggered forward, reducing the distance between himself and the assassin, and the chance that the man could strike again. By the time the assassin realized he'd been gulled, it was too late. He wore no armor; Driskolt's sword, thrust with all his strength, passed easily through his heart.

By then Dris could see that Killeen lay on the ground with one of the little darts rising from his cheek. An assassin's poison had killed his friend, and he'd already gotten vengeance. But vengeance wasn't enough. Wrenching his sword from the assassin's chest, the sidon turned on the swordsman Killy had been fighting when he died.

The last man in the courtyard answered Driskolt's upraised weapon with a predictable defense. Dris changed his stance; the man responded competently. Dris lowered the tip of his sword insolently, deceitfully inviting the stranger to attack. The stranger wagged his wrist behind the steady point of his sword: In the song of steel, this was mockery's tune. Driskolt brought his weapon back to its original position. They were both cowled. Neither could see the other's face. The sidon had revealed a few of his tricks; he settled behind his sword to see what the other man had to show.

The lunge came straight through his guard. Driskolt resorted to his panic-parry—the defense he'd practiced so many times it belonged to reflex, not thought. Steel slid against steel and no damage was done, but Dris had seen everything he wanted to see. He'd allow that there were, perhaps, three men in Walensor who had the strength to beat his sword aside; he could think of only one man who could best him with pure speed. Dris wasn't sure he could win this fight; he absolutely did not want to lose it.

Deep in the shadows, Berika watched as Dris backtracked into the alley until he had enough room to spin around and sprint for the street. His footsteps still echoed when Braydon, who had recovered from the kick in his gut, bolted from the courtyard. Victorious by default, the last swordsman knelt beside Killeen. He kept his weapon arm extended as he closed the youth's eyes, then searched one-handed beneath his surcoat. His hand jerked once; he removed a pendant from the corpse's neck. He examined the assassin more thoroughly before removing something from his belt, but he did not bother closing the dead man's eyes.

When the objects were secure beneath his cloak, he walked cautiously to the center of the courtyard.

"Man-in-the-shadows, are you hurt? Show your face."

Berika had recovered her wits when she recovered the spear and hid in the shadows. She wasn't about to show her face to anyone who could make Driskolt run away. The swordsman kicked the crusted snow where she'd fallen. He approached the exact place where she had hidden herself. She used the spear to lever herself to her feet.

"Who are you?" she demanded, making her voice deep.

"A helping hand."

The swordsman extended his empty hand toward her, but Berika made a shooing gesture with the spearhead. Before she knew what happened, he'd struck the head with his sword. The metals clanged and the spear-shaft vibrated in her hands—but she held it loosely, the way her father had taught her to hold the crook when wolves leapt out of the forest—and it stayed in her hands.

The swordsman retreated; he hadn't expected to hear metal just then. He studied the silhouette more carefully. What he'd taken for a quarterstaff was actually a spear—a Pennaik horse spear, if he had to make a guess. He said a few words in a guttural language, and when the spearman did not respond, he struck the spear with the flat of his sword.

This time the spear spun loose, and before the spearman could react to his loss, he flattened him with a single, off-weapon hand punch to the gut. The defeated man folded onto the filthy snow with a sigh. The swordsman sheathed his weapon, claimed the spear, then threw his enemy over his shoulder.

It was a long haul from the river front to the palace. His lungs were fired before the nightwatch hailed him. He flashed a ring by lantern-light and trudged through the gate as it opened; then he maneuvered his burdens through the tight corners of the old palace backways. The captive over his shoulder groaned whenever his head banged against walls or newel posts. The panting swordsman was tempted to march his captive the rest of the way, but it didn't come to that. After popping an otherwise nondescript wooden plank in the wall of a dim, Brightwater-lit corridor, he dumped his captive hard on the floor.

He struck a light and shed his cloak before examining what he'd brought home from Jeliff's courtyard, where he'd lurked since sundown the last three nights, expecting some form of disaster to strike. The spearman's hair was dark blond and it hung in long, thick plaits that coiled on the floor. He, himself, wore his black hair short, hacking off any lock that fell below his nose or tangled in his collar. Other men wore their hair longer, but no Walensor man wore it long enough to sit on. Merrisati? Kufique? He'd never been outside Walensor and didn't know the fashions of other realms, especially their nether realms.

Kneeling down, he brushed one plait aside—gently, because he did not like the feel of another's flesh against his fingers.

"Godswill—you're no foreign man. You're a woman!"

Taking a deep breath, the woman raised her head. "Yes, midons prince—"

"Godswill, you're the woman in sorMeklan colors. The one who brought me to Aleg's revel."

Chapter Thirteen

Guided only by starlight, Braydon made his way along the tangled streets of Eyerlon. By the time he reached the palace he was only a few breaths short of panic. The nightwatch recognized him and opened the gate.

"I must see my prince," he admitted, hoping the watch would assume the quaver in his voice came from the cold, although cold was the least part of his distress.

"Do you want an escort?" the officer suggested. "There's safety in numbers sometimes. Any man here would risk a golden tirade in exchange for an hour's warmth."

Braydon protested that he'd rather face Prince Alegshorn alone, but the officer insisted and Braydon led three shivering men into the old palace. The corridors were quiet, smelling faintly of bitter herbs. The sorRodion feasted on the last night of Calends. Braydon himself had been in the honor line, saluting King Manal sorRodion as he was wheeled from the new palace to the old in an enclosed chair—the one time during the year the king left his pyramid throne.

Portraits of King Manal were scattered throughout the city, portraits that promised a wise, kindly face in a wreath of snow-white hair and beard. The white wreath was there, and the wisdom—after a fashion, but nothing at all of kindness. And—though Braydon was grieved to admit it—King Manal's face revealed greater depths of malice and cruelty than he'd found in the Wolf when they'd spoken in the tunnel.

And having now seen the tree from which *all* living sorRodion branches grew, Braydon had conceived a fear of his prince. His heart thumped painfully against his ribs as he approached the guarded doors of Prince Alegshorn's quiet hall.

"I must speak with midons prince. Is he still awake?"

"Midons prince is awake all right, but he's not talking," Pretion, the taller spearman, said with a wink. "You'll do better cooling your heels here till we hear the lady slip out the side door."

"I can't stay. I l-left—" Braydon stammered. These men weren't oath-bound like himself. He shouldn't explain anything to these men, maybe he couldn't even explain it all to the prince. But he had to try, and he had to get back to that rubbled courtyard where he'd left his sister. "I'll take full responsibility for disturbing him."

"In a pig's eye," Pretion countered, setting his spear firmly across the door where it was immediately crossed by his partner's. "It's not *your* duty to keep things nice and quiet while he's 'irresistibly detained.'"

Braydon took a deep breath. Back home in Gorse the youths played a game: Whose shout could be heard farthest from the commons. Braydon didn't win often, but he was undaunted by a mere two closed doors and the empty hall between them.

"Aleg!" Then, to Pretion: "Want to let me pass now?" When Pretion hesitated, Braydon filled his lungs again.

"Godswill, man— This better fall on your godswilling head," Pretion swore, but he stood aside.

The hall was dark; the double doors behind him were closed and latched as soon as he was through them. The only light came faintly from the banked hearth; it was enough to guide Braydon to Prince Aleg's unguarded bedchamber door. He cocked his fist and, after a grim moment's hesitation, hammered on the wood.

"Midons!"

He heard a soft-pitched groan followed by a more masculine one, the rustle of linen, the creaking of bed ropes, and the stomp of bare feet on the bedchamber floor. He had belated second thoughts. The inner bolt was thrown with unnecessary vigor and the door cracked a finger's width. Braydon stood at attention.

"Get lost or be flayed." The prince's voice was husky and—Braydon hoped—harsher than intended.

Braydon flung himself against the door as it closed, pitting his desperation against the distracted prince. He won the contest. The door reopened and Prince Alegshorn sorRodion, stark naked and cross-grained, entered his hall.

"Give me your gods-be-damned cloak and talk *fast*."

Braydon surrendered his cloak. "I met with Jeliff, at his request, just a while ago. We waited a long time for another messenger. Jeliff grew anxious, and when the messenger did arrive—it was a bird, midons—he said he could not entrust the message to me, and we must come to the palace together. We left his upper room, but we were set upon before we reached the street. Two men at first, then a third. We were divided; I didn't see clearly, but the man who slew Jeliff was run off by the third man. I did not stay. I-I-thought I should come here and tell you at once, midons prince. I did not think it could wait until dawn."

The prince ground his knuckles into his eyes and returned to the inner chamber. Braydon tried not to overhear the conversation:

"I said now and I mean now."

"But where, midons? If the cook catches me, he'll throw me into the street—"

"Out! Now!"

The command was followed by the sound of a bare-handed slap. A distraught woman ran through the hall, her hastily gathered clothes streaming behind her exposed back. Prince Alegshorn emerged, one cheek noticeably redder than the other.

"See that she finds someplace soft to sleep!" the prince shouted before he settled into his chair beside the brazier. "Godswill, Egg—what went wrong? Put some charcoal in that thing before I freeze."

"I don't know, midons prince. I was very careful. I'm sure no one followed me." He was wary of the silver perched on his weapon arm as he filled the brazier with fresh charcoal and lit it with embers from the hearth. "I cannot stay, midons prince. I must go back."

"Too late," the prince mumbled through his hands. "Down on the river front, bodies don't last the night. *Godswill*—the message! Was it a written message?"

"I don't know, midons prince. There was a sealed tube tied to the bird's leg, about the size of my little finger and dead black, as if it had been charred in fire. Send me off, midons; I'll turn the courtyard inside-out looking for it." The silver didn't burn . . . yet.

Prince Aleg shook his head. "There's nothing left to go back for, Egg. We'd best hope there was Brightwater silver under that char. If the wrong man tries to open it, the message won't survive.

There's no blame on your shoulders; you did what you were told to do, as best you could do it."

Braydon cleaned his hands with the sand and stood up. "I must go back, your highness. I left . . . I left my sword behind."

Aleg dismissed his not-the-entire-truth concern with a wave of his hand. "You'll get another tomorrow. I'm much more interested in knowing everything that happened. Start from when you entered the pickler's room. Leave nothing out, Egg. Let me judge what is important. Tell me about the two men who ambushed you, and the third man. Tell me *everything* about that third man."

Braydon swallowed hard. "Midons Prince Alegshorn, I left my sister in that courtyard. I don't know if she's dead or alive. My oath to you comes first, I know, but— Please, midons, if you will not allow me to go back and search until I find her, please send someone else."

"Your sister? Godswill, Egg—what was your sister doing at the pickler's?" The prince sat up straight in his chair. "Your sister's married to a crippled veteran in your village. Iser's iron balls, what was she doing at Jeliff's?"

Shapeless Au, the creator of all things, had not created a divine patron for sheep or shepherds. When a shepherd was in dire straits—Braydon judged his straits could not be more dire—he laced his fingers together and invoked all the divinities. "As the gods will, midons prince, she left Gorse with the resurrected sorMeklan man held hostage in the Palestra. She was taken by the sorMeklan, by their sidon. Her name is Berika. She wore their colors at your revel—"

"Driskolt's leman!" The prince's voice bridged the gap between astonished inquiry and outrage. "Godswill, Egg—does Dris know?"

"Know what, midons prince?"

"That he's sleeping with a murderess and his dead uncle's woman!"

Ever a stickler for truth, Braydon dared to correct his prince: "Midons prince, I believe the sidon knows everything, but Berika insists that Dart slew her husband. Hirmin was hellfired and cursed. Walensor's well rid of him."

"Well, of course, Egg, a curse always makes murder square—just don't tell the Wolf. Do you have other kinfolk cavorting in high-clan beds?" The prince had settled into sputtering outrage.

Braydon blushed furiously. "No. Berika . . . I was as shocked as you when I saw her in this hall. She is a good and honorable woman, midons prince—"

Prince Aleg laced his fingers until his knuckles popped. "So is my mother, Egg—in her own eyes. I'll have answers, Egg. Now and complete."

Braydon sighed and told both stories—the tale of his sister's escapades with the sorMeklan and the events, as he understood them, in the alley. The prince made a narrow spire with his fingers and hid his face behind it. He was careful not to interrupt until Braydon had run out of words; then he rocked slightly in the chair.

"Tell me again, Egg—what exactly was your sister carrying when she arrived at the pickler's?"

"A spear, midons prince. A beat-up battered spear like none I'd seen before. The tang was long and made of metal but the shaft was short and without a proper butt."

The prince's face disappeared behind his hands. "Dear gods beyond the Web. What happened to the spear? Who had it last?"

"Berika, midons prince, I think. She came to my aid, beating the man I fought. I went down first, midons. I don't know what happened. Perhaps it's still there; the running man did not carry it away. For myself, I-I could not think, midons. I did not think. Please, midons prince, send someone after her," Braydon pleaded. "For my mother's sake, so that all her children might not be dead by sunrise."

"I do not imagine that your sister needs your help or mine, Egg. Any sheep-woman who can get herself so deeply tangled in our affairs is almost certainly capable of getting herself out again. Never underestimate women, Egg. The least of them is cleverer than the smartest man. They see around corners while we walk into the walls. I know only one man who can outthink a woman, and he has no use for them."

But having said this, the prince shouted for his guards and sent one down to the river front.

"Thank you, midons prince."

"They won't find her. I'd imagine Dris came back for her. Godswill it, Braydon. Godswill he got the spear and, godswill, it was not damaged, because if your sister's not talking her heart out to the sorMeklan, she's face-to-face with that third swordsman. And you may be certain *he's* got that spear. How fast was he, Egg? Fast compared to you, or fast compared to me?"

"Very fast, midons prince. Faster than I've ever seen."

"Shit," the prince swore, like any country-common man who'd ever confronted an overripe barnyard. "Shit," he said again. "Dris is going to get himself flayed for this. Butt-naked flayed. Shit."

Braydon scratched his beard, certain the prince did not mean for him to overhear his words. "Midons, are you saying that the sidon of Fenklare was one of the men who ambushed us, that he's the man who ran away?"

"Godswill, Egg—use your wits. Of course Dris was there. First your sister shows up with a dead man—a resurrected man—then she shows up here, in this very hall, with the Wolf on her arm. Next she leaves the sorMeklan residence to talk to you—my oath-bound retainer. And finally she takes off in the dead of the night for the river front. And not just any night, but the last night of Calends, an ill-omened night, as my godsforsaken brother will assure you. And not unarmed, not like any other hysterical woman, oh, no—she's armed herself with the godswilling clan regalia!" Prince Aleg rubbed his brow. "By all the gods awake and asleep, I can't imagine how she did *that*. Godswill, Braydon, I know you cherish your sister, but pray to your private god that Dris retrieved that spear."

"Shepherds don't have a private god, midons prince. Shapeless Au decreed we did not need one."

"Then Shapeless Au is twice a fool for creating your godsforsaken sister. This is worthy of the Wolf—" The prince caught himself mid-thought. "Of course—her path crossed his. The gods are laughing at us, Braydon. Headblind fools that we are, I can hear them laughing." Prince Aleg rose wearily from his chair. "Come on, Braydon. We'd best unravel this to the last thread. Help me dress."

Braydon followed the prince into the inner room. He was puzzled that the prince didn't want the layers of clothing a prudent man would want on a frigid winter night. But he had assumed they were going to the sorMeklan residence to talk with Dris and, one hoped, Berika. His mouth gaped when Prince Aleg locked the inner door before springing a secret panel near his bed.

The narrow passageway was lit with Brightwater moss. It was too dim to read a man's face at arm's length, but bright enough to travel without a lamp. Aleg clicked the panel shut behind them and led the way.

"Where are we going, midons prince?"

"Shhh—"

They climbed more than they walked, and came to a smooth-walled dead end.

Prince Aleg squeezed to the rear behind Braydon. "You first," he whispered. "The catch is straight ahead; the door opens on your right. Give it a good shoulder-shove to get it open."

The prince's tone still hovered on the near side of outrage.

Braydon would have given his life—and Berika's life—to walk away from that innocent-seeming panel, but he was trapped. Blind obedience was almost always the best course for commonfolk, especially in tight places within the palace walls. He found the catch, and then, as he'd been told, gave the panel a shoulder-shove.

His eyes had not adjusted to the light, when something thunked into the door frame, pinning a bit of his forelock to the wood. Braydon felt his heart stutter. Nothing moved except his eyes, which gave him a good view of his own hair and the patterned steel nailed through it. Beyond the hilt of the knife, he could just make out a mannish shape—dark and lean—and untidy heaps everywhere, as if a storeroom guard had taken him and Prince Alegshorn for thieves. He tried to blow his hair out of the way, but his lungs were empty.

Prince Aleg reached over his shoulder to free the knife.

"I'm glad to see you, too—" The prince flung the knife toward its presumed owner.

Braydon's hair no longer blocked his vision. The man-shape resolved into the Wolf's hard features. Braydon squeezed his eyes shut. Prince Alegshorn was about to resolve the brothers' lifelong rivalry—and he was the only living witness. Living for how much longer?

There was a little sound, then nothing. By the time Braydon opened his eyes, Prince Rinchen was secreting the knife in a sheath beneath his sleeve.

"I was expecting you, not a brown-haired messenger. A little warning would be prudent, unless you judge him expendable. Tell him to shut the door."

Braydon didn't wait for an order. He braced his back against the door panel and shut it with his full weight. His eyes saw the princes clasp hands and arm-wrestle. He and Indon used to greet each other that way, but he was still expecting blood when Prince Aleg dropped his older brother hard on his knees, twisting Prince Rinchen's arm behind and between his shoulders.

At that moment Braydon—and quite possibly his prince as well—caught sight of Berika, huddled against the Wolf's bed, wrapped in her cloak which blended with the blankets spilling off the mattress. Her presence here in the Wolf's lair—with clothes dirtied but otherwise intact—could only mean that the Wolf was the third swordsman. Another quick glance around the room revealed the strangely shaped spear Berika had been carrying.

Braydon had barely begun to consider what it all might mean when Prince Aleg released the Wolf's arm.

He turned to Braydon. "I told you that your sister would come up safe," he said an instant before Prince Rinchen took his legs out from under him.

Prince Aleg launched himself at his brother's gut, and the royal princes rolled across the cluttered floor, kicking and cursing. Braydon flattened himself against the nearest wall to keep out of harm's way. But despite the vigor they brought to their brawling, the princes wrought no harm, and slowly Braydon's mind accepted what his eyes could see: The rivalry between golden Prince Alegshorn and the cursed Wolf was as good-natured as the rivalry he had shared with Indon. Braydon couldn't count the number of times that he and Indon had bloodied each other, but if he could have anything he wanted, Compact be damned, it would be to have Indon alive again and at his back right now.

Braydon didn't want to remember Indon just then, so he remembered the upper-room conspiracy on the second night of Calends and the revel the night after. He racked his memory for everything Prince Alegshorn had ever said about his brother.

He wasn't a wagering man, but he'd wager all his precious wealth that the princes had been deceiving the entire kingdom for years. He couldn't guess why they had, or why he'd been allowed to glimpse the truth. Perhaps they trusted the power of the Brightwater silver pinned above his shoulder. But if oath-sorcery could keep him alive, what about his sister? He wanted to get Berika out of the room, and gestured urgently for her to join him by the door. She shook her head, sad but firm.

The princely battle ended when Aleg fell on a lumpy sack. The lumps were metal, and the golden prince lay defenseless with the wind knocked out of him. The Wolf could have killed him easily. Instead, he held out his hand.

"Had enough?"

Prince Alegshorn nodded and took the proffered hand. "I suppose you already know that Jeliff's dead," he wheezed.

"I warned you about him, Aleg," the Wolf snarled, freeing his hand. "I told you to let me take care of him before it came to this."

"He was the only spymaster with eyes inside the Arrizan empire. We needed him—"

Prince Rinchen stood by his worktable, toying with the layers of parchment. "Before Tremontin, not since. He was an assassin first and foremost, and desperate to keep your gold flowing into his purse. It was only a matter of time before he soured. I told you I would not permit that. He killed the sorMeklan ward, the *comes* Killeen barKethmarion avsorMeklan. If Dris had not run Jeliff through, I'd have done it myself." He threw a man-sized ring on a delicate chain at his brother.

Prince Aleg caught the ring but did not bother looking at it. Both Aleg and Berika had blanched when the Wolf mentioned Killeen's honor and title. The *comes* was just another nobleman to Braydon, though he could understand why his prince would blanch. The sorMeklan might declare a pundonor blood feud for this, and if the princes were truly not rivals or enemies, Prince Alegshorn was going to find himself privately stretched between his brother and his closest friend. Watching Berika dissolve in tears, Braydon belatedly guessed barKethmarion was the youth who rescued her from the Wolf the night they both appeared at the revel in Prince Aleg's hall.

There was no way he'd be able to explain this to Ingolde, even if he spent every last flake of silver on Webwork messages. He pursed his lips and shook his head.

"Your hands are no cleaner."

With a jolt, Braydon realized that the Wolf was talking to him.

"How many would have died if I had not been in that courtyard? You brought or lured your sister to an assassin's bolthole. Did you think he'd allow either one of you to see the sun rise again?"

Braydon was speechless, but his prince interceded quickly on his behalf.

"If there is blood-guilt"—Prince Alegshorn duplicated his brother's softly menacing tone—"it starts and stops with me. I employed Jeliff and I hold Braydon's Brightwater oath. If you were so damned suspicious, you could have—*should* have—sent me to mind my own snakes. Trust cuts both ways, brother, or have you forgotten that . . . again?"

The Wolf said nothing. There were signs—narrowed eyes, flared nostrils, a slowly clenched and unclenched fist—of rage barely held in check. Finally, he spoke: "I have not forgotten, but you were not alone . . . again. And I do not ask you to do what an honorable man ought not do. I am careful about these things."

Prince Aleg stared at Berika, then heaved a dramatic sigh. "I would have been more careful myself, brother, but truly, I never expected to find a woman here. I thought you'd have left her for Driskolt."

"Truly, brother, I did not know she was a woman."

Prince Aleg flashed his winning smile, and the tension in the disordered chamber eased. "May I have my spymaster's last message? I assume you found it."

Prince Rinchen rooted through the parchment, found the dull black tube and tossed it across the room. Then he focused his pale eyes on Braydon again.

"You should have accepted my offer."

The Wolf's hard questions still echoed in Braydon's head. He recognized that he had made terrible mistakes, but refusing Prince Rinchen's offer in the tunnel had not been one of them. "Begging midons prince's pardon, but I could not accept your offer without compromising my Brightwater oath to my prince."

"You see, brother, you failed to tempt him," Prince Aleg said, drawing a knife from his boot. "Braydon is an honest man and has absolute faith in his oath. He trusts my friends, even when he shouldn't, and stands apart from my enemies, even when it's not necessary." Aleg rolled up his sleeve and made a sizable gash in his well-muscled forearm. Blood dripped onto the black tube where it sizzled, stank, and left dots of silver amid the black.

"Spit on it first," the Wolf suggested.

"That's chiseling."

"Spit's cheaper than blood."

Prince Aleg cursed under his breath, but he hawked onto the dark metal. The next drop of blood uncovered more of the silver than its predecessor.

Satisfied that his advice had been taken, Prince Rinchen told Braydon: "I am not my brother's enemy. I never was; he does not stand between me and the throne. More to the point, my brother is not *my* enemy, since I hold from him the same oath he holds from you—"

"Tell him the way you got it! You chiseled me for fair."

"There's nothing to tell. It was a spring day three years ago. We were with the army, marching to Norivarl. I left the camp at sunrise—it was my custom, then, to seek solitude while the army broke camp. My brother sneaked along after me until I found a quiet grove and dismounted. I left my sword with my horse—"

"I should have *known* you were up to something!"

Prince Rinchen scowled, but otherwise ignored the interruption. "I appealed to my brother's sense of honor: If he ran me through when I was unarmed, he'd never know in his heart if he was better, or merely lucky. I offered him the chance to settle everything. Only one of us would ride out of the forest; the other would be a corpse tied upon his saddle. It had to look like an accident, the way Vigelan always wanted it to look—whether anyone believed it or not. No swords, no knives, no witnesses. He accepted my challenge."

The brawl, according to Prince Rinchen—and his brother did not interrupt to correct him—was hard-fought and indecisive. They'd pummelled each other from the grove to the verge of a steep ravine. They were both near exhaustion when Aleg got lucky. Rinchen snared his foot beneath a ground root. Bleary from the battering he'd already taken, he fell badly: The paired bones in his forearm snapped like kindling wood. And when he tried to get up, Aleg booted him in the ribs. He'd tumbled backward, down the ravine. Full of fire and smelling victory, Aleg plunged after him.

"There was a brook at the bottom of the ravine, cold and deep after the winter thaw."

"You knew it was there," Prince Aleg interrupted. "You lured me to that exact spot."

"It was our second morning in the same camp, my second morning to ride into the forest," the Wolf conceded. "I knew it would be a good place to settle things between us—but I didn't intend to break my arm or fall ass-over-elbow into that stream."

"Godswill, Rinchen—why won't you simply admit that you chiseled? You *always* chisel. Any time you stumble across a rule, you break it."

"There were no rules, Aleg. It was a fight to the death!"

"By all the gods awake and asleep—you were chiseling when you said we'd fight to the death! You had no intention of killing me. You knew exactly what you wanted, and you chiseled until you got it."

Braydon's eyes and ears opened wide; he kept his mouth shut. He'd seen this happen before: By telling their story to an outsider, Prince Rinchen had resurrected the moment when the brawl took place. The Wolf exhaled through his teeth, avoiding Aleg's glower, then turned his head completely away. Braydon recognized both gestures as the acts of a man about to break the rules—whatever they were—again. He tried without success to catch Prince Aleg's eye, but his prince continued to complain while cleaning the last of the soot off the message case.

"You chiseled. You tricked me. You knew damned well that I swam like a rock. *We* never learned. When, godswill, had you? Did Arkkin teach you on the steppes? Did he find some horse-wallow with mud and throw you in? Damn it all, brother, you knew you were going to founder me in that stream."

The Wolf turned back to face Aleg. "I knew I had to put an end to our fighting. We were too old to be brawling like children. I want what's mine, but I won't buy it with your death. Wouldn't, couldn't and never tried."

The Wolf, Braydon noted, had not answered any of his brother's breathless questions.

Prince Alegshorn had opened the message tube, but set it aside without examining its contents. "You could have told me that. If you'd *ever* told me that—"

"When? How? While Vigelan lived? Sorry, brother, I saw no sense in having both of us die. After the war began? You know where I was then, and after he died we were never alone together. You were surrounded by friends who wanted to prove their loyalty and affection by putting a knife between my ribs. There was no other way to get you to listen."

"It was damned hard to listen with water flooding my lungs."

"The stream wasn't deep. You couldn't drown."

"A man can drown in a godswilling *bucket,* Rinchen, if you hold his head in it long enough!"

"I *need* you, Aleg. I can rule Walensor, but I don't know how to reign. I have no talent for ceremony or largesse. I have had allies, but never friends."

"You wouldn't know a friend if he looked you straight in the eye," Aleg said, doing exactly that.

The Wolf immediately turned toward the brazier. "I inspire loathing, not loyalty. I'm cursed. I destroy what I love; or the gods do, will I or nill I. I *need* you to stand between me and Walensor. I need you too much to risk it all on friendship."

Prince Alegshorn rose to his feet with the bloody knife in his hand. "That was the only day I ever hated you—you dragging me onto the rocks, coughing and spitting. You demanding my oath with bones sticking out of your arm. Me not realizing till after I'd given it, that you'd tricked me. 'By all the gods awake and asleep, by the spirits of my ancestors and the blood in my heart, I swear I will not connive against you, my brother, in word or deed, by my own hands or through the hands of others'"—the knife slipped from Prince Aleg's hand—"'for so long as I live . . .'"

"Have you regretted it, Aleg?"

He retrieved his knife. "No—of course not. You were right. You're always right. *And* you always chisel. That's your curse, Rinchen, your true curse, not some Calends superstition. You lie and you chisel even when you don't have to."

The Wolf's shoulders sagged but he did not deny the accusation. After another moment, Prince Alegshorn shook the contents of the message case—a stained tangle of thread—onto his palm.

"It's red," he said flatly, describing the underlying color of the thread.

"Under the table."

Braydon looked at the parchment-strewn worktable, and with the princes, noticed Berika for the first time in many minutes. She'd stopped sobbing. Her eyes were dry and she regarded them all with a solemn stare.

"We must pay more attention to the assarts," Prince Rinchen said, cold detachment already restored to his voice. "The commonfolk there are breeding too clever and wise. Their lives are not hard enough."

Prince Aleg crawled under the table without answering. He emerged with another tube of considerably greater diameter than the message case. After inserting the knotted end of the thread in a small slit at one end of the tube, he wound the stained thread around it. His face grew grim as the red band widened and the stains aligned into legible writing.

"We needed Jeliff, brother; and would need him, if he still lived, as Hazard lives. The Pyromant reappeared at the imperial court and cleared his name, and then left by himself. The message's dated the forty-seventh of H'roqui—what's that?—the Lesser week of Slaughter?"

"Greater, toward the beginning, I think. Maybe sixty days ago." The Wolf cursed and examined the thread-wrapped tube, but the message was the same when he read it. "If it's true, Aleg—he could be anywhere. Walensor itself. I've had dreams, Aleg. Nightmares—" He unwound the thread and threw it in the brazier. "We're in trouble. I've got to think."

Apparently, this was a signal Prince Aleg recognized. Without another word, he left the table, touched Braydon lightly on the arm, and opened the panel door.

Braydon hesitated. "What about my sister? We can't leave her here!"

"Why not? Where would you take her? Your barracks? *My* bedroom? There isn't a safer place for a woman in all Walensor than my brother's bedroom."

Chapter Fourteen

Berika leaned against the footboard of the prince's bed, which stood against an outside wall and was more affected by the deadwatch wind than any heat from the brazier or the more distant hearth. She tucked her feet beneath her skirt and her hands into the cuffs of her sleeves. Her loose hair added an extra layer of warmth over her shoulders—not that she noticed or cared. She'd seen her name on Braydon's lips as he entered the passage; then Prince Alegshorn whispered something and her brother never looked back.

This long, tumultuous last day of the year had begun at sunrise with Killeen sprawled across her in the huge sorMeklan bed. Now Killy was dead, and she was perched on a hard, narrow bed while the Wolf stared at nothing above the brazier. Between the beds, she'd been interrogated by a bungling sorcerer, stunned by the metal-studded back of Driskolt's gauntlet, and punched in the gut by Walensor's crown prince. Her body ached, and she was wearier than a mother of colicky twins.

The haunting music of the Web as it funneled into the Cascade brought no solace. She wanted to hear the intimate, comforting melodies Dart played on his harp. She wanted Dart himself; she had the Wolf instead.

There was a day in Berika's life that was as important as the day in the forest stream had been to the sorRodion princes. In autumn of this very year she'd whirled herself dizzy beside a Weychawood stream, begging the gods to alter her destiny. Much too late she understood that wise folk were more careful with their prayers.

She'd fetched Weycha's champion out of the forest, but Dart was a perfectly ordinary man compared to Prince Rinchen ruVigelan sorRodion. Dart's unworldliness rarely revealed itself. The Wolf wore his curse like armor. Berika would sooner look into Dart's eyes at their smoldering worst than catch a glimpse from the Wolf.

Nonetheless, Berika would not have left the Wolf's lair with Braydon. The map still spread on the worktable measured how far she'd come from Gorse. If the gods and her naive *basi* had brought her all the way from the muddy assart village to a room in the palace—and she believed that they had—it was much too late to run away.

Berika let her thoughts drift freely, a trick she had mastered while grazing sheep. Wild flights of fantasy had never had a problem in the meadows above Gorse. But in the Wolf's lair Berika's thoughts wandered no farther than the platter of untouched bread and winter delicacies that balanced atop a stack of leather-bound books.

The bright brown loaf of bread loomed large in Berika's mind. She'd fallen in love with honey-bread at the sorMeklan residence and tortured herself imagining this loaf's taste and texture on her tongue. Her mouth watered and her stomach emitted a profound growl.

Prince Rinchen sat upright in his chair. "You—you're still here?"

Berika pressed her hands over her gut, but didn't answer the question. The Wolf stared at her as he had stared at the empty place above the brazier. Men had stared at her before. Berika understood those looks, even if she did not welcome them. The Wolf did not make her feel naked; he made her feel like an unburied corpse. She began to shiver uncontrollably.

The prince scowled and found a jug with two cups inverted over the neck. He wiped the rim of one on his sleeve before filling it. Leaving one foot firmly planted on the floor, he sat on his own bed beside her and laid a hand—a light, hesitant hand—on her trembling shoulder.

"Drink this. It will warm you."

The cup was cold in her hands. The liquid within was colorless and odorless—like water, and though she wondered why the prince would say cold water would warm her, she didn't think poison was a danger in this room, so she gulped it down.

Whatever it was, it certainly wasn't water.

"What was that?" she gasped as her stomach caught fire.

"Shimya'an," the prince muttered. "It comes from the steppes. The word means Water of Life, or Water of Fire. Pennaikmen like their words to have many meanings."

Berika croaked, "Water of fire," just before she started coughing.

Prince Rinchen pried the cup from her grasp. She grabbed his arm, because it was there and because the firewater frightened her. When he pried her fingers off his arm, she clung to his shoulder instead.

"I don't—I'd rather— You're tired." The prince shoved her away and stood up. "You need to go to sleep." He made an ineffectual effort to tidy the bed. "Please—you're here now, just go to sleep."

Berika brushed her hair aside. The fire had breached her skull. Her eyes wanted to see two princes where her mind was sure there was only one. She squinted and got the lean features aligned. "Where will you sleep, midons?"

"Beside you. I do not sleep on the floor in my own room. Neither of us is overly large."

With a sigh Berika attacked the side-laces of her gown. When the cords were loose she rose unsteadily to her knees and hauled the expanse of woolen cloth over her head.

"No, *merou.* Not for me."

Berika continued tugging at the cloth. The prince's bed had an abundance of fur blankets and thick quilts. Whatever his intentions, she'd be more comfortable without the heavy gown.

"I've made vows, *merou.* You will not tempt me."

She got her head out of the gown and studied the two floating princes while she shucked out of the sleeves. The shimya'an liquor made her reckless. "You told me to go to sleep, midons prince. I sleep in my shift." She wadded up her gown and dumped it on the floor.

"I made a vow: no living woman's flesh would tempt me. A man like myself, cursed and incapable of affection, must adhere to his vows or slip completely into the darkness."

Berika wriggled beneath the blankets. They were warm where she'd been sitting on them and she could stretch her legs without fighting cold blankets. "I'm not tempting you, midons prince." She pulled a patchwork fur blanket up around her chin.

He sighed and harvested a feather quilt from the floor, tucking it carefully around her. She felt like a moth snugly wrapped in its cocoon; she'd felt much worse. The Wolf's bed was probably safe—his reputation was unsavory, but she'd heard his vow, and his rumored perversions did not include women. She was hungry, but going to bed hungry was nothing new. Berika closed her eyes, inviting sleep and expecting it to arrive quickly.

But the goddess of sleep had made all her visits to the palace, or perhaps the scowling Wolf scared her away. Berika's eyes popped open and she was wide-awake, staring at the prince while he stared at nothing.

Ash came to Dart's Palestra room in the last hour of nightwatch. She was a changeable creature with large brown eyes that were waiflike one moment and sultry the next. He never knew which Ash would cross his threshold. Tonight it was the waif, looking exceptionally small and fragile in her voluminous white gown. Her hair was infant fine, infant short, and whiter than the robe.

He welcomed her with the traditional last-night greeting: "Safe passage, my lady."

She sobbed and ran to his arms, leaving little red blotches on the knotted carpet. She'd forgotten her shoes. It had happened before. It wasn't a good omen, especially on the last night of the year.

"We must hurry, my champion," she said between sobs. Basilidans spoke with the voice of their gods. Ash tried, but though Weycha had resurrected him to be her champion, she'd always called him Dart, or more intimate names. "We must go to the Basilica. It's almost time. We must greet the new year together from the heights of the Cascade."

Time for what? he wondered, watching her head shake No from side to side as tears flowed from her eyes. She was fifteen when she was herself, and much too young for the things they did at the top of the Cascade. The things they would not do tonight, if he could avoid it.

"Yes, my lady," he agreed, lifting her into his arms. "Indeed we must, without delay."

But he carried the waif to his bed—his chair was hard and spindly—saying one thing, doing another, as she did herself. He held her tenderly across his lap, her white-haired head tucked beneath his chin, her cold, torn feet seeking the warmth beneath his pillow. Reflections in the polished brass candlestick beside the bed notwithstanding, he'd been born more than forty years ago. At moments like this—when they were far from the Cascade—it was easy to imagine Ash as a nightmared child, his own daughter, craving the assurance only a father's arms could provide.

"We must go to the Cascade, my champion," she insisted, sobbing louder than before.

"You're cold, my lady. We'll leave in a moment, once you're warm again."

She closed her fists over his shirt and snuggled deeper against his chest. "We must, my champion—"

He shushed her gently, stroking kitten-soft hair. "Later, little one. Later. Much later."

The sobbing stopped. The fists unclenched.

Her hair began to thicken and flow through his fingers: lustrous chestnut, like autumn leaves or fire.

"Ash," he whispered. "My lady?" he asked, though he knew more certainly than ever that Ash was not his lady. Weycha had endowed him with senses that tingled in the presence of her enemies. They had never been entirely quiet when Ash was near, but they quivered now, like a myriad of burrs stinging his skin. "Ash?"

The girl whose white-tipped, auburn hair now fell luxuriantly past her shoulders, stiffened in his arms; then her legs began to tremble violently. Dart laid her flat on the bed, hoping to keep her from hurting herself as her arms, too, began to tremble and twist grotesquely. He had half a mind to summon a mender, but the other half—Weycha's half—counselled a more discreet and wary course.

"Dart! Dart, please—" She grasped him with unnatural strength, eyes wide and seeing something he could not. "Dart, I'm—"

But her eyes rolled back before she could finish, and when they rolled down again, they were a luminous yellow-green.

"Where—? Where am I?" It was Ash's sultry voice, stronger than ever before.

"With your champion, my lady," Dart assured her, wishing he had Weycha's wooden sword slung from his hip instead of the single-edge fruit knife the spooks allowed him.

"The Brightwater— Where's the hellfired Brightwater?" She seized his shirt, hauling herself up until their noses were nearly touching. "Why aren't we in the gods-all-be-damned Cascade, drowning in gods-all-be-damned Brightwater?"

At that moment Dart was extremely grateful they were not. Ash—if that's who she was—exhaled sour, sulphur breath with every word. Her skin had grown unnaturally warm, and glints of yellow sparked and ebbed in her green eyes. The hair on his neck rose involuntarily and he understood what other men felt when his own eyes glowed with Weycha's power. He squeezed her wrist until she released his shirt.

"Who are you?"

Laughter, rank but melodious. "Your goddess, fool. And you'll be sorry you disobeyed me. But, first we *must* get to the Cascade. Come. Come quickly!"

She began pulling him toward the door. The auburn-haired girl was stronger than she had any right to be, but so was he when face-to-face with Weycha's enemies. When she realized main force would not prevail, her demeanor changed and she spun herself into his arms.

"Please, my champion, my pretty champion. I want to hear the deadwatch bells from the top of the Cascade. There's so little time left. Please hurry, my pet." Her hand slid down his back and below his waist. It followed the curve of his buttocks then came across his hips and into the hollow of his groin, gently kneading the most intimate part of his body. *"Hurry, my pet."*

Ash seduced him regularly, and he succumbed, partly because he was a man, no matter what the spooks said, and partly because he'd suspected that this not-basilidan's true nature lay on the far side of sensuality. She'd proved his suspicions correct, thereby enabling him to resist whatever temptation she raised. But unless Hazard was a red-haired woman—and no one had ever suggested that Hazard was anything other than a mature, military man—Dart still couldn't guess what made this unnatural hoyden Weycha's enemy.

"Who are you?" he demanded, shoving her away. "*What* are you? What do you want?"

She laughed again, less melodiously than before. "The Web, you fool. Weycha's godhead. The essence of a divine forest burning through my veins. Everything my brother wants—only I shall take it from him and make it mine forever instead. Now—COME!"

Hot foul air made a ring around Dart: not *basi*, but something similar. He shrugged it off.

"Not on your life, whoever you are."

Another loop of noxious air, tighter and stronger than the first, dragged him slowly toward the door. There was another peal of malice-filled laughter, followed by the first chime of the deadwatch peal. Her concentration faltered. Dart shed her compulsion a second time and flung her backward against the wall.

"Who are you?" he demanded, pressing a forearm against her

throat. Dart couldn't shape sorcery consciously like a spook—once Severed, always Severed; resurrection hadn't changed that—but a red mist grew at the limit of his vision and he had the power to do what needed to be done. "Answer me!" he shouted over the clamor of the bells.

"Arianna!" She spread her arms wide.

Dart flew backward across the room, striking the outer stone wall with a force that broke several ribs. Arianna, who claimed the Pyromant Hazard for a brother, followed him. Wisps of singe smoke curled from the white robe; charred footprints appeared on the carpet behind her. He braced himself for a desperate, possibly futile battle, but she grabbed the shutter latch instead of him, pulling the heavy planks from their hinges. She shattered the leaded grisaille window with her fist. Frigid wind swept her hair and an eerie, many-colored light flickered over her face.

"It has begun," she said, and as sure as he was of anything at that moment, Dart was sure there was fear in her voice.

"What has?" he countered.

"Hazard's conquest of the Web. He will ride the death rage of ten thousand souls from Tremontin to Eyerlon. Nothing can stand against him now." Pride and terror fought for dominance in her voice. "Not even you. Not even *us.* We could have made a stand from the Cascade. You're a touchstone, champion, a living touchstone. With you to harness the Web, I could have beaten him before the Web went down. Now there's only the wolf and the forest. Damn you, champion, damn you to the hell of cowards and failures. You could have saved the Web."

Weycha wasn't in the Web. Weycha had withdrawn from the Web hours after Berika wished him out of the forest. Weycha was safe, for now, from Hazard, if this Arianna told the truth, but was his lady safe from Arianna herself? 'The wolf and the forest.' The forest and the wolf. Weycha and Rinchen sorRodion. The cursed prince had given the order to bring down Tremontin. What else had he done?—besides promising to pry Weycha's sword and harp free from sorMeklan wards.

Using the wall for balance, Dart climbed to his feet. He ignored the tearing pain in his back. Weycha's implanted sorcery had already begun its healing work, and he'd just undone it all.

"What can you get from the Wolf that you cannot get from me?"

"Obedience," Arianna replied with a laugh that flattened him against the wall again.

His mind's attempt to combine this hellish creature and a black-haired boy clinging to his arm as his horse jumped a briar wall brought cold nausea to Dart's gut. If Arianna spoke the truth— If she'd found some corrupt way to wring obedience from the Wolf, then the Wolf was Weycha's enemy. And the Wolf had been as cruelly cursed by the gods and the gods-of-gods as a mortal soul could be.

If Rinchen was Weycha's enemy, Rinchen would die—but first Weycha's champion intended to deal justice to Arianna. If he'd grasped her laugh correctly, she was proud of what she'd done and would tell him how she'd done it while forest sorcery grew his bones together again.

"Obedience from Walensor's cursed Wolf?" He adopted a tone of skepticism and scorn. "How? His father never succeeded. What hold did you have over him?"

"Why love, of course. Hazard sealed a mote of my soul in a hellfire crystal. We had no idea at the time it would prove so useful, but the boy took a fancy to it and hid it against his heart. I listened to his dreams, champion: little bleak and morbid dreams. Prince Vigelan taught his son about agony, hate, and despair, but the boy dreams of love—any kind of love. The *worst* kind of love—" Arianna's full lips parted, her nostrils flared, and her seething eyes glazed with memories Dart hoped never to share. "His flesh was lusty, easily moved. I reached inside his dreams. I guided him along twisted paths of desire; each one led to death. I tamed the Wolf, shaped him to my needs, and made a pet of him. He does not know the difference between ecstasy and torture, champion. He worships me with his screams, and he *obeys*."

Bile rose in Dart's throat. He gulped the bitter lump down and shook his head. "Extraordinary," he whispered, concealing his disgust. "Beyond mortal measure."

"I could show you, champion." Arianna's too-warm hand traced a curve across his cheek, under his jaw. "Weycha was a lusty goddess, was she not? I think you did not lie chaste beside her all those years. The Wolf's memories are all cut from the same bloody cloth. There are so many paths my pet cannot explore because his imagination is so small. But you, champion—?"

Dart's healing was almost complete. A few more moments and he could hold Arianna's hot hellfire body in his arms, lure her down a tortured path to her own death. Weycha *was* a lusty goddess; he was an angry, vengeful man. He knew how it might be done. She'd caressed his neck and slid her hand beneath his shirt. A talon-sharp fingernail teased the dark, sensitive flesh of his breast. The gambler in his nature told him to match Arianna coin for coin. But his greater self balked: His memories of Weycha—of wild passion that never led to pain or degradation—were too precious to risk or squander.

Red mist clouded Dart's vision. He thrust Arianna away with an anguished roar. She stopped herself before she struck the wall, hovering in midair while hellfire devoured the last threads of Ash's white robe. Her laughter had the sweet stench of corpses left unburied in the sun.

"Wait awhile, champion. I must visit my pet in the palace." She whirled off a sheet of translucent hellfire that wrapped around Dart's body. "It's time for him to understand what I am, what he must do. I, too, need a champion against Hazard. But I will return for you, Weycha's champion. You'll learn to eat from my hand like the Wolf. You'll make a pretty pair."

Dart had the will to destroy her, but Weycha's forest sorcery did not answer to her champion's conscious control. It flared around him in the clean, brilliant colors of spring and autumn, doing battle with hellfire's lurid hues. He was safe against further attack, but paralyzed, too, and unable to do anything as tiny tongues of hellfire erupted through Arianna's skin. The battered, black-scarred body of a mortal woman fell heavily to the floor. Arianna, formed entirely from hellfire, hovered, shrinking slowly. When the Pyromant was no larger than an ember, she flew through the open window, vanishing entirely.

Not long after the deathwatch peal had rung, Prince Rinchen found whatever he had been looking for. Berika watched him scratch swift marks into a wax tablet on the worktable. He kicked out of his boots and clawed free of his shirt. Kneeling beside the brazier box, he nestled an oil lamp in the sand. Several moments had passed before Berika noticed that the Wolf's back was cross-hatched with scars.

Dart, Driskolt, and even Killeen, were scarred men. She assumed scars were the unavoidable price of their steel-filled way of life. But the prince's thick, ugly scars hadn't come from a sword.

Prince Rinchen turned around after he lit the lamp. He saw her staring at him. "I thought you were asleep."

There was a ratty leather thong around his neck with a ratty pouch hanging from it.

"Forgive me, midons prince. I can't sleep. I was woolgathering. I didn't mean to steal—I meant stare."

The prince returned to his chair. The room was cold; he didn't seem to notice. "But you did both, didn't you, Berika-from-the-edge-of-the-forest? Go ahead—*ask.* You commonfolk can hide everything except your gods-be-damned curiosity."

"I have nothing to ask, midons. I did not think a *prince* could be whipped."

"Many, many times, *merou*—if the hand on the whip belongs to another prince and the king looks the other way."

"Your brother?" The Wolf was right: She could hide everything except curiosity.

Prince Rinchen laughed, short and ugly. "Aleg? No, never—unless Vigelan threatened him. And, as the gods will, Aleg knew the threats were real. Vigelan hated failure and we were both failures. Nothing Aleg and I felt toward each other compared to the fear, and the hate, we both felt for him." The prince shuddered, but not, she thought, from the cold. "He'd come at night, mostly. Late, when his eyes and cheeks were red with wine. The menders waited outside the door. No one was allowed to talk about it, but everyone knew. We'd disappear for weeks at a time, but there were never any scars. Never. Until the last time."

Berika decided she did not want to know what the Wolf saw above his brazier.

It was always Vigelan, never Father, in memory's visions. Vigelan with a fist, Vigelan with the back of his hand, Vigelan with a whip. Vigelan standing behind him, standing over him, in a dark and reeking room. Vigelan had been the enemy before he knew Hazard's name. He'd bare his scarred back to the Cascade tomorrow for the sorcerers and noblefolk to see. Perhaps anticipation of that annual shame made it easier to talk to an inconsequential stranger now.

"Berika-from-the-edge-of-the-forest—is your curiosity strong enough to learn how the Arrizan War started—how it truly started?"

The girl's eyes went wide as a forest doe's, but trailing a quilt behind her, she crept across the floor to sit near the brazier's fading heat.

"The Arrizi emissaries arrived just after New Year with their emperor's proposal—one of his daughters was to be wedded, bedded, and brought to the straw by a Walensor prince: me. My sons, when I sired them, were to be raised in the empire; they would not return to Walensor until my death, when they would take my throne and take my kingdom into the empire. Dynastic marriage is the easiest way for one nation to conquer another. Still, Vigelan, the king, and the donitors thought the proposal might serve Walensor's immediate interests. The wedding could take place with all deliberate speed, and if Vigelan got his way, there would never be a bedding. It was worth a gamble, truly. I'd do it myself. The princess Arianna's dowry went directly to the treasure rooms except for a hellfire crystal containing her likeness that I was allowed to keep."

He brushed the pouch hanging from his neck where it had hung since the day they gave it to him—a shimmering glimpse of what might have been. He'd lied to Aleg; Arianna was his only friend. He talked with her every night. She blamed him for the war and tortured him. She loved him, because he was all a dead soul had, and tortured him more. He believed her, embracing the guilt, the pain, the passion. After his family, especially Vigelan, he was grateful for the passion, being already accustomed to pain and guilt.

"Arianna was beautiful: flame-red hair, brilliant green eyes, ivory skin. She was fifteen, a woman, and I— I thought I'd escaped the curse. I would go to the Arrizi capital for my wedding, and I would get her with child immediately. I'd return to Walensor with my pregnant bride and the Arrizi army behind me. I imagined Vigelan's face before I had him flayed. I imagined his screams and blood; it was easy: I knew my own so well. Then I was told I was too young to make the nuptial journey. The marriage would be by proxy, celebrated in both countries at the same time. A wedding of conjury and sorcery to coincide with my own. My uncle would raise my wife's veil and place his knee beneath her skirt—"

His hand went white-knuckled around the pouch. He could hear her calling to him, warning him away from these memories which hurt them both so much.

The girl blundered into the silence. "I remember what happened next. Auld Mag was younger then; she was in the Web all the time. You don't have to tell me. The princess Arianna was kidnapped the morning before the wedding was supposed to take place. Her body was never found, but her bloody clothes turned up in your uncle's baggage. All the Walenfolk were condemned and burned. Hazard and the emperor declared war. My father died at Kasserine, with yours."

He silenced her with a glower and a slow stretch of his arm in her direction. His finger fell a handspan short of her breathless face.

"I said I would tell you the truth. If you would hear it, don't interrupt again."

"I'm sorry, midons prince. I won't."

"I begged to go to the empire for the wedding. Vigelan pretended to relent, but the morning we were to leave, he found reason to whip me bloody. I couldn't walk, much less ride. I was left in Eyerlon—as he'd always intended. I raged, then I began to plot. I vowed that I'd shame him as I'd never shamed him before. I became meek and obedient; he grew lax. I was fitted in cloth-of-gold overlaid with gemstones and pearls to wear when the magicians of both lands joined us together. The night before the wedding was to take place I sneaked out of the room Aleg and I shared—I said Vigelan had grown lax. I removed my wedding clothes from the treasury, and destroyed them bit by bit. I dissolved the pearls in wine vinegar. I tore off the gems and threw them down the garderobe. I burnt the cloth and watched as the molten gold disappeared between the hearth stones. I thought ruining my clothes would solve everything. Remember, I was only twelve, and very foolish. I miscalculated the consequences."

"I know about, consequences, midons. My mother taught me. But I never had the opportunity to practice foolishness on such a grand scale."

Forgiving the interruption, he saw her as a person: a common-born girl with a plain, honest face and lively eyes staring back at him, unexpectedly unafraid. He smiled at her, a chancy gesture on a cursed man's face. A mistake, too; she looked away. He continued, wanting, strangely, to tell it all: a combination last-night and birthday-recitation honoring all his dead.

"When Aleg saw what I'd done, he went ratting. He hadn't wanted to, but I made him go, telling him he'd share what I got when Vigelan came, if he didn't go and get Vigelan himself. I *wanted* Vigelan to know. But dawn came and went without Vigelan. The whole morning passed, and no one came after me. I thought I'd won it all—the royal wedding could not happen because a fool prince had ruined his clothes!" He raked his hair over his eyes, fearing they'd reveal his shame-filled thoughts.

"Gods—what a fool. Vigelan came after the midday peal. I remembered being pleased when I saw the whip. If he meant to bloody me, then he didn't need to show me. Then he came after me like never before. I cowered and screamed, wanting it to be over—usually he stopped when I cried; he knew tears hurt me more than the whip. But not that day. He started talking as he worked the whip, careful to keep me conscious until he was finished. He told me what had happened between the strokes:

"Princess Arianna killed herself in my uncle's tent. She was there with her elder brother who wished to know what kind of man his sister had been bartered to. The princess was like you—listening like a mouse while men talked. When my uncle had said enough, she stole the dagger from her brother's belt and plunged it into her heart. Her brother was Hazard and he killed our emissaries—my uncle and a dozen other good men—right then with hellfire. Then he declared a holy war against us.

"We knew as it happened; there were magga communicants in the tent. We burnt the Arrizan delegation on a pyre made from Arianna's dowry—at least we burnt the part that couldn't be melted down and reminted. I came to when the smoke reached my nose. I was in a cell not far from this room. The menders never came, but an old hostler slathered liniments across the wounds until they began to heal. The cell stayed locked through autumn, winter, and spring—"

Locked, but not unvisited. There were some things he couldn't tell this honest, common girl. Arianna knew; she knew all his secrets. Kept them safe and whispered them in their dreams. He was cursed and deserved what she did to him, deserved what Vigelan did to him—not every night, but often enough—while he was chained to the floor of that cell. He'd have no children; that was the price of what Vigelan did, cursing and sweating and clawing the half-healed flesh of his back. It was just as well. He did not want to pass his curse on to children.

"King Manal didn't ask where I was until after Kasserine, when Vigelan was dead and I'd become his heir. I'd healed lame, scarred everywhere, soul and body, inside and out. The king ordered the menders to work miracles upon me. I balked; with the scars I looked as cursed as I've always felt. We compromised and the menders left my back alone. I had the hellfire crystal throughout my imprisonment. No one thought to take it away from me when I was released, so I've kept it to remember *her* and the scars they took away. Every watch of every day, I remind myself that I'm cursed, that the blame falls on me."

The girl shook her head and frowned. "I thought it was my fault, too, when Hirmin caught me and told me not to tell."

She laid a hand on his arm. Usually he could not bear mortal touch except from Aleg when they were brawling. But this girl frightened him no more than he frightened her and he let her hand remain.

"They lied to you," she said. "All of them, whoever they are, they lied to you."

He got no comfort from her words, only denial. He shook his arm, shedding her hand like a fly. "Don't ever touch me and don't presume, with your country-common ignorance, to tell me what's true and what is not."

Her hand shot back to grip his arm tightly. "Midons prince, explain to me why your uncle would say bad things about you *before* you and the princess were married. Was your uncle a godsforsaken idiot?"

He didn't have to answer; didn't have to listen to this mockery of everything he knew to be true, but finally he said: "No—"

"Then he didn't do it. *Nobody* knows what happened in Arrizan. Your father told you lies, midons. If you were country-common and ignorant, like me, you'd have unravelled it by now, and you'd know that there's a Prince Vigelan in every village, usually more than one. If you were ignorant like me, you'd know you weren't cursed, just common. Cathe weeps, midons prince—he would lie and say the Pyromant and your princess were kin, just to make you feel worse—"

"No, that part is true." He'd come perilously close to believing her. Now he'd caught her in an error; everything else she said became untruth, too, and he could return to what he'd always believed. "I knew I would have a brother-by-marriage who was a pyromant—a magga conjurer, if you will, a master of hellfire. Hazard was very important in my futile dreams. The writ of war bears Hazard's seal above his vow to avenge his sister's murder. I can read Arrizi; I know it's there. As to the rest, I find it easier to believe Arianna killed herself because of me than to believe that my uncle murdered her and left her body for the wolves—"

The brazier gave off negligible heat. The girl began to shiver again; her voice, however, remained steady. "Of course, if you're cursed-special by the gods, everything *has* to be your fault. Princes get cursed by the gods. Country-common boys get beat all the time, but they're not cursed. I guess the Arrizi didn't know the easiest way to conquer a nation is—what did you call it?—dynastic marriage? I guess the Arrizi thought the easiest way to conquer a country is to conjure up a princess, make her disappear, and then declare a holy war. Is there anyone alive who ever saw—"

Rinchen could not—*would not*—endure this. He backhanded her viciously, without warning. He'd busted her lip; blood trickled down. He'd hurt her, as he always hurt anything that got too close. His curse: unloved, unloving . . . deadly, especially when he forgot that he was not like other men. He was ashamed—ashamed of what he'd done, ashamed of what he wanted to do: take her in his arms, kiss away the pain and blood.

Berika cringed when he rose from his chair and lifted her to her feet.

"I hurt you—"

The girl wiped her bleeding lip on her sleeve. "Please don't say you're sorry, midons. You're cursed; I must be cursed, too—how else does a shepherd dare to scold a prince? How else does she wind up in a wolf's lair?"

She thought she'd shocked him; she had. She thought she could free herself; she did. She bolted for the door; but he was faster than she'd ever hoped to be. He wrapped her in an embrace as gentle as he could make it, pressed his lips against hers, tasting the blood. His heart was on fire and his mind echoed with the vows of himself and Arianna which he'd broken by trying to remove the pain he'd caused. She moved within his arms. He gambled that she understood and held her tighter until she was pounding on his ribs. He raised his head, going dizzy and distracted.

"Take it off," Berika gasped, pointing at the pouch with a trembling finger. She didn't know much about hellfire crystals but she knew where one was and that it was evil. "By all the gods awake and asleep—take that thing from around your neck!" Berika could hear the music of the Web pulsing in her ears. When the prince didn't move, she pulled the Web down without thinking and focused her *basi*. "Please, midons prince," she begged, "take it off before it kills you."

The Wolf was headblind, but he was not deaf and he was not immune to sorcery. He lifted the thong over his head. The hellfire crystal swung free. Never taking his eyes from Berika's face, he let the thong and its pendant pouch fall in the sand surrounding the brazier.

Berika lowered her arm and released the Web. Without Brightwater silver or some other touchstone to modulate the reflux, Berika's overreaching sorcery left her nauseous and faint. The Wolf caught her as she fell.

"May I ask what that was all about?" The tone was cold, but not threatening.

Gingerly Berika pushed back her sleeve. Her forearm was scaled and blistering. "Hellfire, midons prince. Didn't you feel it?"

Prince Rinchen shook his head. "Hellfire crystal is like Brightwater silver—except it's clear, and this one has a little image of a red-haired girl. I've stood in the Cascade while I wore it—there's nothing dangerous about it. I'll show you—"

The prince bent over the sand box. A spark singed his fingers.

"Nothing dangerous . . ." Berika muttered.

"It was a coal from the brazier." But he was more cautious the second time he reached for it. There were no more sparks, but a wisp of smoke emerged from the pouch once the knot was loosened. He dropped it back in the sand.

"Reach for the Web again, *merou,*" Prince Rinchen said calmly, forcing her behind him as more smoke seeped out of the pouch. "First, tell the communicant we have learned that Hazard survived Tremontin. Then tell him to get everyone out of the Web until after dawn."

"Why—?"

"Do it, *merou*!"

Smoke thickened around the rafters. It began to glow with hot color. Berika saw two eyes form, a nose, then a mouth—a woman's face, young and beautiful. Arianna. Hazard's sister.

"I can't."

"Don't look," the prince chided with remarkable calm and gentleness as they retreated across the room. "Close your eyes and talk to the spider."

"I—"

"You can."

They were against the bed. The Wolf reached down and withdrew a sword from its hiding place within the bed frame. The smoke hissed like a nest of snakes when he raised the weapon. Berika climbed onto the bed as the prince advanced toward the apparition writhing above the brazier. A tongue of hissing flame flicked toward the sword and withdrew without touching it. She couldn't hear the Web's music; she gathered her courage and her *basi,* just the same. Another tongue of flame leapt from the creature's mouth. Seething orange and magenta, it spiraled down the blade. The Wolf slashed downward, severing the coil from its source. He gave his wailing war-cry and thrust the sword between Arianna's smoldering eyes.

As she had done so many times in the fields beyond Gorse, Berika sent her *basi* leaping out of her mind. She caught the Web on her way down. The sorcerers of Walensor were in a panic. No one noticed an untrained woman clinging to the Web. She waited as long as she could, then let herself fall back into her body.

Prince Rinchen's sword was black and jagged where it had tangled with hellfire. The conjured creature wearing Arianna's face was undiminished. It was clear, even to an untrained observer like herself, that a sword was no threat to Arianna. The Wolf's speed had protected him thus far, but when he tired he would be doomed. There was one sword that might be potent against hellfire conjury—Dart's wooden sword—but it was locked away in the sorMeklan residence.

The prince circled until he was facing Berika and the creature was not.

"Get out, *merou,* while you can."

Berika climbed off the bed. She could see the brazier and the malevolent crystal throbbing in the sand beside it. She froze.

"The crystal! Shatter the crystal."

The prince tried, and lost the tip of his sword in the attempt. He struggled to beat back a fresh surge of attacks. Hellfire wrapped around him. It left a wide, oozing weal across his ribs.

"Wrong weapon," he shouted. "Throw me your silver."

Berika's heart sank. He thought she was a trained sorcerer. "I don't have any."

The Wolf dodged another sulphurous onslaught. He was tiring and barely avoided the next tongue of hellfire. "Get the jug." He feinted recklessly to show her where it sat.

Brightwater would have been perfect. Brightwater brandy might have worked, too—the better varieties were cut with real Brightwater. Berika didn't think blackhead firewater was going to help at all, but she'd already decided she wasn't running away, so she got the jug.

"You'll have to do it," the prince told her when he saw that she had the jug in her hands. "I'll hold her attention while you pour it over the crystal."

Berika was terrified, but the prince was right and there was no other hope. He kept his word, drawing the apparition's attention with doomed attacks as Berika crept to the sand box. The smell of singed flesh mingled with sulphurous hellfire.

"I'm ready—"

"Turn your head away. Protect yourself."

She couldn't, not if she wanted to be certain the liquor fell directly on the crystal. But cursed or not, the Wolf had compassion for the commonfolk pawns he sacrificed, and that, in the moment before she upended the jug, made the sacrifice worthwhile.

Shimya'an firewater splashed over the crystal.

Berika heard a shriek, her own, and an explosion. She felt herself sail across the room and smash against the wall. Then she felt nothing at all.

* * *

A fifteen-year-old girl was dying, naked, on a champion's bed in the besieged Palestra. Dart had gathered her crumpled body in his arms as soon as Weycha's forest sorcery freed him. She'd moaned when he straightened her slender, hellfire-streaked limbs, but that was her body talking. Her mind was locked away in unconsciousness where, he prayed, it would remain. He covered her with a light blanket, then replaced his hellfire-tainted clothes with the warmest garments in his clothespress.

If Weycha's wild forest sorcery could counter hellfire, Dart reckoned it could counter the bit of webwork warding his doorway as well. Arianna had gone to the palace to lay claim to a tortured young man who—sad truth to tell—could hardly be expected to hold out against her. Tomorrow morning, if it came, that same young man would take Weycha's gifts out of Ean sorMeklan's hand. The harp sang with Weycha's voice, her very intimate gift to him. Its sorcery worked in no hands but his own. But the wooden sword was simply a weapon. Anyone could wield it. The Wolf could wield it against Hazard, as he himself intended. Or against Weycha herself; his lady was not proof against the sword she had created. Or against Weycha's champion, and he'd have no defense at all.

Tonight Weycha's gifts were under wards at the sorMeklan residence, and he'd walk through hellfire, if necessary, to retrieve them. Dart was looking for the boots he'd worn to the palace, when a sound as loud as thunder shattered the night. He ran to the open window, expecting to see something awful—flames or hellfire licking at the Basilica dome. But there was only midnight silence and the shimmering of the northern lights.

Perhaps Arianna had lied about Hazard riding ten thousand enraged souls from Tremontin to Eyerlon. For Rinchen's sake he'd like to believe everything she'd said was deceit and falsehood. But it seemed more likely that she'd told the truth from start to finish, especially when, while he watched, a ruddy glow began to stain the heavenly lights in the northeast, where Tremontin lay.

Dart turned away from the window. He had to get to the sorMeklan residence, had to find a way back to Weychawood. His boots were beside the chair. He'd taken one step toward them, when the bed creaked and the dying girl sat up.

"Ash?" Dart whispered; he'd never learned the name she'd been born with.

Not Ash. Her eyes opened with the same color as the hellfire doom burning down from Tremontin. Arianna. More hellfire spewed from her mouth when she opened it. There was an unnatural roar and, of course, the sulphurous stench, but no words. Black lesions opened across her skin, changing quickly to hell-fire's lurid orange, magenta, and green.

Dart couldn't tell if Arianna was aware of him or anything else. He thought the lesions might be wounds—they were very straight—and that she was healing herself with hellfire. Before she'd abandoned Ash's wounded body; now she was consuming it. Transforming it might be a better description: The hellfire blotches simply spread without returning to flesh. Nerves tingled at the base of Dart's skull. Weycha's way of telling him the transformation should not continue.

All Dart had was his bare hands and a fruit knife. Still, her hellfire-pit eyes had not seemed to notice him and Weycha's imperatives were very strong. He put his hand on the knife sheath looped around his belt—

And found himself shrouded in hellfire that squeezed tighter and tighter until he could feel bones breaking and muscles bursting. Seductive voices called upon him to surrender or be crushed. Dart did surrender, but not to Arianna. Weycha's sorcery took command of his body as his mind sought cool shelter in unconsciousness.

Chapter Fifteen

Prince Alegshorn was one of the gods' fortunate creatures who slept soundly every night with pleasant dreams, and awoke in complete command of his senses—even when he had no notion of what had awakened him.

His bedchamber was dark, silent, and utterly still. The door between it and his hall was shut and bolted from the inside; no untoward sound came through it. There were no drafts around his head, as there would have been if the passage door to the Wolf's lair had been sprung. His brother wasn't the sort who retaliated for the nerve-racking jest he'd played earlier in the evening. Aleg knew better than anyone that the Wolf was a killer, never a prankster. If Rinchen ever wanted him dead, he wouldn't know what got him.

Nonetheless, Aleg slid his hand quietly beneath the feather mattress, withdrawing a parrying dagger from the ropes of the bed frame. He whispered his brother's name.

The answer was the slow rumble of distant thunder, which was common enough in summer but virtually unknown in winter. As the prince sat up, bells began to toll. The bells of the palace watchtower rang first and loudest, then the distinctive tones of the residence bells throughout the city. They rang repeatedly, without rhythm; their very chaos conveyed an inescapable message: Eyerlon was under attack.

Still holding his dagger, Prince Aleg entered his hall. The outer doors were open; torchlight cast shadows across the anxious faces of his men. The prince took command, as he'd been taught.

"Braydon—" Berika's brother had remained in the hall; he slept in his cloak beside the hearth. "Rekindle the fire. We need light and heat. You two at the door: one to the throne hall, the other to the watchtower. Find out what's happening."

"It's the Web, midons prince," a torch-bearing guard responded. "Can't you hear it in your head?"

Prince Aleg lowered his dagger. He was Severed but his commonborn men were not. Unless they were headblind, like Braydon, their *basi* was intact. Aleg absolutely could not imagine what they heard, but he guessed the cause:

Hazard, he said to himself, thinking of Jeliff's message. *Godswill.* He unshuttered the nearest window.

The deadwatch sky was a rippling crimson curtain, shot with the brilliant metallic colors of hellfire. The prince was enthralled by the Web's beauty, besieged or not. His men gathered behind him, gasping with horror and awe. A clap of thunder shook the hall. Green flames erupted from the Basilica dome. Prince Aleg placed his hands on the shoulders of the two torchbearers.

"To the throne hall." He shoved the man under his right hand. "The watchtower and the barracks," he ordered the other.

The second man resisted. "Midons prince—I can hear screams and the roar of flames between my ears. It's terrible; I can't make it stop." His face was tight. "What's happening, midons prince? What will become of us?"

He pointed at the door. "I don't know what will become of *me*, but you'll be standing deadwatch forever if you don't get moving."

Aleg *was* a prince. He gave orders whether he was clad in armor, brocade, or an ample linen shirt whose lacy hem brushed the top of his thighs. That single strong belief in himself made his absurd threats more real than hellfire. The guard, anxious no longer, hurried from the hall without a backward glance. Aleg turned to Braydon, who had rekindled the hearth.

"Never thought you'd be grateful you were headblind, did you, Egg?"

Braydon lit a torch before standing up. "No, midons prince. I never thought about it at all. Midons prince, is it truly Hazard? Has he found some way to attack the Web?"

"That's hellfire, Egg," Aleg said, gesturing toward the window with a calm that surprised even him. "Once you've seen it, you never forget it, no matter how empty the space between your ears. You served; you saw men whose skin shimmered like that. You don't need to be a bloody spook and you don't have to know how the Pyromant does it. It's hellfire and it's the enemy. That's all that matters. Shutter it and help me get dressed."

Braydon obeyed the first of the two orders, slowly. By the time he entered the bedchamber, Aleg had shrugged a mail shirt over his linen and was wrestling with a brocade dalmatic. Braydon proceeded to light two lamps with meticulous care before placing the torch in an iron sconce beside the door, adjusting it once, twice . . . and a gods-be-damned *third* time.

"I asked for a hand, Egg."

Braydon came, but with a lack of enthusiasm that fell close enough to insolence to justify a taste of the whip. But insolence wasn't Egg's way and Aleg knew it.

"You're brewing gall in your gut. Go on and spit it out—at me or the floor. It's no shame to be afraid."

"It seems a poor time to be worrying about your clothes, midons prince. Hazard's in the Web. There's no guessing what else has happened, or what could happen, and you're wasting time getting dressed in your finest clothes. You're a prince of Walensor. There must be something more important for you to do."

Aleg shed his charm consciously, transforming himself into a man who was clearly the Wolf's brother and the king's grandson. "Yes, Braydon, I'm a prince of Walensor. I might even be *the* crown prince, heir to my misbegotten brother's throne. Had you thought of that? Our grandfather lives by grace of Brightwater. You're right: I don't know what has happened, or what will happen. The only useful thing I learned directly from Vigelan was to always dress as if I might be king by sundown. But whether I'm king, crown prince, or prince-in-waiting, as I've always been, this is the first day of Greater Ice, New Year's Day—or it will be once the sun rises. If the gods will, I expect to walk to the Basilica at noon with my brothers, sisters, mother, aunt, and assorted cousins to stand under the Cascade until I'm as blue as this cloth.

"You know and I know that it makes no difference; the new year starts no matter what royalty does, but Walensor feels secure when the spiders tell them that all the rituals have been precisely observed. Now, give me a hand with my gods-be-damned boots."

"As you wish, midons prince." Braydon dropped to his knees and held one tall black boot at the proper angle.

"You do know that it doesn't make any difference, don't you, Egg?"

"Yes, midons."

Braydon pulled up on the boot straps while the prince pushed. Aleg was not convinced by Braydon's absent-minded answer. He stamped his booted foot on the floor and paused before lifting his other foot.

"Calends is just the wobbly part of the year between the shortest day of Lesser Winter and first moonlight of Greater Ice, Egg. The spooks have Calends measured until the end of time, I think. They measure it without gods or sorcery, only a bit of webwork."

"If you say so, midons prince."

"It's not what I say, Egg, it's what *is*. The sun rises, the seasons change, folk are born and die, and it has nothing to do with the gods, sorcery, *or* conjury."

He stamped into the second boot, watching closely as his country-common man grappled with words that crossed the line into blasphemy, even heresy. After worrying a handful of whiskers from his beard, Braydon raised his head.

"How do you know this, midons prince?"

"All that my brother said earlier is true. At least five nights a week—since he took my oath and when we are in Eyerlon—I hie myself along that passageway to his lair. He tells me what I need to know, I tell him the same, and then he tells me what he's been thinking about. All men know the Wolf is not like them, Egg; they think they know his curse and judge him accordingly. But ordinary men, like you and me, are content to know that the sun rises in the East; *he* needs to know why. He bandages himself up like a hellfired veteran and goes to afternoon lectures at the Palestra. He argues with the maggas: natural philosophy—moral philosophy, too, I guess. He says they laugh at him because they can't defeat him. They're fools, Egg, our maggas are fools. If the Wolf says there are limits to sorcery, you can bet on his words and win.

"Now, hand me my sword and chain."

Braydon's mouth worked silently. There was a question tickling his tongue; Aleg could see it—and would have answered it, whatever it was, had it emerged. But the man swallowed hard and obeyed his orders. When the sword belt was buckled around his hips and the heavy gold chain of office draped around his neck, Aleg judged himself ready to face catastrophe. "Tuck that in your belt"—he gestured at the parrying dagger he'd left atop his bed—"grab the torch and follow me."

Before they left the hall, a quartet of armed men wearing the king's colors, scarlet and gold, accosted them.

"Midons Prince Alegshorn, you're commanded to the chancery

hall," the foremost of the quartet announced. He and his companions pounced their pennoned spears against the floor, emphasizing their proxy right to command a royal family member.

"By whom?" Aleg challenged, retreating a half-step and fingering the hilt of his sword. "Who sits in the throne?"

"No one," the messenger confessed, losing his composure. "King Manal . . . The king . . . He's . . ."

"Dead?"

The messenger shook his head. "He lives, or did when we left, midons prince, but it's awful in the throne hall. The throne's all busted up. The Brightwater's sour. The magga menders . . ." He made a grim, awed face and shook his head again. "Midons dowager issues commands from the chancery."

"My mother? Who is with her? The Wolf? Has he shown his face? Has anyone gone to fetch him?" Aleg put venom in his voice and cast a wary glance at Braydon. Both he and the Wolf had measured the assart shepherd. They'd planned to make him one of the small handful of men and women who knew the truth—but they hadn't planned to do it the way it happened. Until the Wolf was secure on his throne, their hostile rivalry had to be real enough to fool the Web.

Godswill. The Web.

Braydon avAlegshorn had to play his part; he had to find it first, and by himself. The princes had learned the hard way that *telling* a man how to keep a secret, and a false-face, guaranteed he wouldn't be able to do it in a crisis.

Confusion showed in Braydon's eyes, then vanished. They'd measured him correctly, and Aleg relaxed muscles he hadn't realized were tense. He gave his attention back to the king's man.

"Begging your leave, midons prince, Princess Janna summons neither you nor the Wolf. The Merrisati emissaries surround her and advise her. She's sent us and others to pack everything valuable and movable. The dowager pays no heed to our king, who is neither dead nor alive. We've come here on our own, midons prince. We are the king's men. If he cannot command us, we turn to you, midons Prince Alegshorn. Give us your orders, midons. You're the one we trust, not the Wolf or the lady. Command us, midons Prince Alegshorn; seize the crown before it falls into treacherous hands. We beg you."

The scarlet-clad guard dropped to one knee. He laid down his spear, touched his forehead to his bent knee, and held his hands palms-up.

Suddenly, Aleg doubted his own measure. He'd spun myriad

threads between himself and the moment when King Manal's throne became vacant, but never a thread colored with Hazard and hellfire. Never a thread that did not circle his brother before it circled him. The oath he'd given Rinchen had been sworn over a plain, sharp knife. His conscience maintained it; his conscience could absolve him, if he broke it. The throne was his for the taking— For a price.

Silence grew. Doubts grew in himself and in the men around him. Aleg knew what he wanted, but he didn't know the way.

"Midons prince?" Braydon interrupted. "Was it not your father who said that you must always be dressed as if you would be king by sundown? Forgive me, midons, but your hair stands like unreaped straw, not fitting for a king's crown. A few moments in your bedchamber, midons prince, and you will be ready for a crown."

The way shined, clear and bright. "Absolutely. Absolutely right, Egg." Then he bade the king's man to rise. "Return to the throne hall. Our beloved king must not be left alone, unguarded and unhonored. I will not take your oath until I see my grandfather dead with my own eyes, but I will give you these orders: Defend the crown and the scepter with your lives; they must not be taken from the king's side. These are your only orders. They cannot be changed or overturned, not by the Wolf, not by the dowager, and especially not by her Merrisati shadows. I will come to the chancery to claim what's mine. Now go and obey."

Fortified by straightforward commands, the men in scarlet and gold filed out of the hall. When they were gone, Aleg retreated to his bedchamber, followed by Braydon, who shut the one door behind him and walked directly to the panel door.

"What should I say to midons prince, your brother?"

There was doubt all over the common man's face, trying to hide beneath a shell of courage and confidence. Aleg smiled at him—not the brash grin that served so many other purposes, but a softer, warmer one to melt an honest man's doubt.

"That we must enter the chancery hall together, of course. I didn't lose faith, Braydon—I give you my word on that—I only lost the way until you found it for me again. But until my brother and I are seen together, I can't be seen visiting him. You will sweep the public path to his hall, in case he's coming here himself, although I hold that unlikely. More likely the Pennaikmen will intercept you. Show them your silver when they do, and ask to speak to Arkkin."

"What should I tell Arkkin, midons prince?"

"That I've gone where I belong. I'll wager my brother's stewing in his chair, waiting for me to come through the wall so he can tell me what we're going to do. I'll fetch you when we've gotten everything thrashed out."

Thinking all was settled, Aleg started for the panel door, but Braydon held his ground.

"Midons prince—?" he asked tentatively. "Is the Wolf a good man, or a cursed one?"

Aleg eased around his man, blindly opening the panel. It was not an easy question; gods knew, he'd pondered it all his life. It deserved an answer. "He's cursed, Braydon; doubly cursed. I'd've surrendered. I'd've become a man just like Vigelan. The gods know, Vigelan taught us both to hate and rage. But Rinchen . . . ? Rinchen is different. There's something deep inside him, lonely and cold, but it keeps him pure. He does not love; doesn't dare, but he doesn't hate, either. The Wolf kills without remorse, but he doesn't hurt. I can't measure him with 'good' or 'evil.' There's only the curse he believes in. He's my brother. I was meant to kill him; I'd sooner kill myself instead."

"But can you trust him, midons prince? Can we?"

"I trust my brother as I trust each day to start with sunrise and end with sunset."

Braydon's mouth worked silently with his mind. Aleg willed himself to patience until the man understood.

"The length of the day between sunrise and sunset is longer in summer than it is in winter. You trust the Wolf, but you trust him to different lengths at different times?"

"You're learning fast, Braydon avAlegshorn." This time he smiled his brashest, most mischievous grin. "There's a good future for you, if we both survive."

Aleg ran along the narrow corridor. Night upon night of stealthy passage to the Wolf's lair had taught him which planks were firm and what stride would take him silently from one to the next. He and Rinchen discovered the backway maze through the old palace when they were boys, but Rinchen alone had untangled it during the war years while they were cut off from each other. Despite its location in an out-of-the-way roof corner of the palace, the Wolf's lair was the center of the backway warren. His own hall—which Rinchen had chosen for him—was directly passaged to the lair and a damned long hike through public passages.

Neither of them knew who built the backways, although they

could guess the reasons why. Theirs could not be the first clandestine alliance to mold their kingdom's history.

The clamor of bells came faintly through the walls. The frantic clanging of the residence bells continued unabated, but the palace bells went abruptly silent. Despite the need to reach Rinchen's lair, Aleg paused beside an outer wall and put his ear against the stone. He listened closely for a sound that had not been heard in his lifetime: the muffled sound of great Behemoth ringing alone, her man-high clapper bound in sheepskin to mourn the death of a king.

The one-note peal began; King Manal sorRodion's deathwatch had begun. Aleg's breath caught in his throat. He couldn't think of the consequences until he'd found his brother. The worn, spiraled steps to the lair were in sight when, amid the bronze cacophony, he heard a man's agonized scream. It came from the top of the stairs he took two at a time, wrestling his sword out of its scabbard along the way. He hit the panel brute-force with his shoulder. The door popped off its hinges. Aleg burst into the Wolf's lair sword-first.

Shimmering red light seeped through the shutters, defining the chamber without illuminating it. The ever-present, ever-changing clutter was part of the lair's defense; no one, including Aleg himself, could cross the floor without stumbling over something. He took one cautious stride. His boots crunched on the floor planks, as if the wood had been layered with sand or cinders. He took a breath. The chamber reeked of hellfire. The bells drowned all other sounds, but a sense more subtle than hearing or sight told him that he wasn't alone.

"Rinchen?" he whispered urgently, warding the malodorous darkness with his sword. "Rinchen?"

Something rustled in the far corner. He crouched behind his weapon, too wary to swallow or breathe. After asking himself what was happening, his thoughts threw back the answers; *Hellfire. Hazard. Here.* He'd heard thunder, and the king's guards had told him that the throne had burst apart. But the king hadn't brought Tremontin down on the imperial army. If Hazard lived, surely Hazard knew the Wolf was his most potent enemy in Walensor.

Aleg swallowed the lump in his throat. There must have been two thunderclaps: the one that he'd heard from his hall, and an earlier one, unremembered now, which had awakened him. And now there had been a scream. Hellfire made a man scream.

"Rinchen?"

Mindful of the clutter, he eased his foot forward through the crunching cinders. He thought he heard moaning as well. He took another cautious step. A heavy hand clamped over his weapon-side shoulder, and a steel blade pressed against his throat.

"Lower it," a Pennaik accent commanded.

He dropped the sword altogether, and the choking pressure eased. Sparks flashed and a pool of lantern light revealed the Wolf slumped across the charred, broken remains of his chair. The Pennaik shaman, Arkkin, hovered nearby. Damp linen covered half of his brother's face. It stretched over his heart and flank. Arkkin tipped his head; Aleg was free.

"Is he . . . alive?" he asked in Pennaik. Rinchen spoke Pennaik as if he'd been born in a horsehide tent; he swore the consciously ambiguous tongue was the language of his dreams. Perhaps it was. Despite years of effort, Aleg knew *he* spoke it worse than a milk-tooth toddler.

Usually Arkkin wasted no opportunity to mock his clumsiness; this time he merely frowned. A sound of horror and loss forced its way through Aleg's clenched teeth, but he denied the urge to do more, bitterly aware how unwelcome any affectionate or concerned display would be. He looked away, distracting himself with the details of the ruined chamber.

Sand and cinders were everywhere. The brazier box was a patch of charcoal splinters, the brazier itself a torn and twisted mass of metal. Across it lay a corroded, shortened sword. Aleg picked it up and ran his thumbnail along the pitted edge. Flakes of rotten steel came loose. A bead of amber hellfire glared briefly.

It took a rare breed of courage to face hellfire armed only with steel. Aleg set the ruined weapon carefully aside. Godswill, if Rinchen died, he'd never part with that sword.

"He made a fight of it," he said, though the Pennaikman ignored him. "Hazard hasn't beaten us yet."

The shepherd girl, Braydon's sister, was bundled in the Wolf's bed. One arm was above the quilts and blankets. A thick, meat-colored scab covered her forearm from wrist to elbow. Aleg deduced his brother must have been conscious after the battle; without Rinchen's direct command, Arkkin never would have mended a woman's injuries first.

Hellfire wasn't mere fire. It ate through a man's flesh and then it got into his blood. Once hellfire was in a man's blood there was nothing a mender could do except to prolong his agony or grant him a swift death. Aleg thought of the Wolf standing back while the girl was mended, while hellfire ate his flesh. He cursed softly.

His brother had chosen a gods-be-damned poor moment to discover gallantry.

Arkkin agreed. "Wasted a fight," he muttered, spitting at the remains of the brazier.

The cloth was almost dry. Arkkin peeled it away delicately; even so, the Wolf's body went rigid and a groan escaped through his taut lips. His arm flailed in a feeble, half-conscious effort to push the shaman away. Aleg snared it easily—and catching the Wolf had never been easy. Holding his breath, he watched as Arkkin uncovered the hellfire wound.

A malevolent weal traversed Rinchen's cheek and neck. It crossed his ribs above his heart before curling to an end on his flank. A thick scab—the mender's hallmark—solidified quickly over the lower half of the serpentine wound, but the upper portion remained dark. Rinchen's ice eyes fluttered open. The pupils widened and a tremor raced down the arm that Aleg held.

All three of them understood that hellfire circulated through Rinchen's veins.

Arkkin spoke first: "I will sacrifice a stallion and purify its blood with salt. We will try again tonight, my lord, when the moon first rises. If you had listened to me—"

"It was my choice," the Wolf snarled. He freed his wrist without acknowledging who held it. "She saved my life. If the king can live without his lower half"—he straightened himself in the broken chair—"I can live with a little hellfire." Rinchen tried to turn his head. He winced and rotated his whole body instead. "Jeliff's warning came too late. Hazard found a way to usurp the Web."

"He used the souls of his dead," Arkkin added.

A sour taste filled Aleg's mouth. "Necromancy?"

Walenfolk remembered their dead and sometimes honored them, but they rigorously excluded their dead from sorcery. Necromancy, the magical discipline which harnessed the essence of death as sorcery harnessed *basi*, the essence of life, filled gods-fearing, Compact-abiding Walenfolk with reflexive loathing. Prince Aleg held himself a properly gods-fearing man.

"I don't believe it. Necromancy is anathema; the dead can't reach the Web—"

Arkkin spat a second time. "Fools. White-livered fools. You get what you deserve." He walked away with the linen cloth, gesturing emphatically and muttering to spirits only he could see. He took a long pull from a shimya'an jug, then confronted his hellfired prince. "If you trust him so much, why haven't you told him the truth?"

"What truth?" Aleg demanded, looking from Arkkin to his brother.

Rinchen sighed and with obvious effort explained: "The Web *is* souls, Aleg. All our souls, forever. It's what happens when folk die beneath the Web—It's what happens when the likes of you and me were Severed. Our souls always belong to the Web, never to us. But when sorcerers die, they take their memories with them. They live on in the Web forever."

"Godswill— Where did you learn these things?" Foolish words; he knew the answer to that question.

"No gods," Arkkin interrupted. "Only twice-damned fools thinking they could cheat death. Thinking that they could become immortal. Not even gods are immortal."

"I asked questions," Rinchen said softly, careful of the eroding flesh near his mouth. "I thought about what was missing from the answers I got. And I remembered what it was like before I was Severed, and after."

"Rinchen, they Severed you the day after you were born. It was New Year's Day—just like today." They'd had this discussion before. "There were a hundred witnesses. They all swore the Brightwater ran red around you. Nobody remembers what happened the day they were born. Not even you. You're just another headblind dolt, like the rest of us."

"Headblind now, but not the day I was born. I know what Hazard wants from the Web. Every spook in Walensor does."

Aleg narrowed his eyes. There was one exception to the Severance ritual: If a noble child was born with manifest *basi*, it was whisked away to the Palestra, fostered among the sorcerers, and forbidden to inherit noble—royal—power. It had always seemed to him that if Rinchen's *basi* had been manifest, Vigelan's problems would have been immediately solved. If a prince wasn't Severed, he couldn't become king. It was as plain and simple as that beneath the Web of Walensor. Rinchen had been Severed, therefore Rinchen's *basi* could not have been manifest.

"If you weren't born spook-ish, how *were* you born . . . ?" he whispered.

"Cursed. The maggas didn't want me either."

"Could you—?" Aleg asked, then added, even more hesitantly: "Would you?"

The Wolf shrugged, and cringed from the pain he inflicted on himself. Aleg took his brother's hand again, hoping he could get away with it. The supreme irony was that the Wolf hurt more easily than most men . . . most boys. You learned such things about a brother when you lived together, fought together, slept together for the first twelve years of your life, and you trusted your gut when it told you that a brother hadn't changed. Rinchen couldn't ride over pain the way he could; Rinchen had to go through it, under it, bear its weight on his back.

Aleg squeezed the hand he held and, miraculously, it squeezed weakly back.

"The Brightwater ran red, Aleg. Maybe if I lived as long as Grandfather—"

"Grandfather!" The moment shattered. Aleg lifted both hands to push his hair off his forehead. "Godswill! The king's men came to me, saying the throne was blasted. Hazard attacked you both. Grandfather's dying; listen to the bell."

Rinchen closed his eyes, listened, and heard. His eyes remained closed. "They didn't come to me. Maybe they thought I was already dead."

There was no surprise in the Wolf's voice, only a trace of bitterness and a world of despair. A sickly green bead of hellfire appeared on his blackened cheek. Aleg averted his eyes.

"It's time," he said, thick and awkward. "The king neither reigns nor rules. We go down together, or I—I can go down alone."

The Wolf rose slowly out of his chair. "Then hellfire or no, we go together. It is my right, brother. I hold you to your oath."

Aleg looked up in time to see another hellfire bead lengthen and submerge. "You can't," he said, fighting tears. "Godswill, Rinchen, you can't. It's too much, even for you. I can stall for a day. It's not about oaths, Rinchen."

"You said it yourself: The king neither reigns nor rules."

The Wolf rummaged one-handedly through a heap of clothing, selecting an old, loose shirt and shaking out the cinder-sand. Arkkin pulled the garment out of his hand.

"Listen to him, my lord. If you don't rest, you'll be dead by sundown."

"I'll die King of Walensor."

It was, Aleg thought, the first time Arkkin had agreed with him. Too bad he was going to change his mind. He snagged another shirt from the chaos and draped it across Rinchen's hand. If the Wolf wanted Walensor's blasted throne while Hazard ruled the Web, he wouldn't have his younger brother standing in his way.

Arkkin larded them both with Pennaik epithets that defied

translation. He also bandaged Prince Rinchen's ribs and helped him dress. The hellfire weal burned with malevolent color before they were done. Aleg found Vigelan's coronet in a battered kettle. He settled it on Rinchen's brow, but metal crossed the weal. Blinded by pain, Rinchen threw it to the floor. Aleg picked it up as it rolled past his foot.

"Leave it," the Wolf commanded in a voice as ominous as his throbbing face.

Aleg offered the hollow circle before him, inviting his brother to hold the other side. "If the Web is filled with dead souls, as you say, then may the gods, or Hazard, grant that Vigelan sees us share his crown."

The Wolf grinned with the unmaimed half of his face. "May they grant it, indeed."

He took his half of the crown.

Chapter Sixteen

Ean ruEan sorMeklan paced the hearthstones of his lower hall: seven strides in one direction, seven in the other. The Severed Donitor of Fenklare knew less about the catastrophe in the skies than the dirtiest beggar. He'd dispatched partisans and kinfolk throughout the residence and deep into the city. Ignorance made him frantic and ill-tempered, like a young husband banished from his bedchamber while his wife gave birth.

Drina's screams had been no harder to endure than the relentless clanging of Eyerlon's bells, including, of course, the sorMeklan bell. The bells served no good purpose. Although the Web and the sorcerers were obviously besieged, there was no tangible danger to anyone else. The Basilica was shrouded in towering, unnatural flames, but it was the only building so engulfed and Ean knew by harsh experience how little ordinary folk could do against hellfire. He could have silenced the sorMeklan bell, but he would not, nor would his counterparts in the other residences. The brazen clanging, like his own pacing, was a desperate defiance of impotence.

In addition to the bell-born headache, he endured the discomfort of two quilted wool layers beneath a mail shirt that absorbed the heat of the hearth beside him. He had not been in his residence when the conflagration erupted, but with his only son, wandering the river front, looking for bodies and the centerpiece of the clan regalia.

He and Dris had found two corpses, stripped of everything valuable, in a derelict courtyard. One was Killeen barKethmarion, the sorMeklan ward—any other time explaining that boy's death to his adoring kin would be the most troublesome thought in Ean's mind, but without the Web to convey the message, that concern was irrelevant. The other corpse bore the distinctive torso tattoos of a Kufique assassin. Dris had expected to find two additional bodies: shepherds from an assart village in far Fenklare, and the spear.

When his son came scratching on his bedchamber door in the waning hour of nightwatch, confessing to his river front escapade, Ean had been strongly tempted to beat the boy senseless. Now, in the depths of deadwatch, he was glad he'd resisted the temptation. No beating could have hurt Dris more than the sight of Killy stretched across the garbage. He'd stood well aside while his son struggled to wrap his cloak around that stiff-frozen, naked corpse, letting the enormity of folly burn deep into Dris's conscience.

They had no sooner hoisted the body between them when the sky erupted with hellfire, and he'd become doubly grateful for his earlier restraint. Even a Severed man could see that no one was going to get their bruises mended for a while.

By the time they'd wrestled the corpse to the residence, clouds were hiding the hellfire in the sky. Whatever was happening in the Web, Ean believed that Walensor's sorcerers were getting the worst of it, but he kept his judgment private. He sent his eyes and ears into the night and kept his son with him in the lower hall.

Driskolt sat in a corner, empty-eyed and unmoving. Ean wasn't blind to his son's anguish. The regalia was important; a ward's life was more important; a friend's life was most important. Endangering them—*losing* them—was unpardonable. He couldn't forgive his son. Donitors, and those who would become donitors, inevitably made mistakes that were unpardonable. They each had to find and follow the treacherous path through responsibility and despair; otherwise they lost their souls in darkness. He'd learned his lesson years ago, when he'd nearly killed his younger brother in a sword brawl—that same brother who'd drunk himself to death a few years later and was now resurrected.

Ean racked his memory for words that would help Dris find the sword's-edge path a noble conscience must tread, if it would survive. "We'll find them," he said, running fingers through hair that matched his own. "That assart shepherd and our spear. Her hedge-sorcery won't help her now. There will be justice, and vengeance."

The boy raised his head, anguish floating in tear-filled eyes. Ean waited, but his son's chin sank without a word.

Driskolt couldn't think about justice or vengeance, not when he hadn't told his father everything about the debacle. He couldn't guess what had brought the Wolf to the courtyard. A lifelong and unquestioning hatred of Aleg's brother urged him to blame everything on the cursed prince: the escape of Berika and her brother, the loss of Rodion's spear, and, especially, Killy's dishonored death through an assassin's poison. Surely Prince Rinchen had played *some* role; no one was in that courtyard by happenstance. Including himself—and he'd brought Killeen. To make a man of him, just as he'd brought him to the bolthole conspirators meeting, just as he'd steered him and Berika into the same bed. The possibility that he, himself, was more to blame than any ten-times cursed prince loomed in his mind, but he couldn't face it. Not yet. Not when he couldn't explain that skilled and blindingly fast swordsman—

Godswill, but the Wolf sang a grand song of steel, all speed and finesse. And cursed, Dris reminded himself quickly. He risked his own soul admiring a cursed man. The blame *must* fall on the Wolf. It took a curse to confound so many good intentions. He'd meant no harm involving Killeen in his affair. Even Berika must have had good reasons for what she'd done; she had *influence,* but not a curse. And her brother, Braydon? Dris couldn't imagine a good reason that put Aleg's newly oath-bound partisan in the company of a Kufique assassin— Assassins were maggots, feeding off death and honor; and a foreign assassin was the worst of all. But Braydon *was* oathbound; that silver on his shoulder constrained his behavior as surely as bridle and spurs constrained an unruly horse. There had to be a good reason for everything—

Except the Wolf, who wore his curse like some perverse armor, taking small mistakes— Truly, he shouldn't have brought Killy to the alley, shouldn't have sent him up to Berika's room. Killy'd had women telling him what to do all his life; he resented women, didn't like them. Dris had hoped wise, gentle Berika could settle him. But she couldn't work miracles—especially when he'd never told her what he was trying to do. He could have managed everything better, should have and would never make a similar mistake in the future—

But it took the Wolf and his curse to turn mistakes into disaster.

With his back wedged into the hearthstone corner, Dris swore to himself that he'd learn from his mistakes. That still left Prince

Rinchen. A cursed man couldn't escape his curse. He was what he was and couldn't change. Killeen's death had created a pundonor between himself and the Wolf—an outrage so private and potent that it could only be remedied with blood, preferably the last drop of black blood from the Wolf's black heart.

"What shall I do with these, midons Ean?" Horsten Rockarm asked from the stairs.

Driskolt's head jerked upright, cracking against the stone wall behind him. He stared at the odd-contoured sack in Horsten's arms, guessing its contents: his uncle's touchstones. Weycha's harp and the wooden sword.

"Keep them close," his father said. "We'll take them to the palace. Gods know what good they'll do my brother now. How does it go?"

The one-eyed armsmaster was a grizzle-haired veteran, and being a commonborn, unSevered man, had accumulated enough *basi* to, in his own words, think like a spook when he needed to. "Almost over," he said softly. "The screams are not so loud, and somewhere—beyond the Web or deep in it—there's laughter."

"Hazard?"

It was a logical guess, considering the malevolent colors rippling through the snow clouds and the flames shooting through the Basilica dome, albeit an incredible guess, after the victory at Tremontin.

"I've laid low all my life, midons Ean," Rockarm said, shaking his head for emphasis. "I'd rather not poke my head up for a look, if it's all the same to you."

Ean didn't argue. "I don't suppose you found Nishu?"

"I don't hear *him* screaming. He's gone to ground somewhere. The spider will crawl out in his own time. How fares Maryele?"

Maryele was their mender, a true daughter of one of the lesser septs, and, unlike Nishrun, genuinely cherished by the clan.

"She lives," a woman's weary voice interjected from the top of the stairway. "She drank some wine and went to bed, but we're all dreams to her."

"My lady—" Lord Ean opened his arms to his wife.

Horsten shouldered his burdens and claimed a piece of wall near Driskolt.

"Midons," she replied, bowing her head as she approached the hearth. Drina, Lady sorMeklan and Driskolt's mother, was a small-statured woman who could stand beneath her husband's outstretched arms without mussing her sleekly coiled braids. "There's nothing more cruel than a mender in need of mending.

Gods will it," the lady challenged fiercely, "I'll arm myself with *basi* and do battle with Hazard myself!"

"That would be a fearsome thing to see," Ean agreed with complete sincerity. "Were you able to talk to her? Did she say anything?"

"Only names while she tore her hair. A litany of the dead . . ." The lady's voice faded and she put her hand over her mouth. "The dead," she whispered. "It's not yet dawn. The dead of the year, but not yet the new year. From Kasserine to Tremontin, there's been too much death beneath the Web. The dead have come back to continue the war."

Drina's explanation was better than any Dris and his father had discussed while carrying Killy's poor corpse. Dris saw Killy, then, in his mind's eye, both dead and alive. His heart wailed in silence—he'd lost friends in the war, but nothing like this. He let his head thump against the stone wall, mere bruising pain a satisfactory distraction until he heard his mother say:

"We owe your poor brother an apology."

But before she could elaborate, a clamor arose from the cellar storeroom. Prodded rudely from behind, Nishrun stumbled face-first into the lower hall.

"Midons, we found him cowering behind the wine barrels with the other rats," one of the partisans said, booting the dazed spider as he tried to stand.

"Enough!" Ean sorMeklan shouted, and the armed partisans took a discreet step backward.

Nishrun knelt cautiously. His face was bruised and scratched, but the blood was dry. The partisans hadn't beaten him; probably he'd hurt himself finding a place to hide. Dris judged his father's spider a coward, start to finish, but something more than the usual grovelling terror filled Nishu's eyes when he finally raised them.

"It's too horrible, midons donitor. I cannot describe it. Horror, hellfire, and death . . . Living thoughts captured and enslaved. Souls extinguished. You cannot imagine—"

"I do not need to imagine," Lord Ean replied harshly. "I commanded the reserve at Kasserine. I was on the ridge when the slag broke free."

Nishrun bowed, and banged his head on the stones. "Yes, midons donitor. Yes. You understand, midons. You know the fear, the terror: Your friends are dying, and there's nothing you can do."

The sorMeklan didn't need a coward lecturing them about helplessness. Driskolt's father reacted without thought, hauling the spider to his feet by the crimson leather neckband of his robe.

"If you had enough *basi* to vanquish Hazard, we would still have found you with the wine—"

"Hazard? Gods awake! Not the Pyromant. Not *Hazard*."

Like a cat with a mouse, Lord Ean lifted the spineless sorcerer off the floor and shook him violently. "You tell me, Nishu."

The coward's eyes glazed. "Hot," he croaked. "Burning hot. Windy. Gall and brimstone. Hellfire." His sightless eyes widened. He pulled his hands over his face and his knees up to his chest. "Hazard. He comes. His face is huge, the color of old blood. He's carrying a sword as bright as the burning sun. His hand—"

Nishrun's face froze in terror so potent that Lord Ean opened his fist. The sorcerer fell heavily to the stones.

"We owe your poor brother an apology," Lady sorMeklan repeated faintly. "We owe him his touchstones."

Ean nodded, but his attention remained on Nishrun. The abject sorcerer clawed at the hearth-stones; his fingertips bled. From the look on his father's face, Driskolt judged that he wasn't the only man who doubted that an overgrown acorn and a wooden sword would prevail against the pyromant who had stolen the last shreds of Nishrun's dignity.

Horsten held out the sack. "I have them here."

The acorn *thrummed* through the cloth. Driskolt looked up at the sound. He noticed only that these were two more sorMeklan treasures lost to the Wolf. It was more than an honorable man could bear.

"Listen," Lady sorMeklan said, looking up at the ceiling.

Annoyance flashed in the donitor's eyes. The bells were ringing as they had for hours. Nothing had changed.

"Listen," she repeated, touching his sleeve. "Behemoth. The passing bell. How long has it been ringing?"

Squinting his eyes and straining his ears, Driskolt heard the muffled voice of the great bell.

"He's gone . . . King Manal's gone. Hazard's taken the king," a partisan murmured.

A communal sob spread through the partisans, but not the noblefolk. Driskolt knew he didn't have a head for politics, but even he understood that something had turned rotten in King Manal's mind. He'd been in the throne hall with his father when the king lashed the Wolf with sorcery.

Godswill, if it took sorcery to slay the Wolf, he'd not get in the way, but sorcery from the throne was another matter. Sorcery and any sorRodion in the same thought filled a man's bowels with dread. Except Aleg. Godswill, Aleg was his friend. Aleg was a good man and he'd be a good king.

If the gods willed, Driskolt swore he'd make Aleg king himself: the pundonor between himself and Rinchen. The cursed prince's blood staining his sword.

"The Wolf must not take the throne." He pounded his fist against the wall, then turned to his father. "Leave the touchstones behind, midons father. Take me instead."

Ean looked at his son and saw a foolish stranger. Driskolt's friendship with Prince Alegshorn, which he'd encouraged, fed an unreasoning hatred of Prince Aleg's older brother. Before the war, when the golden prince had all the advantages and fratricide seemed likely, Driskolt's prejudice had been harmless. But lately Prince Alegshorn pursued the Wolf with less vigor—possibly because he'd had no success catching him. Wise men, among whose ranks the sidon was not yet numbered, were starting to hedge their bets where the succession was concerned.

Ean had formed his opinion of Prince Rinchen many years earlier. He'd never believed in curses, never thrown in with Prince Vigelan—his brother was Vigelan's friend, not him. He'd spotted the shrewdness in those icy eyes while Rinchen was still a boy. He'd distrusted the Wolf then, and he distrusted him now, but not because of superstition.

Vigelan's oldest son had no partisans; he was beyond influence. He haggled like a commonborn merchant, but he wasn't greedy; he couldn't be bribed or bought. And, if all that weren't enough, the Wolf understood Eyerlon.

The city's growth had been an unforeseen consequence of King Manal's accident. Because the king could no longer travel through the kingdom, mighty noblefolk, like himself, were forced to visit Eyerlon. As much as Ean disliked the raw, royal city, he'd realized that having the kingdom's chancellors near its sorcerers had kept Walensor alive during the Arrizan War.

It had also severely curtailed the traditional power of the donitors.

King Manal did not comprehend the masterful government he'd inadvertently created. Prince Vigelan, had he lived, and Prince Alegshorn, if he managed to seize the crown, were traditional men. With proper encouragement, Walensor could return to the old ways of wandering kings, rooted sorcerers, and donitors ruling their donits as they saw fit. Prince Rinchen was another matter altogether. Raised in the royal palace—if one dared to say he'd been raised by his sorRodion kin, not merely driven wild and mad—the Wolf's only significant curse, in Ean's weighty opinion, was that he understood the city's potential.

Ean's mind threw up a vision of the dark prince in the dark, pyramid throne—never mind that the Wolf would not rule from there. He could live with that, he supposed, and Dris would learn, but he didn't want his son within shouting distance of Walensor's probable king this New Year's Day.

"I need you here, Dris. There's no guessing what will happen once the sun rises and the folk learn that their king and the Web are gone. I place the sorMeklan honor and safety in your hands." Then he pulled his wife close and whispered down to her ear, telling her the barest details of barKethmarion's death, concluding; "Our son's gone brittle, my lady. He needs a firm but gentle hand. Your hand, not mine."

Lady sorMeklan glanced at her scowling son before looking up at her husband. "As you will, midons. But surely there's no need to take the touchstones today? Wait a bit yourself. Surely now you'll be able to give them back to Dris—your brother, I mean."

Ean kissed her lightly; Drina had always been fond of his roguish brother. Never enough to make him jealous, but enough to bridge peacefully between them in that last year, before Dris *died*. "Need? No, there's no need, and all the more reason to bring them. What I give to the Wolf on the first day of his reign, I expect to have returned many times over."

"He is cursed, midons," Drina said with the same voice she'd used to speak of Hazard. "I do not want anything of his beneath my roof."

"Then, my lady, I shall confine the Wolf's largesse to the stable, where I'm certain it will be more comfortable."

After a final kiss, Ean called for his cloak and shouted the names of those partisans who would accompany him to the palace. His wife gave orders as well, commanding two partisans to carry the still-babbling Nishrun to his quarters and sending her sulking son to the counting room. Driskolt might have argued with Ean, but he knew better than to argue with his mother.

The bells penetrated every corner of Eyerlon, even the Palestra and Basilica, where no one needed them or noticed them—except in a dusty corner behind a narrow bed in a modest chamber of the deserted northwest tower. Resurrection aside, Dart sorMeklan couldn't hear the screaming Web, but he could hear those bells as he hauled his mind up to consciousness.

His hands were pressed against his temples before he was fully alert, and long moments passed before he could distinguish the brazen voices from the throbbing inside his skull. Never in all his squandered youth had Weycha's champion suffered such a walloping hangover, or been so certain that he was stone-sober. His room was lit by a single oil lamp; the tiny flame hurt his eyes.

He was cold-cramped and naked and not quite certain how he'd gotten that way, except it hadn't been pleasant. Sinews tore like split green wood as he crawled onto his bed. The linens were cold, but otherwise intact. This sparked some surprise within the throbbing; it hurt too much, just yet, to wonder why he'd expected something different. Moaning the name of his forest goddess, he waited for the aches to subside. The healing would come—true healing, not such webwork as the menders bestowed. He had *basi*; he needed patience because there was nothing he could do consciously except to reconstruct his memory, a process in which, courtesy of the inquists, he'd become quite expert.

Ash. Arianna. The first a waif shivering in his arms, becoming the second: Hazard's hellfire sister. Arianna had visited him twice. Her second visit gave him the wounds that forest sorcery was beginning, now, to heal. But earlier . . . Straining against paralysis, Dart turned his head toward the wall and closed his eyes, craving privacy as he remembered what Arianna had said about Prince Rinchen. No forest sorcery could ease the ache those words left behind. He cared about that ice-eyed young man who'd promised to free his harp and sword from sorMeklan wards *without* giving them to the sorcerers first. He'd felt nothing untoward in Rinchen's presence.

Stretched across his bed, numb from cold and tingling with sorcery that was independent of the Web, Dart reminded himself that he'd told Arianna the simple truth: He was Weycha's champion. Nothing else mattered. He'd given no oaths to Rinchen sorRodion. Insofar as Arianna had vowed to usurp his lady, he had another enemy to defend her from. But the Wolf was no true concern of Weycha's, or his.

Dart raised his head and opened his eyes. Gods-be-damned if the Wolf was no concern of his. His harp and sword were supposed to pass through the Wolf's hands on their way to him. If Arianna had compromised his integrity, Rinchen *was* another enemy. If she hadn't, then the prince had earned a champion's help.

Fretting about Rinchen and the immutable pace of his own healing, Dart lost track of time and place until blankets settled over him. He was seated bolt-upright before he considered the wisdom of such an abrupt move. Everything squeaked like dry, binding wood, but the paralysis was gone.

"I—I'm sorry. I thought you were asleep." Halwisse sorJos retreated toward the door.

Dart collected his scattered thoughts. Halwisse had aged years in hours. Her face and hair were dulled, her shoulders stooped, and her eyes had become hollow bruises, rimmed with crimson. Tears dribbled steadily down her cheeks; she did not seem to notice them.

"I was almost awake and you startled me," Dart explained, modestly knotting the topmost blanket around his waist before swinging his legs over the side. "Thank you all the same. The window got blasted . . ." He let the thought go unfinished. He had an idea what Halwisse had been through since deadwatch began. "I'm the one who should be sorry. There was nothing I could do. Please believe me."

Halwisse's tears disappeared into the already damp blue wool of her gown. A few lucky women became more attractive when they cried, but Halwisse sorJos was not so lucky. Dart extended a hand. She found her voice when their fingers touched.

"We didn't listen."

He held her as he'd held Ash not long ago. Poor Ash—gone, dead, Arianna's discarded pawn, with only a stray thought to mourn her. But the living needed comfort more.

"We didn't listen," Halwisse repeated, her tears making warm streams down his back. "Everything you ever said was true. I—*I* looked within you. *I* felt Weycha's marks upon you. I should have known, anathema or not, you were a goddess's champion. I should have stopped the inquists. I should have stopped Ash." She raised a haggard face. "They're gone, Dris—*All* the basilidans, almost all the magga communicants and inquists. Feladon. He was consumed; there's nothing left, not even bones. The Cascade ran with blood before the dome burned through. The marble baths crashed to the floor. The Brightwater pool . . ." Her head fell against Dart's chest. "I was so sure that you and Ash had died when the baths fell, but I couldn't wade into that pool to find you. It took all my courage just to come up and stand in your doorway to say goodbye. But you were here. Alive. *Healing*."

When a magga mender spoke of healing, not even grief concealed her awe.

"If only we had listened to you."

"Nothing would be different," Dart said as gently as he could. "My lady foresaw none of this, yet she was prepared. She withdrew from the Web. She sleeps among her trees until Quickening. When I return to the forest with her gifts, I will be ready for Pyromant Hazard. That is where and how I will defeat him." He didn't mention that Ash was neither dead nor a basilidan, but Hazard's sister and an enemy he didn't yet know how to conquer, nor did he mention Prince Rinchen, but Halwisse made a connection on her own.

"The gifts. Weycha's gifts." She sat up straight and dried her eyes. "You were"—she hesitated—"*dead* for a long time. The Wolf became everything Prince Vigelan feared he would become. There are many who would prefer to see Prince Alegshorn as crown prince. There have been conspiracies and some who would commit murder to ensure a favorable succession. The sorJos have conspired, recently, and hired assassins, too. My fault. The Wolf survived; we paid an honor-price, but that was not enough. Somehow he'd learned that your gifts—which you had successfully hidden from the inquists . . . from all of us—were under wards at the sorMeklan residence. He forced a compromise: If Lord sorMeklan surrendered your sword and harp when he swore his liege oath on New Year's Day, there would be no formal inquiry by the inquists."

Dart blinked, his sole concession to surprise. So, *that* was how Prince Rinchen planned to acquire Weycha's gifts. The prince was an opportunist of the first water. The man Dart had been was approving; the champion that he was worried about Arianna and integrity. The less time the harp and sword spent in Prince Rinchen's hands, the better.

Better still if he intercepted them before the liege oaths were taken.

One bell rang as the sun cracked the eastern horizon. Muffled Behemoth, the passing bell, the mournful sound of death. Thinking only of the sword, Dart cocked his head toward the window.

"Will anyone take the liege oaths today?"

Halwisse sniffled and shivered. "I don't know. Without the Web . . . Some of the younger sorcerers seem less afflicted. They've gone to the palace, but I know of none who have come back. Behemoth's rung like that for hours. I don't know." She settled against Dart's shoulder.

"I've got to go to the sorMeklan residence," Dart said as he disengaged himself. "It's barely dawn. I must speak to my brother before he goes to the palace, if I can."

There were a few garments left in the clothespress. Halwisse still sat on the bed, absorbed by her losses, when he had finished dressing. He paused in the doorway—the wards across his door had fallen with the Web—and called her name repeatedly, but she never acknowledged hearing him, and he left without looking back.

Chapter Seventeen

Dart wandered through the Palestra searching for the door that led to freedom. Eventually he found an unlocked postern door, but only after he'd found slain sorcerers everywhere, some serene in their final sleep, but most blasted and reeking with hellfire. He met survivors, too, as dazed and racked with grief as Halwisse. Their eyes were focused inward, on loss. They did not notice him, and after the first few, he willed himself not to notice them.

He thought it would be better outside, in the cold of New Year's Day. It was. The sun shone brightly and an easterly wind had already purged the stench of hellfire from the air. If he'd been eye-blind as well as headblind, or if he'd never looked up . . . But the Basilica loomed over the Palestra, as it loomed over all Eyerlon; no one could look up and not be appalled by the sight.

Hazard's hellfire onslaught had consumed the dome's gleaming gold skin. The arched timbers that had supported it were miraculously, obscenely intact: a charred-black skeleton of the Web against a cloudless sky.

Paying unnecessarily close attention to the cobblestones, Dart marched through the unguarded Palestra gate, determined to ignore what he could not have prevented. Hoarfrost collected on his lips and chin. He marched past the Basilica itself, where no wind short of a gale could have swept away the stench. Disregarding his resolution, he climbed the empty steps to the portico, pausing between the open, hellfired doors.

The Cascade was gone. In the great pool where Brightwater had splashed amid ever-changing rainbows and mist, liver-colored ichor churned fitfully. While Dart watched, bubbles burst and fouled the air. Red smears stained the white marble walls and floors. He didn't think the blotches were blood—mortal blood should have darkened by now—but he couldn't be certain from the doorway. By birth and rebirth Dart sorMeklan had little love for spooks, but no one deserved Hazard's carnage. He sincerely hoped that those who had survived, Halwisse and the other living ghosts he'd encountered in the Palestra, would be able to restore the Basilica to its glory after Hazard was gone.

After he was gone as well.

Weycha had given him the strengths and gifts to slay the Pyromant; Dart had no doubt of that, but suddenly he also knew that he would not survive the slaying. Weycha had lifted him out of death for a single purpose, which was Hazard—not Berika, not Rinchen, not even Arianna. Once he'd achieved that purpose, the goddess would have no further need of him and he would die.

Dart retreated unsteadily down the Basilica steps. He imagined himself as an arrow at the peak of flight, unable to change his course, unafraid of his landing, and very aware that the cloudless sky was the most beautiful shade of blue that mortal eyes could see. His heart skipped a beat. When its rhythm was restored, he started walking toward the sorMeklan residence.

The streets of Eyerlon had grown more numerous since he last walked them eighteen years earlier, but the main ones had not changed and he made his way across the city, hoping familiar sights would eventually stir his memory. Citizens crowded the streets, as they would on any New Year's Day, but they did not gather to exchange the traditional good-will greetings. At each step, he overheard similar conversations as commonfolk, with their variable *basi*, compared memories of the most horrific night of their lives.

When he lived the noble life of Fenklare's sidon and Prince Vigelan's boon companion, Dart had staggered home to the half-built residence blind-drunk more often than he returned sober. Allowing those old instincts to guide his feet, he eventually came to a barred green-and-ruby gate. Dart had no idea what he'd say to his brother, Ean. Words would come and he would not leave without the gifts his goddess had given him. He hammered the heavy door-knocker against the flat bronze plate beneath it. An unfamiliar, mail-coiffed face appeared at the grate.

Remembering his noblefolk manners, Dart snarled at the partisan: "Send word to midons Lord Ean, donitor, that his brother claims hospitality."

The partisan studied Dart's hair and cocked his head to get a look at Dart's eyes before answering: "The donitor is not here. He's gone to the palace. Hie yourself there if you want him."

Dart was gratified to see that the partisan knew how to recognize him, but disappointed to learn that his ever-dutiful brother had already gone to the palace, as if this New Year's were the same as any other. He concealed both reactions beneath an indifferent shrug. "I can get what I want from the sidon or the lady, or whoever is in charge. But not you, I'm certain."

The partisan grimaced. "Aye, not me." He raised the bar and opened the gate wide enough to let Dart in. "The lady's in the counting room, midons—" The honorific was reflexive courtesy. He was not *midons*, which declared a right to dispense justice, a right which Dart, because his lands and title had reverted to his brother after his death and had not been reconfirmed, did not have. "All the same, I'll be asking you to leave your weapons here. I'll give you an escort."

There were a half-dozen well-armed men in the courtyard, two of them with bows and nocked arrows. Dart opened his cloak to show that he carried nothing more deadly than a fruit knife in his belt. Bows were lowered and an archer sauntered over. He inspected Dart from head to foot. Dart had the distinct sense that they had known each other eighteen years ago, not politely.

"Figured you'd show up on a godsforsaken day like this one."

"Figured you'd be here to greet me," he responded with an equally toothy smile. He'd always been a gambler, able to bluff regardless of the stakes. Weycha hadn't tampered with that when she resurrected him. Furling his cloak over his sword-arm, he bowed with mock grandeur, and allowed the unremembered archer to lead him to the counting room.

Lady sorMeklan and her son were both in the counting room when Dart arrived there. Already adapting to the demise of sorcery, Lady sorMeklan was dictating messages for hand-delivery in Relamain and the clan's honor-estates. Driskolt moped on a bench behind her, springing to his feet with a drawn knife the moment he saw Dart, his uncle.

The lady quenched her son's ardor with a wave of her hand as she stood up. The younger Driskolt sheathed his knife reluctantly.

"Lord Dris—" Drina began warmly, then caught herself with a smile. "You call yourself 'Dart' now. Welcome, Lord Dart." She dismissed her scribe and the archer, then held out her hand.

Dart kissed her fingers while his mind filled with sparks of memory. Drina sorMeklan, his brother's wife, who by rights should have taken Ean's side in every quarrel, had fostered compromise between them instead. He had always been in awe of her; he still was. "Dart, midons," he suggested, releasing her hand. "Plain and unadorned."

"Drina," she replied. "Plain, unadorned, and gone to grey."

Through the tail of his eye, Dart watched Driskolt fumbling with his knife again when Drina embraced him warmly, tilting her head upward to receive the affectionate brother's kiss she never forgot to claim. He could imagine Driskolt's sour thoughts, but kissed Drina all the same. One didn't know if the opportunity would ever return.

"Do you come from the Palestra?" she asked hesitantly as they separated. "We know very little of what has happened."

Dart nodded. "I was looking for Ean—" He caught a glimpse of his nephew's still-smoldering expression and adopted a more respectful tone. "For midons Lord Ean. He holds certain things of mine."

"Your wooden sword and that big acorn with the harp inside?"

His hopes lifted, but she dashed them quickly with a sigh. "Midons has taken them to the palace, to give to the . . . to Prince . . . no, King Rinchen."

"Iser forbid," Driskolt swore. "I said midons sire should leave them behind."

Dart judged that did not mean Driskolt would be happy to return them to their rightful owner, merely that he despised the Wolf more than he despised a resurrected uncle.

Lady sorMeklan looked from her unhappy son to him. "Midons Ean has done a rightful thing for rightful reasons. He made this clear to me before he left. Both of you think he was wrong. I want to know why."

She shoved her own padded chair toward Dart, but chose the scribe's abandoned high stool for herself. "You first." She nodded to her son. "Your foolishness forced the bargain."

Dart suppressed a smile as he took his place in the padded chair. Perched upon that stool, the lady towered over both him and Dris.

Under his mother's benign, but implacable, guidance, Dris spoke of Berika and the *influence* Nishrun had discovered in this very room less than a day earlier. He admitted watching Berika take the spear to the river front courtyard and described how he and Killy had nearly frozen while Berika, her brother, and a stranger—an assassin—conferred in an upper room. Driskolt's voice thickened when he reached the surprise and counter-surprise of the skirmish that had claimed Killy's life.

"Prince Rinchen didn't kill him," Dart corrected. "The assassin did. And you killed the assassin."

"The Wolf kept Killy off-guard; the assassin did the killing for him."

From what Dart had seen of the full-grown Rinchen sorRodion, the prince didn't need help when it came to killing. But he recognized animosity when he encountered it, and chose—wisely, he thought—to keep his opinions to himself.

Then Drina turned her quick wits on him.

"You flinched when I said that midons Ean had taken your touchstones to the palace. You do not trust Prince Rinchen either. What are *your* reasons? How does a man who has been lost these last many years come to share my son's distrust of our royal wolf?"

Dart had been constructing and changing his story all the while Driskolt told his. He'd stroked the wooden chair-arms as he'd often stroked a set of wooden dice, and began with Halwisse sorJos, a name he knew would be recognized.

"Little Halwisse," the lady repeated, confirming that she remembered what Halwisse hoped everyone had forgotten.

Before Dart could go further, there was a knock on the door and a partisan announced:

"Midons donitor has sent a messenger back from the palace."

"Send him in," Drina said.

A youth in sorMeklan colors dropped to one knee on the threshold, but not before his eyes betrayed his shock at seeing the donitor's resurrected brother in close-confidence with the donitor's son and lady-wife. He stammered constantly while telling them that King Manal had not died after all. And a moment's notice confirmed to Dart and the others that Behemoth no longer rang. But, the boy said, the king lay so near to death that a mirror held beneath his nose was scarcely clouded by his breath. The dowager princess Janna had given the order to toll the passing bell, but when her sons appeared in the chancery hall and learned the truth, they had silenced it together.

"Her *sons*?" Lady sorMeklan spoke before Dart or Dris could find their tongues. "Prince Alegshorn *and* the Wolf?"

Wringing his hands, the messenger nodded. "I was there at

midons donitor's side when they came through the door together. The Wolf is hellfired; Prince Alegshorn held him steady on his feet whenever he faltered. They held their father's coronet in their hands between them."

The lady shook her head. "Wonder upon wonder."

"The Wolf sits on a window ledge," the messenger continued. "With his hellfired cheek against the cold glass. The coronet sits on a cushion at his feet. Prince Alegshorn stands aside, whispering in his ear; but I think—begging midons' pardon—I think that the Wolf speaks his own mind regardless."

"Godswill!" Driskolt swore, pounding fist against palm. "It cannot be. Aleg wouldn't tolerate it."

"Midons sidon, I swear I speak the truth. Prince Alegshorn is hale and whole. His shadow falls in its proper shape on the floor—I saw it with my own eyes. The Wolf bears no weapon; his left arm is bound inside his shirt. Prince Alegshorn bears his sword on his hip, but when midons dowager commanded him to make good use of it, Prince Alegshorn replied that there was no good use left since Prince Vigelan is already dead."

Dris leapt to his feet. "Aleg would never say that! The only grudge Aleg bears is against the Wolf, not his father."

"Peace." Lady sorMeklan laid a restraining hand on his arm. "There was always a whisper that midons Prince Vigelan feared his own father, the king, liked young Prince Alegshorn too well, and that he, himself, would never sit on the throne. You do not remember, my son, because you were as young yourself, but your friend felt his father's rage often enough. Both boys had cause to fear their father, maybe cause to hate him. Prince Alegshorn seems to have grown up well enough, but he is a sorRodion and their thoughts run dark. When the women talk, there has always been a thought that Vigelan had raised his sons to hate their father more than they hated each other."

"Aleg would *never* make common cause with the Wolf!"

Dart had been sitting back in his chair with his fingers steepled over his nose. When Dris concluded his outburst, he lowered them. "What of the touchstones midons donitor brought with him to the palace?" He addressed the messenger directly, though it was a breath of rank within the clan. "Did he surrender them, and to whom?"

"Midons donitor had them still when I left. Beyond that I cannot say."

"I'll take my chances with Ean," Dart decided. He rose to his feet. "My lady—" He bowed his head toward his brother's wife.

"It was good to see you once more. The years have not changed you, gods grant that they never do—"

The convoluted courtesy of noblefolk farewells gave Dris time to seize Dart's shoulder, spinning him rudely around.

"*You* didn't finish. What do you know about the Wolf that you aren't telling?"

Dart failed to shrug out of his nephew's grasp. He chose his words carefully, hoping to keep a bad situation from turning worse. "I don't know what might happen if my lady's gifts are touched by hellfired hands."

His vision hued toward bloody red for the second time since his arrival in Eyerlon—perhaps the sorcerers had done something to keep his eyes from glowing as he knew they were glowing at Dris now. Perhaps the destruction of the Web had freed him.

"Hellfired hands . . ." Dris repeated. "Cursed hands . . . The Wolf's cursed hands. The Wolf was born in deadwatch before New Year's morning exactly twenty-three years ago. You were dead for eighteen years; now you're a goddess's champion against Hazard. The Wolf's been alive for twenty-three. What does that make him, I wonder?"

"I'm not saying anything like that, Dris—"

"It's all coming clear to me: the curse, the hellfire . . . Aleg standing next to him, doing nothing. Hazard has the Wolf on a chain. Hazard's *always* had the Wolf on a chain—"

"It's not Hazard—" Dart shook his head and left the thought unfinished. Mentioning Arianna wasn't going to bring this dispute to a quick or peaceful end. "A curse isn't always evil, it's just different—like being Severed, or being left-armed in a fight. Sometimes it's an advantage. I don't know where Prince Rinchen's curse puts him between hellfire and my lady's gifts. I'm hedging my bets, that's all—"

"Godswill—I've *seen* what happens when you gamble."

Dart cursed himself for forgetting a night in Relamain when misfortune and an ill-considered grudge brought him face-to-face with Dris over a gaming table. That encounter, more than Berika, had brought him here to Eyerlon. But he was a gambler, a better gambler than his nephew and—more importantly—a luckier one. He raised the stakes and rolled:

"You're right, lord sidon—" No need yet to flatter him with a *midons*. "I don't know the two princes well enough to hedge my bets successfully, but you've known them all your life. You'll know the truth when you see it. Come with me to the palace. Help me sort it out before it's too late."

Driskolt eyed him suspiciously. "Yes," he murmured mostly to himself, then "Yes," again with growing resolve. "I'll help you get your touchstones back from the sorRodion Wolf."

Dart knew better than to trust his nephew. Still, he could always roll the dice again.

A New Year's court unlike any other in Walensor's history unfolded itself in the chancery beyond the new palace throne hall. The kingdom's mighty men crowded together like beggars on the alms porch. The air was stale but vastly preferable to the throne hall, visible through two sets of open doors, which released an undercurrent of hellfire, a testament to the unseen—from the chancery—destruction.

Prince Rinchen sat on a wide window ledge, soothing his hellfired face against the cold glass. His brother stood at his shoulder, an extra pair of eyes and ears, since his own were none too reliable. His plain shirt was damp with Brightwater, Aleg's also. It was the closest they'd been able to come to the Immersion ritual, what with the Basilica in ruins, all the maggas in shock or worse, and the rest of the sorRodion clan under armed guard until they accepted the hitherto unimaginable: He and Aleg were going to rule Walensor together.

Or they would, once King Manal died. The menders would not guess what was keeping the king alive. There wasn't enough Brightwater left in the kingdom to mend a broken toe. But a clutch of disciplined menders—young, resilient, and uncertain of their craft in the best of times—insisted they could find a pulse, and holding a piece of glass beneath his nose, proved that the king still breathed, if only intermittently.

It was past the traditional time for the six donitors to begin the liege-oath ceremony. Not one of them had budged from his—or her, in the case of the Survarl donitor—knot of supporters. Watching their reflection in the window glass, Prince Rinchen did not doubt that every one of them was stalling in the hope that both he and his grandfather would be dead before long.

They might get their wish. He felt the hellfire creeping beneath the bandages Arkkin had wound around his ribs. He'd borne the pain so far, with Aleg's help, but if Arkkin's blend of stallion blood and salt didn't work, he'd be dead by morning.

Walensor's gods might be dead—their basilidans certainly were—but they'd gotten the final laugh. After a lifetime of bartering with his curse, hoping to wrest some meaning from existence, he'd be king for a single day: uncrowned, neither ruling nor reigning, and unable to free his mind from hellfire pain. *That* was all the meaning of his life.

Rinchen wanted their liege-oaths as a matter of pride. He wanted to give Dart his harp and sword as the one tangible act of a very short reign. The noblefolk were waiting for him to die; he was waiting for a messenger to return from the Palestra with Dart sorMeklan in tow.

A purple-robed bard—not the man he'd sent to the sorcerers—returned from the Palestra alone.

"He's not been seen, nor the basilidan who was with him, nor have their bodies been found. It was their custom," the young man said circumspectly, "to pass the deadwatch hours in the Cascade. Of those who were known to be in the Basilica when Hazard struck, there have been no survivors, midons Prince Rinchen. No one—" His voice broke and he needed a moment before continuing. "We have not searched the pool."

The prince's vision blurred. It had to be hellfire; he hadn't shed a tear since the door to his cell was unlocked after Kasserine.

"Say something. Everyone's waiting," Aleg whispered.

He made a fist with his weapon hand, the only one he could move. He struck his thigh, then unclenched his fingers.

"Fenklare's here," Aleg continued, "in force, along the back wall. They've got the champion's touchstones. Lord Ean knows why you wanted them, and he knows it's too late. Far be it from me to tell you how to rule, dear brother, but you *could* curry favor with Fenklare. Hellfire and Hazard aren't our only problems. Please say something courteous to Lord Ean, or I will."

With a strangled groan only Aleg could hear, he tore his face from the window. A moment passed before the purple blur resolved into the bard's robe. "Return to the Palestra; comfort the living. There is no time to look for the dead, or the lost." Every word was agony, but Aleg was right. If he could get Fenklare's support, for a day or a year, he could get the others. He caught Lord sorMeklan's eye and invited him to come closer.

The donitor shouldered his way through the crowd. Horsten Rockarm, his half-Pennaik armsmaster, trailed close behind, carrying the touchstone bundle. Lord Ean had been visibly stunned when he and Aleg appeared sharing Vigelan's coronet, but Aleg swore—based on his friendship with Lord Ean's son, Driskolt—that Fenklare's donitor was a practical man who valued sense, not prejudice.

*   *   *

Lord Ean clasped the hand of the bard as they passed each other. He paused again, not taking the bundle from Horsten Rockarm's hands, but bending down to pick up the ruined sword Prince Alegshorn had ordered down from his brother's lair. He did not doubt the story Aleg told while he held the weapon for all to see, and—truly—he did not begrudge the Wolf his hero's moment. The ice-eyed prince was dying before their eyes, eaten from within by hellfire—a death they'd all hoped never to see again after Tremontin. Ean admired compassion in a strong man. He was pleased to see it in the sorRodion prince who would become their king, Prince Alegshorn, and he felt it himself for Weycha's champion.

Dart had always been a troublesome rogue, but he was a brother, and the sorMeklan were not the sorRodion. Ean swore silently that he and Horsten would give Dart a proper mourning as soon as they could. But for the moment he was the donitor of Fenklare, with a wooden weapon that might—even without its proper owner—be more effective against Hazard than the Wolf's steel sword had been.

Twenty years ago he would have kept the sword. He would have gone to Weychawood, where he'd hunted all his life, and he would have faced Hazard himself. But it wasn't twenty years ago and he wasn't vain enough to think he could better the cursed prince's performance. Maybe Prince Aleg could, or one of the sorMoreg cousins, though Ean doubted any living man could do better than the Wolf. It was a tragedy that Prince Rinchen had not had the wooden sword when he needed it.

A bead of poison-green hellfire slid along the edge of the black weal on the Wolf's jaw, enlarging it slightly.

"You aren't having second thoughts, are you, Lord sorMeklan? If you'd surrendered them when I first asked, we might not be standing here like this."

The Wolf's fist was clenched. Prince Alegshorn made a fist of his own and nudged it into his brother's flank. The Wolf uncoiled three fingers that lay like knives against his thigh. Prince Aleg whispered something in his brother's ear and withdrew. A code, and not devised since Hazard's deadwatch attack. A wealth of idle questions sprouted in Ean's mind; he swept them all aside as moot. The Wolf was dying; Prince Aleg's scowl as he moved away had told him everything else he needed to know.

"You're right on both counts, midons," he agreed. "If I had yesterday back, I'd live it differently. But I don't, and you don't have tomorrow, so, for my brother's memory, I'll give you today. What do you want, Prince Rinchen ruVigelan sorRodion?"

The prince's hellfire weals were momentarily quiet. He took a deep breath and let it out with a sigh. "I want the sword and the harp you hid while your brother was sequestered; you forfeited them when you refused to send your son to the inquists. They are yesterday's and have nothing to do with today. For today, and for your brother's memory, I want your New Year's oath—your liege-oath—sworn to me and to my brother as well, honestly and openly before these assembled witnesses."

The court held its collective breath; Prince Alegshorn came close beside his brother again.

"But the king is not dead," a faceless, nameless voice muttered from the depths of the audience.

Ean sorMeklan ignored the voice. He wasn't a gambler—he'd always left gambling to his brother—but he liked what he saw as Aleg set his wide-fingered hand on his brother's shoulder. He hadn't cracked their code, but he would if he had to, if the Wolf survived . . . And if King Manal survived? Ean knew his own mind: He'd sooner trust a cursed prince and his amiable brother than a sorcery-wielding king who'd cheated death twice. Still, a man had to bargain:

"You ask much for the memory of a man you hardly knew."

"For Lord Dart sorMeklan's memory," Prince Rinchen said slowly, "I will return the spear of the sorMeklan—"

Ean felt his jaw and fists clench. Prince Aleg's hand tightened, too, and beads of hellfire bloomed on the Wolf's face.

"—and the thief who stole it."

Outraged questions filled the donitor's mind. Hellfire wriggled on the prince's immobile face. Ean banished his questions with a sigh. It didn't matter how his son's damned *influential* woman had fallen into the dying prince's hands. "Send her to the residence, but bring the spear here. I'll swear your oath with Rodion's spear in my hand."

Chapter Eighteen

Dart would have gotten himself royally lost inside the new palace without Driskolt to guide him. Courtesy of his friendship with Prince Aleg, Dris knew both halves of the palace as well as anyone who did not live there. His face was known to most of the king's partisans, who passed him through the chambers and corridors without noticing a cowled stranger, Dart himself, trailing along behind. Dris set a pace meant to impress his uncle, and it did—though probably not as Driskolt intended. As much as he could regret anything with thoughts of the harp and sword clamoring in his mind, Dart regretted that there'd be no time to repair the damage of their first few meetings. If circumstances had allowed, he'd have forged a friendship with his brother's son; Ean had raised him better than they'd been raised themselves by their own father.

But circumstances would not allow—not if Dart got his heart's wish: Weycha's touchstones in his hands once more.

He thought of Hazard, then remembered the untamed sensuality of his own goddess, and dared to hope that she might still have a need for him after his destiny was fulfilled; he wasn't giving heed to Driskolt, who stopped short on the throne hall threshold. They collided hard, with Dart taking the worst of it, because nothing was going to push Dris into that hellfire-blasted chamber.

King Manal's throne hall, though by far the largest chamber in either half of the palace, was smaller than the dome-roofed Basilica. Its destruction was more intimate, especially with the seared and shrivelled corpses of the king's companion menders lying in puddles of soured Brightwater, their blackened arms held stiffly before their faces. Dart understood that folk died in that posture, a final, instinctive attempt to protect their heads, when they died of fire. Nonetheless, it seemed as if they'd been praying—as perhaps they had—to gods who had not listened.

The hellfire assault had destroyed the black pyramid throne; slimy splinters carpeted the floor. The door to the menders' waiting room, which the throne had formerly concealed, was plainly visible and open. On the far side of the menders' room, beyond the clutch of disciplined menders in their blue-banded grey robes, another open door revealed the many-colored backs of the high nobility.

"The chancery," Dris said with a curt nod. "They're holding the liege-oath court in the chancery."

Setting his lips in a thin line, Dris crossed the throne hall threshold, picking a course that carefully avoided the turgid puddles of soured Brightwater. Dart followed. They were several paces short of the menders' room when a tall, reedy sorcerer approached them. He left a gap in the menders' circle that gave the two sorMeklan men a glimpse of King Manal's emaciated, shrunken body, but he blocked the doorway with a wide stance and outstretched arms.

"Can't you see what we're doing here? The king's life hangs by a thread. Our work is difficult enough, without you noblefolk and your partisans traipsing through."

As part of his display of familiarity with the palace and its denizens, Driskolt had consigned their heavy cloaks and cowls to the watchtower guards. When the sorcerer looked at Driskolt, he saw a nobleman's sword and gold-embroidered shirt. When he looked at Dart, he saw nothing at all, not even the much-rumored, many-colored hair or faintly sparkling eyes.

"We're trying—" Driskolt gestured at the crowded room which at that moment erupted with cheers and shouts.

The king's new, less-experienced menders looked up. The reedy sorcerer, who was apparently in command, ordered them to pay attention only to their work; then he turned back to him and Dart.

"No," the grey-robed man said emphatically. "The sooner everyone leaves, the better. I don't care who you are, you're too late. It's too crowded already. We can't do our work. There're too many distractions."

Before they could react to stop him, the sorcerer slammed the door loudly and latched it.

All the grudges against sorcery and sorcerers that Dart had harbored in silence since he returned to Eyerlon, all the anger he had swallowed, all the anguish he had suffered at their hands, crystallized around that one young mender who hadn't noticed him. The serenity with which he had endured the indignities of his repeated interrogations and mendings shattered, and his temper, dormant since Berika called him across the stream outside of Gorse, broke loose.

"My lady's gifts are mine! I want what belongs to me," he snarled, cocking his fist at the door. "I'll give you a distraction you won't soon forget!"

Driskolt seized Dart's arm before it struck wood. "There's another way," he said. "Follow me."

Dart was trembling. The outpouring of pure rage banished the lethargy and resignation that had determined his resurrected life. He was himself again, wiser and endowed with a champion's power, but otherwise the same: fully capable of a noble tirade. He needed another moment to reorient himself, but he didn't get it. Dris was retreating across the throne hall. If there was another way to the chancery and the touchstones, he'd never find it on his own.

Once again, they stopped short of their destination, in a window-walled gallery which was as crowded as the chancery beyond it.

The crowd had long since sorted itself by rank and prestige. Dris and Dart found themselves staring at the drab backs of the burly partisans who had escorted their more-important patrons to the palace. None of them wore badges of sorMeklan green and ruby and none was willing to surrender their place to latecomers. Dris exercised his frustration by jumping up and down, snatching glimpses of distant activity. By contrast, Dart stood near the windows, nurturing his anger.

"I see it!" Dris exalted, breaking Dart's concentration. "I see Rodion's spear!" He leapt again, as much for joy as to catch another glimpse of the battered weapon.

The sidon's celebration ended abruptly. One of the partisans spun around, saying: "Aye, midons, the Wolf had it locked away in his lair and made Fenklare swear liege-loyalty before he'd give it back."

"What?"

Another partisan turned around. Both men wore the red and white badges of the sorLewel clan. The feud between Prince

Alegshorn and the Wolf was not the most notorious in the kingdom. That dubious honor fell to the sorMeklan and the sorLewel. Rooted now in his old self, Dart not only remembered the details, he felt the outrage.

Reasonable and wise after the Escham River recarved its channel, the sorMeklan merely claimed their customary half of the river revenues. And—simply because it had appeared on their side of the river—the new silt-rich farmland between the old channel and the new. The damned sorLewel claimed for their own the entire river and its revenues *and* the new farmland. King Manal refused to issue an edict settling the issue, and a dozen sorMeklan men and two dozen sorLewel had died before Weycha claimed Dart eighteen years ago. One look into those red-and-white-partisan eyes and he knew the feud had only gotten worse since then.

"It's true," the burlier of the two partisans insisted. "All of a sudden guards came bursting through. They wore the king's colors, but it was the Wolf's blackheads that came back with Fenklare's spear. Damn careless to lose it to the Wolf in the first place; damn poor trading on Fenklare's part to get it back, if you ask me, midons."

Neither Dart nor Dris was wearing the sorMeklan colors. The sidon did not have to: His manner and appearance all proclaimed that he dwelt at the pinnacle of power, where individual identity was more important than the clan. Dart wore the drab clothes the sorcerers had given him. It was simple luck that placed them face-to-face with some of the few partisans in Eyerlon who, because of the river feud, could not recognize them. Dart knew what Dris was feeling: a gut-level need to teach these sorLewel fools a lesson; he was feeling it, too. But this was neither the time nor the place to indulge family honor. He controlled his own urges and was grateful when Dris did the same.

They withdrew to the windows.

"Did you hear that?" Dris sputtered.

"They're sorLewel. They're trying to rile us into doing something foolish."

"They didn't recognize us."

"They're still sorLewel, and they'd lie to anyone about the sorMeklan. We don't know what's happened up there. We don't know what Ean did, who has Rodion's spear, or what's become of my lady's gifts." It was the last question that dominated Dart's thoughts. He had questions for his friend the Wolf, but he didn't want to ask those questions in the crowded chancery. "I've got to wait," he muttered, as much to himself as his nephew.

"Wait!" Dris exploded. "The Wolf killed my friend. He had our spear; he must have had Berika and her brother, too. He's put Aleg on a leash and taken our oath . . . under duress, godswill; we don't have to honor an oath under duress. He's got your gods-be-damned gifts and he's hellfired besides. Iser's balls, what are you waiting for?"

"I don't know!" Dart snarled back. Until that moment he hadn't overlaid Driskolt's grievances with his own fears. He hadn't considered the possibility that Berika had been with the Wolf when Arianna arrived, but the imperatives that Weycha had sealed inside his champion's soul were implacable. He couldn't care about Berika. He couldn't worry about the prince. He could not think about anything but recovering the gifts–they were so close now, he could feel them. "If Ean walks out here with the spear on one shoulder and my gifts under the other, then I'll be as happy as any man can be. If he's got the spear, but not the gifts, I'll go looking for the Wolf." He was talking to himself more than his nephew. "But I can't fight my way in; it wouldn't work. I'd get myself killed. Can't you see, I've got to wait until the paths are simpler?"

Driskolt *should* see. Dart's world had gone red again, and the sunlight streaming through the window had to reveal his hair for the unnatural growth it was.

Dris nodded slowly. "Wait here. I'll shove to the front. I'll send midons sire out to you."

Dart was at war with himself. He ignored his nephew's thoughtful, slitted eyes and said nothing before Driskolt began asserting his gods-given right to be at the front of any gathering, gradually winning the argument. The sorLewel partisans appraised him with sidelong glances that left Weycha's champion wishing he had something more potent than a fruit knife hidden in his boot.

He tried to keep himself inconspicuous by the windows and waited for the audience to end. A few partisans broke out of the throng almost immediately, but they weren't sorMeklan men. Dart began to pace, seven paces to the right, seven to the left—the habit of another lifetime.

The court concluded with the sort of cheering normally heard before a battle. Dart eased forward, avoiding the sorLewel. He was not the only one caught by surprise when the great nobles decided it was time to leave. The churning mass immobilized him amid cursing, shoving strangers as the great nobles swept a path from the chancery, protected and propelled by a growing wedge of partisans. He saw the spear and shouted his brother's name, but it was hopeless. Although he was trapped for only a few moments, the spear had disappeared from sight by the time he was free.

He hesitated in the rapidly emptying corridor, then sprinted toward the partly closed chancery doors. He pushed the doors apart, expecting to see the Wolf surrounded by menders. But Prince Rinchen was gone. A well-dressed young man stood by himself, wearing Prince Vigelan's coronet at a rakish angle atop golden hair.

"Midons Prince Alegshorn?"

Prince Aleg opened his mouth, but said nothing as the color drained from his cheeks. "Godswill—you're supposed to be dead." He unsheathed his sword.

Unsure what the younger sorRodion prince knew about him or anything connected to him, Dart spread his hands quickly, proclaiming in the traditional way that he harbored no ill-intent. "I've been in the Palestra since the second day of Greater Hoarfrost."

"A bard came in here not an hour ago and told us you died in the Cascade when Hazard stormed the Web. Are you come back to life a second time?" Prince Aleg held his sword between them.

"I've only died once, eighteen years ago. I was in my bed when Hazard struck the Web." Dart hoped a single slice of truth would satisfy the nervous prince. "I'd hoped to find my brother here, or yours."

The chancery air was hot and stale. Prince Aleg sheathed his sword and wiped his forehead, removing the coronet with the same gesture. "They've both gone. Lord sorMeklan left with all the others. My brother's gone to his hall. If you're looking for your sword and harp—they went with Rinchen."

Dart sighed. "Midons prince—how is your brother? I've been told he was hellfired. Is he *changed* at all? This sullen alliance of yours, was it made of your own free will?"

The prince chuckled and sheathed his sword. "No dancing about the point with you, is there?" He threaded his arm through the coronet and began walking toward the gallery. "It's not a 'sudden alliance,' and if free will includes having someone hold your head under water until you're half drowned, then, yes, it was made of my own free will. I support my brother's legitimate right to rule and—whatever else *he* may have told you, I count him my friend as well as my brother and lord."

There were layers of meaning in the prince's words, but he

hadn't told Dart what he wanted to know. "I meant today. Has he changed since deadwatch? Since he was hellfired?"

Prince Aleg's expression hardened royally. "Since deadwatch our spooks lost the Web and our king lost his throne, but my brother fought hellfire with a plain steel sword." His smile was bitter. "It takes more than some damned Arrizi pyromant's hellfire to change the Wolf."

"She failed," Dart mused. "She didn't compromise him."

"She? The shepherd girl? He says she saved his life." Prince Aleg stared at the coronet. "For all the good it did her or him."

"For all the good it did?" Dart muttered. Hearing the prince talk about Berika when he'd been thinking about Arianna had unsettled him. "I don't understand."

"You don't?" the prince began spitefully; then his voice softened and he nodded. "No—you wouldn't. You didn't live through the war. You don't know about hellfire. It burns like fire at first, but it's more than fire. It burrows through a man's flesh. It gets into his blood and, finally, into his soul. The menders have to work fast to save a hellfired man, but somehow my brother got Arkkin to mend the girl first. Arkkin's Pennaik; he doesn't use the Web. He mended the girl, but he didn't have enough left for my brother. Arkkin will try again, but with hellfire, there comes a point where mending's no mercy—" Aleg hid his mouth behind an anxious hand. He stared out the window, even closed his eyes, before finding the will to continue. "He'd exercised his curse-talent for saying the wrong thing at the wrong time. I thought Lord Ean would walk out, but my brother showed a different kind of curse with hellfire oozing down his face. The bard had just announced that you were dead. Lord Ean buckled: 'For my brother's memory,' he said, 'I'll give you today.' And he did. Godswill, he did." The prince fingered the unadorned coronet.

"Every man or woman of rank followed Fenklare and swore liege-loyalty to the two of us. My brother's face looked like the slag at Kasserine when he walked out of here."

"Fenklare led the way? My brother, Ean?"

"Who else but a brother?"

Dart didn't answer. The chancery was quiet enough that the conversations of the menders in the next room were audible through the door. Prince Alegshorn broke the silence.

"Is there more? It's time to tell my dear mother that the situation's not as hopeless as she's undoubtedly told the Merrisati it is, but, if you're like-minded, I'll take you to Rinchen's hall first. It's not an easy place to find."

"I'd like that very much. I'm also relieved that you don't think the situation is hopeless. Do you and Rinchen have a strategy?"

"I don't and he's dying—" Another pause as the prince's voice cracked. "I don't *want* to be king," he whispered, words Dart sensed he should not have heard. But the golden prince recovered quickly, flashing a brilliant smile, and with a hearty laugh, wrapping a conspiratorial arm around Dart's shoulder. "You're alive. You're Weycha's champion. You swore you could kill her enemies. You swore you could kill the Wolf, with or without your wooden sword, and *he* believed you. *That*, Dart sorMeklan, restores hope in the darkest corner of our beleaguered kingdom."

Aleg steered them toward the menders' room door. "We'll take the backways, through the waiting room and the throne hall. It's faster, but it's not going to be a pleasant sight to see."

The prince's carefree charm did not fool Dart, but he was honored to be included in the tradition of sorRodion deception rather than merely its target.

King Manal's condition was unchanged. The menders were doing their best. They swathed the king in linen, dampened with Brightwater which they had created with their innate *basi* rather than with the Web. But the reedy mender who'd boldly upbraided Driskolt sorMeklan bowed his head to the prince and confessed that he did not believe their efforts were significant.

"Brightwater was King Manal's blood. Without it, without the magga menders who controlled and directed it, he should not be alive. It is a mystery to me, midons prince. A deep mystery."

"These are deeply mysterious times, good mender. I am taking Weycha's champion to my brother's hall, then retiring to my own. You will send a messenger to both those places if anything should change. *Anything*. And you will not, under any circumstance, send a messenger to my lady mother. Do you understand?"

The mender bowed lower, then raised his head and looked directly at Dart. "If I had realized that it was you—that the champion had cheated death a second time—Forgive me, but I saw only your friend. If, by chance, you are looking for him, he came through here not long after midons Prince Rinchen. Perhaps you will all meet in the Wolf's lair."

Dart touched Prince Alegshorn's arm. His voice was a whisper; he could not make it louder. "Dris has gone after Rinchen. He's going to kill him."

"Midons?" the sorcerer asked.

But Prince Aleg wasted no time with questions. He'd heard

enough and was already halfway across the throne hall when Dart started after him.

Prince Rinchen walked slowly through the backways. It would have been easier to drag the touchstone sack behind him, but he wrestled it in his good arm instead. Hellfire oozed with each step he took. The pain was defeating him; he'd gotten only as far as the dusty attic passage above the tunnel between the old palace and the new one. His vision was blurred on one side; his ear was ringing. He wanted to rest, but didn't dare.

By the time he heard the footsteps it was too late.

"Damn you to a cold hell!"

His hellfired ear garbled the words and there was no time to turn his head before the attacker slammed into his injured flank. He lost his balance. The sack slipped out of his hand, but he landed a solid kick in his attacker's gut before he collapsed in blind agony on the floor. The other man went down, too, and there was the distinctive sound of steel clattering against the wooden floor. Rinchen groaned. So close to death already, he still didn't want to die. But he had no defense against a sword except to lock his legs around his enemy's torso and keep them both on the floor until his strength gave out.

A *thrumming* rose from the sack, reminding him that one of Dart's touchstones was a sword. After dragging himself and his enemy across the floor, he slit the sack open—hellfired or bandaged, the Wolf went nowhere without a knife hidden in his sleeve. When his good hand felt the familiar contours of a sword-hilt he loosened his leg-hold, rammed a heel into his enemy's groin, and forced himself upright.

"Driskolt." Rinchen recognized his attacker as he came on guard. "There's no need, Dris—"

"Be damned there's no need." Aleg's friend retrieved his sword with a snarl. "You stole everything. You killed him, you godswilling bastard."

By then the prince had gotten a close look at his own weapon. It had the heft and length of a battle sword. In the open attic it should have had a considerable advantage over Driskolt's shorter city-sword, if it had not been made of wood. He prepared to defend himself, knowing it was futile.

"An assassin killed barKethmarion. You know that, Dris—"

Dris responded to his logic by gripping his own sword double-handed and slashing into Rinchen's blind side. Rinchen parried, quick and careful, despite the cost, absorbing the shock with his body, since a piece of wood could not take the full force of steel. He read Driskolt's stance as he had in Jeliff's courtyard, and saw repeated invitations for attack, but he was a different man now and could not make use of them. Dris backed him across the attic.

"Yield," Driskolt demanded, "and be damned."

Rinchen was an arm's length from the wall. He had to take the brunt of Driskolt's attack with the wooden sword, risking it and, of course, his life. The blades met with a metallic clash, surprising Rinchen, but not—Rinchen observed—Driskolt. Hellfire mixed with sweat, etching fresh wounds beneath the bandages, but the strange wooden sword hadn't splintered.

"Be damned yourself," he countered, beating the lighter sword aside now that he had confidence in his own weapon.

Footsteps echoed on the new palace stairway. Neither combatant risked disaster with a sidelong glance, nor paid any heed to shouted words, until a man-shape thrust itself between them. Driskolt sorMeklan went sprawling. His sword spun out of his hand. Rinchen had an instant to recognize his brother's golden hair in the tangle of arms and legs before he was seized from behind. An unfamiliar hand tried to disarm him.

He'd have none of that.

Despite the agony beneath his bandages, he writhed, kicked, and did his best to ram the ebony hilt into some unprotected part of his captor's body.

Dart placed his hand over Rinchen's on the hilt. "Not with my sword, you don't," he whispered into the prince's good ear.

But neither of them was prepared for what happened next. Summer-green sparks showered from the wooden sword's tip. They formed a stream that spiralled the length of the blade. When it wrapped over their clenched hands, Dart gasped and Rinchen stiffened with a scream.

Dart heard the music of the forest in all its distant splendor. He held a helpless Prince Rinchen in his arms as the sparks spread over the hellfire weals.

"Weycha honors your courage and forgives the death of her sister-self," he explained, hearing his goddess's voice in her music. "But, when I told you about Ash's red hair, you might have told me about your lady-love."

Verdant sparks reached the prince's face. As the wild-forest sorcery joined the battle with its enemy, the Wolf howled and went limp.

"Godswill!" Driskolt swore.

Prince Alegshorn, transfixed by the war of magic playing out across his brother's body, did nothing to stop Dris from retrieving his sword, so Dart aimed the sparkling tip of the wooden sword at his nephew's heart.

"Don't be a fool, Dris."

Dart let his sword fall. "I don't understand," he muttered.

Dart eased Rinchen onto the floor. The prince was conscious. His eyes were wide open and filled with terror, but his body belonged to the sword . . . and Weycha. When his hand finally slid off the hilt, the wild green sorcery continued to swirl above his wounds.

Prince Aleg cast a measured glance at Driskolt's fallen weapon before asking Dart: "Is he going to live?"

"My lady chooses to heal him."

Hellfire did not die quietly or easily. The air around the prince crackled. Snakelike tongues of amber, purple, and poison-green slashed through the sparks.

"You're certain?"

"The sword is a living part of Weycha's will. She could have killed him with it, but she chose to heal him instead. See for yourself: The wounds are already growing smaller."

"I'll take your word. I don't intend to come any closer. What did you mean 'Ash's red hair'?"

"Hazard's sister never died. She was her brother's ally from the start, I think," Dart explained. He shot a glance at the hellfire-green and forest-green flames hissing across Rinchen's face and hoped he was unconscious at last, before he told Aleg, and Dris, about his encounters with Arianna. "She said she visited his dreams. He'd kept a touchstone from the betrothal gifts, a hellfire crystal, she said. I'm certain he fought her, not Hazard, last night."

"Arianna. Iser's cast-iron balls," Prince Aleg mused. "I never guessed. Never came close. All that nonsense about oaths and vows. Will he or won't he? Does he or doesn't he, with whom or what? And all the while my brother's been lovestruck while Hazard's sister visits him in his dreams. Poor bastard. I'll wager she gave him a pretty nightmare or two."

The sorcery-shrouded lump between them all groaned, and with extraordinary effort lifted a closed fist and held it there until his strength failed completely and his arm fell heavily back to the floor.

Chapter Nineteen

"I feel like a fool, Aleg. I fought beside you in the war. I trusted you with my life. *I invited you into a conspiracy against your gods-be-damned brother!* I was going to kill him for you. His cursed blood on my hands so you could rule clean. Godswill, Aleg, has it always been this way? Another sorRodion scheme to keep the clans in disarray, as Manal does with the river? Godswill—I never cared about the rest. I was content to be your friend, and now I feel like a damned fool."

Dart laid the now-inert wooden sword on the floor beside him and, after assuring himself that forest sorcery was slowly winning the battle against hellfire, sat on his heels to watch. Even a fool could look at Prince Aleg's face and read that he wasn't going to thank the man who killed his brother. Driskolt's voice hurt to hear, but he wasn't angry yet, and might never be, if Prince Aleg could say the right words quickly enough.

Prince Alegshorn picked up Driskolt's sword. He held it out, hilt-first: an unspoken declaration of continued trust and friendship. "Vigelan rode us hard before we knew better, and there were acts that couldn't be forgotten, couldn't be talked about. Even now—" Aleg glanced at his brother's hand which lay still. "It was real enough, Dris, until he won. He chiseled, but he won. He's had my oath for three years. I resented it at first, but not anymore. Vigelan's dead. We've talked; we've forgiven—" The prince's eyes never left his brother's unmoving hand. "I've forgiven," he corrected quietly.

"You lied to us, midons prince." Dris lapsed into formality; anger had begun to show. "You made fools of us, of me. Your friend. I asked if you would take a stand against the Wolf, and you said you would." He refused to accept his sword.

"Harsh words, Dris. I took advantage of your prejudice—it's something I've learned from the Wolf. I told you I would stand with you *if* he acted as you believed he intended to do. And I would stand with you, even now, if I did not have my brother's oath that he will not."

"What good's a Brightwater oath anymore?" Driskolt was in no mood for reconciliation.

"Not Brightwater, just a plain oath sworn in blood over red-hot steel. Trust grows, but first you have to plant the seed." Prince Alegshorn waggled the hilt. "Ask yourself: What were you doing in that courtyard last night? Why didn't you kill the shepherds when you had the chance? Jeliff was *my* man, Dris, a spy sworn to me before Rinchen and I made our peace. He ran a web inside the Arrizan empire, he gave us useful knowledge, but the Wolf never trusted him, wanted to cut him loose after Tremontin. The kind of man Jeliff was— The kind of man my brother is— That meant killing him, and I'm the one who balked. Rinchen wanted him dead, but he wouldn't touch him against my will—

"Now ask yourself, Dris: What was the Wolf doing in that courtyard?"

The attic was quiet, except for the sound of sorcery: then Driskolt snatched the sword from Prince Aleg's hand and snarled: "Watching out for his own. Damn you, Aleg—he was looking for answers. Just like me."

"You deserve answers, my friend. And I love you as a friend, Dris. I've kept an eye out for your honor these last three years, knowing that I couldn't tell you the truth: *my* decision, again. I could have persuaded Rinchen, but I judged the risk to you too great. Now it's time for us to have a long talk—the truth, as much of it as you want to hear—then I think we'll get very drunk."

Driskolt slammed his sword into its scabbard. "I don't understand. I don't believe I can understand, but I want to, Aleg. And I want to get away from here." Then, after he wiped his face on his sleeve, he said, "Killy's dead, Aleg. Did you know that? Jeliff, *your* man—your *assassin* slew him where he stood. He was my responsibility. My father told me to make a man of him. I made a corpse instead: naked, frozen, thrown away like garbage. What for, Aleg? What for?"

"For Walensor," Aleg answered, wrapping his arms around a stiff, reluctant friend. "For Walensor, because her kings and princes have become too skilled at deceit. I swear to you, Dris, it's over— *We* swear it, my brother and I: No more deception."

Slowly Driskolt's arms rose and tightened over the prince's shoulders. "I want to believe, Aleg."

"Come to my hall, we'll start there—" Aleg paused, looked up, and caught Dart's eye. "We can, can't we? Your goddess is quenching the hellfire, isn't she? My brother's going to live?"

He nodded. "As Weycha wills. He'll be hungry as—a wolf and sore, but definitely alive."

He watched the relief spread over Aleg's face and wondered how anyone had ever believed the princes opposed each other. Except he had believed. Taking advantage of prejudice, Aleg had called it, and done it very well. His nephew looked like a man thoroughly taken advantage of, as the prince, his arm still on Driskolt's shoulders, led the way to the far stairs. But Aleg had the royal grace which the sorRodion had lacked for generations. The pair would be friends again, stronger than ever, before the sun set.

"Join us in my hall, when you can," Prince Aleg called back from the top of the old palace stairway. It was not a request. "I'll have food waiting for both of you."

They departed and Dart retrieved the acorn from the slit-open sack. He ran his hands lovingly over the acorn's rough cap. The nut split, freeing the harp. His fingers traced idle melodies over strings that never required tuning. With his back to the ensorcelled prince, he wove private songs of joy and loneliness. The songs had no words—at least none that needed singing. When his song was complete, he rested his head against the bark-covered pillar and Weycha guided his hands through countermelodies.

Prince Rinchen moaned when he heard the harp sing with Weycha's voice. His arm and legs thrashed against the floor. Forest-green sorcery had conquered the hellfire, but it didn't fade. Dart's hands played mirth, his own and his lady's. The Wolf lay still again. Then the harp played compassion and the aches of love denied. The music changed slowly, creeping toward joy and other bright passions as the Wolf, himself, crept toward the harp once his body's healing was complete.

Dart recalled another bitter cold winter, eighteen years past, when music wrung tears from his rogue's soul, transforming him into the goddess's champion. Weycha had no mercy for the men she used. When she was finished, the Wolf would not be the same.

"You carry a goddess in your hands," the prince said, sitting now with one leg curled beneath him and the other bent, supporting his chin. His weapon hand lay palm-up beside his ankle; the other one was still bound beneath his shirt. His eyes were their usual silver—Dart had wondered about that, knowing what forest sorcery had done to his. Rinchen's face was whole, returned to ivory pallor.

"Only her voice," Dart said, bringing the melody to an end. "Weycha sleeps in winter. She dreams the future, but she does not know which dreams will come true. Her dreams transformed me into her champion. She made the harp so we could be together when we were not dreaming. She never dreamt that I would leave her forest. She never dreamt that her enemy would destroy the Web."

"Pyromant Hazard."

"Necromant," Dart corrected. "He seized the Web with the usurped souls of ten thousand Arrizi soldiers. They used you, midons prince. Hazard intended a war from the start, never a marriage. His sister was his accomplice. They must have hoped Kasserine would be enough, but four thousand Walenfolk souls proved insufficient—or unwilling—to storm the Web. He waited until he could sacrifice his entire army. The death of Tremontin filled my lady with dread because Weycha is Tremontin, not because of the Web. She never dreamt Hazard's entire plan. And she did not dream that her enemy had an ally."

The Wolf bowed his head. "Two."

"I told you that I knew Ash was wrong, but I didn't know how wrong until it was too late. Arianna used you worse than Hazard ever planned. She had designs for Weycha, designs for you; but my lady has healed you. I accept her judgment. You were used, my friend, but never dishonored."

Rinchen turned away, rejecting compassion. "Everything I did—*Everything!*—served my kingdom's mortal enemies. I've ruined the only thing I dared love. My curse haunts me. I cannot outrun it." The proud, brittle prince sat with his face hidden behind his knee. Heaving shoulders hinted at otherwise mute anguish.

Words had failed, so Dart took up the harp again. The light coming through the arrow-slit windows above the tunnel had grown dim before Rinchen raised his head.

"I'm going to fall on my sword."

Once again Dart ended his song. "Pardon me, but I won't wager on the outcome," he said lightly and the prince glowered at him, clearly unprepared to hear his dire promises dismissed by a chronic gambler.

"Why, by the gods, *not*? I've destroyed everything. Nothing's too big for my curse to swallow: forests, kingdoms, Webs, *goddesses*! You of all people— You—" The prince's voice, which had been gaining volume, faded to a whisper: "You know about Arianna. You should let me use your sword."

"I did, and look what happened. There's not even a scar."

Rinchen touched his cheek. "Godswill . . ."

"Beyond a doubt. Now, my friend and my prince, will you accept a dead man's advice?" He took the Wolf's scowl for assent. "There's precious little difference between being cursed and being champion."

"I hear no advice in that, not even truth."

"The harp tells me that Arianna's followed Hazard to Weychawood. I'm only one man; I need another. Avenge yourself. Set aside your curse and come with me to the forest. Help me save my lady and all the rest you love."

Rinchen stared through the arrow-slit windows at a lavender twilight sky. Stars appeared.

"I cannot refuse," he said, making it clear that it was not an easy or simple declaration. "Were I a champion, I wouldn't trust a cursed man. I'd kill him now, before his curse struck again. All the same, I would welcome vengeance. I'll go with you to the forest. You, to your lady goddess. Me, to my . . . Me, with my curse. I'll be ready."

Dart smiled a bemused smile as Rinchen stripped off his shirt. The prince used brute force against the tough linen strips, but whoever had bandaged him, knew him well. The knots were sealed with wax. The harder Rinchen pulled, the tighter the knots became. Already drained by the healing, Rinchen was panting exhausted before the first knot yielded. Dart removed the fruit knife from his belt and sliced through the bandages. He was about to chide the prince for stubbornness, when he saw the scars that Weycha had not touched.

He didn't need to ask questions. A lifetime ago, he'd lived in Prince Vigelan's world. He'd seen that handsome face turn raging purple when his firstborn's name was spoken. The scars were at least a decade old. It took very little to imagine the beatings Rinchen had taken before Kasserine.

Then he thought about Arianna poisoning a young man's

dreams year after year, and wondered what other horrors were written in the Wolf's memory.

In his efforts to remove the bandages, the prince had clawed his skin until it bled. The wonder was not that Rinchen believed he was cursed or succumbed to mindless savagery; the wonder was that, mostly, Prince Rinchen was a sane, sometimes gentle, man. Dart unwound the remaining linen gently, in respectful silence.

Weycha's healing sorcery had extracted a greater price from Rinchen's body than it had taken from Dart. The prince was gaunt beneath the bandages and remained on the floor, gathering strength, while Dart shoved the noisome linen through the arrow-slits. When he returned, he offered Rinchen a helping hand to stand up. The prince eyed it suspiciously.

"I don't *bite,* my prince. A few splinters, now and again . . ."

Another man might have laughed, or blushed. Rinchen shook his head until his shaggy, uneven hair fell before his eyes. But he took Dart's hand firmly and accepted a bit of help getting to his feet.

Still hiding behind his hair, he muttered: "Thank you."

"I should thank you for returning my lady's gift— And for returning Rodion's spear."

"Godswill!"

Rinchen turned away so suddenly that Dart thought the prince was fainting, and lunged to catch him. "What's wrong?"

Gaunt as he was, the Wolf was still quick. Dart failed to touch him. "Nothing. A stray thought. There's something I must do before we leave. Lord Ean will hardly be pleased with his bargain once he learns that I have not died. I don't have a sweet tongue for persuasion, but I must try. How much time do I have before we leave?"

"My lady is safe until the forest quickens," Dart said, repeating what he'd felt when he first touched the sword and what the harp had confirmed in his arms.

"Two full months, forty days—that's more than I dared hope."

Dart shook his head. "Not the calendar's Quickening, the forest's quickening. Hazard is already in Weychawood, using the Web to warm the ground. We have days, maybe weeks, but not months. Let me help you with Ean."

"No, the girl betrayed you in Relamain. I can't ask you to help. Won't. It wouldn't be right."

"Berika?"

"She saved my life last night. Today, Lord Ean thought you were dead and I was dying. He was in a mood to be generous, and so, unfortunately, was I. I returned the thief along with what she had stolen."

He'd heard the tale from Driskolt at the residence. "You had no choice. She stole Rodion's spear and Ean knew it. Once you admitted you had it, he would have asked about her. If you hadn't surrendered her, you'd be harboring a fugitive from clan justice—a bad precedent for a new reign."

Ean's retribution was nothing he'd wish on an enemy, much less a country-common shepherd, but it was a distant concern, now that he had the harp and had heard Weycha's warning. If he and Rinchen were going to Weychawood, they barely had time to prepare for a hard, winter journey. Berika could, and would, take care of herself.

"Berika often does things that she should not do—remarkable things—but she survives."

"Remarkable things like luring you away from your goddess and betraying you? I don't expect you or Weycha to forgive her, and I don't expect Lord Ean to withhold clan justice, but she saved my life. I must plead for her. I returned that damned spear no worse for its adventure; that should count for something. You sorMeklan get stiff-necked and foolish about Rodion's spear. You got so drunk congratulating yourselves when you found it, you never noticed Rodion bedding the queen. By the time you were sober again, her belly had swelled and the throne was his—" Rinchen laughed, a humorless chuckle. "I know—I'll tell Lord Ean that she used it against me . . . Maybe he'll adopt her into the sorMeklan."

Dart reassembled the acorn pieces around his harp while the prince pulled on his shirt. He recalled the grand feasts in Relamain when regalia was paraded through the hall, and he found, to his dismay, that he didn't like hearing the sorMeklan myths debased by Rodion's ice-eyed descendant. His neck did get stiff, and he needed a moment to convince himself that this was what Prince Aleg called his brother's curse-talent for saying precisely the wrong thing.

"If you want the sorMeklan to treat Berika with mercy rather than justice," he said then, "you'll have better luck pleading your case to Driskolt."

"Need I remind you that Dris just tried to kill me? The only way I'd persuade Dris to give Berika mercy is if I got on my knees and begged him to flay her slowly over a fire." Rinchen picked up the knife he'd used to slit the sack and examined its edge before sliding it into the sheath beneath his sleeve.

"I don't think you'll have to go that far. Your brother's been plying him with food and wine. In fact, he's ordered us to join them. Dris will be in the mood for noble gestures. Persuade Driskolt, then let him persuade Ean. Ean won't let Berika, or even our 'damned' spear, create a rift between himself and Driskolt. We stiff-necked sorMeklan don't devour our young, unlike certain barbaric Pennaik marauders."

Rinchen frowned. "They drove you to an early death—but I'll try."

The first nightwatch of the new year progressed through several of its hours while the four young men, two sorRodion princes and two sorMeklan sidons—present and former—sat in front of the hearth in Prince Alegshorn's hall. Driskolt sorMeklan was on his feet and snarling at the Wolf more than once. Aleg's knuckles grew sore from the clenched-fists signals he shot at his brother. Dart guessed the essence of the code, adding a second voice to that silent conversation and soothing melodies whenever it threatened to disintegrate completely.

In the end a compromise was reached: Berika would be confined in the sorMeklan cellars for a week—she had, after all, stolen the single most valuable item in the sorMeklan regalia—but she would not be beaten, and when she emerged from the cellars the clan would arrange a respectable marriage for her.

"She has *influence,*" Driskolt concluded, "and no small amount of intelligence and beauty. When this is over, and order is restored, we will find a disciplined spook to marry her. Surely some worthy man has survived. Beri's no fool. She'll understand that what we offer is better than returning to her village to herd sheep."

Dart found himself challenging the arranged marriage. "Berika's earned her widowhood," he countered, but they outnumbered him and he had no stomach for an argument that might force him to admit that whenever he thought of his beloved goddess, she wore Berika's face. He wove a persuasive chord and the discussion meandered to simpler matters, like food, drink . . . and the fate of Walensor if Rinchen did not return from Weychawood, or even if he did.

Considering how it began, the day had gone better than Rinchen dared hope. A renegade goddess had healed his hellfire wounds, and the clans had accepted his right to rule the kingdom with his brother openly beside him. He'd survived another assassination attempt and reached an honorable compromise with that would-be assassin in the matter of the commonborn shepherd who'd saved him from Arianna.

Arianna was another matter entirely. Courtesy of Dart's goddess, there was a bright and wholesome light shining into his life. He wasn't sure he liked it; the contrast was too great. Throughout the war, he'd shared his most private thoughts with a hellfire crystal. He'd loved Arianna in darkness, believing that what she offered—bitter memories, torture, anguish, and an unshakable belief that he died each time he dreamt about her—was all a cursed man deserved.

Weycha's light left no place for shame. He preferred the dark. He clutched two loaves of bread he'd taken from Aleg's hall, and Vigelan's coronet, tightly in his arms. Then he ran up the stairs to his hall, pausing at the landing where firelight and droning voices spilled from an open doorway.

A gust of snow struck Rinchen as he stood on the threshold of the hall his Pennaikmen claimed for themselves. They had made their own compromises with palace life, removing the glass and shutters from the windows. Arkkin led the chanting from the hearthstones. In one hand the shaman shook a rattle made from the skull of a horse, in the other he held a ladle made from the skull of a man. A large kettle hung above the fire, releasing vapors that were as noxious as hellfire.

The chanting ebbed when the Pennaikmen saw their prince. Arkkin continued alone for some moments; he scowled when he looked up. Leaving the ladle on the stones, he approached the doorway, shaking the rattle with every step. He probed Rinchen's healed cheek with a stiff forefinger, then pinched it hard.

"Who did this?" he demanded, shaking the rattle on either side of the prince's head.

"The goddess Weycha, through her champion's sword."

"What price?"

"No price I do not willingly pay. We will accompany the champion to Weychawood. There is—" He stopped short of explaining himself. The Pennaikmen were fiercely loyal, the shaman in particular, but they had not offered their service until he was sixteen. They'd never expressed an interest in the origin of the Arrizan War, and they kept their opinion of his curse to themselves. "There is something I must do in the forest."

He had not spoken loudly. Between the wind and the hearth fire, there was no reason for his voice to reach the corners of the hall, yet it did. While Arkkin stared into his eyes, the six other Pennaik warriors rose to their feet.

"The girl with hair of fire," Arkkin said to the others in their native tongue. Allowing for ambiguities—and Arkkin was a master of ambiguities, often loading four or five meanings into a single phrase when the men gathered around a summer bonfire—he might also have meant: wildfire raging across the steppes or a mother who roasts her children. "It is time," he added with a more straightforward inflection.

Rinchen felt cold. "Time for what?"

Arkkin returned to his kettle. He threw powder into the flames; they hissed and smoked. Then, with no greater warning, the nomads began to pack their meager possessions. Rinchen swallowed hard. Winter journeys required extensive and deliberate preparations. There was no way he and Dart could leave Eyerlon before the end of Greater Ice, no reason for the Pennaikmen to be packing—

Unless they did not intend to accompany him to Weychawood.

The Pennaikmen gave Rinchen their service, not their oaths. He could not command them and felt suddenly, deeply foolish that he had come to rely upon them. With a bitter voice, he repeated his question. They ignored him until he strode across the threshold, then Arkkin aimed the horse skull at his chest. The shaman uttered a Pennaik word that meant, among other things, "impure," and he retreated.

"Are you leaving?" Rinchen asked, choosing Pennaik words that implied both abandonment and cowardice.

Arkkin swirled the horse-skull rattle. "We prepare to meet your destiny, in Weychawood. We will be ready," he replied, then added, in ordinary Walens, "Sleep well, my prince."

The shaman's words in both languages were susceptible to varied interpretations, as was the sly smile on his face. Rinchen continued up to his hall with none of the contentment he'd felt moments earlier. There were two more Pennaikmen standing guard by torchlight inside his otherwise empty hall. Each held spears identical to the one Berika had stolen from the sorMeklan, and stoppered jugs that might have contained shimya'an but were more probably filled with Arkkin's noxious brew. Neither Pennaikman seemed surprised to see that he was hale and whole. Except for their stares, which followed him the length of the hall, neither man acknowledged him at all.

He squared his shoulders and entered his private chamber. He'd barely gotten the door closed when he was blind-sided. His small attacker was not at all skilled in rough-and-tumble arts, and with little more than a shrug, he dumped the unfortunate fool onto the floor.

"Berika!"

She wore an absurd assortment of her own linen and his clothes. In the shadowed, flickering light, he could see that she'd been crying. She flinched when he reached for her hand, but he seized it anyway and hauled her upright.

"Godswill, Berika, what happened? Why are you still here and why are you frightened?"

She started crying and he put his arms around her gingerly. He meant to console her, but his awkward efforts only fed her terror, until he was inspired to hold her hand against his healed cheek.

"It *is* me, Berika. I'm healed. I held Dart's wooden sword, and the forest goddess healed me."

Her head sagged against his shoulder. "He said I stole your life, midons prince. He said he was going to keep me here until the moon rose and then he was going to cut my throat and take the blood out of my heart—"

"He? Arkkin?"

Berika nodded.

"I would not let him do that," he insisted. But he knew that if the brew of salted horse blood and shimya'an didn't purge the hellfire from his body, Arkkin would have added a woman's blood to the brew, and he wouldn't have been in any condition to object.

While Berika shivered against him, he cast a glance around his room, looking for the sorMeklan spear, relieved when he did not see it. The room itself was still scarred from the previous night. Sand was scattered everywhere and the ruin of his chair sat in the charred splotch where the brazier had exploded and burned. But there was also a cheerful fire in the hearth and a set of empty dishes beside it.

"Did you eat before or after they came for the spear?"

"Both. The old blackhead didn't want to take any chances that I'd be short of blood. He made me take off my gown, midons; then he wrapped the spear in it. He said there'd be no questions after he slit my throat."

Rinchen knew Arkkin wasn't above spinning tales when it suited him. The spear had been naked when it arrived in the chancery. The Pennaikmen carrying it—neither of whom had been Arkkin—swore that the thief had been escorted to the sorMeklan residence. He was inclined now to interpret Arkkin's "sleep well" in a completely different way.

"There's nothing to be afraid of. I'm healed and the moon's

been up for hours. All we have to do is find you some respectable clothes and you can return to the sorMeklan residence. Everything may have worked out for the best. Whatever story got passed back to the residence, Dart and Dris will have pleaded for you. By the time you get there, they may well have decided on a suitable husband, a sorcerer—"

Berika wriggled free. "Midons, I won't! Never! Midons, I'd sooner the old blackhead cut my throat. I'd sooner have frozen in that courtyard or died of hellfire. I won't be sold and I won't be married off to some rat-faced Nishrun. I'm a widow, midons prince. I have earned a widow's rights!"

"Dart said your husband was a beast who deserved his death, but you're too young to be a widow the rest of your life. You're a beautiful woman. Surely you don't wish to live without a husband? Dris agreed that your services to the clan outweighed your crimes against it. If 'rat-faced Nishrun' is not to your liking, name another . . . The sorMeklan acknowledge their responsibility. It is not a question of being sold. They will pursue your interests."

Where marriage was concerned, Rinchen knew himself to be a poor advocate. He recognized the panic that widened her eyes. He'd have felt the same way if he'd thought four men had calmly plotted his life, regardless of his "best interests."

She was looking for escape, and he let her go. She stood still a moment, scanning the room like a frightened animal. There was one window behind heavy shutters and it was sealed with leaded glass. There were two doors, not counting the garderobe. One was hidden among the wood panels, and if she remembered it at all, she'd remember that his brother had emerged from it last night. Women flocked to Aleg, but his bedroom was scarcely a sanctuary for a woman seeking to escape the domination of men. The other door led to his hall and beyond.

He caught her effortlessly as she spurted for that door. "What ails you, Berika?"

She struck with fists and feet, shouting: "I don't want to have my life chosen for me. If I can't have anything that I want, then I just want to be left alone. I want to live in a quiet room, by myself."

Rinchen was not without empathy. "How would you live in a room by yourself? You would have to eat, unless you chose to starve. You would need wood for a winter fire, unless you chose to freeze. You have only those skills the gods grant to every woman. Is marriage truly the worst fate you can imagine?"

Berika hissed and struggled. "I want to be free to live my own life."

"Then, dear lady, you would be freer than a king or prince—and I cannot help you. No shepherd may be freer than royalty." He was bitter, thinking of his own life—of the Severing rite which had begun it, and ended it. He enjoyed nothing more than the hours he spent in the Palestra, swaddled in a veteran's bandages and arguing philosophy with the maggas. He could live without the throne, he thought, if they'd left him whole to use the Web. But he was cursed, and they hadn't.

Berika, not surprisingly misunderstood. "What would you do to help me, midons crown prince?" she snarled, spitting acid into his title. "Nobody tells you how to live your life! You live the way you want, midons *prince,* and damn the whole world." She freed one arm and backhanded him across the jaw.

Three months as Driskolt's leman had not softened this shepherd's work-hardened muscles. Vigelan would have approved of her aim and force, and for a moment Rinchen battled a murderous rage. He'd promised himself that once he was grown to manhood no one would strike him without regretting it. The vow had served through the war and with assassins; but it failed with Berika. Maybe it was Dart's goddess who'd put light in the dark places. Maybe, but he didn't want to exchange a curse for a goddess. Better—easier—to admit he was simply tired. He shoved her away, a bit forcefully, and rubbed his stinging jaw.

Berika stumbled but kept her balance, and her defiance. She fully expected the Wolf to lunge for her throat, but to her astonishment, he lowered his arms and spoke gently:

"Open your eyes, Berika. Look around you. This is living alone, leaving them alone and being left alone by everyone. Godswill, woman—is *this* what you want?"

"I want to be happy. I want to make lace and sell it for gold to noble ladies. I'll live in a warm room. I'll sit by a big window, making my lace, and watch the sun set every afternoon. I don't believe in curses, midons prince. I make my own luck; the sorcerers said so. I'll work very hard, but only for myself. I'll come and go as I please, with no one to tell me otherwise."

"Do you know how to make lace?"

The simple question vanquished Berika's rage, leaving her with wobbly knees and blurred vision. "No, it's a dream, midons prince. A foolish dream."

"Then, please, dream it while you're sleeping. I was bone-weary when I opened the door; I still am. We are back where we were before. I will not turn you out if you have nowhere to go, but I do not sleep on the floor in my own room. Get into bed and pray for dreams of lace." To emphasize his point, he began to unlace his pants.

"Midons prince, I won't mind the floor." Berika clutched her borrowed clothes and moved no closer to the bed. "Everything's changed . . ."

"Berika—I resisted the temptation to break your neck when you struck me. I swear to you, I will resist the temptation to rape you should your leg brush against mine while we sleep. Godswill, Dart swears you slept like kittens all the way across Fenklare. Tell yourself I'm Weycha's champion and *go to bed.*"

Embarrassed and appalled, Berika bundled herself into the bed while the prince banked the hearth and lowered the bed curtains. She was determined that no part of her would touch his leg or anywhere else, but, unfortunately, the prince not only wanted to sleep in his own narrow bed, he insisted on sleeping square in the middle of it. She balanced precariously on the edge of the mattress, with her back against the cold wall.

The Web was quiet, unnaturally quiet, which was at least better than the echoed screaming she'd heard all day. She did not waste her time with a prayer to Mother Cathe for lace or anything else. She took the prince's advice and thought about Dart.

But the palace wasn't a Fenklare haystack, or even the Knotted Rose Inn in Relamain where they'd stayed while she was sick. She'd been blinded by Hirmin's brutality while she and Dart were together, rejecting a man who—she knew now—loved her, because she believed Dart's love would be like Hirmin's love, and all love was the enemy. If she could return to that moldy haystack or the Knotted Rose, she wouldn't sleep with her back to his, but burrow into his arms, welcoming whatever he offered her and cherishing it forever.

Berika thought about Dart; she listened to the Wolf settle himself in the linen and begin to draw slow, steady breaths. The Wolf wasn't a beast, like Hirmin. He wasn't even a good-natured tyrant like Driskolt sorMeklan. With King Manal dying, the man lying beside her was the most powerful man in Walensor. He was also a lonely man, with horrible scars on his back and—she was certain—elsewhere. He was cursed and took life without a second thought, but he hadn't raised a hand to her, although she'd given him cause.

Arkkin said he'd sacrificed his life to save hers.

This is living alone, the Wolf had said when she told him her dreams. *Godswill, woman—is this what you want?*

Was it what he wanted? Did either of them need love as an enemy? Not lasting love— Berika wasn't foolish enough to think love between a country-common shepherd and a prince could last. But who knew how long any love would last, and was not knowing an adequate reason to call love the enemy?

"There's more to life than survival," she murmured.

"Go to sleep."

Holding her breath in the bed-curtained darkness, Berika stretched her arm until her fingertips touched the ropelike scars. Habit and all the voices of her conscience tried to pull her arm back, but she overcame habit and conscience alike. Her fingers brushed gently over the ridges of his shoulder. There were fresh scabs, despite Weycha's healing. Berika shuddered, thinking of Hirmin's hellfired flesh. Prince Rinchen shuddered, too. She couldn't guess his thoughts, but he neither turned toward her nor pulled away.

Berika dared again—wriggling closer until she could mold herself to his back. Locks of soft, shaggy hair tickled her forehead. Her lips touched the line between scars and smooth flesh at his shoulder. His heart was pounding beneath her fingers, and he breathed with shudders and gasps. But, otherwise, the Wolf didn't move. Last night he'd mentioned vows, undoubtedly made to Arianna, the hellfire apparition who'd nearly killed them both. Surely last night's vows did not apply tonight.

She kissed him lightly, and—truth to tell—mistakenly, amid the scars. He made a noise somewhere between a growl and a moan.

"My lady, that is not chaste."

She kissed him again, still lightly, still amid the scars. "I know, midons," she said, and marvelled at the sound of her own voice.

"I have no wish to hurt you."

"I'm not afraid."

The prince moaned—a small, sad sound—without the passion she'd expected. "I am," he admitted, barely loud enough for her to hear. He turned in her arms. His touch was gentle—gentler than her own, his kisses, lighter still. The Wolf did nothing Berika did not do first, and then hesitantly, almost reluctantly. Thinking of Hirmin, Driskolt, even Killeen, she was puzzled and impatient. Men were men; she expected certain, sometimes unpleasant, things to happen.

Perhaps men were not born knowing, any more than she had

been. Perhaps men had to learn what happened between men and women when their bodies pressed close together.

And Prince Rinchen did not know, had not learned.

She pulled him close and taught him.

Later, when they lay twined in each other's arms and much more comfortable than before, Berika discovered that the shame she had borne since Hirmin first thrust her into a corner and tore away her clothes was gone. She was free and safe, and unafraid to say the words she had never needed to say before.

"Midons, I—"

He sealed her lips with a finger.

"Call me by my name, and know that I treasure this and you. But don't talk to me about love. I have no place in my soul for love. I am content to live without it. I do not hurt what I do not love and it does not hurt me. We have the moment, and for the moment we have each other. That must be enough."

Chapter Twenty

Over the next few days, Berika settled into another corner room tucked beneath another roof in a much larger residence. The Wolf's old palace lair was larger than her sorMeklan room and solidly walled with plastered stone. Between the hearth and a new brazier, the room was comfortably warm. It was also very isolated; Berika saw more of the Pennaik shaman, Arkkin, than she did of her prince.

Prince Rinchen began his days at dawn on the practice fields; Berika understood that part of his life. But he couldn't retreat into privacy each afternoon, and his evenings were as crowded as his days. The Web had unified Walensor. Without it—or so her prince said when she saw him—ruling his still-moribund grandfather's kingdom was difficult; meeting the challenge of Hazard's usurpation was almost impossible.

Each night, after a light supper, he'd sit in his chair—a new one—staring at the hearth, until his brother came through the panel door. The princes would talk until the deadwatch peal had rung and been forgotten. Berika didn't understand a quarter of what she overheard, but she understood that Walensor would be a very thoroughly ruled kingdom if Dart and Prince Rinchen wrested the Web back from its Arrizi usurpers.

One matter she did understand was that of Prince Rinchen's Merrisati bride, presumed to have begun her tiresome journey from her maritime kingdom to Walensor; without the Web there was no way to confirm her progress. Berika's heart ached each time she heard Princess Thylda's name, but she held fast to Rinchen's advice: Treasure the moments they had; the future would come of its own soon enough.

On the fourth day of Greater Ice, Arkkin hauled a large green-and-ruby box to the lair along with her midday meal. He seemed as curious about the contents as she was, but the blackhead shaman still made her nervous, and she refused to open the box while he was there. He scuttled about the lair for hours muttering in his incomprehensible language before finally leaving—she hoped it wasn't a curse. She waited until the bells struck again before untying the ribbons around the box.

The sorMeklan had sent her things to the palace, acknowledging her relocation, with all that implied. Her lace-making pillow, her needles, and her spools of thread were neatly arranged in the topmost layer. Beneath them were clothes, boots, a set of combs for her hair, and a small purse filled with bright and uncut silver coins. There was no way for her to know who had prepared the box, but because of the coins, she suspected it had come from Dart; he'd remember and understand that she needed the peace of mind only minted silver could provide.

Berika played with her coins and practiced her lacemaking after that. She mastered the simple stitches she'd learned from the crone at the sorMeklan residence and used her silver coins to make new lace-patterns or parchment scraps. She was ready for another lesson, and the prince would have arranged it, had she asked—anything unfamiliar seemed to fascinate him. He'd wanted to thread the needle himself and experiment with each of the stitches she knew. Berika considered this a waste of their moments together—especially as he was better at the fine work than she was.

Prince Rinchen surprised her in other ways. Shy, lonely, and strangely unsure of himself around her, he seemed content to ask endless questions about her life, Gorse, and the sheep; he revealed little about himself, and that with such reluctance that she stopped asking questions. He was more interested in teaching her to sign her name than he was in taking her to bed, where, more often than not, they slept—as Dart would have it—like kittens in each other's arms.

She knew the moments wouldn't last. If Princess Thylda did not arrive, some other royal daughter would. Their days were numbered, like the squares on the stained counting board she found beneath his worktable. Rinchen swore he didn't love her, or anyone else. Then he'd place his hand over hers, guiding her through the snarl of lines he said was her name, and she'd feel his pulse hammering.

Several days later Prince Rinchen made an unexpected afternoon appearance in his lair. Berika sat at the worktable, making circles with her silver coins on the counting board. She tried to slide the coins unobtrusively into their soft leather purse, but Rinchen was faster, as always.

"They came in the box from the sorMeklan residence," she explained hastily. "Dart put them there."

"Not very likely." He spilled the coins from one hand to the other. "Dart did not ask Lord Ean to restore his property, and Lord Ean did not offer anything before he left Eyerlon. I offered to endow him with lordless sorRodion land, but he says he has no interest in land or money. He only wants to get out of Eyerlon more quickly than I can arrange. These coins come from Dris, to rankle me."

The coins clattered onto the counting board where, one by one, Berika returned them to the purse.

"Dart cares about money. He does very well with dice, especially wooden dice."

The prince took her hand and the coin that it held. "True, but if Dart had won these coins, some would be clipped, some would be worn, and they all would be tarnished. These coins are all clean and bright as the day they were minted. They've been behind sorMeklan treasure wards for nearly eleven years."

"Maybe Dart asked for them?"

"No. I'll wager against every one of these coins that Lord Ean gave Dris permission to dower you, and Dris chose these coins to let me know that he's forgiven you, but never me."

There was still much Berika did not know about her prince, but she knew he didn't gamble. "How can you be so certain?"

Rinchen flipped the coin she held. There was an inscription that she could not read and a crude profile she could not hope to recognize. "That"—he pointed out one half of the inscription—"is my name. And this is Arianna's. King Manal struck these coins for our marriage. They were never circulated. I thought they'd all been melted and reminted, but the sorMeklan collect more than our spears. If you're going to live up here where the air is thin, you must learn to be observant."

The coin slipped through Berika's fingers. It bounced once on the counting board and vanished into the clutter. "There's too much. I'll never learn. I can't learn to write my name. I can't read, midons." She couldn't call him by his given name, no matter that she loved him. "I can't even read what's on a silver coin, midons."

The one thing he'd asked from her, and she couldn't give it. He never reminded or chastised her, and tried to hide that he noticed. She wouldn't have known that he had, if he hadn't been standing so close that she could feel the quiver race through his body.

"Reading isn't hard, Berika," he insisted, and perhaps it wasn't, for a prince, but not a shepherd. "Writing can be troublesome, but I'll teach you to read while we travel to Gorse."

"Gorse?" Berika's tongue stuck to the roof of her mouth. Of all the places in her memory, Gorse was the last one she wanted to revisit.

"Yes, Gorse—where did you think Dart and I were going?"

Berika hadn't thought about it at all. She knew that amid his other duties Rinchen was making arrangements for the confrontation which he and Dart meant to have with the Arrizi pyromants. And she knew the confrontation would take place in Weychawood, but Weychawood filled a whole corner of the Walensor map.

"I never thought you'd go to Gorse; it's as far away from anywhere as a place can be."

"It's also where you fetched Dart out of Weycha's forest. All in all, Gorse seems the most logical place for us to enter Weychawood. And it seemed logical that since your brother has already asked if he can come with us, you'd wish to come, too. Braydon thought you would."

Her head sank and her shoulders sagged of their own volition. His hand touched her cheek, gently urging her to meet his eyes. She pushed against his arm instead. His fingers trembled before they moved away.

"I always thought common families were *different;* and your brother seemed to care about you and your mother. You don't have to return to Gorse. You can stay here while I'm gone. I'll tell Aleg . . . and bolt the panel— Ah, I saw that: You almost smiled."

Berika spun around so he could not see her face at all. Each time the younger prince visited the lair, he made her blush with his mischievous smiles. Berika knew the alliance between the brothers was deep, but she didn't know how wide it was. And she couldn't guess what Prince Aleg might do while his brother was gone, nor what the Wolf might do when he got back. The only thing that could unnerve her more than the thought of Prince Aleg coming through the panel door was Prince Rinchen, Dart, her brother, and—above all—her mother in the same room without her there to defend herself.

"I'll come with you to Gorse."

"There is no need—"

"No, I want to go, but Gorse is so far away."

"Twenty leagues, but the winter has been cold. We will use sleighs along the Escham until Relamain, then travel overland to Gorse. It will take a week and a half, a bit more if the weather turns ugly."

"Gorse is more than twenty leagues away for me, midons. I lived there all my life, never walking farther away than the Flayne market. Now I'm in Eyerlon, I can't imagine living in Gorse again. I don't have a home anymore. Not in Gorse. Not here either. I've lost my roots, midons."

He cupped her chin again. His hands were always cold and as calloused as any laborer's. Gentleness did not come naturally to her prince. It was an act of will, appearing without warning, vanishing the same way, like a shooting star.

"Look at me, Berika. I have provided for you and the sorMeklan have provided for you. No matter what happens in the Weychawood, you will not have to remain in Gorse. Arkkin will take you wherever you want to go."

"Arkkin wants my blood for his stewpot," she retorted, ignoring, but not forgetting, the other words he'd said. "He's fattening me up. He says so himself, every day, when he brings my meals up from the kitchen."

"He doesn't bring them up from the kitchen, Berika. Arkkin doesn't trust the palace kitchen; doesn't like the food we eat. He's cooking your meals himself. In all the years I've known Arkkin he's never eaten in my presence or offered me a taste from his pot. Never."

Berika felt her cheeks betray her. "No," she murmured, hiding her embarrassment behind a curtain of hair.

"My lady, you have stolen a champion from a goddess and Rodion's spear from the sorMeklan. Arkkin is awed by your audacity, and your success. You are a woman he respects, probably the only one he's ever met. If he could convince himself you were a respectable tribeswoman, he'd give you the sun and the moon on a platter, and more cause for blushing than my brother ever will."

Her face burned furiously. "I'll never learn. I never should have left Gorse. I belong there, herding sheep." She stood up and meant to walk away, but wound up with her arms locked around him.

"I will not keep you from your sheep," he whispered. "But I would miss you."

Sheep receded quickly from the center of Berika's mind. Rinchen's lips lingered against hers and he did not spring away when she touched them with the tip of her tongue. His right hand wove through her hair. The other slid along her back, reaching below her waist for the first time. She was surprised and disappointed when he pushed her away heartbeats later.

"I must go." He kissed her fingertips. "Aleg and I dine with our beloved mother tonight. The dowager has sent messengers throughout the kingdom. She calls us usurpers and offers herself as regent while the king lies unconscious and, after he dies, until our younger brother, Gilenan, comes of age. She's taking bids for our sisters' dowries, and not even the gods can tell us what she's told the Merrisati. Aleg does not want her running rampant while I'm gone; it takes both of us to stay ahead of her schemes. It will not be a pleasant meal; I will not return here tonight."

Berika knew better than to complain, but not how to conceal her thoughts from a man raised on royal treachery.

"You would not want me here. I get angry sometimes, very angry, and I want to do forbidden things. I had Arianna before—" His eyes widened and glazed with memories that could not be pleasant. "You are good and gentle, Berika—better than I deserve. I will not risk my anger with you. Wait patiently until tomorrow, when we leave for Gore. When Eyerlon has fallen below the horizon, we will have time for each other."

Berika smiled weakly. She would have welcomed the gentle caress of his fingers against her face and hair forever, but his eyes were still wide open with memories. Empty black pupils obscured almost all of the silver, and she was not entirely sorry when he headed for the door.

Arkkin and a pair of Pennaikmen brought her supper and rummaged through the mess gathering clothing, weapons, and other items. Berika put everything she owned into the sorMeklan box and barely constrained her tears as one of the younger Pennaikmen carried it away.

"I come at dawn," Arkkin said as he closed the door.

Berika took no chances. She heaped sacks of chain mail in front of the panel door and bolted the door to the empty hall. After lighting every lamp she could find, she sat in the prince's chair with the fire-poker gripped across her lap. She was wide-awake when the palace bells rang the start of deadwatch, but her eyelids grew heavy. Pinching herself hard enough to raise a bruise was not enough to keep her awake.

She awoke with Arkkin pounding on the bolted door, and didn't have her wits together until she'd been shuttled to the courtyard between the tunnel and the outer gate. Prince Rinchen was already there, mounted on a black stallion and cloaked against the cold in shaggy wolf pelts. Berika wanted to see his face before she disappeared into the sleigh. It was a tiny wish, but it caught the shaman's attention.

"None of that," he growled as he lifted her up to the door.

The sleigh was crowded with provisions for the journey. There were no benches as there had been in the sorMeklan sleigh and there were no other passengers, which at least meant that there was no one to complain when she rolled up the leather curtains. As sunlight filled the courtyard, she caught her first glimpse of Dart since a sleety Hoarfrost day in a sorMeklan river boat.

There was little left of the ragged forest-fetch who'd chased her and her sheep from the Weychawood stream. Dart was a prince's noble companion, now, carefully groomed and radiating confidence. The wooden sword hung in an elaborate scabbard at his waist. The acorn harp-case, distinctive despite the tasselled blanket in which it had been wrapped, was lashed behind a stallion's saddle. The stallion, fractious in a nervous stableboy's hands, calmed to his touch and words. Berika remembered him saying he rode horses, remembering using it as another excuse to berate him. Her heart skipped a beat as he furled a fur-lined sorMeklan green cloak over one arm, mounted the stallion, and took the rein expertly in one hand. Prince Rinchen joined him and they conversed as equals.

No—there was nothing left of the man who'd called her name from the anvil of sorcery, nothing at all. Berika kept her wishes well restrained, and he never noticed her as he rode past the window.

Prince Alegshorn appeared in the old palace doorway. Rinchen dismounted. The brothers clasped hands and wrestled for advantage; brawling competition seemed to be the only way they could express the affection between them. The golden prince had come to the courtyard amid his men. Berika caught one of them staring at her and realized it was her brother. She lowered the curtain and sat nervously waiting for Braydon to open the door, but he never did and she had dozed off by the time the sleigh lurched into motion.

The sleigh's steel runners screeched on the cobblestone high road out of Eyerlon. Berika pressed her hands to her ears. She thought she would be raving if the sound went on for ten days, but they left the road not far from the city gates and descended to the frozen river.

She opened the curtain again, but the runners threw up plumes of ice crystals that made her eyes water, so she closed it again and made herself a nest amid the sacks of grain. The monotonous drone of the runners and the swaying of the sleigh itself swallowed her thoughts.

Although the horses were rested regularly, giving the travellers opportunities to stretch their legs, Berika chose to remain inside the sleigh. The cramps she got from sitting hour after hour were easier to bear than Braydon's disapproving stares. She realized, as well, that there was no way she could be near Rinchen without also being near Dart, and she hadn't found the courage to talk to Weycha's champion.

Matters improved slightly when they stopped for the night at a river-town inn. Befitting her unique and ambiguous status, she was whisked upstairs with the prince's baggage. She ate her supper alone and listened through cracks in the floor to Dart's harping.

"Why didn't you come downstairs?" Rinchen asked much later, when the inn was dark.

"I was tired," she answered, which was a lie. She hadn't done anything but sleep all day.

"Are you avoiding Dart? Your brother? Me?"

"No." Another lie.

"Are you unwell?"

"No, I'm just tired." Berika returned to her original lie, adding a new one: "It will be better when we get to Gorse."

Rinchen accepted her claims of exhaustion and did not pursue his promise to teach her to read. Their routine, once established, did not vary for the five days they travelled along the thick river ice. Then, near the sorMeklan stronghold of Relamain, they left the river and travelled across Fenklare to Weychawood, following the same King's Road Berika and Dart had walked in late autumn. They stayed in charterhouses that knew how to fuss over a royal visitor. And if that royal visitor was travelling with a lady, the keepers would make a fuss over her, too . . . no questions asked. Berika found it simpler to accept the unwanted attention than concoct excuses to avoid it. She sat on the prince's left side, sharing his plate; Dart always sat on his right. Rinchen ate as if he were afraid of food, leaving plenty for her, and she used him as a shield against Dart's glances or words.

After eating, she didn't have to pay for a warm seat near the roaring fire. Folk who would never notice a shepherd girl eagerly surrendered their place to a prince's lady. Serving girls who knew no more about Prince Rinchen than Berika herself had known before she reached Eyerlon stared at her with endless, slack-jawed, wide-eyed envy—and she began to understand why noblefolk pretended they couldn't see commonfolk. It was easier all around.

When Dart played his harp, which he did every night in the charterhouses, he paid no attention to his mortal audience. With his eyes closed and his cheek resting against the rough wood pillar, he told his goddess that he was coming, and the fortunate folk heard music that would echo forever in their dreams.

The less fortunate—noblefolk, burghers, and any sorcerers who'd survived Hazard's usurpation—huddled around Prince Rinchen instead. Wherever the travellers stopped, these sadder and wiser folk peppered the prince with questions that varied little from one night to the next. Rinchen answered as best he could, but he could not give them the reassurance they craved.

The Wolf never lost his temper with his audience, but he became irritable with his companions. When he snapped at Berika after they'd been on the King's Road for five nights—chiding her for humming snatches of Dart's melodies—she was content to crawl silently into the bed. He was still in his chair, staring at embers, in the morning.

The sky was ominous the next morning, as was the Wolf's mood. It didn't take sorcery to know there was a thick blanket of snow waiting to fall from the dull grey clouds, and a tantrum brewing in their prince. An argument broke out between the Pennaikmen and the other Walenfolk over the wisdom of leaving before the storm had come and gone. Rinchen ended the argument by riding out of the charterhouse yard alone.

Snow was falling by the time the sleigh caught up with him, whereupon Arkkin announced that he'd seen two crows flying against the wind. The shaman swore he could not proceed one step farther until he had interpreted the omen by moonlight. This time there was no argument. The Pennaikmen dismounted, Prince Rinchen and Dart dismounted, the Walenfolk dismounted, and for the first time since they'd left the palace courtyard, the sleigh was completely emptied.

The ominous crows had been flying through a sheltered hollow between several small hills when Arkkin spotted them. There was a copse of trees to shelter the horses, another to shelter the pavilion where the Walenfolk would sleep, and a third where the Pennaikmen would make their separate camp.

"Too damned convenient, if you ask me," Braydon swore to his sister. It was the longest statement he'd made to her since the journey began. "I didn't see any damned crows, and I was riding right behind the blackheads."

Berika watched the neighboring copse where the prince was bedding down the horses. She knew immediately that if Arkkin hadn't seen crows he would have seen something else. "Rinchen needed a rest," she said, as much to herself as to Braydon.

"*Rinchen!* Godswill—your *Rinchen*'s a sorRodion prince! He's the gods-be-damned Wolf, and you're calling him by his name. Have you completely lost your mind? The sidon of Fenklare wasn't enough for you . . . you've got to climb into bed with the gods-be-damned Wolf! If our king still had a cock, would you be chasing him, too?"

If Braydon had stopped with the prince's name, he'd have gotten the better of her. She was shamed that she could think his name and speak it easily to another man, because she still couldn't say anything but 'midons' to his face. But Braydon went too far. Unfortunately, before she vented her tirade, one of the officers shouted Braydon's name and he headed toward the emerging Walenfolk camp.

Without a second thought, Berika scooped up a handful of fresh snow, packed it into an icy ball, and hurled it accurately at her brother's thick neck. It struck squarely; Braydon himself had taught her to throw when she was a little girl. Braydon proved he hadn't forgotten anything, either—anticipating her dodge before he launched his own, somewhat softer, snowball that spread chilly white powder into her hair and eyes. She had no idea who threw the next snowball—except that it hit Braydon from behind and he assumed it had come from one of the men grappling with the tent. He spun and retaliated accordingly.

The hollow erupted with snowballs, both splattering-soft and hard-packed ice. There were any number of repressed grievances and an unlimited supply of snow. In a very short time the Pennaikmen were under attack, too. Battle lines were drawn: Pennaikmen in their trees, Walenfolk in theirs. The prince and Dart, ignoring common pleasures, hunkered down in their distinctive cloaks in the safety of the horse lines.

Berika crouched to one side of the Walenfolk, sniping at her brother until she, too, caught a snowball from the rear. She whirled around, gathering snow as she spun, but there were only softly curved mounds of snow wherever she looked. Standing puzzled and an easy target, she got hit in the back again, and without hesitation threw her snowball at Braydon. Then she heard laughter. A good many of the Walenfolk and Pennaikmen were laughing by then, but the particular, unfamiliar laughter that caught Berika's attention came from behind.

Along with another snowball.

She spun around again. There was snow in the air and snow on the ground. Nothing more. Nothing less.

"Who's there?"

No answer, not even a snowball. She turned back to the main battle and counted heads. Everyone was there, including Dart and the prince, still sitting in their cloaks near the horses. They hadn't moved. They hadn't moved at all.

Berika cupped her hands around her eyes.

"I think she's figured it out."

That was a voice Berika remembered all too well, which could only mean that the laughter came from the prince. She'd never heard him laugh.

"I think you're right."

For a moment Berika heard them both chuckling. She refused to turn around. There were no more snowballs from Braydon or anyone else and the mock battle sputtered to a halt. The Walenfolk went back to their camp; the Pennaikmen returned to theirs. Berika went hunting. She found two sets of footprints and the disturbed places behind the crest of the hollow where they'd flattened themselves between snowballs. Before she'd completely satisfied her curiosity, she heard the song of steel rising from the hollow.

Dart and Rinchen had armored themselves in chain mail and were swinging swords at each other in slow motion. Braydon stood by himself, watching. Fearing the worst, Berika hurried to his side.

"Are they fighting?" she asked as the prince slowly parried Dart's sword-stroke.

"No, your precious prince isn't fighting with your precious champion. They're taking each other's measure," Braydon assured her. "They've never crossed steel before and they don't want to take a chance they'll hurt each other. There's nothing for you to worry about."

Braydon had been getting lessons from Prince Aleg's armsmaster. Berika expected arrogance; that didn't mean she had to like it. She stuck her tongue out at him, then watched closely as Dart and

Rinchen exchanged attacks. They were taking turns exactly as Braydon said.

"Why are you being so mean?" she asked when the song of steel proved less exciting than she'd expected. "It's my life and it's not as if I had any honor to lose."

"I don't like to see you used by the Wolf."

"I was *used* by Hirmin. The prince does not *use* me."

"He won't marry you, Beri. He'll stick you with a bastard and leave you in a gutter. It's what they do."

"He won't. The sorMeklan gave me money. The prince has promised me more. I know it won't last forever, but I'll be able to take care of myself. And I won't be bearing any man's bastard; I've got more than enough *basi* to keep that from ever happening."

Braydon twisted his face into a disbelieving sneer. "I thought you were smarter than that, Beri. You can't go playing spook's tricks. You didn't have enough *basi* to reach the Web."

"I've got enough to take care of myself," Berika hissed, too angry and hurt to explain what she'd learned from Nishrun. "That's all that matters, isn't it? You don't have to worry that I'll ask you to play father to my bastards."

The prince and Dart called more complicated attacks at a faster pace. The swords made different sounds as they struck against each other. There was grace and beauty in the movements of the men wielding their weapons, and suddenly Berika understood why the deadly art was called the song of steel and why men loved it so much. Fascination overcame her fear, and neither she nor Braydon could look away as the swords moved fast enough to blur and sing.

"They're good, Beri," Braydon said in hushed awe when they stopped calling their attacks. "Neither one of them's pulled back. It's all clean-fought: attack and counterattack. They aren't making any mistakes. The Wolf's as good as I've heard, and your champion's taking it all in stride."

"Dart's not my champion," Berika said wearily, "and Prince Rinchen is not a wolf. Please, Braydon? It's going to be hard enough when I face Ingolde. Please don't make it worse."

"Tell her they've given you money. Better yet: Tell her they've promised you land. You should ask your prince for land. Everyone says he's going to confiscate half the land in Walensor and then sell it to the highest bidder. Money's just money, Berika, but land is forever. Get him to give you land and everyone will think you've gotten the better of him."

"I don't want to get the better of Rinchen. I love him—" The words were out before she suspected they were on her tongue. For an instant, they hung in little puffs of steam; then they escaped forever. "Sweet Mother Cathe—don't tell Ingolde I said that. Please, Braydon, swear to me that you won't tell Ingolde."

"Is it true?"

"No."

"You're going to get hurt, Beri. You're going to get hurt in places Hirmin never touched."

That had already happened. Berika whipped her cloak tightly around her and ran away in tears.

"Berika! Come back!" Braydon started after her. He was getting close when she heard the Wolf's voice.

"Egg! Aleg asked me to teach you a lesson or two when I had the time. I've got the time. You need a lesson."

Braydon stopped, swearing. Berika continued her blind, reckless stumble through the falling snow to the crest of the hollow. She found one of the depressions Dart and Rinchen had used during the snowball battle, its edges already blurred with fresh-fallen snow, and dropped to her knees. The tears came in aching sobs, released by Braydon's harsh words, but fueled by deeper feelings she would not name.

"Berika, it's me, Dart—I want to talk to you."

Linking love and the prince hurt, but not as badly as any thought of Weycha's champion. When she heard Dart's voice, another wave of sobs threatened to burst within her. She loved Prince Rinchen because he needed someone to love him—the way the sheep needed a shepherd to care for them. And she was a shepherd, a good shepherd who took good care of her sheep. Maybe—the thought was practically treasonous, equating the Wolf with a lamb—maybe she *cared* for the prince more than she loved him.

And maybe she loved someone she hadn't cared for very well.

"Berika . . . Please?"

Dart wasn't a sheep. The prince wasn't a sheep. They were men, complicated men. She loved them both in very different ways, and at that particular moment she wanted nothing to do with either one of them. "Go away."

"We need to talk, Berika."

"Not now. Go away. *Please.*"

"No, Berika. We have to talk now—while Rinchen's pounding manners into your fool brother's head. You've been afraid to look at me since we left Eyerlon. Don't be. I stopped blaming you the moment I found out who I was. I treated you badly on the river boat because I didn't know what I was heading into and I thought Driskolt would take care of you."

"He reminded me of my brother," Berika said between sobs.

"That lout—?"

"No, my other brother, Indon. He's dead, you never met him."

A little laugh. She could see Dart smiling in her mind, and ground her bare knuckles into her eyes until the vision went away. For all the good it did: He sat in the snow beside her.

"With me Berika, you can't be sure. I don't apologize for what I did on the river boat; I'd do it again, but I do apologize for hurting you and leaving you to think that I blamed you for what had happened. When I was out of my mind in the Palestra, I used your face to find my way back to light and life. I never meant to hurt you that badly. Will you forgive me?"

She couldn't answer through the sobs, but forgiving Dart was as easy as taking his hand, which she did.

"Another thing. Rinchen is a friend of mine. You could say we've been friends a long time. I met him first when he was a scrappy, beat-up little boy. I liked him then and I like him now. You're alike in many ways: both afraid of happiness and terrified of love. He's got his reasons, you've got yours. I've told him he shouldn't be afraid of you, and I'm telling you the same thing—"

The words brought more anguish than Berika could hold. She threw herself into Dart's arms. "It should have been you. I loved you from the moment you waded across that stream, but I was afraid. I was afraid because of Hirmin. I was afraid because I thought you were a demon. And then I was afraid because I thought you might be a highborn man. But mostly I was afraid because I loved you. Now it's too late. I want to love you, but it's too late."

He rocked her in his arms. She stopped crying when she realized he was trembling harder than she was. She tried to wriggle free, but his hands were locked in her hair and there was no way she could see his face.

"Berika— You were wise to be afraid. It was always too late for us. My life was never my own. If you'd let yourself love me and I'd loved you in return, I'd be hurting you right now. I'm not coming out of the forest, Berika. I *died* and I was brought back to life for one purpose: to protect Weycha from her enemy. Now Hazard's in the forest, and it's time for me to do what I am meant to do. I will face Hazard, and I pray to the gods of the gods that

I destroy him, but win or lose, Berika, I'm not coming out of Weychawood. I'm not afraid of dying a second time, but I'd like to see you happy before I do. I'd like to see Rinchen happy, too."

He was wrong—wrong in countless ways, but Berika loved him too much to contradict him.

Chapter Twenty-one

Dart and Berika had been dusted by falling snow before they released each other. Their footprints had been softened, but new, sharp-edged prints cut the crest of the hollow. Someone had come close enough to see a man and a woman in a desperate embrace, then turned around and walked away, backtracking through his own footprints. Berika thought it must have been a Pennaikman, maybe Arkkin who could be as quiet as a shadow when he chose; Dart would not offer his opinion.

Two fires burned bright, and the promise of a hearty dinner blended with the snow. Braydon's lesson in the song of steel and manners was over. He squatted by the Walenfolk fire, tending the stewpot. The prince sat nearby, using a black oilstone to remove burrs only he could perceive on the edge of his sword.

Braydon's moustache was stiff with blood that oozed from his nose and froze on the bristles. The flesh around his eye was swollen and turning dark. A length of clean linen was wound around his weapon hand. All-in-all, his injuries were more typical of a bare-knuckled brawl than the song of steel. Faced with the question from his sister, Braydon conceded that he'd tried to surprise Prince Rinchen with the trick he'd seen Prince Alegshorn use on the practice field.

"I held my sword by the blade and swung the hilt at his head."

"As if Aleg knows something sly that he didn't learn from me," Rinchen interjected between honing strokes. "Throw the blade away, fool, when you swing wide."

"I tried, midons Prince Rinchen."

"You gave it to me," the prince corrected. "I had two swords, you had none. Very foolish."

"He threw both swords aside," Braydon admitted later, when Berika retied his bandage for the night. "And came after me with his fists. I thought I knew how to brawl, Beri, but never touched him. Never came close. Never saw the punches coming. Learned my damn lesson, I did."

Braydon didn't say which lesson he'd learned, but there was peace between him and his sister, peace that she treasured. Her brother offered affection without passion or tragedy. He'd still be nearby when Dart stayed in Weychawood and when the prince walked out of her life, as he inevitably would, no matter what Dart said or hoped. Braydon would return to Eyerlon and remain there. He'd marry, have children, invite his lace-making sister to join his family whenever tradition demanded a gathering of blood-kin. She'd tell his children about her adventures, then go home to her quiet room.

It was a dream, but it was the best dream she had, and she needed peace with Braydon if she had any hope at all of making it true. Meanwhile, Berika endured an exquisite torture beside the campfire, sitting between Dart, playing Weycha's harp for the snow-wrapped trees, and Prince Rinchen, honing the sword he intended to put through Arianna's heart. She was not sorry when wiser heads let the fires burn down.

She slept in the warmth and safety of the Walenfolk tent, among a dozen men, three of whom she loved.

They left the hollow the next morning. The mounted men took turns cutting a path through the fresh snow for their companions and the sleigh. Two days later they came to the end of the King's Road and the king's charterhouses. Two days after that they entered Flayne, the market town where the villagers of Gorse sold whatever they could spare and bought what they needed.

It was not market day and Flayne was nearly deserted. Peeking beneath the leather curtain, Berika saw no one she recognized. Nor was there a single shopkeeper standing at his open door from whom the prince's men could requisition the extra food and forage they needed to bring to Gorse, if the village was going to survive their visit. While the Walenfolk scrounged provisions door-to-door, the prince made a thorough study of the town from his stallion's back. Berika thought she saw astonishment on his face and wondered if he'd ever seen how country commonfolk lived, and wondered, as well, what he'd think when he saw Gorse—smaller, poorer, and even more drab than Flayne.

She thought they'd spend the night at Flayne's squalid little inn when the scroungers didn't return until midway through the afternoon. But Braydon—her own brother, who surely remembered that Flayne was more than a half-day's journey away, especially in winter—said they could reach Gorse by sundown. The driver cracked his whip and the sleigh began to move along a track that was less familiar than it should have been. The sleigh stopped again when the sky was turning pink. Berika thought they'd be spending another night in tents and was deciding what sharp words she'd say to Braydon, when she heard a familiar voice:

"This be the assart land of the village of Gorse, granted by King Manal sorRodion on the day he was crowned. What we owe, we owe only to the king himself. You'll find no sorMeklan hospitality here. Turn your horses around and go back where you belong."

Trust herself to forget that the horse-drawn sleigh could travel faster than any man could walk. Trust Rimp the alderman to speak first and blunder badly. Berika heard the slide of steel as men drew their swords.

"I am Rinchen ruVigelan ruManal sorRodion, Crown Prince of Walensor." The prince's voice was mean and dangerous. "And I neither need nor claim sorMeklan hospitality. I had not believed that a sorRodion assart—an assart granted by my grandfather—would deny a girl-child's right to reach the Web or hound a goddess's champion until he fled for his life, but now I see how commonfolk abuse their assart privileges. I have returned with Weycha's champion to right the wrongs that were done then and since. I am of a mind to put a torch to every dwelling and formally return this assarted land to the goddess. What say you now?"

The villagers were Berika's folk, and she'd wished them the worst many times in her life, but she never meant to wish them an angry Wolf. Through her little window, she could see the Pennaikmen with their swords drawn, the back of Dart's green cloak, and a bit of Prince Rinchen's wolf cloak. She couldn't see Braydon or any of the villagers. Berika waited for her mother to speak up, but there was only silence.

Since that horrible moment when Nishrun had battered her with inquist sorcery, she had anticipated the moment when she would demand an explanation from her mother; and although she knew that many sorcerers had perished in the Web's fall, she had never considered the possibility that Ingolde might have died. The distance between love and hate was very short in an orphan's eyes.

"I say that you would be committing a crime, midons prince. Gorse is assart land. Our alderman is rude, but he is not wrong. And if anyone is to blame for the hounding of Weycha's champion, it is I alone."

"Ingolde." Berika put her shoulder to the sleigh door and leapt to the ground. "Mother!" She ran to Ingolde's side, then turned to the prince.

"Please, midons—I told you: Gorse is far away from everywhere. There's no Web now to tell anyone that you were coming. Nobody here has seen a prince before. You can't blame them for not recognizing you. You can't destroy their homes just because they didn't bow to you."

Prince Rinchen sat back in the saddle and appeared to give the matter serious thought. "As you wish, my lady. At least I know how you came by your temper. Do I have your permission to enter the royal assart of Gorse?" The Wolf was never entirely predictable, never entirely harmless. His smile, unlike Prince Aleg's, almost always revealed his teeth.

Berika nodded and the villagers gasped with astonishment at the respect a prince showed to *their* Berika. Rinchen raised his hand and the Pennaikmen put up their weapons. The Walenfolk, including Dart and Braydon, had not drawn theirs. Seeing that the danger had passed, Rimp hobbled forward on his crutch.

"A thousand welcomes to your assart, midons Prince Rinchen. I have a fine house for your comfort. My wife will be honored to serve your pleasures."

There were only two dwellings in Gorse that could, with generosity, be called houses at all: Rimp's two-story stone house beside the millpond and, at the upper end of the common, the unpainted timbers of the shepherd's house. The rest were snow-covered cottages set into the side of a hill. The prince looked from one house to the other and from Berika, still holding her mother's hands, back to Rimp.

"My thanks to you and your good wife. Some of my men will be pleased to accept your hospitality, but I'll stay with the hedge-sorcerer—if she's receiving visitors."

The black stallion reared up and pivoted in the snow until the prince faced Ingolde; then it stood with one front leg extended, the other front leg bent, and its head bowed low. The Walenfolk, villagers and riders alike, held their breath in wonder. Berika looked up at her mother, who shook her head: Whatever made the stallion dance, it wasn't Ingolde's hedge-sorcery. Then Berika looked at Arkkin, who was grinning, and Dart, who'd covered his mouth with his hand.

"Ingolde Braydswidow, will you allow us across your threshold?"

Ingolde shed Berika's hands and met the infamous ice-colored eyes without flinching. "I would be honored, midons prince. But, please leave your horse outside, midons prince; the floor is not strong enough to bear his weight."

Berika wasn't sure if there was humor in her mother's voice, but Dart's shoulders were shaking and the prince was either very angry or biting his lips for some other reason. Then Ingolde led the royal party up the path to her home. Berika kept her head down, avoiding the prince, and was startled when someone grabbed her elbow.

"Cathe weeps, Beri—you've come back with your fetch *and* a prince! Are they both your lovers? If only Ingolde had known you were coming!"

Berika and dark-haired, lively Heldey had grown up together. That, and that alone, was the strength of their friendship. Widowhood, thrust upon Heldey with Indon's death, did not suit her at all. She opened her cloak and flirted with each of the Walenfolk men as they rode past, drawing the line at the Pennaikmen, and retreating behind Berika when one of them chuckled appreciatively.

"Was that your brother, Braydon?" she whispered when that danger had passed. "Mounted and wearing a sword? You've got to tell me everything. Oh, Beri—who would believe it? You, of all folk! How did you get a prince to notice you?"

"I threatened him with a spear," Berika replied as she started up the path.

With her hands hidden inside her cloak, Berika folded her fingers into the Horns of Cathe, a ward-sign against misfortune of all kinds. The only home she'd known in Gorse was called the shepherd's house because her father was a shepherd. It should have been called the weaver's house, since Ingolde had earned the coins that built it. In other villages the shepherd was a poor man, selling his fleeces for a smattering of black grit coins. In Gorse, Ingolde spun the fleece into fine yarn and wove lengths of cloth that sold for three silver marks each. When the snows came, she set up her loom between the hearth and the front door and wove cloth until spring.

When Berika was little, Brayd had built a second, half-scale loom. After that she followed her father and the sheep in summer, and learned the weaver's trade from her mother in winter. She got a smattering of black grit coins for each half-size length of cloth she wove. After the Arrizi declared war and the price of cloth had gone up, Berika got a flake of silver for her short lengths and Brayd had marched proudly to Kasserine, never to return. Silver couldn't bring her father back, or protect her from Hirmin, but it told her what she was worth and gave her a measure of joy.

A few years later Hirmin Maggotson came back from Norivarl with hellfire scars on his face and soul. Ingolde had said Hirmin would never do a man's work again. If Berika didn't want to starve with her children, she'd weave until her back burned and her fingers bled. Ingolde had taken Berika's hoard of silver and commissioned a second, full-sized loom from a guild carpenter in a distant city. Berika wove each winter after that, but the joy and pride were gone. Her full lengths of cloth were never as fine as her half-lengths had been, and after she fled Gorse she'd never considered the weaver's trade. When Driskolt sorMeklan told her about lace, Berika had recognized it as her proper calling. Lace was cloth made entirely from knots, and knots were a weaver's bane.

Halfway up the commons now, Berika spied Ingolde's loom through the open doorway of the shepherd's house. A yard of fine woolen cloth marched down its warps. Her courage failed and she veered off the path. She meant to visit the open-roofed fane where the villagers made offerings to the forest goddess whose land they farmed.

But the fane was gone. A round clearing amid the brambles had replaced the small, vine-covered building. The old, lightning-struck tree trunk within it had been reduced to bits of charcoal poking through the snow.

Berika crumbled some of the charcoal and sowed ashes across the snow. Auld Mag had said that the villagers would know that Weycha had forgiven them for clearing her land when she sent green life back to the tree in the fane.

Another lie. Weycha wouldn't forgive Gorse any more than Berika was going to forgive Ingolde for ruining her life. She plowed across unbroken snow to the shepherd's house.

The bridge over the millstream was too narrow for the sleigh. The men from Eyerlon had to haul everything up the hill on their backs, no doubt wishing that their prince had accepted Rimp's invitation. The village could not stable twenty-four horses. There were stalls for the stallions in the shed attached to Rimp's stone house, but the other animals were tied in lines near the sleigh. As Berika watched, Heldey and another young woman, Embla, struggled with a sack of grain. Berika met them on the path and lent a hand.

No one expected a prince to haul boxes or bales. Prince Rinchen stood outside the shepherd's house answering the same questions he'd answered everywhere else. He did not acknowledge Berika as she walked by plucking coarse-cloth fibers from her fingers, pausing to make Cathe's Horns one last time before entering her mother's house.

A single fire served the house for both cooking and heating. It burned in a circular pit dug into the dirt floor and was vented through a gap in the thatch above. Between the pit and the vent, an iron kettle hung from a roof-beam chain. Ingolde leaned over the pit, stirring the kettle. The moment when Berika feared for her mother's life had passed. Her anger and resentment had returned, hotter than the fire. She hung her cloak on its peg beside the door and waited silently until Ingolde noticed her.

"Midons prince brought a hog's haunch for his supper. Someone should have told him there's no spit in Gorse strong enough to turn it," Ingolde said, leaving no doubt who should have known and who should have told him. "If he wants meat, he'll have to chunk it out of his stew like a common man. The knife's sharp and on the board."

Berika scuffed her feet in the dirt, fighting the habits of obedience. It was as if she'd been in the undercroft with the sheep instead of gone for months.

"Berika! Don't stand there like a slack-jawed fool. There's work to be done if the prince and his men are going to eat their supper before dawn."

"I have to talk to you."

"Talk while you're chopping. I'm not going anywhere."

"Auld Mag was supposed to help me. This far from Eyerlon a hedge-sorcerer is supposed to tell the spider when a child has enough *basi*. You should have helped me. You knew; you must have known. It's supposed to be an honor when your daughter goes to Eyerlon. The sorcerers shower a common girl's family with gold when she leaves them. You would have been rich. You should have been proud."

Ingolde stood straight. She swept strands of hair from her sweaty forehead and met her daughter's fierce stare. "You were exceptional. You would have been a magga and you would have died with them. How proud would I be now?" She went back to watching the kettle. "You'll get that fine gown dirty cutting the meat. Take a shirt from the chest."

"You admit that you knew and you did nothing. Why, Mother, why?"

"Mag was our hedge-sorcerer."

"You could have taken me to Flayne and paid the sorcerer there. We had the silver. *I* had the silver."

The ladle clanked against the kettle. "It's over and done. Consider yourself lucky, Berika, and let it rest."

"I can't let it rest." Berika's voice rose. "What did you get when you sold me to Auld Mag and Hirmin?"

"Not now," Ingolde hissed. "Lower your voice."

Berika marched closer to the fire-pit, keeping her back to the door. "What was the price of my soul, Ingolde?" she shouted. "You know what Hirmin did to me. You could have stopped it. You could have sent me to Eyerlon, but you never did. Why? Can't you please tell me why?"

There was no answer that would have erased the shame, but at least Ingolde's hands were shaking.

"Later, Berika," Ingolde whispered, gesturing toward the door. "Midons prince is waiting for you."

Berika turned, stiffened, and felt faint. Rinchen wasn't the only one who'd come into the shepherd's house. Braydon, with Heldey firmly attached to his arm, stood awkwardly inside the doorway. Their shadows darkened the house. Prince Rinchen squatted on the floor examining the warp weights of Ingolde's loom. She wondered how long he'd been there, what he'd overheard, dreaded the probable answers.

"Ingolde wants someone to cut up meat for the kettle," Berika said, gamely pretending that nothing unusual had occurred. "Could you two do that for her?"

Braydon allowed Heldey to guide him to the table. Berika took their place in the doorway. She stared through the twilight, hoping to see Dart, hoping he hadn't decided to stay with Rimp. The village was quiet, except for the Pennaikmen in their camp on the far side of the millstream.

"He went to the forest," the prince told her, without getting up from the floor. "He'll be back. We both want to talk to the hedge-sorcerer before we go."

Berika pushed the door shut but left it unlatched. She stood beside the loom, caressing its smooth beams. "My mother is a weaver. She came from a faraway city to marry my father. He built her this loom as a wedding gift. My father was a kind and gentle man, but I'm my mother's daughter."

"My mother is a poisoner. Vigelan gave her me for a wedding gift. She believes I deliberately chose the ill-omened hour of my birth and my appearance, just to shame her. I tell her I may be cursed, but I'm not a fool. If I could have chosen, I would not have been born at all. Not to her and Vigelan."

A long, straight row of nut-sized clay weights hung beneath the loom. Each was tied to a small sheaf of warp threads that descended from the half-woven cloth. The prince held the end-weight a handspan away from the others, then released it. An instant later the weight at the far end of the row jumped without anyone touching it.

"Sorcery—?" Berika whispered, retreating as the weight the prince had held jumped toward his hand.

"Trickery. Sit. I'll show you."

Berika sat. Three children joined them. They were no kin to Berika, but the offspring of Embla, another widow, whom Ingolde had taken in before the youngest was born. Ingolde practiced charity, just not with her own daughter. The children were entranced by the fine-dressed man who played with forbidden toys. They had no idea if he were a prince or a Wolf, merely watched with eyes of wonder while he made the weights dance. Rinchen taught the oldest before getting to his feet.

"Ingolde gets angry when her warps get tangled," Berika said as she stood. "She'll never forgive you."

"I'll survive, and so will you. So have you. Dart and I will go into the forest, do what we have to do, and—gods be willing—Hazard and Arianna will be memories by tomorrow's supper. We'll go home to Eyerlon and you can forget this place."

"So soon?" Berika meant to sound hopeful, but she wasn't thinking of the Arrizi pyromants, or leaving Gorse behind. She was thinking about losing Dart and maybe the prince, too. He was confident, but Arianna was a formidable enemy. "Don't you need to rest or plan?"

"We had the whole journey to plan, and as for rest, Dart was all for crossing the stream the moment we got here. Berika—look at me: I'm not going to die. I'm going to kill Arianna and then I'm coming out of that forest if I have to drag myself out."

But Berika would not look at him and he went back to playing with the children. Dart returned before the stars came out, red-cheeked and dusted with fresh snow. The snow sparkled as it melted, and so did his eyes. Weycha's champion looked straight at her, straight through her.

"Do you know where we're going?" the prince asked, separating from the children again.

"I found the place where we'll enter the forest. Where's Ingolde?"

Without a word exchanged, Berika took her mother's place beside the kettle. Dart was not himself; or perhaps he was, and the man she thought was Dart was merely a shadow. His eyes continued to flash with spring and autumn colors as he hammered Ingolde with questions. The two of them were still going at it, with Rinchen absorbing both questions and answers, when Berika announced that the stew was ready.

Braydon stood in the doorway and shouted the message to the entire village. Everyone came, even Rimp and his very pregnant wife, drawn as much by the promise of a meaty stew as by the once-in-a-lifetime opportunity to break bread with royalty. There was plenty of stew left in the kettle after Berika filled every crude bowl and hollowed loaf of bread, but there was no place for her near the door, where Ingolde sat between a champion and a prince. So she sat on the edge of the loft with Embla's children, listening to the sheep in the undercroft, and feeling badly done by.

Dart finally sat back. He and Ingolde ate a cold supper. The villagers passed him the acorn. They gasped appropriately when he broke apart the pieces, but when he touched the strings the sounds were sour and pain filled his face.

"Hazard's in the forest," he murmured. "He listens to everything. He could find me. He could find my lady." He reassembled the acorn, picked up the sword, and went outside.

The mood, which had not been cheerful, collapsed completely. The other villagers and the Eyerlon men who were staying with them filed silently out of the shepherd's house. They twisted their fingers into the Horns of Cathe and were careful not to touch the grim young man with the uncanny eyes who stood just outside the shepherd's house, slapping the unsheathed wooden sword against his palm. When only the women of the shepherd's house, their children, Braydon and the prince remained, Dart came inside. The sword glowed with a deep green light that only Berika and her mother could see.

"I don't like it," he said, staring at the darkness beyond the village. "The smell of death is everywhere. Trees die while they sleep, but this is different."

Prince Rinchen closed the door. "Tomorrow."

"Tomorrow," Dart agreed, sliding the sword into its scabbard.

He started toward the loft, where he and Braydon would sleep. Berika intercepted him. She couldn't say the words she wanted to say—*Come home safely*—so she threw her arms around him, not caring about anyone else in the house or the world. Berika had promised herself she wouldn't cry, and by reaching deep into her soul, she found the strength to keep her promise.

"Sleep well, Berika."

Dart kissed her hair because she had her head down, staring at her feet. She could see the Wolf's boots as well.

"Do you want me to wake you up before Dart and I leave?" He hooked his finger under her chin. "I told your mother that I would not turn all the women and children of this house out of their bed. I will sleep in the loft."

Berika fought the pressure against her chin. "I thought you did not sleep on the floor."

"This is your mother's house, not my room. Do you want me to wake you?"

"No, we can say goodbye now."

"As you wish, my lady—but I would prefer to say good night."

Berika said neither, and the prince joined Dart and Braydon in the loft. The children were already bundled in the middle of the bed. The fire had burned down to embers. The house itself was still warm from the cooking and the villagers, but it would not remain that way for long. Embla kicked off her wooden shoes and tied rags around her feet before sliding fully clothed into bed beside her children. Heldey reluctantly followed Embla's example; if Rinchen had turned them out, she would have slept with Braydon in the loft. A man and a woman nested down among the sacks of fleece in the loft might not be any warmer than four women and three children crowded into one bed, but they were certain to be less aware of the cold.

Ingolde blew out the lamp and called her daughter's name. Berika replied by wrapping herself in her cloak and sitting by the dying fire. There was an outburst of creaking and coughing; then the shepherd's house was as quiet as it was dark.

"All right, Berika," Ingolde said softly, wearily. She was wrapped in her own cloak and carried an additional blanket which she draped around them both as she sat. "I don't believe it will help, but I'll tell you why."

"I'm listening."

"Not everyone who can reach the Web becomes a sorcerer. I was fifteen when I heard the music. I told no one. I was happy with my life. Sorcery did not tempt me. My father was an older man who owned a clothworks in Dunking; I was his heir. He'd arranged a marriage with one of his journeymen, a man almost as old as he was. A daughter could not inherit the clothworks, but a widow could. Chlodrin was bald and ugly and utterly without imagination, but he could give me children and the clothworks. Eyerlon could not offer me more."

Her mother had extolled the virtues of widowhood before, but Chlodrin was an unfamiliar name. Berika learned that before Chlodrin and Ingolde celebrated their lopsided marriage a group of young noblemen invaded the town. They'd come to hunt in Weychawood—a different part of the same huge forest that bordered Gorse—but mostly they'd come to run wild in the taverns and chase the town's women. They descended on the clothworks, exercising noble rights which no common man, even a rich man like Ingolde's father, could refuse.

Ingolde was exiled to the attic workrooms but not before she caught the eye of a handsome youth. Her father reminded her of her impending marriage, but bald and ugly Chlodrin had met his match. Ingolde traded her clothes with a kitchen wench.

"His hair was dark-honey gold, his eyes sparkled when he laughed, and his smile could light a room—"

Berika thought of Prince Alegshorn. If Ingolde could be dazzled by any man, it would have to have been a man like Prince Aleg.

"We coupled like cats," Ingolde continued—and her daughter was grateful for the darkness. "We could not get our fill of each other. We dreamed wild, wonderful dreams. He said he would take me to Relamain to live in the stronghold. He said he would persuade his father to allow us to marry. I would be Lady Ingolde, and he would be my lord. My head knew better, but my heart ruled whenever he was near. My heart was broken when he left with his friends. He said he'd return for me in the spring, and gave me a burnished gold ring for remembrance. He gave me something else—a belly that swelled as soon as he was gone.

"I'd been brazen and foolish. Chlodrin wouldn't have me and my father turned against me. He threw me out of his house and locked the door against me. I came to Gorse—to Mag, my grandmother's sister. There was nothing else I could do. Nowhere else I could go."

"But you had *basi*. . . ."

"I was past seventeen by then. It was too late."

"There are other uses for *basi*," Berika muttered, grateful once again for the darkness.

"But you must want to use it in those ways, and I did not. I loved him, Beri. My life was already ruined. All I had was the ring and the child. I was sick to death when I arrived at Mag's home. Hirmin was a baby—Mag called him her 'autumn child.' He had no father, but Mag was the hedge-sorcerer, and allowances were made. There was no way she could keep me and my child, not in a place as small as Gorse. If I would not give up the child, I would have to marry. She found me a husband—Brayd, your father—but he would not take a bride far-gone with another man's child. There was a way, but it was dangerous. Mag said we could work a sorcery that would make the child grow small, and keep it small until I was safely married.

"Our sorcery was dangerous. It broke the Compact—we tampered with life. Brayd was a good and gentle man, and I would have my lord's daughter. We knew it was a daughter. Mag had a price: my daughter for her son, but it did not seem so high then. We worked our sorcery in fear and secrecy—Eyerlon deals harshly with hedge-sorcerers who dabble with anathema—but we were successful in every way except one. When my child was born, she was Indon."

Berika sat upright. "Indon?"

"You, Braydon, and Indon are all my children, but Indon was a nobleman's son. He was not the image of his father, but there was a likeness. Sometimes I would look at Indon and see my lord's face. Do you remember how he would lower his head in his hands and scowl over his fingers? That was his father, Beri. But he did me no good with Mag. We shared a terrible secret. We grew uneasy with each other, distrustful. She wanted my daughter for her son. When Braydon was born, she accused me of cheating her. I miscarried twice between you and Braydon; both were daughters, and both times she accused me of anathema. When you were born she finally had her payment and there was a truce between us. But there was never peace, because there was always what we had done, and what she accused me of doing.

"She threatened me. She said that she would go to the sorcerer in Flayne and swear my children were tainted with anathema. I would have died, and my children would have died. If I had tried to spirit you off to Eyerlon, Mag would have destroyed us both. She told me so many, many times, and I never doubted her. I knew what I'd done was terrible—worse than anathema—but I knew you were strong. I knew you would survive."

There were only a handful of coals left in the fire-pit when

Ingolde reached the end of her story. Several of them winked out before Berika had her thoughts in order.

"I survived," she said with a sigh. "I have the best *bad* luck beneath the Web. Why didn't you go to Relamain instead of Gorse?"

"Relamain was dreams, Berika. When I was in love, I believed the dreams. Afterward . . . I was better off in Gorse."

"What was his name?"

Ingolde strangled a laugh. "I don't remember. Isn't that odd? I love a man, he ruins my life . . . I can remember his body, but I cannot remember his name. I called him 'midons,' as you call your prince 'midons prince.'"

"What about 'midons sidon'? What about Ean ruEan sorMeklan?"

"The donitor?" Ingolde laughed again. "Don't be foolish."

"I'm not. The donitor has a son, Driskolt ruEan sorMeklan. He scowls over his fingers, and sometimes when I looked at him, I thought he was Indon."

"Cathe weeps."

"The best bad luck beneath the Web: The donitor of Fenklare has promised to find me a suitable husband. I guess I truly am the daughter he never had," Berika said, and began her own story.

When Berika's tale was finished and the fire-pit was dark and cold, Ingolde had only one question: "Have you fallen in love, Beri? Have you succumbed?"

"Yes."

"With midons Prince Rinchen?"

"With them both."

Ingolde rocked her daughter gently while she cried, and stroked her hair until she fell asleep. Ingolde dozed. She knew every sound the shepherd's house could make, and she knew when the two men Berika loved rose from their blankets. The house was almost as dark as it had been at midnight. Ingolde listened as they stumbled into their clothes and buckled their sword belts. She heard the latch and felt a blast of cold air as the door opened and closed. She waited a few moments, then shook Berika awake.

"If you love them, go after them—Dart has left his harp behind."

Chapter Twenty-two

A finger's depth of snow had fallen during the night, but the dawn sky was clear with a crescent moon lingering above the western horizon to greet the sun as it rose. Dart and Rinchen left parallel tracks across the millstream bridge. The Pennaik camp appeared as quiet as the village, but Arkkin was waiting for them. He simmered a pot of foul-smelling pitch over a small fire, which the two noblemen slathered over the seams of their boots to waterproof them. Arkkin had the other provisions that Rinchen had brought with him from Eyerlon: oiled leather leggings to bind over their breeches, fur-lined mittens with overlapped palm-slits, and two pairs of teardrop-shaped snowshoes.

Rinchen laced the snowshoes over his boots with the confidence that came from practice. After a struggle that left him sitting in the snow, Dart threw his aside.

"It's easier to walk on top of the snow than plow through it," Rinchen chided, "and no chance that you'll plant your foot in a hole by mistake."

"I don't know—"

"Exactly. You don't know where we're going, how far we have to go, or what we've got to cross to get there. Your goddess may have given you everything you need to vanquish Hazard, but you keep saying she sleeps all winter. You don't know winter. I talked to men from Norivarl. They know winter, and they said we'll need these."

While Dart fought a second, triumphant fight with the snowshoes, Rinchen collected embers in a waterproof firepot which he placed in an already bulging satchel. Dart took his first unsteady steps atop the snow to satisfy his curiosity. Along with the firepot, Rinchen was carrying a tinderbox, a cone-shaped pot, a ladle, a flint-and-steel sparker, coils of leathery dried meat, and an abundance of bright-colored silk strips.

"You're not leaving anything behind," Dart commented, holding up a length of red silk.

"Nothing except you." Rinchen snatched the silk out of Dart's hand. Friendship was a new sensation for him, and the thought of losing it left him surly. "When I told my loving mother of the danger I faced, she offered the gown off her back to ensure my safe return." He didn't bother making the lie believable. Janna was under guard in her new palace rooms, vowing vengeance on disrespectful sons and brewing gods-knew-what in her crystal crucibles. She could do whatever she wanted, so long as she didn't conspire with her Merrisati kin while Aleg was alone.

Rinchen shuddered doubt from his thoughts. Aleg could handle Janna. Aleg could rule as well as reign if he didn't return to Eyerlon. He was the one who lacked the full measure of kingly talents, making enemies easily because he did not dare have friends or love. The curse tainted everything. He was losing Dart, and dreaded to think what might happen to Berika before his curse was through with her. Mostly, Rinchen dreaded what would happen to him, to his kingdom, if he lost Aleg—

Maybe it would be better if he died with Arianna.

"Are you ready?" Dart asked, nudging his arm and drawing his thoughts back to the immediate.

He nodded and slung the satchel over his shoulder beneath the wolf-fur cloak.

They hiked upstream until they came to the place where Dart said Berika had fetched him out of the forest. Rinchen tied his first strip of silk to a tree on Weycha's side of the stream. Although the snowshoes left an unmistakable trail in the unbroken snow, he paused every few hundred paces. Once they were well into the forest, Dart stopped complaining, and admitted, with an uneasy laugh, that nothing was familiar and the only woodlore the forest's champion knew was what he remembered from his life as Driskolt sorMeklan.

In contrast to the fields surrounding Gorse, Weychawood was

carpeted with old snow. The thick, granular crust rarely cracked beneath their snowshoes, but on the occasions when one of them broke through the crust, there was water running beneath the snow, and they were grateful for the pitch sealing their boots. Around mid-morning they came to a hollow that was thawed and muddy at the bottom but snow-crusted around the crest.

"You ever see anything like this before?" Dart asked casually.

Rinchen tied yellow silk to a branch before answering: "In autumn, when the ground still holds the warmth from summer, but not in Ice. Even if the air warms, there shouldn't be enough sunlight to melt the snow from the trees in Ice."

Dart swore softly.

They plodded around the hollow's crest, avoiding the mud, saying nothing, when misty tendrils began rising from the thicker snow banks. The mist clung to the trees like fleece; the tendrils thickened into a blanket of musty fog. Rinchen marked the branches more frequently with his scraps of silk. Fallen branches littered the ground, atop the crusted snow. Carcasses lay scattered through the deadwood: birds, small game, deer, and predators, all bloated or burst, none eaten.

The prince prodded a carcass with a stick. "Whatever it is, it's not starvation and it's not disease. There are poisons that will drop an animal in its tracks," he said, thinking of the various concoctions that Janna kept in her locked cabinet, "but not every animal—"

"And every tree," Dart added, testing a branch of a young oak tree. It broke clean and loud. "They're all dead. The sap has dried out. You could burn this wood tonight and there'd be no smoke."

"What could kill trees *and* animals?"

Dart swung Weycha's wooden sword like a scythe to cut through an oak tree. As the thigh-thick tree crashed to the ground an acrid stench polluted the air. "Hazard," he said, scabbarding the sword.

"Are we too late?"

"No. You were right—the air's too cold and there's not enough sun. The thaw makes my lady restless, but it has not awakened her."

"Are we getting close?"

"Closer than Hazard," Dart replied cryptically and started walking.

Rinchen knotted silk around a branch and caught up. The fog thickened, obscuring the sun and the treetops. The forest echoed with the sounds of dripping water and falling wood. For an hour or more, the only living sounds they heard were those they made themselves. Then a flight of ravens flew above the fog.

Dart seized the prince's arm. "She's close by."

"Arianna?" Rinchen shrugged his cloak back from his shoulders and loosened his sword.

"My lady."

Dart released Rinchen's arm and forged through the fog as fast as the clumsy snowshoes would allow. Rinchen called out once, but his command fell on deaf ears. He put all his energy into keeping Dart's grey silhouette in sight, forgetting his silk strips. The fog closed within an arm's length. Rinchen lost Dart's silhouette; the sound of snowshoes ahead was his only guide.

Then, as if it had been cut with a knife, the fog ended at the edge of a clearing some forty paces wide. A ring of giant oak trees marked the perimeter of the clearing, the boundary of the fog. With branches intertwined well above his head, the clearing was locked in twilight and nearly bare of snow, but the ground was frozen hard.

Rinchen stood between two trees in a space barely wide enough for his shoulders. The trees on either side were as broad as he was tall, but the oak tree at the center of the clearing, the tree toward which Dart ran, was the largest tree he'd ever seen. Ten men could have stood with their arms outstretched and faces pressed against the bark; their fingers would not have touched.

They'd reached the heart of Weychawood, where the goddess dwelt with the avatars of her sister-selves. Dart cried with joy, but Rinchen was awed and cautious, careful not to touch the trees as he removed his snowshoes. He kept a wary eye on the tangled branches where huge acorns hung like boulders. Ever-observant, he calculated that there had once been twenty-seven oak trees in the outer ring, but six trees had vanished completely and a seventh lay on her back with her crown fallen outside the circular clearing and hidden by Hazard's unnatural fog.

Tremontin.

Suddenly oblivious to all else, Rinchen made his way to the fallen giant. He reached into the naked roots, half-expecting them to twine around his arms, but they remained lifeless. A voice cried in his conscience, enjoining him to fall on his knees, to repent, and beg forgiveness from the forest he had destroyed, but Walensor was his only god. He'd sacrifice every one of the trees in the clearing if it would preserve the kingdom. People—flawed, ordinary people and monsters like Vigelan—were more important than trees or gods.

Rinchen regretted Tremontin's death, but he'd not repent and he wouldn't beg forgiveness. If the goddess did not understand—Well, he was used to being misunderstood.

A strong hand clamped over his shoulder, catching the leather binding of his mail shirt. It hauled him backward, out of Tremontin's embrace.

"I told you to be careful around old trees. You can't undo the past. Weycha forgave you. Nothing else is important."

Rinchen shuddered and stared at Dart's face a moment before recognizing him. "I wasn't trying to undo the past. She gave me a chance to say I was sorry, but I couldn't: I'm not. I didn't know Hazard wouldn't die."

He looked past Dart's shoulder. There was a gaping hole in the trunk of Weycha's central tree. "We're too late."

"No, we got here in time."

"What happened there?"

"I happened there. This is where I was reborn."

Like him, Dart had shed his snowshoes. He clambered easily into the bark-lined cavity and stretched his arms apart; they touched the opposite sides.

"If Fate and my lady will it, this is where I'll return."

The bark shimmered. Rinchen rubbed his eyes, but the blurring was not in his eyes or imagination. "Dart! Get out—"

But it was already too late. Weycha was swallowing her champion.

If the tree *was* Weycha— If Hazard hadn't deceived them and defeated them. He lunged toward the tree, thrusting his mittened hands into the cavity as it closed. He felt the wool of Dart's cloak, felt greenwood splinters pierce his skin.

Then the tree spat him out. His fingers were naked, stiff and gnarled like root wood. And they hurt. He fell to the ground, waiting for the pain to stop, but fainted before it did.

Berika prepared to follow Dart and the prince. She wore two pairs of her father's breeches beneath her skirt, with a layer of straw between them. The fleece-lined boots she'd worn while she rode in the sleigh had kept her feet warm, but their soft soles were not meant for lengthy hikes over uncertain ground. With her mother's help, she bound more straw over the boots and a set of boardlike wooden patens over the straw.

The crackling straw awoke the children, who woke everyone else. Braydon was not surprised that the noblemen had gone off quietly, he wasn't even surprised that Berika was determined to follow them, but he was astonished that Ingolde was helping her, and said so. He thought it was a terrible idea and recited the dangers, both natural and unnatural, that she might face in Weychawood. In short order he was layering himself in deadwatch gear and wondering aloud if he would ever learn to keep his mouth shut. Braydon belted on his sword, but followed Berika's example and took his old shepherd's crook from the collection behind the door.

Berika's crook had belonged to her father. It had a clutch of brass bells bound below the hook and a wrapping of iron around the straight end. With Dart's forgotten acorn slung over her shoulder and the musical crook in her right hand, she was ready to face Weychawood.

The moon had set and the sun was well above the eastern horizon when she and Braydon followed the tracks across the bridge. They saw the tracks to the Pennaik camp, and would have ignored them, but Arkkin hailed Berika by name.

"Pay no attention," Braydon suggested and took his own advice, floundering to his knees in the deep snow by the stream.

Berika saw the ungainly objects Arkkin waved over his head and matched them with the odd tracks her brother was obliterating. "He wants to help us."

"Iser's fist, Beri, he's a blackhead spook. We don't want his help."

"I do. You can wait here or come with me, whichever you want." She started toward the Pennaik camp.

"I can't let you go in there alone." Braydon swore as he followed her.

The snowshoes that Arkkin offered them differed from the ones the prince and Dart had worn in that they were fresh-made from willow withies and strips of leather the Pennaikmen had scrounged from their own gear. Braydon admitted that the snowshoes would make their journey easier—he knew men from Norivarl, too—but it galled him to accept blackhead charity, particularly from one of their spooks. Though once he'd taken the snowshoes, he needed little persuasion to slather his boots with blackhead pitch.

Berika gratefully discarded her patens and hitched her gown up to her knees. She recognized the place where Dart and the prince had crossed the stream, although she did not explain its significance to her brother. They both noticed the fluttering silk and had no doubt which of the men they were following had tied it to the branch.

"First, the blackhead and his snowshoes, and now this. It's like the damned Wolf knew you were going to be following him."

"He's just being careful. Rinchen is always careful, and anyway, there were *four* snowshoes. How did he know you'd be coming with me? Did *you* tell him?"

"Don't talk nonsense." Braydon put his head down and followed the silk-marked track.

It wasn't long before they came to the melted hollow. Berika wasn't headblind or Severed. "Hazard's been here," she said grimly. "He's thawing the soil wherever he goes. If he makes the soil warm, the trees will quicken and the goddess will wake up. Once she's awake, he'll be able to find her."

Braydon looked around, as if the Arrizi pyromant might be hiding in a nearby tree, until Berika observed that there were no footprints. "He must look down from the Web with pyromancy."

"You're sure?"

Berika said she was. It was only a half-lie. She felt Hazard's malign presence in the sky overhead and in the darkness beyond her *basi*. She had felt it every day since the pyromant usurped the Web, and consoled herself with the hope that she was too small to interest a goddess-stalking predator. The malignant sensations grew stronger with every step that she and her brother took toward the heart of the forest, but they were weak compared to those she'd felt in Eyerlon. She thought they were safe.

They entered the fog and walked among the fallen branches. Berika felt the presence of the dead animals before she saw them: specks of emptiness in the fog. At first she did not guess what they were, but the specks grew numerous and finally she connected one with the bloated carcass of a rabbit. She said nothing to Braydon, who looked neither right nor left as he marched through the forest a few paces ahead of her. She hoped to spare him the knowledge that everything around them had died a sudden, unnatural death. Then they came to the place where one set of snowshoe tracks stopped squarely in front of a dead badger. Braydon never hesitated, and Berika understood that he was trying to shield her.

The fog thickened. Rinchen's silk markers lost their color beyond an arm's length and disappeared completely beyond that. They followed the cuts the noblemen's snowshoes left in the crusted snow, but Hazard's fog consumed the snow; the tracks were disappearing.

"If we're not lost already, we will be soon," Braydon announced. "What do they need that damned harp for anyway?"

Berika let her *basi* out slowly. The fog remained thick before her eyes, but in her mind she saw faint shadows were Dart had touched the forest. "That way," she said, pointing at shadows her headblind brother could not see. "I'll lead now."

Braydon caught her arm and would not let her pass by him. "If they want to die like heroes, that's fine—for them. But not us, Beri. There's no reason for us to be here. We're just little folk caught up in something big. We can still slip away. If Hazard and Arianna go down and the Wolf walks out alive, I swear I'll be the first to kiss his feet. But if he doesn't— Life never changes in places like Gorse, no matter who's in the Web or on the throne."

Something grim and predatory passed silently overhead. Berika breathed in her *basi*. Braydon stared at the hidden sky.

"Life *will* change," she whispered. "Anyone with *basi* can feel the changes coming if Dart and the prince fail. Even the headblind can feel it. We've got to help. We've got to keep going."

"What happened just then?" Braydon gripped her arm tight enough to hurt. "Tell your poor, headblind brother what that was."

"Nothing," Berika insisted, surging ahead.

She was exposed as a liar moments later when the fog transmitted desperate yowls and thrashing. Something was in the fight of its life. She grabbed Braydon's cloak.

"Hurry. Make your mind empty and follow me."

Braydon opened his mouth to protest or complain, but before he said a word, the yowls changed pitch. They'd both seen enough pigs slaughtered to know the sound of death. They couldn't go fast and they didn't get far before Berika heard something rumbling through the fog.

"Mother Cathe, protect us," she whispered.

Berika closed her eyes and imagined an open chest in the middle of her mind. She imagined all her *basi* flowing into the chest, then locked it shut with heavy, iron locks. When she opened her eyes, she couldn't see her feet through the fog, much less Dart's shadow tracks. The rumbling had become inaudible. She'd Severed herself from the Web, and made herself invisible to it.

If she'd been alone, she could have stayed right where she was and escaped notice, but she was with her brother, who was merely headblind. Before she could think of anything that would protect him, the ground shook and fire reared up in front of them. The fog evaporated and the hellfire shaped itself into the wraith she had seen in Rinchen's lair.

"Help me," the wraith pleaded.

Berika shook her head. There was nothing this side of death that could tempt her to help the echo-voiced apparition, but Arianna was talking to Braydon, not her. Berika was certain her brother saw something quite different.

"Help me," Arianna repeated, sprouting what Berika perceived as arms of hellfire. "Hazard hounds me from one end of the forest to the other. My strength is almost gone; I can resist him no longer. If only I can reach the trees at the heart of the forest, I'll be safe. I'll vanquish him for Walensor. Please help me find the trees."

"We're going to the trees at the heart of the forest," Braydon replied before Berika could stop him. "You can come with us. I'll carry you."

"We?" The pyromant's empty black eyes swept left and right. "We?"

"My sister and I. We're taking the harp—"

Berika sprang the locks on her *basi* and smacked Braydon across the face with her crook. "It's Arianna, Hazard's sister. Don't listen, Braydon. Don't tell her—"

Arianna loosed a bolt of hellfire. It caught Berika squarely between her breasts and lifted her off her feet. She hurtled through the air, screaming as the viscous flames made a spiralling cocoon around her body. The last thing she felt was the harp case shattering beneath her as she struck the ground.

She was unable to scream or close her eyes as the hellfire swirled over her face. There was no pain, no heat, no stench—nothing at all except the vibration of the harp through her spine. Death was not as bad as some parts of life had been; Berika surrendered quietly, but did not die. Weycha's harp played its own angry music against the hellfire. Hours passed before the orange and magenta beads vanished in oily smoke.

Berika was disoriented and sore when the haze cleared. Several moments passed before she remembered who she was and how she had come to be spread-eagled in the mud at the base of an old oak tree. Several more passed before she found the muscles that moved her arms and legs. She stood up slowly and looked down at the harp that had saved her life. The acorn was shattered and singed, but the harp was unharmed. Clutching it in front of her like a shield, Berika looked for her brother. She found the foul and burnt circle where Arianna's hellfire column sprang from the ground, but the pyromant was gone.

And so was Braydon.

Rinchen's fingers were rigid sticks. His wrists squealed like warped doors on rusty hinges. Close examination in the soft twilight beneath Weycha's trees revealed tufts of greenwood protruding from each and every swollen pore, from fingertip to the base of his palm.

The wooden cavity into which Dart had disappeared had become a bulge in the great oak's trunk.

Basilidans said they spoke the words of the gods and that the gods were real. Rinchen accepted that the gods existed, because he had no way to prove the basilidans were wrong, but he had faith only in himself and his curse. He and Dart had discussed their roles many times during the journey from Eyerlon. Dart and the wooden sword would confront Hazard. Armed with his speed and steel, he would confront Arianna.

If Hazard himself marched into Weycha's grove, Rinchen knew he stood no chance, but if flame-haired Arianna appeared, he'd find a way to keep his promise.

He sat cross-legged with his back against the bulge in Weycha's trunk. He put his teeth against a numbed knuckle of his weapon hand, withdrawing a single splinter. The pain was sharp, but passing, and he worked without rest until the ground became littered with grain-sized bits of wood. A raven flew down to investigate. The black bird was larger than any hawk in the royal mews. It pecked at the splinters and found them acceptable fare. Other ravens flew down. They devoured what was already on the ground and fought for each fresh splinter the prince withdrew. The boldest bird hopped onto the Wolf's knee.

Rinchen met the bird's bright, black-eyed stare. "If you want to help"—he held up his left hand—"help here. A man's sword-hand is his own responsibility."

Weycha's raven pecked the back of the Wolf's left hand twice before withdrawing a splinter. The goddess's ravens were more intelligent than other ravens, but they were still birds. They flocked and they fought and there was no way he could maintain the distinction between his two hands. Conceding defeat, Rinchen set his hands on his knees and allowed the birds to undo what their mistress had done.

Mirth radiated through the oak bark. He considered himself unjustly mocked, and hammered the bark with his elbow. The ravens took flight amid squawks and feathers. Mirth became unmistakable laughter, and Severed though he was, Rinchen had a vision of what the goddess and his friend could see: a too-serious young man, cloaked in wolf-fur with ravens wheeling around him, and a stray black feather sticking upright from equally black hair.

In the vision, and in reality, the largest raven of the flock swooped down to land atop his head. Deliberately, and gently, it pecked, then pinched his nose. He stared, cross-eyed, into bright black beads that shimmered with the colors of spring and autumn.

"Enough!" Rinchen leaned back against the tree, dislodging the bird. "You win. I'm *silly*. Go ahead and laugh."

They did, with swaying branches, falling leaves, and ravens swooping drunkenly at his head, until he laughed too, and laughed until his sides ached.

The ravens finished their work. They loitered on the ground while the prince exercised the aches and stiffness out of his hands. They flew up into the branches when he drew his sword for shadow-practice. Rinchen thought he'd scared them away, but he hadn't. Moments after they'd disappeared, Braydon Braydson appeared beside Tremontin's fallen oak. Rinchen flexed his fingers around the sword hilt.

"I have found Arianna, midons prince. She is waiting for you. She needs you."

Rinchen glanced over his shoulder. Weycha's oak was unchanged. The bulge did not shimmer with life. He raised his sword in a salute, then turned back to Braydon.

"I'm ready."

"Follow me, midons. I will take you to her."

Rinchen followed Braydon. Weycha's ravens followed the Wolf.

CHAPTER Twenty-three

Berika heard ravens above the fog. She veered after them, but the harp strings cried softly and the instrument became heavy in her arms. With a sigh, she backtracked and the birds flew beyond earshot. A tree uprooted many winters earlier stretched before her, and with the harp's silent permission, she sat down to rest.

The heartwood harp was her only guide in the forest. After losing Braydon, she'd wandered recklessly, searching for the shadows Dart left on the snow, ignoring the harp's soft sounds and getting lost in the process. Finally she listened to the harp, which was silent when she followed the path of its choosing and cried when she strayed from it.

Or rested too long.

Wearily, she swung her snowshoes over the tree trunk, persevering through the fog with the harp held awkwardly before her.

Without warning, she entered the cold, crystal air of Weycha's clearing. She thought that by some miracle she'd arrived first; then she saw two abandoned pairs of snowshoes.

"Dart?" The harp echoed her voice, but there was no reply. She called out Prince Rinchen's name, and her brother's, with the same disappointing results. "Weycha? Weycha, can you hear me? Do you know I'm here? Are you safe? Am I?"

A breeze rippled a melody from the harp strings which, for the first time, did not merely echo her questions. The great oak shuddered from roots to crown, and acorns larger than the harp case plummeted from the high branches. Berika stumbled toward a great, overturned tree as fast as her clumsy and now unnecessary snowshoes allowed. After shoving the harp in ahead of her, she tore off her snowshoes and crouched in the root-tangle beside them and the harp.

All the trees shook their branches. A gusty wind swirled down to the ground. It gathered the acorns, the snowshoes and everything else except for the harp, and flung them into the fog outside the clearing. The harp sang louder than Dart had ever played it, and Berika wedged herself deeper into the roots. She watched in awe as the great oak yawned and brilliant light filled the clearing.

Weycha's champion descended from his birthplace.

Dart's eyes glowed with the greens of spring and summer; his hair shimmered with the radiance of autumn. He carried his lady's sword in his right hand. Flames rippled along the blood-colored blade, but the wood was neither scarred nor consumed. The harp hailed Weycha's champion with joyous music. He saluted Tremontin with the burning sword.

Berika closed her eyes and prayed.

Rumbling erupted beyond the clearing. Berika kept her eyes closed until it stopped. She caught a whiff of hellfire. The fallen tree in which she hid trembled beneath heavy footsteps as something—Hazard—emerged from the fog. Dreadful curiosity pried open Berika's eyes. She looked upon the face of Hazard through the veil of Tremontin's tattered roots.

The Pyromant was a large man, but not an impressive one. His face was broad, hung with fleshy jowls. His eyes were close-set beneath a heavy brow. He was nearly bald; his scalp was mottled with livery blotches. What hair he had formed a greasy fringe along his neck, behind his ears. He was naked, with withered loins and a belly gone slack with age.

But in his right hand Hazard carried a golden sword that pulsed with the light and heat of molten iron. It was, by chance, pointed at Berika's heart.

At least she hoped it was by chance.

With a sweep of his wooden sword, Dart invited Hazard into the clearing. The Pyromant leapt over the roots where Berika hid, attacking as his feet struck the ground. He battered Dart with a succession of quick thrusts and slashes. The noxious colors of hellfire flared each time the swords touched. Hellfire itself flowed down the wooden blade, but was absorbed before reaching the ebony hilt. Hazard disengaged and retreated to take his opponent's measure.

Twice more the Arrizi pyromant launched blistering attacks. Dart parried each stroke cleanly. When the champion did attack, he began with a feint that successfully drew Hazard's sun blade beyond his body. The wooden sword pierced Hazard's forearm and opened a gash that leaked hellfire, not blood.

Hazard bellowed from the pain, and acorns fell from the giant trees.

Berika hoped for an easy victory, but her hope was crushed when Hazard's arm sealed itself. Hellfire shot from the sun-sword's tip. Dart impaled the noxious fireball and flung it to the ground, where it dissolved into black scum. Hazard hurled more fireballs; they all spread harmlessly over the ground. Berika saw the battle between Rinchen and Arianna replayed on a larger scale: Dart had the skills and resources to defend himself, but his attacks were futile. Hazard had the power of the Web and all the time in the world. And Berika had no shimya'an firewater.

She did have Weycha's harp. For one foolish moment she considered playing it, or heaving it at the back of Hazard's head, but Dart had begun to shift the battle lines. Berika watched and waited.

Each time Weycha's champion defended himself, whether from a gout of hellfire or the sun-sword itself, he rotated the conflict to his left. The tactic seemed dubious. Dart was supposed to protect Weycha, not let Hazard get between him and her tree, which was what, step by small step, he was doing. Berika imagined Hazard running for the oak trunk cavity and plunging his sword straight into the heartwood.

It seemed the Pyromant imagined the same. Once his back was to Weycha's tree, he refused Dart's rotations, and his retreats outdistanced his attacks. The distance between his back and the tree shrank.

Berika clenched her fists and made desperate wishes with her *basi*, but she stood no chance against hellfire and wild forest sorcery. Dragging the harp behind her, she crawled out from Tremontin's roots. She thought to use Weycha's voice to distract Hazard while she warned Dart, and got as far as plucking a heavy-handed chord from the strings.

Hazard looked directly at her. His eyes shone like the sun; her warning died in her throat. He whirled one gout of hellfire at Dart, another at the harp and her. He sprinted to the cavity. Dart couldn't catch both gouts of hellfire *and* reach the oak before Hazard plunged his sword into Weycha's heart. Berika watched with horror and guilt as Dart grounded the second hellfire gout before he charged after Hazard. He didn't have the speed to catch him. The Pyromant raised the sun-sword high above his head as he stood on the cavity's rim. The searing blade spouted hellfire as he began a downward slash.

Dart held the wooden sword before him like a lance, skewering Hazard from back to front before the slash struck living wood. He put his weight against the ebony hilt and pushed until its quillons were against Hazard's back.

The Pyromant roared. His body spewed hellfire and the cavity churned with metallic colors. Dart disappeared in the flames. The harp screamed and twilight became midnight as the oak trees swayed in a howling storm. Rancid fumes filled the clearing. Berika fell to her knees among Tremontin's roots, losing hold of the harp. Her eyes burned and her vision blurred, but she kept her head up.

Hellfire gushed from the cavity reaching perilously close to Berika's shelter. She was sure each breath would be her last, but the fallen avatar never ignited. Through the stench and smoke, Berika understood that Weycha's champion had acted deliberately when he rotated the battle and that her own contribution, while foolish and ill-considered, had not changed anything.

The champion and his lady held Hazard in hellfire, like meat roasting on a spit.

Gradually hellfire ceased to dominate the conflagration. Real flames in the amber, red, and yellow of burning wood licked the rim of the cavity, and Hazard's roars became wails as Weycha cleansed herself with honest fire. A dark, man-shaped shadow reappeared in the flames. The air remained foul and gusty, but Berika ventured into the clearing.

Weycha's champion was as black as the ebony hilt he clutched in his hands. Berika could not tell if he survived or if he was dead, and stiff like charred-through meat. The golden sword had melted; precious metal trickled out of the cavity. It puddled amid the ground roots. Hazard himself had been reduced to shrivelling hellfire, impaled on the burning sword, doomed but not quite dead. Berika watched him shrink until he was no larger than a rat. Then, with one final shriek, he vanished. The wooden sword crumbled into bright embers and Dart toppled like a statue.

Berika rushed to Dart's side while flames still lapped at the blackened cavity. His hands were burnt, but the rest of him was merely crusted with greasy soot. Folding strands of her hair, she held them before Dart's mouth and nose to see if there was any breath left in him; the ends fluttered weakly. Berika wiped his cheek with the snow-soaked hem of her cloak.

Dart's eyes opened; they were fire-red from lid to lid, without irises or pupils.

Weycha's champion had won his victory, but the man she'd called Dart was gone. She cradled his head in her lap. Tears fell unnoticed and unchecked on his face. The fire burned down to cold ashes, but the wind persisted and the clearing remained dark.

There had been two pyromants in Weychawood. Hazard had been the more powerful, but Arianna, hiding somewhere until Hazard and Dart destroyed each other, was just as dangerous, maybe more. If Prince Rinchen—a very mortal man with many flaws—could not destroy the woman of his dreams, Dart's victory would go for naught.

Berika shivered and held Dart's unconscious head against her breast.

Braydon was possessed, Rinchen decided. Arianna's imperatives pulled the shepherd through the forest like a fisherman hauling in his line. He forged a path over rocks, trees, and treacherous ice which no sane man—no cursed man, either—would follow if he had any choice. Rinchen had none, not if he wanted to find Arianna. He minded his feet and fell less often than Braydon, but had little attention to spare for his surroundings until Braydon stopped short. They nearly collided at the crest of a moderate hill.

"She awaits," Braydon said flatly, opening his arms.

Rinchen looked down the slope. His breath caught in his throat. He'd known Arianna would wait for him in Weychawood as she waited for him in his dreams: a flame-haired vision wrapped in translucent silk, surrounded by moonlight roses each with sharp, black thorns. He'd known and sworn to Dart that he'd be untempted; he'd lied. Arianna's blood-red lips parted, touched by the tip of her tongue, which glistened a brighter shade of red. She knew his secrets, knew what a cursed man wanted from the depths of his dark, tainted soul.

He stole a glance at Braydon, whose eyes were bright and wide; then he drew his sword.

Arianna radiated sadness and disappointment. "No, my love. Let us start over, as it was meant to be."

He walked toward her as visions appeared in his mind: she was naked, they were together, upon the roses, with blood and pain and passion. He died, screaming, inside her; she brought him back—again and again. He could not tell where conjury ended and his own yearning began. He walked further, scabbarding the sword as he stepped onto the pale roses. The pyromant caressed his cheek, leaving a stream of warm blood behind.

Pain was pleasure. Pleasure was pain. Death was the best of both.

He loosened the silk and drew his love, naked, into a tight embrace, kissing the delicious blood from her lips.

"Don't! You godsforsaken wolf—*stop*!"

Stunned and lethargic, Rinchen watched Braydon charge down the hill. He couldn't guess which of them, him or Arianna, the man intended to kill. And he never found out. Arianna cast away her glamour. She became the flaming creature he'd fought in his lair, and blasted her bower with hellfire. Rinchen dove and flattened himself in the mud.

Braydon was much less lucky. Noxious flames of hellfire enveloped his body. His screams were swiftly reduced to mindless whimpers; then he was silent, but not dead. Hellfire did not kill quickly.

Rinchen pushed himself to his feet. He unclasped his cloak, allowing it to fall to the ground. Then he brushed the clots of mud and snow from his clothes—particularly from his sleeves and especially the inside of his left forearm, which was hardly wet at all.

He ignored Braydon's living corpse when he got to his feet, but he'd seen it and made a silent promise. Arianna had not restored her glamour. Shimmering magenta hair writhed over her bare breasts. Patches of hellfire flickered on her skin.

"He would have slain you," she explained.

"But you saved me. Be as you were, my love. Let me see the face I remember."

The pyromant closed her eyes and with apparent effort became a beautiful young woman again. She re-created the translucent silk gown, but the roses withered as quickly as she made them. "I dare not reach for the Web until I am certain Weycha's champion has slain my brother."

"I understand. I know what it's like to be hated by close-kin and abused." He slid his right arm behind her waist. With his left hand he traced the curves of her face and the hollows of her neck. "It cannot have been easy for you, my love, with Hazard ruling your life. Our dreams together could not undo the damage we suffered at other hands. We are each friends of despair." He buried his face in her hair, and whispered: "You have looked into the depths of my soul. You know I am the only man who can give you what you want." He kissed the pyromant's ear with his teeth, lapping blood with a soft tongue.

The pyromant's mortal pulse quickened beneath her breasts. Her lips were warm and moist and dangerous on the prince's neck. "We will find the ecstasy beyond blood and pain."

"Beyond blood and pain, my love"—Rinchen lowered his left arm and shuddered; the knife beneath his sleeve, which he had loosened when he brushed off the snow, fell into his hand—"there is no ecstasy—" The Wolf slid the blade through her breast. He thrust it upward, until he felt her mortal heart quiver against the steel. Deep blue eyes went wide with disbelief, her mouth opened. "—only death." He kissed her as steel pierced her heart.

Arianna struggled wildly, but he held her tight. Twisting the knife, swallowing her blood as it flowed through her lips. She could not heal herself fast enough, far enough, to survive the leap to hellfire. When her body grew warm, he let her go, retreated, and drew his sword and swung it double-handed. The weapon deteriorated as it passed through her body, but he swung both hard and fast. It severed her neck before it corroded.

Rinchen watched until there was nothing left of the woman he had loved. He considered retrieving what remained of his knife but placed his withered sword over the knife instead. Then he knelt beside Braydon Braydson. Streaks of hellfire scintillated on what remained of Braydon's skin; their colors proclaimed that the shepherd still lived.

In the war, it was his royal duty to walk the field after a battle, searching for men destroyed by hellfire as Braydon was. He'd kneel beside a faceless stranger and grant him a merciful death. His sword and knife were gone, but Rinchen knew ways to kill with just his hands. He stared up through the trees. The forest was darker than it had been, but that was no more than the natural end of a very long day. The fog was thinner; he could see Weycha's ravens roosting in the branches.

Weycha had forgiven and healed the destroyer of Tremontin. Surely she would heal a shepherd.

Rinchen wrapped Braydon carefully in wolf-fur. The ravens took flight when he lifted the shepherd's body. He relied on the birds to lead him back to the clearing, but ice crystals hung in the air as Hazard's conjury dissipated. The crescent moon rose, scattering light through the tiny crystals and he had no difficulty finding Weycha's circle and did not hesitate before entering it.

He called Dart's name as he carried Braydon through one of the gaps in the outer ring. There was no reply, but there was a small campfire burning on the far side of the great oak, near the cavity. Adjusting his burden for the last time, he wondered if he was too late, if Weycha had already claimed her champion forever. He stumbled, almost losing his man-shaped burden. His body was weary past measure, but his heart was wearier with the thought that his curse had cut him off from a single, simple favor: the chance to say goodbye.

But the cavity, though enlarged by fire, was empty. Dart sat beside it, leaning against Weycha's trunk, his eyes closed. Resting, Rinchen thought, or sleeping. He laid Braydon beside the fire and dropped to his knees beside the man he'd dared to call a friend.

"Dart," he called softly, without response, and gently touched his arm. A fire-maimed hand slid to the ground. The Wolf held it tenderly, shielding the broken flesh from the sting of his tears.

"It's not right," he whispered. "We did what we came to do. All we asked was the time to say 'well done' and 'goodbye.'" He restored the maimed hand to its place in Dart's lap. "It's not right," he repeated in a louder voice and pounded his fist against the scarred trunk. "I couldn't say goodbye the first time. That's all I wanted. Why couldn't you wait?"

His forehead fell against Dart's shoulder and his fist slid limply to the ground. Moments passed. He heard footsteps; he didn't need to look. Dart could not have built the fire. Braydon would not have come into Weychawood alone.

"Hazard's gone," Berika said, dumping an armload of wood.

"And Arianna," Rinchen replied. He found the strength to lift his head. "It's over. We won."

Berika reached out to touch the wolf-wrapped bundle beside the fire. "What hap—?"

"Don't!" he lunged, but for once—when it mattered most—he wasn't quick enough.

"No . . ." Berika wailed, letting the fur slip through her fingers. She sat down heavily, eyes closing quickly while she trembled with grief and horror. "No."

And her brother began to wail, too—horrible thin sounds pushed through blackened lips. They stopped when Berika opened her eyes again:

"Where's the wooden sword?" Rinchen asked.

"Gone. Burnt." Berika rocked from side to side, unable to cry. "He's suffering. We've got to do something to save him. Oh, gods—how did it happen? Were you with him when it happened?"

Rinchen touched Dart's cheek, then returned to the fire. "Yes. Arianna found your brother before she found me. He led me to her. Dart and I had a plan: I would let her think she had seduced me. Dart was sure she would conjure a mortal body that I could kill, if she thought I was blind to her intentions. And she did, but something went wrong; she lost her hold over Braydon. He tried to warn me . . . or stop me." Rinchen held a stick of firewood in the flames. "Your brother never had a chance. I'm sorry."

"He never liked you. He never truly trusted you."

"Is that why he came into Weychawood after us?" He stood up and flung the burning stick out of the clearing; then levelled an accusing finger at Berika. "Is that why you both followed us? If you couldn't trust me, couldn't you at least trust Dart? Godswill, Berika—*we knew what we were doing*! Why did you interfere?"

Berika fussed guiltily with the hem of her skirt. "You left the harp behind. We brought it with us. It saved my life when Arianna found us."

He raked the campsite with a critical eye; the harp wasn't in sight. "Dart left it behind deliberately . . . for us." His voice was tight. Rage licked at his thoughts. "For you and me. He wanted us to remember him when he'd gone back to his gods-be-damned lady." He sat and watched the fire. The rage burned inward, quenching Weycha's healing light, leaving him alone in familiar darkness. "Nothing is ever saved, it always slips away. Dart, your brother, the harp—" He caught himself before he added Arianna's name to the litany of what he had lost.

"We still have the harp," Berika said softly. She ran to the roots of Tremontin to retrieve it.

First they leaned it against Braydon's hellfired body, and then they placed it gently in the arms of Weycha's champion. They prayed for a miracle and were bitterly disappointed. Clouds welled up to cover the crescent moon and an icy wind filtered down through the oak branches. Winter had returned to Weychawood.

Rinchen shivered and warmed his hands over the fire.

"It's time to say goodbye." He uncovered Braydon's head. "When you're done, tear off a length of your linen, please. I must wrap my hands before I touch him. It will be quick, I can promise you that."

He sat beside Dart and took the harp into his lap. There'd never been time to learn to play the harp, or anything else, but he liked music, could sing along, soft and unnoticed, with any tune. He was patient and methodical because those traits were immune to his curse and kept him alive. He plucked the strings one at a time, then compared them to the melodies he remembered.

Berika's eyes were dry when she joined him. "I wish we could put my brother inside Weycha's tree."

By then he was plucking the strings out of sequence, mapping his way across the instrument, finding patterns that approximated his memories. "We could try, but Dart is her champion."

"Will you . . . ? Will you *kill* Dart, too?"

He pretended not to hear the question until he'd finished his experiment: One note at a time, he re-created a phrase from one of Dart's melodies. "Yes."

"I wish you didn't have to."

"I wish a lot of things, Berika, but I promised my fr—" His voice caught on another word, like 'father,' which he could no longer say. He curled around the harp's rough-wood pillar, hiding from everyone, including himself. "I swore to Dart that I'd take care of him . . . of his body. I told you that the first night, before Arianna. I am very careful of my vows."

"I wish you didn't have to, that's all. No man, even a prince with a curse, should have to kill his friends.

"I don't have . . . any." He attacked the second phrase of the melody, in lieu of hearing Berika's sympathy. The instrument had no magic in his arms, but he was nothing if not persistent until the thought crossed his mind, sudden and irresistible, that he should stop.

"Are you ready?" he asked.

Berika nodded and reached beneath her skirt to tear off a strip of her linen. The prince left the harp against Dart's arm. He wrapped the linen carefully around both hands; then, holding his breath, placed one hand on either side of Braydon's hellfired neck. He took a deep breath and closed his eyes.

Dart found his voice: "No. Wait! I like Berika's idea better."

With a shout of pure joy, Berika bounded around the fire. She wrapped him in an exuberant, exquisitely painful embrace. He kissed her lightly on the cheek, but his eyes were for Rinchen hunched over beside the fallen shepherd, gasping for air and not getting any. Very conscious of his ruined hands, Dart put his arm over Berika's shoulder. She helped him stand and walk.

"Suddenly I heard you talking—I couldn't answer, not at first. My lady . . ."

He rested his forearm on Rinchen's shoulder. The prince heaved himself sideways to escape. Rinchen was breathing easier, but not ready to talk. They stared at each other; then the Wolf, his eyes still wide with panic and exhaustion, tried to crawl away.

"You have no one to blame but yourself." Dart snagged Rinchen's arm despite the pain in his hands, forcing him to stop. "You are, beyond a doubt, the worst harpist beneath what is left of the Web. You make mathematics, not music. My lady realized she would have to listen to you for a lifetime and allowed me to come back and throw her voice to the fire."

"Touch it and you'll die a death your gods-be-damned lady won't be able to undo."

Dart retreated, unprepared for the heartfelt sincerity of his friend's warning. "I've got to touch it, Rinchen; I've got to persuade her to take Braydon instead." He turned to Berika. "There's no other way."

Berika looked down at her brother. A thread of magenta hellfire wormed over the ruin of his cheek. Rinchen had not administered his mercy before Dart stopped him.

"Will the goddess have him?" she asked.

"My lady will have him or no one. It is wonder and bliss with her, but it is not what I choose." He touched Rinchen's shoulder again. "Rinchen? Friend? Help me? I can't carry him myself."

Sighing but otherwise silent, Rinchen carried Braydon to the charred and larger cavity. Weycha was not pleased with the substitute offering. Her branches clashed. Falling acorns sent them running for cover, and the cavity refused to close. But Dart took the harp and began to play. The melodies were ragged at first—his hands were burnt to sinew and bone. The goddess healed them, so he could hear her empassioned arguments for his return.

Berika and Rinchen huddled together beneath her cloak. Dart played a counter-melody that put them to sleep; then he played for his life and his freedom.

The dialogue between Weycha and her reluctant champion lasted far into the night. The campfire burned down; the sky cleared and a blanket of frigid air dropped from the stars. Dart played without stopping until, at last, his fingers grew cold. He set the harp aside and felt his way to the cavity.

You are a willful, stubborn, and clever man.

"And I love my lady all the more because she has set me free to be a man again."

Braydon's body rose out of the cloak. The hellfire streaks faded.

He is a poor figure of a man.

"As I was when you found me. He will serve you well."

The goddess laughed and the cavity began to close. Dart grabbed Rinchen's tattered wolf-pelt cloak at the last moment, and with it wrapped snugly around them all, fell asleep between his friends.

CHAPTER Twenty-four

The Web sighed when Hazard's power was extinguished. Across the length and breadth of the kingdom weary, grieving sorcerers, Ingolde and Arkkin among them, lifted their heads and their *basi.* It might be a generation or more before the glory of Walensor's sorcery was restored, and it would never be as it was. Much of the knowledge was lost forever, consumed by the Pyromant's greed.

But in the tiny assart of Gorse, on the edge of Weychawood, the Web's sigh had special significance.

At midnight, the hedge-sorcerer and the shaman met on the millstream bridge, halfway between the shepherd's house and the Pennaik camp.

"Hazard fell from the sky," Arkkin said, solemnly displaying the charred, cracked shoulder blade of the stallion he had slain on New Years's Day. "The girl with the hair of fire is gone."

"You tell me what I know for myself," Ingolde replied, fingering the age-polished weaver's shuttle that was *her* touchstone. "Tell me what I do not know. Have you seen my children?"

Arkkin turned the plow-shaped bone over. There were fewer cracks on the underside, but they were deeper and the bone had cratered around them. "Too soon. It is not settled."

Ingolde studied the shaman's black bone oracle and then turned her attention to the moon. "Sunrise?"
"Sunrise," Arkkin agreed.

They met again at sunrise and began walking toward Weychawood. The Pennaikmen were arrayed behind Arkkin. Ingolde Braydswidow led the able-bodied men and women of the village as well as the Walenfolk who had accompanied the prince and her own son. They followed the snowshoe trail to the stream. Once in the forest they followed Prince Rinchen's markers; the silk ribbons shone like gemstones in the bright sunlight. At mid-morning they met a cold and hungry trio coming toward them.

There were cheers and hearty embraces. There was grief too. Four had gone into Weychawood, but only three came out. They had accomplished all that they set out to do, but Braydon was gone. The shepherd-turned-guard had been chosen by the goddess. His name would be remembered.

And he was gone.

Ingolde stood aside from the celebration. When everyone else turned around for Gorse, she continued alone to the heart of the forest. She returned the next morning, wearing a grim face, but satisfied that Weycha would treat her son properly, with love and honor.

The sleigh was loaded and the horses were being harnessed as the hedge-sorcerer climbed the uneven snow from the stream to the bridge. Berika gave her mother the invitation Heldey desperately wanted:

"Will you come with me to Eyerlon?"

Ingolde looked past her daughter to Dart and the prince, mounted on their stallions.

"With those two looking out for you, Berika, you won't need, or heed, a mother's advice." She hugged Berika. "A tree will grow in our fane this spring; Weycha will not be forgotten or neglected, and Gorse will be her special place. There will be enough work to keep weavers and hedge-sorcerers busy the rest of their lives."

Berika wrapped her arms around Ingolde's neck. "I'll miss you."

"We'll meet in the Web. What the spiders spin, weavers have to finish."

Then Ingolde walked over to the bridge to the huddled villagers.

The sleigh and its escort retraced their route across Fenklare to the King's Road, along the King's Road to the frozen Escham River, and down the river to Eyerlon itself. Berika did not have the training to mark their progress in the Web's tattered remnants; Arkkin lacked the interest. Even so, the charterhouses on the King's Road were packed with commonfolk and, especially, surviving sorcerers who wished to honor the heroes who had defeated Hazard and freed the Web.

There were sorMeklan partisans and kin at every charterhouse, too, but Lord Ean sorMeklan waited until the sleigh was on the Escham River. He rode out of Relamain onto the ice with a small escort. The sleigh stopped and Berika witnessed a restrained, but heartfelt, reunion between the donitor and his brother. Then Lord Ean invited the prince to ride privately beside him behind the sleigh.

Rinchen agreed and they were moving again, with Berika in her usual place, balancing a wax-covered tablet on her knees. The prince had remembered his promise to teach her to read, and to write, as well. He scratched lines into a wax tablet each morning, while the men harnessed the horses, and expected her to copy and memorize them during the day. As a teacher, Rinchen was knowledgeable and fair. He made allowances for the swaying sleigh, and never raised his voice or belittled her efforts. All the same, he made it clear that he expected Berika's best efforts, and radiated disappointment when her attention wandered.

With the man who might be her brother's father riding behind the sleigh, Berika's curiosity got the better of her efforts. She set the tablet aside and went to work uncovering a tiny rear window. After fighting with rusty nails and stiff leather, she peeled up one corner in time to see the donitor hand a wrapped parcel to the prince.

"You will appreciate that I have taken considerable risk in bringing this to you," Lord Ean sorMeklan said in an ordinary voice, which by quirks of the cold air and smooth ice, was perfectly audible inside the sleigh.

The donitor's hair was darker than Ingolde had described it, and streaked with grey. There were wrinkles around his eyes and mouth. It was hard to imagine him stealing her mother's heart; it was difficult to believe that Ingolde had ever had a heart that could be stolen. Berika kept her eye close to the opening and tried to decipher which of Lord Ean's features Indon had inherited.

Rinchen accepted the parcel. "You will remember, Lord sorMeklan, that my brother and I hold your liege-oath. You would take a far greater risk if you had not told us."

"With King Manal alive and awake, there is some question about how many kings Walensor can sustain, midons prince. Your grandfather sustains himself without sorcery now— At least without a covey of menders surrounding his throne. He holds you and your brother as usurpers. You're wise to return quickly to Eyerlon. You'll do well to watch your back once you get there."

"Do I detect concern, Lord sorMeklan? Could it be that you have a preference as to which sorRodion wears the crown? You do not have to worry about the kingdom, Lord Ean. You have only to worry about upholding your oath."

Berika listened and cringed. Yes, the donitor was concerned, and yes, he had a preference. It showed in every line of his face. But her prince, who truly didn't recognize a friend—an ally, at least—when he saw one, seemed determined to make Lord sorMeklan regret whatever choices he'd made.

"You have a year to grapple with your brother, your grandfather, your mother, and the Merrisati. You are a hero now, midons prince, but a year is a long time. Much can happen in a year."

"I will be disappointed if it does not, but not as disappointed as you will be, Lord Ean, if the sorMeklan forget how tightly they are tied to my brother and me."

"There is no need for threats, midons." Lord Ean's voice was weary. "The Merrisati have long had designs on Fenklare's coast. Where King Trench is involved, I foresee no conflict between the sorMeklan and the sorRodion princes."

While Berika watched, the noblemen exchanged calculated glances; then Lord Ean smiled. Indon had inherited his smile from his father. But she didn't dwell on the similarity. Mention of the Merrisati had turned her thoughts toward Rinchen's impending marriage, which she'd successfully forgotten since Eyerlon.

For three weeks she'd shared his life and bed. Despite Dart's assurances that Prince Rinchen loved her as she loved him, his affection had turned as chaste as snow and he'd resolutely avoided all mention of the forbidden word. The Wolf wasn't the young Ean sorMeklan. He made no promises that were not easily kept, and although his name and hers were already linked in bardic tales that would, perhaps, grow into legends, Berika doubted there'd ever be more.

That didn't stop her from feeling anxious and prematurely lonely.

Lord Ean and the prince rode in silence for a bit longer; then the donitor reined his horse to a stop. The parties separated, and Prince Rinchen concealed the parcel in a compartment of his saddle. Berika studied him as she studied her columns of words, committing the subtlest shape and gesture to memory, until she realized he was looking at the sleigh, at the window, and at the peephole she had made in it.

Gripped by shame and guilt, she let the leather fall back into its accustomed place. She replaced the nails as best she could, and piled everything in the sleigh against its rear wall. Nothing helped. She had spied on him; she'd violated the trust that spanned the vast distance between a prince and a shepherd. But the sleigh did not screech to an immediate halt. She was not called out onto the ice, lectured, and abandoned. Nor were there accusations when they stopped for the night at a river inn. There was another reading lesson, a jostling, noisy supper in a crowded room, and finally—the moment Berika both longed for and dreaded—an escape upstairs to the quiet room where they were alone.

She stiffened when he touched her neck, but it wasn't murder that was on Prince Rinchen's mind. He wound his always-cold hands in her hair. He kissed her lips with what was, for him, uncommon passion, then whispered in her ear: "I think I would like to hold you in my arms again—if you would have me?"

How strange that a prince—of all men—would ask a question that no one else, including her, deemed necessary. Berika gave him the answer they both wanted, and after that, took greater faith in what Dart had told her. The four days they spent on the frozen Escham river, and especially the nights, blended into a single, seamless moment of quiet, undemanding bliss.

The sleigh scraped up to the wharf at Eyerlon during a steady snowfall. The door opened and Arkkin lifted her to the snow-slicked dock in time to see Prince Alegshorn greet his brother with an embrace which swiftly deteriorated into a wrestling match. The golden prince performed the same ritual with Dart, but he gave Berika a hug that left her breathless.

"Braydon was my oath-bound man," Prince Aleg whispered while his arms still held her. "I mourn the loss of a good and honest man. If there is anything you need—anything at all—come to me." He stole a kiss, then let her go.

Berika stared at her feet, waiting for the heat to fade from her cheeks. Prince Aleg called for the horses to be led up from the river ice. He herded the travellers toward the shore.

"A heroes' feast awaits at the palace. Grandfather wants your head served as the main course." Prince Aleg jabbed his brother's well-padded shoulder. "Mother would like our livers served raw with dessert. The Merrisati are slicing intrigue hot from the spit. And little Gilenan says he's the one who should be king. Welcome home, brother. I was beginning to fear you'd decided to become a tree."

Rinchen took his stallion's reins and remounted. "I thought we were going to keep our lady mother locked up where the Merrisati couldn't find her. How did she get out?"

"It's a long, boring story, but I supposed you'd want to hear it. That's why I waited for you down here."

Prince Alegshorn mounted quickly and started up the streets to the palace beside his brother. Berika hadn't had time to wonder what would become of her before Dart appeared at her side, leading his own stallion.

"Maybe we could say we're sick," Dart proposed as he put his foot into the stirrup. "We could dash for the sorMeklan residence. Driskolt would be sympathetic, I think; I'm sure he's had supper with the sorRodion." He settled in the saddle and held out his arm. "Grab on, I'll lift you up behind me. The food's bound to be better at the residence. I never developed a taste for raw liver, have you?"

Berika landed sideways across the stallion's rump. The horse grunted and gave a sidewise cow-kick that forced Dart to reach behind and steady her.

"How can you makes jokes?" she asked, holding onto his arm until he pulled it away.

"Humor is our only hope, Berika. We're living on sorRodion charity now, which is like living on air." Dart's voice turned less lighthearted. "Prince Rinchen wants the crown, but he's going to have to fight for it. His enemies are our enemies, and his most dangerous enemies are in his family. Hold on tight."

Dart meant to the saddle, but Berika deliberately misunderstood and wrapped her arms around his waist instead. She rode through the streets of Eyerlon with her cheek pressed against his cloak.

When the deadwatch peal rang that night, Berika was alone in the Wolf's lair, shivering despite the blankets, and convinced that Dart had told the truth about the royal family. King Manal was alive and awake and thoroughly insane. He accused all three of them—Dart, Berika, and Prince Rinchen—of conspiring with Hazard to usurp his throne. Then he accused every sorcerer left alive of joining the conspiracy. He condemned everyone to death by flaying. Berika felt a surge of hostile *basi* when the king talked of death: not enough to hurt, but enough to destroy her appetite.

The sorRodion supped together every night, and trusted each other so little that their food was awash in peppery poison-neutralizing spices. No matter what a dish looked like—and there was, thank all the gods, no raw liver—it tasted like fire. She was blotting tears from her eyes throughout the ordeal and knew she owed Arkkin a debt of gratitude for preparing her food.

Janna, the dowager princess, was a shrill viper, surrounded by Merrisati foreigners. Her youngest son, Prince Gilenan, whom she put forward as the true heir to the mad king's throne, was a petulant little boy who threatened everyone with a variety of tortures. And if the three sorRodion princesses had names or voices, Berika didn't hear them.

If Prince Rinchen had been beside her, Berika would have calmly told him to either kill every member of his clan—except Prince Aleg—or run away as far and as fast as he could. But the Wolf did not return to his lair that night, nor the next. She saw him briefly the following morning, between chancery skirmishes, and though he made an effort to be cheerful, Berika felt the cold rage seething just beneath the surface. She gave him the advice she'd been saving since their arrival feast.

"It may come to that," he acknowledged, rummaging through the clutter on and beneath his worktable.

"I'd go with you, if you have to run away. It doesn't matter to me whether you're a prince or a king or a common man."

Rinchen found the scrap of parchment he was looking for. He stuffed it absently in his boot and studied her through slitted eyes. "I could almost wish it didn't matter to me, my lady, and we could run away together, but it does matter, and I'll kill them all before I show them my back."

He kissed her before he left and promised he'd return before deadwatch rang.

The prince had not been gone long when Arkkin brought her a visitor. The grey-robed neophyte recited a message from the new Magga Sorcerer, Halwisse sorJos. The Palestra needed help reconstructing the Web. A plea had gone out to every sorcerer and hedge-sorcerer, through those pathways in the Web that had been restored, seeking the names of Walenfolk who had the *basi* for sorcery, but had, for whatever reason, never come to Eyerlon. Berika's name had filtered back from several sources. If Berika was willing, the Magga wished to meet with her personally and immediately.

"Do you want to be bothered with those white-livered fools?" Arkkin asked.

"It can do no harm to talk with the Magga," she replied with more confidence than she felt.

The shaman hawked into the glowing brazier. "Shall I tell my prince you've left him for spooks?"

Berika crossed her hands over her heart. "No, absolutely not! I'll talk to the Magga, but I'm coming back here, no matter what." Then she remembered how Dart had been swallowed whole by the Basilica and that the name of the magga who succored him after each interrogation was Halwisse sorJos. She also recalled the prince telling her that she had earned Arkkin's admiration, and decided to put it to the test. "Arkkin, if I have not returned by sunset, *please come and fetch me home*!"

Arkkin smiled broadly, revealing black and jagged teeth. "I will do better than that, *merou*. I'll come with you now, and stand outside the door."

The shaman paced loudly outside the door of the otherwise quiet room where Berika met with the new Magga Sorcerer. Halwisse sorJos looked worse than perturbed by the sounds; she seemed anxious and almost frightened.

"I'm supposed to ask you why you think you have sufficient *basi* to reach the Web and why you did not present yourself before your seventeenth birthday," Halwisse said with some embarrassment and sidelong glances at the closed door. "Considering what I've already been told, that won't be necessary. By sheer *basi* you would stand in the disciplined ranks at this very moment, and you could expect to wear a magga's color eventually, but, Berika, you're undisciplined in the purest sense of the word. You would have to unlearn everything before you could begin to earn your silver. It would not be easy. It might not succeed and it won't be pleasant."

"What you're really saying, midons Magga, is that it's still too late for me. I've got the *basi* but I can't become a sorcerer."

"No, Berika." Halwisse's voice softened, and a measure of the hollow weariness in her eyes lifted. "You *are* a sorcerer, a hedge-sorcerer, and a very powerful one at that, but you have not been taught how to use Brightwater silver to concentrate and control the power of the Web. If ever you wanted to try to become a disciplined sorcerer, with silver of your own, the doors of the Palestra are open to you. I can promise you a room of your own, with a west-facing window, if that's what you want."

Berika squinted at the woman seated opposite her and tried to remember with whom besides Prince Rinchen she'd shared that particular dream. No other names sprang into her mind. She already knew that the Wolf was not above meddling in her life.

"What would you do, midons Magga, if you were me?"

Halwisse sighed. "I was afraid you were going to ask me that." She rose from her chair and stared out the window at the ruin of the Basilica dome. "I want it back, Berika. I want to see the Cascade again before I die. I want a sorcerer living in every one of these empty rooms. I want you to put on a grey robe and start at the very beginning so you can help me. But if I were you, I'd find myself an interesting bit of stone and I'd make myself a hedge-sorcerer's touchstone. I will offer you a bargain, Berika: Help me reweave the Web with your hedge-sorcery, and I will keep that room here for you."

"When do I have to decide, midons Magga?"

"Whenever you're ready. Whenever you need the room. Truly, whenever."

Berika knotted her fingers until they hurt. "Who told you about the room? Midons Prince Rinchen?"

"No," Halwisse sorJos said gently. "Dris. Driskolt sorMeklan."

"Thank you, midons Magga, but I'll have to think about it." She got to her feet without looking at the Magga's face. "But I'm not ready yet."

Arkkin escorted her back to the old palace without comment. He offered her supper, but Berika refused, saying she wasn't hungry, when she simply wanted to be alone. She found the parchment map of Walensor and spread it across the worktable. The markings were no longer meaningless. She found Merrisat in the empty space beyond Fenklare's green borders. No one had mentioned the princess's name in Berika's hearing since her return to Eyerlon, and she had no intention of asking. When Princess Thylda arrived, it would be time to retreat to the Palestra.

Nightwatch began. Berika lit a lamp and stayed at the worktable, sounding out all the names on the map and waiting for Prince Rinchen to keep his promise. The nightwatch was in its second hour when he stormed in, slamming the door hard enough to shake plaster from the walls.

"I've changed my mind. We leave at the top of deadwatch. Can you be ready?"

"What happened?"

"Will you come with me?"

"Yes—of course, but what happened?"

"Aleg has forsworn his oath. He's betrayed me and sided with our mother. The Merrisati have promised him an army. I've tried to rally the donitors, but with the Web in tatters, it's impossible. I need someone with me—someone I trust—who can reach the Web for me." Rinchen rampaged through the chronic mess, rearranging it thoroughly.

"Prince Alegshorn, midons? Your brother, midons? I don't believe it."

Rinchen paused with a chain-mail shirt in his hands. "Why would I lie?" He shrugged the metal links over his head and shoulders, then covered them with another shirt. "I suppose you'll want to say goodbye to Dart. Do you know where to find him?"

She shook her head and he gave her detailed instructions.

"But remember, when deadwatch rings, you're to be down in the tunnel between the palaces. I can't wait for you. Bring only what you can carry on the back of a horse. Do you understand?"

He stormed out of the room as soon as Berika nodded her head, leaving her with a mouthful of questions and only one place to go for answers.

She'd taken few opportunities to wander the old palace warrens, but the prince's directions were very clear and the unmistakable voice of Weycha's harp guided the last steps of her journey. She knocked and was invited in.

"I've come to say goodbye."

Dart set down the harp. "Goodbye? Where are you going?"

"I don't know. I'm leaving with Prince Rinchen at the top of deadwatch. Prince Alegshorn has forsworn his oath and the Merrisati are giving him an army."

He gestured for Berika to take his place on the bed, as he had no chair, and preferred to pace, scratching his chin before saying: "This is very . . . *sudden*, Berika. Who told you Prince Alegshorn has forsworn his oath?"

Berika recited the conversation she'd had with the prince.

"I'm glad he suggested you say goodbye to me," he said when she'd finished.

"I think the prince knows you wouldn't betray him. But he said he needed someone who could reach the Web. I'm sure that's why he's taking me, and not you."

"Undoubtedly."

"Do you think he'll be able to rally the donitors?"

"It's hard to say, Berika. Who knows who might get wind of this plan and stop him. He might not live long enough to get out of the palace."

Berika worried the hem of Dart's blanket. "It's so hard to believe. I thought they hated each other at first, then I thought that it was more than just an oath. I thought they trusted each other and were friends. They deceived everybody together, then Prince Alegshorn deceived Prince Rinchen."

"Deceit is the sorRodion war-cry, Berika." Dart pulled Berika to her feet and gave her a hug. "I'm certain the Wolf's got more surprises hidden away. Are you certain you want to do this with him?"

"I love him," Berika whispered. "It's strange. If he stayed here and became king, he'd marry that Merrisati princess and we'd be separated. But now that Prince Alegshorn has betrayed his oath, we can be together."

"Very strange," Dart agreed. "But if you're going to be ready, shouldn't you go back upstairs? Suppose the Wolf decided he had to leave early?"

Dart listened to Berika's retreating footsteps until he could no longer hear them. Then he belted on a steel sword, furled his cloak around his shoulders, and took the shortest route from his room in the old palace to the chancery in the new one. As he expected, a Pennaikman and a spearman from the king's guard stood outside the doors. Both men recognized him, and he entered without challenge or announcement. Prince Rinchen was hunched over a sheet of parchment and did not immediately look up.

"In the name of all the gods awake and asleep—have you lost your mind?" He got the prince's attention. "Of all the chiseling, dirty tricks you could have pulled to get rid of a woman when you were tired of her, this is the worst. Aleg's in bed with the dowager and the Merrisati are giving him an army—have you told him that? I'm sure he'll get a good laugh. Godswill, we all need one—all except Berika."

The prince rose slowly to his feet. "I thought you'd understand."

Rinchen deceived everyone by hiding his emotions, but when one did show on his face—as confusion did now—it was probably sincere, which infuriated Dart all the more.

"Do you have any idea how much Berika loves you? Do you have any idea what she's been through at the hands of men? Can that icy heart of yours beat fast enough to understand how much this stunt is going to hurt her? If you want to be done with her, you didn't have to deceive her. You could have at least told her the truth, Rinchen. Godswill—you could have told *me*."

"I thought it would be easier this way."

Rinchen walked around the table. They stood an arm's length apart, talking much louder than was necessary.

"Easier for whom? What do you truly have planned, midons prince? Is Berika going to disappear tonight? Will her clothes turn up in some Merrisati baggage next week when the princess arrives?"

The Wolf lunged for his throat, as Dart had anticipated. He wasn't fast enough to deflect the attack entirely, but he got in a few blows of his own before they crashed to the floor. They fought with more fury than skill until the guards managed to pull them apart. Both of them were bloodied. Rinchen had the beginnings of a black eye; Dart nursed the numbing ache of a dislocated thumb. The guards looked anxiously to the prince for orders.

"Leave us. Don't interrupt again."

The guards hesitated, then obeyed.

"I'm not finished," Dart warned as the doors shut. He squeezed his injured hand and winced as the bones snapped together. "I want answers. Good, honest answers, if you know the meaning of the word. Why have you deceived Berika?"

"I haven't deceived her."

"What do you call it? Are you planning to be in the tunnel at the top of deadwatch?"

"No, you are. I sent her to you. It's not as if you don't love her; I heard you in the snow. I knew you would know what she said couldn't possibly be true. I assumed you'd understand what I had in mind."

"I'm beginning to think you don't have a mind, Rinchen. I'm not a part of this. Berika doesn't love me; she loves you and she thinks the two of you are going to ride out of Eyerlon at the top of deadwatch. I call that deceit. How deep does your deceit go? You've deceived me: I thought you *did* love her."

"I destroy what I love."

"Godswill—let's not start *that* again."

"All right—I didn't know what love was before the gods put her in my life. She lies beside me at night, soft, gentle, and trusting. Her arms surround me when she falls asleep. Her breath is warm on my neck. What more could a man want?"

Dart said nothing. When the man in question was Rinchen sorRodion, perhaps that was all he wanted. He'd listened to both Arianna and Rinchen describe their unspeakable passions, and he'd been so repelled by Berika's excuse for a husband that he'd killed the man when he had the chance. A love that consisted of gentle hugs and soft breathing was, probably, all either of them truly wanted.

"If I could have the throne and Berika too," Rinchen continued, "there'd be no problem. But there is a problem, and she's headed here with her father's blessing and twenty ox-carts of gold. I thought about having Aleg marry the princess; that creates more problems. I've got to marry her, and her father's blessing and the twenty gods-be-damned ox-carts of gold. I could keep Berika as my leman; godswill—I think she loves me enough that she wouldn't refuse. But she loves you, too, and since you love her—"

"—You expected me to explain to Berika why you can't marry her and won't keep her as a leman?"

"I expect you to marry her and make her happy."

"We'll move back to Gorse and raise sheep? I can't marry Berika or any other woman. In case you've forgotten—I'm a dead man, midons. I've been restored to my clan, but I've got no land to my name, no living, no title. I subsist on sorRodion charity."

"I've offered you sorRodion land and title, and you consistently refused to take them. Finally I've realized you're not simply a dead man, you are a dead *sorMeklan* man, and you'll never be happy with anything I could give you. So, I've bargained with Lord Ean and he's agreed to provide you with honorable sorMeklan land and title." Rinchen retrieved a scroll with a fringe of lead-sealed ribbons from his table. He waved it before Dart's face. "The honor of Kethmarion, lately gone extinct, with the promise of the assart village of Gorse, once I'm crowned and it passes into sorMeklan hands. Sign it, and it's all yours."

It had been easy to refuse the prince's earlier endowment offers. He hadn't expected to survive his contest with Hazard, and the honor itself was a hodgepodge of Pennaik hills and valleys.

The honor-estate of Kethmarion, in the heart of Fenklare, was harder to resist.

"And forget about living in Gorse and raising sheep. Jemat sorLewel's the one I'm putting out to pasture. The title I offer you is Marischal of Walensor, and I expect you, and Berika, to live in Eyerlon with me."

A lot harder to resist.

Dart took a deep breath to steady his voice. "Do the sorLewel know you're offering the title they've held for generations to a sorMeklan man? They won't be pleased, midons. The river feud will pale in comparison."

"The feud is settled as well; that's in the agreement with Lord

Ean. But no, the sorLewel don't know, and won't know until you say yes. There's no reason to stir *that* hornet's nest without cause. Everyone will raise a hue and cry when they learn the marischal will no longer be a donitor. I've doubled the voice of the sorMeklan in our council. Lord Ean wanted Dris to get the title; I said one Driskolt sorMeklan is as good as another, but if you don't want it, maybe I'll let the other one have it instead. Aleg will be happy—"

Impossible to resist.

"Enough!" He spread the fringed parchment across the table. "But you could have talked to us, Rinchen." He signed his name beside his brother's and passed the pen to his prince. "You should still talk to Berika. She'll be angry at first, but she'll understand."

"If I'd known love was going to hurt this much, I would have made damn sure she went back with the spear. If I see her, I'm going to change my mind."

Dart repeated the suggestion, then let the matter drop. There was an hour-candle burning on the worktable. It had melted down to the last line, and given the vagaries of nighttime drafts and boredom in the watchtower, the deadwatch bells could ring at any moment. The prince produced his final gifts: a small sack of gold and the name of an inn not far from the gates which his brother recommended.

Dart had everything he ever wanted, and was prepared to take it. Growing up a younger brother in the sorMeklan clan hadn't been pleasant, but it hadn't left him so distrustful that he couldn't take gifts when they were offered, or enjoy his own good fortune. Which was more than could be said for Rinchen, already returned to the worktable, head down, poring over another vast, nearly illegible sheet of parchment, scratching words onto a wax tablet like a common merchant's apprentice.

The prince gave every appearance of a man who'd just resolved an annoying, but not terribly important problem. Dart took what he saw as truth—for a moment—then walked around to Rinchen's side of the worktable and dropped a hand onto a wiry, suddenly tense shoulder.

"You'll be late," Rinchen said without looking up.

"You're a better man than you give yourself credit for. She *would* stay beside you, princess-bride or no, and no one"—he squeezed the shoulder slightly, to convey that he especially included himself in that statement—"would judge you harshly."

"I would. I want Berika to have more than I can give her. You, too. I'm happy for you, truly. I'll enjoy seeing you together—"

"Liar."

Rinchen shrugged, and the shoulder in Dart's hand relaxed.

"I want to see one happily married man and woman before I die."

"Maybe she won't be so bad—"

"Pigs will fly, Dart— She's my mother's cousin. I've read their letters. Now, get going—I've got a kingdom to govern."

Dart loosened his grip. Taking a lesson from Rinchen's brother, he gave his friend a light, affectionate punch. He'd started to turn away, when a cold hand clamped around his wrist.

"You'll come back, won't you?"

"Don't worry, runt. We'll both be back."

Once he left the chancery, Dart headed directly for the tunnel. Two horses, blanketed and drowsy, waited in the torchlight. Berika huddled in the doorway behind them.

She was stung by Prince Rinchen's deceit and enraged by his manipulation of her life. She was also very cold and wormed her way inside his cloak when he let her. He found himself defending the prince until he was almost as cold as she'd been. As the numbness crept past his knees he took refuge in the one argument he knew she couldn't resist.

"I'm your fetch, Berika. I'm the demon you wished out of Weychawood. When I was empty-headed, I held on to your face, your name. I loved my lady because she was my goddess, but I fell in love with you when I first saw you, and I've loved you ever since. I love the prince, too, and I feel sorry for him, because he does love you—loves you very much. But when all is said and done, he loves Walensor more, and Walensor needs that Merrisati gold and the princess who comes with it."

The deadwatch peal rang out, deafening them, and halting conversation. Dart took advantage of the moment to do what he'd wanted to do since Berika had wriggled inside his cloak: He kissed the woman he loved and held her until her stubbornness melted.

"Your eyes still sparkle," Berika said softly. She circled his eye with a very cold finger. "They're green now. They were gold and red."

"Spring is coming. I'll always be a demon-fetch, your very cold demon-fetch."

"We could go inside—?"

"We can go to an inn. I've got a purse of gold. I swear to you that we can take the best room in the inn, complete with a mattress and blankets and a fire in the hearth. And we'll stay there until the snow melts."

"I'd like that."

Dart mounted one of the horses and lifted Berika up before him in the saddle. They rode through the palace gate and disappeared into the streets of Eyerlon.

Glossary

av — In noblefolk names, a prefix indicating that an individual has been formally adopted into another noblefolk clan. In commonfolk names, the prefix indicates that the individual has given a binding oath to either a clan or another individual.

Basi — The energy of Walensor's magic. *Basi* is an intangible substance that exists in varying amounts in all living creatures and some inanimate objects. By its nature, *basi* increases over time, albeit at an unpredictable rate.

bar — In noblefolk names, the prefix that denotes an estate or other piece of property particularly associated with an individual.

Calendar — Walensor's year is divided into eighteen months. Each month consists of two ten-day weeks. The Greater Week corresponds to the waxing moon; the Lesser to the waning moon. The solar and lunar cycles are corrected annually at the Calends festival, which lasts from the winter solstice until the next new moon.

Donit — One of the six (Arl, Escham, Fenklare, Norivarl, Pennaik, and Survarl) geo-political subdivisions of the kingdom of Walensor. Donits are ruled by clan aristocracies that are bound by blood ties, marriage alliances, and oaths.

Donitor — The hereditary title of the overlord of a donit.

Hedge-Sorcerers — Walenfolk magicians who practice sorcery without the benefit of Eyerlon training are called hedge-sorcerers. Hedge-sorcery is the sorcery of the commonfolk.

Leman — A commonfolk woman (occasionally a man) taken into a noble household by one of its legitimate members as an intimate companion. A leman makes no vows to the noblefolk clan and assumes no noblefolk privileges. Lemanage is the only noble association founded on affection or friendship.

Midons — A noble title that means "justice-giver." It denotes the right of one individual to pronounce judgment on another and is used reflexively by commonfolk when dealing with the noblefolk. The title is also used by a noble individual to address another noble of higher rank; *lord* or *lady* is used to address a peer of lesser rank.

ru — In noblefolk names, a prefix meaning "child of" and referring to whichever parent is of higher aristocratic rank.

Severance — A ritual which prevents an individual from ever using his or her innate *basi* for any sorcerous purpose. Noblefolk children are Severed within days of their birth unless they are born with "manifest" *basi*, in which case they are fostered immediately to the sorcerers in Eyerlon.

Sidon — The title of a donitor's heir, usually the donitor's oldest son and confirmed when the heir attains his majority at age twenty-two (seventeen, if the heir is female).

sor — In noblefolk names, the prefix denoting an individual's clan lineage.

Sorcerers — Walenfolk magicians who are educated in Eyerlon are called sorcerers. Sorcerers of significant ability are generally accepted into one of several sorcerous disciplines: bards, who entertain and serve as the kingdom's architects and engineers; basilidans, who intercede with Walensor's gods; communicants, who govern the Web; inquists, who ascertain the truth; and menders, who tend the sick or injured.

Sorcerers who rise to the top of their discipline are called maggas. The magga sorcerers choose one of their number to become the kingdom's Magga Sorcerer.

The Web — An ancient and unique network of sorcery that spans the borders of Walensor. It binds Walenfolk to their gods, to each other, and to their past.